Master's Touch

By
David Nimer

Book 1
Talent Master Series

To my amazing, supportive and all around perfect wife for being my soundboard, main editor and having the best advice and plot structure I could ever ask for. You truly kept me on the correct path while traveling through the Illusion Forest.

And to Andrew, Ethan and Rachel --thanks a million for your faith in my storytelling and listening to all my consistently repetitive conversations about the Talent Master.

David Nimer
Visit my website at www.davidnimer.com

Printed in the United States of America

First Printing: November 2019
Kindle Publishing / IngramSpark

Library of Congress Registration Number #TXu 2-159-619

ISBN: 978-0-578-58731-8

Contents

Chapter 1...1

Chapter 2 7

Chapter 3 16

Chapter 4..19

Chapter 5 23

Chapter 6 27

Chapter 7 28

Chapter 8 33

Chapter 9 40

Chapter 10 43

Chapter 11.. 49

Chapter 12... 65

Chapter 13... 69

Chapter 14 81

Chapter 15... 91

Chapter 16 94

Chapter 17... 96

Chapter 18 112

Chapter 19 122

Chapter 20... 130

Chapter 21..148

Chapter 22 153

Chapter 23 162

Chapter 24... 175

Chapter 25 186

Chapter 26 189

Chapter 27 203
Chapter 28 217
Chapter 29 223
Chapter 30 237
Chapter 31 244
Chapter 32 252
Chapter 33 258
Chapter 34 263

Chapter 1

Destiny

"*L*et me get this straight." Ean paced the room while his parents and the stranger Jon Henric sat stiffly on the couches in his family home, "We're from another planet? Are we even human?" He paused and held out his sun-tanned hands to study them, "Or am I going to grow mutations?"

Jon rolled his dark brown eyes, "You are still human...only from another world and unique."

"But *you're* not human." Ean stated, running a hand through his own blondish-brown hair.

Jon smiled, his white teeth contrasting his ebony skin. "No, I am not... I am an Arturian by race, a shape shifter from the world Natura. I have been on Earth protecting your family for 400 years. And before you ask, I will likely live to be more than a thousand years old."

"So why did we come to Earth? *How* did we come to Earth? Do we have a spaceship? Can I drive it?"

"Jason, how could you not teach him about his heritage?" Jon reproached Ean's father.

Jason's white knuckles clenched around his wife Emily's hands as he fought to control his temper. "Ean is only 16! I meant what I said 14 years ago...we are done with this so-called 'family destiny'."

Ignoring him, Jon turned to Ean. "Your family is not a normal family. In your family there are Talent Masters--people with extraordinary talents, skills, and strengths--who can combine these with dragon magic to protect, lead and serve the inhabitants of Natura. *You* are the next Talent Master."

A cold chill ran down Ean's spine as he remembered the dragons plaguing his dreams since his last birthday. He couldn't shake the image of their hot breath and sharp teeth reaching for him. He looked up to see his parents and Jon watching him.

"What is Natura?" Ean turned a folding chair around across the coffee table from Jon and straddled it, resting his athletic arms across the backrest.

Jon grinned and leaned forward, "Only the best place in the Universe! Imagine a world where magic is a part of life; where people share their abilities to help each other; where love, harmony, and peace flourishes; where mythical creatures thrive, where some people can change shape within the blink of an eye; where there is no limitation, segregation, or starvation. Natura is paradise."

"If Natura is so great, then why are we here and not there?"

Nodding, Jon sat back. "Good. Right to the point--over 400 years ago, an unknown person by the name of Abigor began pulling strings at the University of Islandia. From there, he gained a foothold into the military's upper ranks, causing an overthrow of the monarchy. In one sweep he slaughtered the entire royal family...all except your ancestor, an infant at the time. With the help of a dragon, I rescued and brought him here through a magical portal for protection."

"Where is this portal?"

"Dublin, Ireland, at the famous Tara stone," Jon replied. "Incidentally, it is also called the Stone of Destiny...and you, Ean, as a Talent Master, are destined to return to Natura."

"Enough!" Jason stood and pointed a finger at Jon. "Don't you *dare* do this to my son. Don't you *dare* tell him he belongs anywhere else than here with us!" Jason shook his head. "I know you think someday our family will produce a Talent Master, but here we are--four centuries later--and nothing. Sooner or later you need to realize there isn't going to be one-- our family is unable to produce a child with the abilities you seek. Did you consider we can't because we don't live on a magical planet like Natura? It is time you face the facts: there is no Talent Master and there never will be one. You're stuck on this planet for the rest of your life and Natura is going to survive without us."

Jon bolted up to his feet. "I haven't been wasting my time waiting for the next Talent Master. Your son is remarkable, as I'm sure you know. He excels in English, science, math, sports, and whatever else he tries. In fact, whenever he started getting recognition for his talents, you moved your family in an attempt to hide from me. Despite your best efforts to elude me, you never did. I've been with you the whole time, watching him and waiting."

Jon's expression became somber. "This mobile lifestyle has been hard for Ean," he walked over and put a hand on Ean's shoulder. "In fact, going into hiding to offer him a 'normal' childhood backfired on you. You never gave him the chance to build lasting friendships. He got picked on as the new kid more often than not. His successes made him seem too perfect, too smart, and only succeeded in making him an outsider.

"Whether you believe it or not, I have been helping you keep him a secret through damage control--declining scholarship offers, deterring scouts of prestigious athletic schools from approaching him, and protecting him from nosy school counselors. Don't get me started on the times I had to take care of a bully or two. Poor kids will need therapy after what I did to them."

"What did you do?" Ean couldn't contain his curiosity.

A mischievous grin appeared on Jon's face. "I changed my appearance a few times in front of them."

"How scary for them," Emily interjected, thinking about when she saw it the first time years ago. Deep down, however, she was grateful someone had been looking out for Ean because of the secret difficulties he had been facing. "Ean, is it true kids picked on you?" She asked her son with concern.

His mother's worried expression made self-pity well up in Ean. He shrugged, looked at the floor and mumbled, "Maybe." If he said more, he'd end up getting all emotional over something that happened a while ago. One thing Ean learned moving around so much is there is always at least one bully in every school. The latest school wasn't so bad though. It helped having someone like Jeff Killwell, his skinny exuberant red-headed friend, stand by him when the bullies came around. Ean cleared his throat and addressed Jon, "How did you know?"

"Like I said, I watched over you," Jon replied. "The reason kids pick on you is because one thing is clear: you don't belong here. You are destined for bigger and better things than what is offered here. You belong in Natura, with your own kind!"

"My own kind?"

"Yeah," Jon, with excitement in his eyes, stooped down to face Ean. "On Natura there are wonders you couldn't even begin to imagine. It is a place where you can fly with dragons; An enchanted world where the very air is filled with the undercurrent of magic and where your own magic, locked up in here--" He tapped Ean's chest, "Will come alive, flowing from you like Master Musician. Come with me Ean. Let me show you the world of your ancestors, a world where you are destined to be King. You will be the greatest Talent Master in the history of our world!"

"That's it! Get out!" Jason roared, stabbing a finger at the front door.

Jon stood and started backing toward it, hands up. "Look, all I'm asking you, Jason, is to let him try. Let him put his hand on the Stone and find out if the portal will open. Doesn't he have a right to learn of his destiny?"

"His destiny is what he makes it, not what you dictate to him." Jason ushered him through the door. "As long as I have any say, you will not disrupt our family. So help me, you will not even so much as speak to my son. Do you hear me?"

"He was born to be a king..." Whatever else he said was cut off as Jason slammed the door, his red face shaking with suppressed rage. Emily came to his side and took his arm to calm him.

"Dad, what did he mean magic is inside of me? And what is a 'Talent Master'? Why don't we prove to him I'm not one?"

Jason rubbed his forehead to soothe his growing headache. "I have nothing to prove to him."

"But what harm would--"

"I said, NO! Now go to your room."

Stomping upstairs, Ean's face flushed with anger as he slammed his bedroom door. If he showed Jon he couldn't open the portal, it proved he didn't possess the abilities Jon looked for and the Arturian would leave them alone. Why couldn't his dad understand that?

Disturbing thoughts crept into his mind. *What if Dad doesn't want me to try it because he is afraid I am a Talent Master? What if I can open the portal? Is that why Dad won't let me try? Is he being overprotective and trying to shield me from what Jon said could be my destiny? Or could it be that Dad had gotten his hopes of being Talent Master dashed when he was unable to open the portal? Is he jealous I might be able to do it?*

No matter what the reasoning was behind his dad's reluctance, Ean didn't care anymore. All he could think about was how easy the Talent

Master test would be. He could go to Ireland, put his hand on a rock and then he would know one way or the other.

Something small hit his window with a tap. Curious, Ean went over to investigate the cause of it. Below Jon stood behind some bushes holding a handful of small pebbles. He looked up expectantly at the window.

An idea started to form in Ean's mind.

Chapter 2

The Journey

*D*ear Mom and Dad,
Please don't be mad, but I decided Dad was right: I need to make my own destiny. But I need to know what doors are open to me (and by doors, I mean portals). I decided to go to Ireland with Jon. Don't worry, we'll be safe and I expect I'll be home soon. I love you both so much.

Love, Ean

P.S. With everything going on, I forgot to tell you Jeff and I are both going to go to the University this fall! If you don't disown me by the time I return, could you please submit the completed registration paperwork? Also, we need to look for a place to live up by the University. Could you help find somewhere for Jeff and me to live? I'd commute, but it wouldn't be reasonable. Thanks!

∞ ∞ ∞

Jon and Ean shuffled through security. Ean took one last look back, then turned toward the gate leading them on the first leg of their trip to Chicago.

The two travelers boarded the plane without a hitch. They had first class tickets, so they entered the plane among the first passengers. As Ean relaxed in his seat, he glanced at the faces of the passengers filing past; several people dressed in business attire carrying laptops, some couples, a few people presumably traveling for vacation.

One young mother traveling with a toddler and infant took their seats across from him, with the toddler sitting by the window. The boy tried twice to climb out of his seat--once by standing on the seat and almost falling backwards, the second when he put up his food tray and tried to stand on it. While scolding him, his mother used her free hand to pull him back into his seat, making it clear he should remain seated. Afterwards the boy sat with his arms folded and a deep scowl on his face.

Ean chuckled, remembering when he himself had made that same face a time or two when his family moved. On the other side, the mom looked rather tired. Ean assumed it was because her little boy had an over-abundance of energy--like a puppy freed after being penned up all day. Ean smiled again at the boy's defiant attitude as he wiggled in his seat, while still keeping his arms folded. Then the boy slid off the chair and started pulling things out of the seat pocket in front of him. Before his mother could respond Ean began to laugh. The mother scowled over at him before she too began to laugh.

"He's always such a busy boy," she apologized.

"No problem. Do you mind if I offer him my phone to play with? It might help."

Her gratitude was obvious, "Sure, if you don't mind."

"No problem at all. By the way, I am Ean McMurrin."

"I am Elizabeth, and this is Jacob and Rosemary." She lifted her left shoulder to reveal the sleeping baby's face.

"She's beautiful!" The little girl had porcelain skin and a deep reddish brown hair unlike her mother's light-brown hair. He wondered if Rosemary had her green eyes.

He turned his attention back to the toddler and offered his phone to Jacob. "Here you go, little Buddy. Try this game." He had downloaded a car racing game that worked by tilting the phone side to side to move the car.

Not long after the plane took off, Elizabeth fell asleep with the sleeping Rosemary securely cuddled to her in the baby wrap. So for the next few hours Ean helped Jacob move from one app to another, keeping him entertained while his mother and sister slept.

When the plane descended, Elizabeth awoke to find Jacob still had Ean's phone. "Sweetie, time to give the phone back to the nice young man."

"NO! Mine!" He grasped the phone to his chest.

"Jacob, give it back right now," she instructed with a firmer voice.

The boy hung his head, "Okay, Mama." With his eyes down he handed the phone over.

Ean smiled, "Why thank you, Jacob."

Elizabeth leaned toward him making eye contact. "Thank you for lending him your phone."

"No problem at all," Ean responded with a smile.

Jon cleared his throat for Ean's attention. "Come on, we need to make our next flight." As they walked off the plane Ean overheard Elizabeth asking a flight attendant where to find the connecting flight to Dublin, Ireland.

Surprised, he turned and blurted, "Are you going to Dublin too?"

"Yes. Wait, are you two taking the same flight?"

"I think so," Ean responded. Then, with the polite manners his parents ingrained in him, he added, "Can we help you with your carry-on bags?"

She hesitated, then took a deep breath and said, "Sure, some help would be wonderful."

Perceiving her concern, Jon held out a hand. "Hi, I am Jon Henric and I promise we won't run off with your belongings."

Elizabeth looked embarrassed. "Was it that obvious?"

"No, you were concerned about the motives of two men whom you just met."

They each shouldered an extra bag so the mother could carry Rosemary and use her extra hand to hold Jacob's arm as they walked to the next gate. Again they all boarded early with first class tickets. Jon struck up a conversation with Elizabeth, leaving Ean to listen to Jacob ramble on about airplanes and fighter ships. As the plane took off Rosemary began to fuss and Ean, not knowing why, offered to hold her.

Much more relaxed now, Elizabeth said, "Sure, but please remember to support her head...and be careful to not bump the soft spot on her head...and oh! Please put on this sanitizer first." She dug a travel sized bottle from her bag.

Jon smiled. He had seen the same motherly protectiveness throughout the past few centuries he had spent on Earth. Some things would never change.

Watching Ean cradle the baby in his arms, Jon sighed. If only the McMurrin family produced more than one child in each generation, he would have been able to return home to Natura by now. His thoughts lingered on his homeland, one familiar image overshadowed all the rest with her beauty and grace, her contagious laughter and playful smile. He wondered once again what it would be like to be reunited with her. Did she move on to someone else in his absence? Or would she still be there, waiting for him with open arms?

"Jon? Earth to Jon!" Ean's chuckle at his own joke interrupted Jon's thoughts and brought him back to the present. Once he had Jon's attention, Ean leaned closer and whispered, "When we arrive, what's the plan?"

"Simple. Hail a taxi, head to the stone and go home." Jon grinned, "It will be great! There are wonders only to be dreamed of in this world. And *you* will be an amazing king and Talent Master. Wait until you unlock the magic--oh the things you will be able to do!"

"Yeah, it all sounds great, but I am beginning to...well, you know..."

"Feel a little nervous about it?"

Ean nodded. "I'm not sure how to be a king or Talent Master, or anything. Maybe this wasn't a good idea after all. I don't know..." He sighed.

"Missing your parents?" Jon nodded knowingly. "That's normal. I would worry if you didn't. I promise you, your experiences in Natura will be worth it. As for your worries about running a kingdom, don't worry, I can help you there." He grinned, "I will be with you every step of the way. My duty is to look out for you and your best interests, as I did for your father."

"What was my dad like at my age? Was he excited to try opening the portal?"

Jon chuckled. "Though scared to leave his parents, he put on quite the show of bravado to compensate. He swore he would be the best king ever. By the time we arrived in Ireland he moped and pouted all the way to the stone about how he didn't choose his destiny. When unable to open the portal, he became angry and sullen toward me. He had to blame someone, so I became, in his mind, the enemy." Jon shook his head, "He always was a high strung boy."

Ean could imagine his father reacting the way Jon described. How strange to talk to someone who knew more about his family than he did. *Maybe after we arrive to Natura, Jon and I can talk about all the things Dad never told me.*

He felt less nervous about his future the more he dwelt on how his dad kept him from knowing about Natura and his family's royal inheritance. *There's a possibility I'm a king!* Ean let his mind daydream about what living in a castle and having people wait on him would be like. It was all he could think about for the rest of the flight.

After disembarking, collecting their luggage, helping Elizabeth collect hers, and saying goodbye to her and the kids, Jon and Ean made their way to the airport doors. Jon hailed a taxi as they heard a young woman squeal with excitement, "Lizzy...Lizzy!"

A young woman rocketed over to embrace Elizabeth, who waited nearby with Jacob and Rosemary. The ecstatic girl--an older version of the baby Rosemary--grabbed Jacob in a vast hug, bestowing many kisses on him before he could squirm away. She then scooped the baby out of her mother's arms.

Turning to Elizabeth, whom she had called Lizzy, the young woman gave her a one-armed hug, still cradling the baby girl in her other arm. The two ladies conversed with swift glances in the direction of Jon and Ean. Jon waved for a taxi and one pulled up to the curb. Before the driver got out of the cab, the boisterous newcomer--no more than 16 or 17 years of age-- came up to them.

"We are in your debt, Mr. McMurrin and Companion, for the help and assistance you gave my sister and her kids." She said with a light Irish accent.

"Think nothing of it." Jon replied, handing his bag to the driver who had reached them.

She was looking at Ean though; whose face felt like it lit on fire. She had an expression reminding him of his Mom when determined to get her way. So he did the only thing he could--stare right back into her dark hazel eyes.

She continued undaunted, "Well, gentlemen, we owe you. So I plan on giving you some good old Irish hospitality while you're here in Dublin. Where are you staying?"

Jon cleared his throat, "Ah, Madame, we are heading right out of town to a local tourist attraction...Ean, your bag." He indicated Ean should give his bag to the waiting driver.

"Yeah," Ean added, handing his bag over. "We hear the Hill of Tara is pretty this time of year."

"Oh?" She seemed disappointed they weren't staying in town. Then she perked up and said, "I can take you there, Mr. McMurrin." Her free hand shot out and grabbed Ean's bag, preventing the driver from putting it in the trunk. "I insist...no charge."

"That will not be necessary," Jon said.

Ean realized he had better intervene before Jon offended her. "Why not?" He turned to the driver. "Sorry, I guess we won't need your services after all."

"What?!" Jon was incredulous. "Ean what do you think you are doing?"

Seeing the determination on Ean's face, the driver, unhappy about the loss of a customer, let the teenager take Ean's bag. Then he dropped Jon's on the curb with a thump. Ean turned back to the girl. "We would be delighted to accept your offer on one condition." She raised an eyebrow in expectation. "Call me Ean. Mr. McMurrin is my Dad."

She smiled and handed Rosemary to him so she could retrieve the car. Elizabeth walked over, joining the group. "Sorry for my over-zealous sister. I won't hold a grudge if you decided to make a quick run for it."

Though they didn't run, Ean thought Jon considered it. Instead he acted like a gentleman and thanked Elizabeth's sister when she returned. Acknowledging his gratitude with a nod, she helped the group settle inside the SUV. Elizabeth drove them into town, keeping up a constant commentary about Dublin's historical sites and some of the great pubs and restaurants they should try before leaving Ireland. Ean didn't hear much of her commentary--he couldn't concentrate with her sister sitting next to him.

Then Elizabeth said, "How silly of me! Here I am going on and on about Dublin and forgot to introduce my own sister! Gentlemen, this is Adair O'Conner, my baby sister."

"Oh hardly 'baby,' Sis," Adair replied, giving her sister a stern look.

The older sibling chuckled. "Sorry Adair, even though you age every year, you will still be my little sister. Some things never change."

During this banter, Ean tried hard to avoid looking at the beautiful Adair. At the same time he wondered if he was about to suffer a heart attack; he was short of breath, speechless and lightheaded. When he did try to respond to questions, he mumbled and made somewhat incoherent statements, at which the ladies giggled. Jon took a quick look at Ean, rolled his eyes and returned his attention to outside the car window. Ean still couldn't believe the resemblance of Adair to Rosemary. The car turned a corner and the sun radiated on Adair, her skin glowed and her red hair shone with a mixture of subtle highlights.

Adair changed the conversation by asking questions about little Rose to Elizabeth. Ean turned his attention to Jacob, who was playing with a toy F16 airplane. Ean asked him what he was playing and in return received a quick animated boyish response, "Planes go down!" He mimicked his plane flying with a zoom-zoom description, then 'ka-boom!' The boy was winning the pretend war, though the sound effects caused Elizabeth to stiffen up in her seat and glance back frequently with a sad, stricken look in her eyes.

A short time later they parked in front of a two-story town home narrowly stacked within a block of identical homes.

Elizabeth and her kids got out; Adair gave her a quick hug and promised to be back before dinner time.

Jumping into the driver's seat, Adair asked, "Alright, you want the Hill of Tara?"

"Yes, please," was Jon's response.

"Then that is where you'll go."

They headed out of town. Adair inquired if they wanted to check into a hotel or stop for lunch before leaving town. She started to recommend a local café when Jon cut her off, "No thanks--just the hill and then we will no longer be a burden to you."

She scowled at this comment, but gave no rebuttal to his statement.

Ean piped up, "We recently ate on the plane, and since the Hill of Tara is not more than an hour away, there is no need to check in to a hotel at this time." Jon gave Ean a stern look as if to say 'Don't interfere.'

Ean shrugged his shoulders and continued watching the scenery. After a few of Adair's attempts at conversation, the car became silent for the remainder of the drive, with the exception of the sound the tires made as they drove on the road.

When they arrived at their destination, Ean emerged from the car to grab his duffle bag, throwing the strap over his shoulder. In an attempt to smooth over his earlier conversational stumbling, he thanked Adair for the ride and asked her to say their goodbyes to Elizabeth and the kids.

Adair looked rather shocked at Ean's obvious goodbye. She objected, "I'm not leaving the two of you stranded on this hill. At times there are not many visitors here--like now--and you have no way of getting back to town!"

Jon jumped in, "We will be fine. Thanks again for everything--and have a safe drive home." He tugged on Ean's sleeve and indicated they walk up the hill.

"Now you wait a minute," Adair thundered, storming after them as they began the hike toward the Stone of Destiny. "Wait up!" she demanded.

Jon whirled around and growled through clenched teeth, "Your services are no longer needed. I am very familiar with Ireland and we do not require your assistance in getting to our destination." Jon turned back and continued up the hill.

Ean had also stopped and was about to say Adair should wait in the car for them when Jon looked at him and nodded toward the stone, indicating they move along.

Following him, guilt gnawed at him for how poorly they treated her. The more he thought about how hurt and angry she must be, the angrier he became at how rude and pushy Jon was being toward her. Why not let her come up the stone? She has as much right as anyone else! Determined to invite Adair along, Ean turned to her; The emotions of anger...hurt...and confusion briefly flickered across her face before she hid them.

"Ean," came the sharp command. Jon nodded again toward the Stone of Destiny. Ean shook his head and began to walk toward Adair. Jon reached out and grabbed his arm, "Leave her be," he whispered into his ear.

Ean jerked his arm away, "No!" He stomped back to the beautiful young woman. Taking a deep breath, he said, "I am so, so sorry for how we have treated you. We have been rude and ungrateful for all of your kindness. Please forgive us."

Adair recovered her composure with miraculous speed. She smiled, "I was beginning to wonder if Americans had any courtesy left."

Ean gave a deep bow, "Might I correct this perception by offering to escort you to the Stone of Destiny?"

"Why sir," She said with mock playfulness, "That would be lovely." Adair took his proffered arm in such a vice-like grip, he wondered if she was trying to make sure he couldn't make a run for it.

Jon had made it to the Stone and was fuming at the turn of events. As the teenagers reached the stone, Jon growled through clenched teeth, "She should not be here!" He turned to her, "You must leave now and don't look back."

"Jon!" Ean's voice rang with indignation as he stepped between the two. "Adair was nice enough to give us a ride here and is willing to give us a ride back after we are done. The least you could show her is an ounce of civility when talking to her."

"She must leave now--before this goes too far!"

Concerned, Adair asked, "Before what goes too far?"

"Nothing. You're not supposed to be here." Jon responded curtly. Then Jon turned with a quick intake of breath as he heard the sound of an approaching vehicle.

"Be *here*?" Adair gave a mirthless laugh. Her cheeks glowed a deeper red, her hands balling into fists as she shouted, "This is *my* country sir, if anyone shouldn't be here, it's *you*."

Jon looked her in the eye, his quiet reply in stark contrast to her retort, "You're right. Time to go home Ean." He grabbed Ean's right hand, pressing it down hard on the Stone of Destiny.

Then they were gone.

Chapter 3

Emily

hree days later Emily McMurrin paced in the study, upset over the fact her son ran away and Jason rebuffed her insistence they call the police to catch him at the airport. In fact, this disagreement had been the last sign of her husband's normally strong-willed temperament. Now the man, usually so confident and steady, wandered around the house, lost and defeated. This new uncharacteristic behavior concerned her like never before.

She remembered the day her husband and his parents, Arthur and Magnolia, sat her down and explained an old family friend had some sort of guardianship claim on her son. How that could be, she didn't know. She did know Jason and her in-laws believed it was in the best interest of the family if Arthur and Magnolia went their separate ways and Jason and Emily kept a low profile.

This meant they moved anytime something happened which might make one of them stand out, such as the time a local newspaper covering Ean's track meet featured a photo of Ean, claiming he could be Olympic worthy. Then came the time Ean qualified for the national spelling bee before Jason and Emily realized the amount of public recognition he would receive. They moved again when his mandatory science fair project won top honors and then because of his noteworthy participation in debate and math team competitions. Each time they moved, Jason and Emily made up new ways to discourage Ean from pursuing further the subjects in which he excelled.

Emily wanted to home-school her gifted son, but Jason said it would be good for Ean to make friends. But Ean didn't end up making many friends. He gave up getting to know other kids, knowing his family might pick up and move at a moment's notice. He also never told his mom about the bullies or difficulties fitting in at school. Though not her fault, she blamed herself; as his mother she should have known of his problems.

She did know he didn't make many friends. She remembered being ecstatic when Ean invited Jeff home. Yet still it pained Emily her son kept unpacked moving boxes in his closet, so he wouldn't need to pack them up again the next time they moved.

Now, despite all their efforts and the sacrifices they'd made to protect their son, he left, leaving a short note behind. This would not have happened if they were more supportive. They failed their only child.

Jason previously told his wife about his own failed attempt to prove himself as Talent Master, and though she wondered if the whole thing was a delusion made up by Arthur, she now faced the fact that her son may even now be on a different planet. Not until the world news reported a brilliant light beam and screeching noise echoing through the countryside of Dublin that her deepest fears had been confirmed--Ean was gone!

She also learned Ean and Jon had not been alone. Reports circulated of a missing teenage girl, Adair O'Conner, last seen in the company of a man and teenage boy fitting the descriptions of Jon and Ean. Adair's older sister, a recently widowed young mother named Elizabeth, publicly plead for anyone with information on her whereabouts to step forward. If Jason's predictions of Ean's potential birthright were correct, then 16-year old Adair was most likely gone, too.

Sitting at her computer, Emily scrolled through the captured online images of the event in Dublin, obsessed with anything having the potential to do with her son. A newly uploaded video caught her attention. A history professor from the University of Dublin had been filming an amateur video about local historical sites for her class near the base of the Hill of Tara when the event took place. Emily played the clip. Then she played it again. As she clicked on it for a third time, she stopped the clip right where the light appeared out of nowhere and the screeching sound began. Her heart skipped a beat--for there, faintly outlined in the bright brilliant light, three people stood next to a stone pillar. Hand trembling, she clicked the play button. The screeching continued, the light grew brighter and then, as suddenly as the light appeared, it was gone--and with it, the people.

The implications of what happened set in; her mixed emotions once again veered toward anger. If the girl had gone with them, then she and Jason could have gone with Ean too. Regardless of the choices causing her to be separated from her only son; she made a commitment: No matter what it took, she was going to find him.

Chapter 4

The Arrival

*D*eafening blackness. The instant his hand touched the stone, Ean was sucked into a dimension devoid of senses. After a brief moment of nothingness, one speck of light sped toward him, followed by dozens of multicolored streaks. Swirling, they spun quickly in looping circles until they formed shapes that moved as if in fast motion. A high pitched ringing sound reverberated through the air, increasing in volume as the lights swirled around. The tone resonated within his body as every fiber of his being vibrated with the sound. He was only faintly aware of the Tara Stone glowing a radiant red, the ground stones also pulsing red, before swirling beams of red light shot straight up into the sky, engulfing Ean and his companions.

"Can someone travel faster than the speed of light?" Ean vaguely wondered as he experienced indescribable sensations. Later, he would describe it as an overwhelming sensation of warmth radiating throughout him while being hugged tightly by encircling light. Then it disappeared; replaced by an icy coldness that swept over him as if he'd gotten drenched with mountain lake water. Shivering, he opened his eyes to a blurry green line and concentrated on it until a distant line of trees came into focus. He studied them until his eyes adjusted and zoomed in on individual trees, revealing far more detail than he should be able to see.

A flicker of warmth started from within his chest, building in intensity to a flame, then a small fire. The blood pumping through his veins was heating up, the tips of his fingers and toes tingled as though electrified, and his skin felt like it could move and change of its own accord. For a moment, he wondered if he could leave his body and fly through the sky, alive and without limitations. He was *magical*.

The thought hit his mind as the new sensations abruptly stopped and he was himself once again. It took him a moment to regain his breath, which was lost again as soon as he realized they weren't in Ireland anymore. Speechlessly, he took in his surroundings, his mind asking one impossible question after another.

Ean found himself standing on a hill similar to, yet very different from, the one he had left. Upon the flat ground stones, there was an identical stone to the Stone of Destiny, surrounded by equally large stones forming a U-shape. Beyond the hill a vast forest of dense green trees spread outward. Ean could hear the deep thrum of water behind him and turned to spot what he assumed was an ocean, crashing against the base of the hill.

He turned to ask Jon about it, but couldn't see him anywhere. A few feet away Adair lay unconscious on the ground. Rushing to her side, Ean lifted her head and felt relieved when her eyes opened. It only took a moment for her to realize who held her.

"Hands off!" Adair demanded as she scrambled away from him in fear.

"Okay--I'm moving...I'm moving." Put off by her reaction, Ean moved to stand a good distance away in the ring of stones. The grass, wet and frosted, sounded like he walked on miniature icicles--just like when he lived in Georgia and winter humidity would leave frozen drops of ice clinging to the blades of grass.

The sound of the water caught Adair's attention. She gazed toward the expansive body of water to her right, then swiveled her head to take in her surroundings. "Whoa!" she murmured. "This place is...amazing!...Where are we?"

Ean's brow furrowed. "I think we're in Natura. The Tara Stone was supposed to be a portal between Earth and this world. Jon, I can't believe it worked!" Ean turned to talk to Jon, but he was nowhere in sight. He yelled out, "Jon?" When no response came, an uneasy idea emerged.

"Oh, no. Jon's might still be on Earth...or worse...." He couldn't bear to consider what else might have happened to Jon.

"What do you mean we're not on Earth anymore? Take me back! We need to go back right now!" Adair scrambled up and raced toward the middle stone. She put her hand on the rock and pushed. When nothing happened, she turned and cried out, "Help me!"

Ean hurried over and put his hand on the stone. The stone turned red and a pulse of energy hit him, throwing him backward a few feet.

"Ean! Are you okay?" Adair called.

Getting up, Ean said. "Yeah, but I don't think we can go back to Earth through this stone."

Adair fell to her knees in despair and started crying into her hands. A lump formed in his throat; they were stranded in a strange world with no one to help them.

"What are we going to do?" Adair wailed.

"Continue on your journey, of course," came a voice.

Ean spun around to see who had spoken, but no one was there. "Who's there?"

A flash of green fire flared to his right and their attention was drawn to the ground in front of the center stone pillar, where a lizard stood, no more than a foot and a half long from its nose to the tip of its tail. It had light green scales on its belly and dark green scales on its back, which shimmered in the sunlight.

"What a minute...have I seen you before?" Ean asked. "I think I had a dream about you, only you were..."

"Bigger?" The little lizard chuckled. Then he began to grow in size until he towered over them. The teenagers scrambled back and Adair stepped to Ean's side, grabbing his arm in a vice-like grip for the second time that day.

"What are you?" Her voice wavered as she spoke.

Wings unfolded from the sides of his body; so it wasn't a normal lizard...

Adair gasped, "A dragon?"

Nodding his head in agreement, the dragon said, "You may call me Drake."

"But didn't you...I mean do you...eat people?" Ean voice trembled despite his attempt to remain calm.

With a grumbling chuckle, Drake replied, "Not today."

Shaking off the shock from seeing the dragon from his dreams, one question came to the front of Ean's mind. "How come you can speak English?"

The dragon snorted and a puff of smoke curled up from his nostrils. "I am not speaking English, yet you hear it because all Earthly languages are derived from dialects found in Natura. You may find you will be able to understand many--if not most--of Natura's written or spoken languages." Straightening up, the dragon spoke to Ean. "You are the Talent Master we are waiting for."

"Talent Master?" Adair asked Ean. "What's that?"

"I found out about it a couple of days ago. I'm still not sure myself."

"This is not the time to answer your questions. Your life is in danger. Make haste; we must enter the Illusion Forest. Its magical boundaries will protect you from your enemies. Follow me." The dragon turned and launched himself into the air. His massive wings flapped to gain altitude to clear the tree tops.

Adair turned to Ean. "What should we do?"

He shrugged. "Follow him. I don't think we have any other choice at this point."

"That's reassuring," Adair said as the two set off, running after the dragon into the Forest.

Chapter 5

The Lost Son Returns

*A*s it so happened, Jon did make it to Natura. He hated leaving the humans at the portal alone, but he knew he had to talk with the Emperor of the Arturians before the discovery of new arrivals. Familiar with his way home, he was now walking through the capital building of Ferreglen.

At the end of the hall, he approached tall golden double doors, embedded with diamonds and other precious stones, creating an image of a beautiful garden oasis bordered by jewels depicting flowers and vines intertwined with fairies, unicorns, dragons, and other mythical creatures.

Jon slowed his step as he neared, nodding his head to acknowledge the two guards on either side of the door. With a casual flick of his right wrist, he turned his hand so the back of his hand was toward the men and the hallway light reflected off the ring on his middle finger, causing the guards to flinch in recognition. Following his movements with amazed eyes, they made no move to prevent him from entering the Elders' council chambers.

His entrance halted the conversation in mid-sentence. Jon walked to the near end of the conference table, surveying each of the ruling Elders seated at the table before turning his attention to head of the table, where the leader of Ferreglen sat. He appeared to be a handsome middle-aged man, his dark hair speckled with grey along the sides of his head. Though dressed in a dark tunic and pants like the Elders, his manner exuded a quiet, yet powerful air of authority. Silence hung in the air as the Elders examined the newcomer.

"Father, I am home."

The room erupted with an uproar of denials and accusations.

"I thought your son was dead!" one resounded.

"It can't be!" cried several others.

Jon held out his ring for their inspection. Despite the evidence, there was a heated debate until the Emperor's voice thundered above the rest, "Enough!" The room fell silent. His gaze passed over each of the Elders, coming to rest on Jon. "There is only one who can wear that ring...the heir to Ferreglen's Empire. My son is home."

Jon continued, "I brought with me a boy--the heir to the throne of Islandia and a true Talent Master."

Again the room broke out into disagreements. "Impossible! The entire bloodline is dead!" one Elder thundered.

"Where is this heir and how can you be certain he is a Talent Master?" another questioned.

"Even if he is, what use is it to us now?"

"He could be a blessing to our kind..."

"Or a curse to Natura!"

The debate continued on for several minutes and when it was obvious the council members would not relent, the Emperor stood. He waited for the members to cease their objections. "We can discuss the heir later. For now we will allow our historian to give a brief summary of Natura's history since my son's absence." The Emperor signaled an attendant to bring a chair for Jon and nodded to an Elder to begin the historical monologue.

After Jon had been given an update of Natura's unstable state of affairs, he was troubled. The information most disturbing was this same Abigor who had overthrown the kingdom of Islandia over 400 years ago still had control over much of the planet. He ruled over all citizens--with the exception of the inhabitants of Illusion Forest, including Ferreglen and Eden, the city of the dragons. Eden was still hovering above the planet, where the dragons had placed it for protection during the revolt. The magical barrier surrounding it ensured no one could enter or leave the city, nor could it be destroyed from the weaponry below.

The tyranny of Abigor was not the only crisis. After the update he received on Natura's state of affairs, Jon recounted his lengthy mission on the earthly realm. Almost finished, he described their return to Natura, "and when I placed Ean's hand on the stone, the stone sang its praise, flared its flames of color, and transported the three of us to--"

"What do you mean 'three' of you?" The Emperor interrupted.

Jon stiffened. Though he had exposed the fact there was an unauthorized human in Natura, this was the reason he had left Ean and Adair at the portal by themselves. He had come here alone to explain the situation and hope it would be enough to spare Adair's life. "There was an Earthling with us when Ean activated the stone. She was transported with us to Natura."

"This is an outrage!" declared a red-faced Elder, spittle flying from his lips as he pointed his finger at Jon, "You have broken the decree regulating passage of persons between worlds!"

Jon addressed the angry Elder, "It could not be helped Augustus. The heir was at the stone and it was his actions causing the girl to be there. In essence, he approved her to be with him at the stone and even the decree includes a clause that the Talent Master may make exceptions."

"Just because you bring a descendant who has the ability to open the portal does not mean he is a Talent Master," responded Augustus. "Until you can prove to us he IS a Talent Master, we assume he is not. Therefore, we must follow the protocol for the violation of the Inter-world Portal Decree."

A younger member of the Elder Council spoke up, "What are the ramifications for the breach?"

Silence echoed throughout the room when no one answered the question. Finally the Emperor pronounced, "Death."

Even though he had known the verdict, Jon's face paled. After a few silent moments, he rose from his chair, "Elders of the Council, since there is some debate as to the validity of Ean's authenticity as Talent Master, I say we table the matter before further action against the other Earthling. When you have tested Ean and found him to be a Talent Master--and I have no doubt you will--then the exception to the decree will be valid, and the girl will be granted amnesty."

The Emperor nodded his head, "It is fair if the descendant proves himself and vouches for the girl's presence in Natura, then she should be granted immunity and the council's protection and assistance. How says the council?"

Romearus, the oldest Elder, rasped, "First the boy and girl must face the tests of the Forest protecting Ferreglen from unwanted visitors. *If* they survive those, then I say we test the boy and both of the Earthlings' fates will rely on the outcome."

"It has been motioned the heir of Islandia must pass the challenges of the Forest and validate his claim as Talent Master, upon which the fate of the two humans will be determined." The Emperor restated.

"Motion seconded," voiced an Elder. Jon had to hide a smile. The council of Elders always assumed their vote mattered in the decisions of Ferreglen; though by law and general knowledge, only the decisions of the Emperor counted.

The Emperor, however, humored the council's delusions. "Those in favor?" All the council members raised their hands in agreement. "The vote appears unanimous in favor of the mandate. Let us adjourn the meeting."

The council members stood and shuffled out the doors, many passing by Jon to shake his hand or pat his arm affectionately. A few, however, ignored him or gave him hooded glares instead.

As the last Elder disappeared from view, the Emperor gave a sigh of relief. "These past 400 years have been rough without you. Having you back is a blessing for a man as old as I." He strode forward and gave Jon a strong embrace. "Let us retire to our quarters. We have a lot of catching up to do."

Jon smiled as his father placed his arm around his shoulders and walked with him through a set of double doors to the private family quarters on the top floor of the capital.

Chapter 6

Shock

*A*bigor stood on the balcony of Islandia's tallest tower when the beam of swirling red light lit up the clear blue sky in the far distance. He stepped forward to grip the top of the stone railing with both hands, thoughts of what it could mean crossing his mind as the light faded from view. Abigor knew deep down something changed in his world, but he had no idea what happened or if it benefited him.

"Guards!" He barked. The two standing as sentinels outside his private quarters burst in, tumbling over each other in their haste.

Weapons drawn, they looked around for the danger. "Sire?"

"Out here, you fools!" They rushed to the balcony where Abigor paced along the ledge. "Find the general and tell Mars to stand at full alert. Something is amidst in our land and I will find out what it is." He commanded. Saluting smartly, they backed out of the room not daring to make eye contact with Abigor.

Chapter 7

In the Forest

Following the dragon, Ean and Adair ran through the dense forest for a few minutes before Adair gasped, "I need to stop..." They stopped so she could catch her breath.

"Welcome to the Illusion Forest, a sanctuary to the magical creatures in this world." Drake, having returned to his small lizard self, was perched on a stump ahead of them.

"So now what do we do?" Ean asked.

"Journey to the City of Ferreglen and speak with the Emperor. He has always been an ally of your family and can help you with your quest."

"What quest?" Ean wondered.

Drake huffed, "Hasn't Jon told you anything? You must take back your kingdom of Islandia, free the inhabitants from the evil tyranny, and fix all the damage done during the last 400 years."

"Oh, is that all?" Sarcasm dripped from his voice.

"No, you must also sire another heir to the throne."

Ean's eyes grew wide and his cheeks turned bright red. *How embarrassing! And in front of a gorgeous girl!* Ean could have sworn Drake snickered at his discomfort.

Adair cut in, "Wait a minute, I'm missing something here." She looked from one to the other. "What are you two talking about?"

"Allow me to explain," Drake said. For the next hour Drake detailed the history of Ean's royal lineage, the rebellion culminating in his ancestor being taken to Earth for refuge, and the expectation for Ean to be the next

Talent Master. Adair and Ean sat speechless as Drake explained how the current dictatorship was causing the starvation of many citizens and a large number of homeless children. Desperation led to extreme measures: a child showing remarkable talent was often sold to the University, while children with less talent were sold into slavery. In order for Abigor to keep control of the people, he made sure to pay the citizens well if they turned in anyone speaking against his dictatorship or engaged in revolutionary behavior. This resulted in a general overall distrust between the citizens.

Politics within the University were also appalling--talented citizens who desired to improve their circumstances through school or employment opportunities were required to use mandatory drug prescriptions given out and controlled by the University. Once on the drugs, however, the user could not stop taking them; the pills altered biological mechanisms such that if the user stopped taking them, their organs would shut down and they would die. It was well known if someone on the drugs offended a high ranking University official, their prescription would be revoked and they subsequently died a painful death.

"How awful!" Adair cried. "This place is evil--I want to go home." Tears welled in her eyes.

Ean reached over and took her hand in his. Squeezing it, he said, "I'll get you home. I promise."

Drake flew from his stump over to Adair's shoulder. He landed on her shoulder and wrapped his tail around the other side of her neck. Adair discovered she was oddly comforted by his close proximity. "Earthlings, if we are ever going to make it to the City of Ferreglen, we had better start moving."

After a long time walking, it took all of Ean's strength to move forward. The scenery of the dense forest never changed, always mud pulling at his shoes and strands of vines tripping him up at every step. His discomfort was increased by the sloshing and suction-like sounds coming from his shoes as he walked. He glanced at Adair, who walked with ease in almost a straight line. For some reason this made him grumpy.

For the last couple of miserable hours, Ean reflected on how his life changed. A couple of days ago, he was home with his parents. His main worry had been how his parents would react when he left home for college.

Then Jon revealed himself, turning his world upside down. Now Ean was kicking himself for his decision to go with him to Ireland. Why did he allow himself to be so easily convinced in trying to open the portal? Why did he run away and why didn't his parents call him or try to stop him from going?

Regardless, it was too late to turn back. He had gone too far. He never should have run away. But he did and now he would never be able to talk to his parents again. Looking at Adair, Ean's stomach was like a ton of lead. He had abducted her, like those UFO stories of an alien kidnapping humans—he just never imagined *he* would be the alien taking a human from her home planet--

My planet, he corrected himself. *I'm both Earthling and Naturan--that should mean something. I don't know...If only I listened to my parents this never would have happened.* He shook his head, *Wait! What am I saying? If my parents had been honest with me from the start this never would have happened! They are to blame, not me.*

No matter who was at fault, the fact remained...he would never set eyes on them again. The weight of this knowledge was heavy. He glanced at Adair again. She appeared to be taking everything in stride, as if it were normal for her to be hiking through the forest in an alien world. *I have to find a way to send her home. She shouldn't be trapped here because of my mistakes.*

He tripped, yet again. Ean called to Drake, "Hey, Dragon, we've been traveling for hours. Where is the City of Ferreglen?"

"Ferreglen is located in the southeast corner of the Forest, near the border to the black wasteland. We entered by way of the northwest side of the Forest, so we have some distance to go. I give you a forewarning: the Forest is magical, our destination arrival time is not certain. To protect inhabitants, the Forest tests those who enter. Those who prove themselves worthy will reach their destination. Those who do not demonstrate their worthiness, spend the rest of their lives in the Forest, unable to reach their destination, nor even able to leave."

"You couldn't have mentioned that *before* we entered the forest?" Ean asked. The lizard ignored him.

"How long will it take us to prove worthy?" Adair asked.

"Depends on Ean and how fast he learns." Adair studied Ean, sizing up his capabilities. Drake continued, "The Forest sees it as his responsibility to protect and guard you."

Adair didn't like the sound of that. She looked around fearfully, "Protect me from what?"

Sensing her concern, Drake added, "Don't worry, you are safe for now. This young one here," Drake indicated Ean, "needs to learn more before the challenges begin, so for now we will continue to stroll through the Forest."

"Easy for you to say!" interjected Ean, "The vines and mud are everywhere! Can't we rest for a moment?" Drake conceded it would be a good time to stop for the night and the trio set about finding dry ground where they could rest without becoming entangled in vines. As they scattered leaves for their beds, a brisk wind kicked up. Adair shivered and goose bumps appeared on her arms. Heading over to where he dropped his duffel bag, Ean pulled out a flannel shirt. "Here, put this on."

"What? Oh... thanks. It's colder now. I wish we could make a fire."

Jumping off Adair's shoulder, Drake grew in mid-flight to the size of a Mastiff. He turned to face a boulder a few feet away. Clearing his throat, a rumble began deep in his chest. The scales on his chest began to glow, as spreading light traveled up his throat. Drake opened his mouth, releasing a jet of green fire toward the rock until it glowed white with heat. Satisfied, Drake closed his mouth and a puff of smoke rose from his nostrils. Seeing the stunned expressions on the Earthlings' faces, he said, "What good would a dragon be if he can't keep the chilly air at bay?"

Adair moved closer to the rock with her hands extended toward the heat. "Drake, you are the *best*!"

Not wanting to be outdone by a lizard, Ean mumbled, "Here Adair, take some more of my clothes to stay warm--and keep the bag as a pillow."

"Thanks, that's thoughtful of you." She took the bag from him and turned away from him on the pretense of getting settled for the night. Despite the kindness extended by Ean and Drake, tears started to form in her eyes. Tonight was supposed to be different. She was supposed to spend time with her sister, who had arrived from the United States. Adair should have been with Elizabeth, the children and her father--the family together again. The pain in her heart was almost unbearable as she sat down on the ground, moving rocks around to try to make a more suitable bed. Her back to Ean, she lay down facing the warm boulder and tried to sleep.

Drake settled into a flower bed of lilies, content to stay there for the night. After Ean was sure Adair was settled in for the night, he walked over to Drake.

"Hey Dragon--can we talk for a moment?"

"Sure human, what's on your mind?"

Chapter 8

Bathroom with Perks!

*T*he next morning Ean awoke disoriented and tired, not having slept much the prior night. After speaking with Drake, Ean had attempted to go to sleep, but getting comfortable had been elusive as the temperature was below Ean's comfort level. He had spent much of the night trying to figure out how he and Adair could survive in the forest. They needed the basics: shelter, warmer clothing, bedding, and food to eat. At one point he considered eating the little annoying dragon, but Adair was growing an attachment to the lizard and he didn't think she would approve of his idea. Plus it wouldn't be a good idea to eat his fire-starter and guide. Realizing most of his plans to survive required supplies he didn't have, Ean gave up trying to come up with unusable survival strategies.

During the rest of the night, Ean's mind kept wandering back to all that had happened in the last couple of days, which seemed like a lifetime ago. His early morning hours were spent dealing with the horror of Natura's situation. The plight of Natura's people pulled at his heart-strings and he wondered what he, one person, could do to help them.

After a few stretching exercises, Ean walked around to clear his head until he came across something not there the day before--a trail running through the forest.

"Hey guys, check this out!" Ean called.

Rolling over, Adair rubbed her eyes. "Oh, savage. I hoped this had been a dream." She sat up and ran her fingers through her hair, trying to dislodge the leaves tangled within. "What's so exciting?" Adair asked.

"There's a trail here now!"

She jumped up for a better look. "That's good, right?"

"Most likely," Drake answered. "Before we continue our journey, we should eat our morning feast."

Right on cue Adair's stomach growled, "I second the idea because I don't know about you, but I am *starving*!"

"Great idea, Dragon," Ean stated, "Do you suggest starting with a leaf salad or a mud pie?"

"Pie sounds good," Adair said. "So do crepes with strawberries and cream cheese, Danish pastries, and triple berry muffins. I also wouldn't mind polishing off some eggs over-easy and a tall glass of cold orange juice..."

Ean snorted, "Yeah, let's talk about what we *want*, but don't have. I want a stack of buttermilk pancakes, a grapefruit, a large bowl of scrambled eggs and a side of hash browns. Throw in steak for lunch, with a pile of rolls, mashed potatoes and gravy, and a six-pack of coca-cola...wait--I also want a supply of trail mix, a two-liter bottle of water and a candy bar to top it off."

Adair scoffed, "Trying to out-do me McMurrin? Well then for lunch I want a large deli sandwich with pickles and baked chips to the side. Then for dinner I want citrus glazed salmon, steamed vegetables, and *lots* of milk to drink. Forget about candy bars for dessert--I want cheesecake smothered with fresh berries and whipping cream."

Drake looked at both of them with an amused expression, "Quite the tall order." Drake stood up, stretched and walked over to Adair. With a leap and a couple of flaps of his wings, he landed on her shoulders and stretched out, his tail hanging over one arm, swinging casually.

Ean fought off the urge to grab him and throw him.

Nonchalantly, Drake turned to Ean. "You want it, you can have it."

"What do you mean?"

"All Quester's receive one visit to Louie Lou's Shop."

"What is Louie Lou's Shop?" Adair questioned.

Drake turned his head and looked up at her. "I would assume it is obvious. It's right behind you."

Ean and Adair turned around. Right in front of them was a tree house--or more accurately a tree that *was* a house, complete with a door right in the middle of the trunk. On the door hung a sign carved on a piece of bark: 'Louie Lou's Diner and Shop Extraordinaire: Walk-ins Welcome." Amazed, Ean and Adair exchanged surprised looks, opened the door and took tentative steps inside to view an empty dining area with the ability to seat 30 people. Magic was most definitely involved, because from the outside there was no way there would be so much room inside. Nearby and to the left of the door stood the hostess, a thin female about four feet tall with long black hair and green eyes. Her stunning tan skin looked the same color as the surrounding wooden walls.

In a high squeaky voice she exclaimed, "Excellent! New Questers! Come in, come in please! You'll need seating for two and--wait a minute! What do you have there? Oh my, I have never seen one before but I do believe that is a dragon. Yes, yes...this must be a great Quest indeed!" She snapped her fingers and three menus appeared in her hands, "Please, follow me."

They were led through the room, skipping the vacant tables. At the back of the room was a hallway with doors. Behind the first door to the right was a smaller room with a large circular table in the corner. Red curtains surrounded the table, giving them a sense of privacy. Once they had been seated, the small hostess handed Ean and Adair menus and placed Drake's on the table. "My name is Shena. We received your custom orders, but you are welcome to look at the menu for anything else you might desire."

Drake spoke up and added "An eighteen-pound roast--cooked medium-rare, and Louie Lou's famous sixteen-berry shake, one for each of us--with mine in a punch bowl please."

"Yes, Sir, right away," Shena turned to Adair and Ean. "Do you want to add anything to your orders?"

Adair spoke first, "No, thank you, everything sounds perfect." Then she leaned close to Shena and asked in a hopeful whisper, "Is there a place I can freshen up?"

"There sure is," Shena placed a hand on her hip and gestured, "Straight across the hall of this room is a place for each of you to freshen up. I'll go check on your orders then." Shena turned and walked back the way she came.

"Wow Drake, sounds like you have a healthy appetite," Adair commented. She had been considering keeping him as a pet, but if his appetite was this big, there was no way she could afford to feed him.

"Yes, my dear, I do. Plus the shakes are unforgettable."

"Well, if you two will excuse me," Adair stood, "I'll go and freshen up."

Drake jumped from her shoulder to the floor in front of the table.

As a second thought, Adair turned to Ean. "Ean, you should freshen up too. And *please* wash those shoes--they stink."

Ean's cheeks turned bright red as he too left the table.

Entering the restroom, Ean almost bumped into a very chubby bald man with stumpy legs and arms. The man held out a rolled up washcloth, what looked like a ring box with a slit in the top, and a flat plastic-like card to Ean. His voice wheezed as he spoke, "Here are your ordering supplies and a hot towel for your face. Open the ordering sheet, pictures of items will appear above it. Point to what you want and slide the picture into the box. If something you need is not pictured, Speak the name of what it is into the box. Don't worry," he added, "There's no cost." After handing Ean the items, the man plopped himself in a chair in the corner of the room and dozed off.

A row of doors leading to small convenience cubicles lined the other side of the room. A very uncomfortable Ean chose the cubicle farthest from the man. Opening the plastic card, Ean jumped and bumped back into the stall door when a glowing 3D pictures of objects filled the air. It took Ean a few minutes to figure out how the objects were organized by group and how to move them for better viewing.

The object categories included survival gear, miscellaneous outdoor equipment, cooking supplies, clothing and a series of weapons; bombs, poisons, and dangerous chemicals. He skimmed through them, sliding into the box pictures of every object he thought he might need to survive in the Illusion Forest. At least his lack of sleep now came in handy--he was grateful for the night hours spent thinking of what items he wished he had with him. To the chosen arsenal of equipment he added a pistol, sword, machete, knockout gas, dart gun, and one very deadly poison. He reasoned that since a weapons category existed, he was bound to need them. Then he ordered a significant amount of food--a small amount of perishable food and a much larger amount of non-perishable food. He had no idea how long it would take him to make it to Ferreglen.

Ean stepped out of the room and washed up before speaking to the man in the corner, "My list is rather long and there's no way I'll be able to carry everything. Can I add transportation to the list?"

"Anything you need, you can add. There is one catch--all means of transportation in the Illusion Forest must be animal powered."

Ean thought about it for a minute and then whispered into the box what he would need. Thanking the guy, Ean handed him the box and card and stepped back out into the diner.

By the time the food was served, Adair still had not returned from the bathroom. Ean began to eat and was halfway through his food when Adair arrived. She looked amazing...she had showered and changed into a whole new outfit--from the hat on her head to the boots she strode over in. The clothes were rugged enough for the forest, but stylish enough to walk down Broadway Avenue. A slight floral fragrance infused the room as she seated herself.

Ean sat in his seat, gawking like a school kid before he came to his senses and closed his mouth. "Wow, you look amazing!" His reply came out in a higher pitched voice than expected. He cleared his throat.

Adair blushed and a corner smile appeared on her face as she picked up her fork. "This *food* looks amazing." She lifted her fork to take the first bite and heard a loud growling sound. Drake had grown to the size of a horse and was swallowing his food whole. Adair laughed.

Drake, ignoring both of them, lowered his large head and gulped down his roast in one swallow. He then slurped up the berry shake with three quick licks of his bowl. After licking the outside of his mouth with his long tongue, Drake gave a toothy grin and started shrinking. He diminished in size until he became the small dragon he had been moments before.

Their gaze on him, Drake turned to them, "What? I was hungry. If I ate in this mass it would have taken hours to finish it all. Larger size speeds things up a bit."

"Drake," Adair said, "Are there other dragons living here or are you the only one?"

"There are other dragons, only they live in the city Eden. I'm the only dragon in the Illusion Forest. I don't know how many there are; it has been some time since I have been home, but there are hundreds of thousands, I would say."

"Okay," Adair squeaked. It was difficult to absorb the fact she was on a planet populated with large dragons.

Lingering long after the food was gone and following another trip to the restroom, the trio got up to leave the diner. Passing into the front room, they discovered the tables were now packed with customers. They passed what appeared to be leprechauns wearing dark green vests, dwarfs, trolls (or ogres, Adair couldn't tell which), stone gargoyles, and a few humans--at least they looked human-like, but Adair was startled when a petite blond woman morphed into a stocky brunette female when turning to greet a neighboring dwarf. Adair craned her neck for a second look and whispered to Drake, "What are they?"

Knowing what Adair meant, Drake replied, "They are Arturians. An Arturian is a human-like being who can change form, including size and clothing, to another form of the same gender. You might be surprised to know their life expectancy spans thousands of years."

They stepped out the door, where three men greeted them, each leading a beautiful horse. The grey Arabian mare and chestnut Arabian mare bobbed their heads, saddled and ready to ride. An all-black Friesian stood harnessed to a small cart loaded with gear. With the agility and speed of the Arabian and the strength and large stride of the Friesian, the trio could make good time on their journey to Ferreglen.

Adair gasped. "Where did they come from? How did horses from Earth get *here*?"

Drake commented drily, "The better question to ask, Adair, is how did these breeds get to Earth?"

Adair strode up to the horse in the lead. She thanked the man and took the reins from him before swinging up into the saddle.

"Hey, don't I get to choose which horse to ride?" Ean called. "After all, I was the one who ordered everything."

"True, Your Highness," she replied, "So you should lead the pack horse...we wouldn't want to lose all the supplies you ordered." She took her horse off on a gallop down the trail.

Drake chuckled as he flew to catch up with Adair.

Irritated, Ean stalked up to his horse. 'Your Highness,' even in jest, was something to which he wasn't accustomed. Grumbling, Ean led the remaining horses down the trail after them.

Chapter 9

Family Confession

*E*ver since the incident aired on CNN News the previous week, Emily had avoided answering the phone and questions about Ean from his closest friend, Jeff Killwell. Emily answered the first call from Jeff the day after she found the note Ean left. Concerned Ean had not come over like they had planned, his texts were unanswered, and calls went straight to voicemail, Jeff resorted to calling his friend's parents.

Emily covered for her son, telling the friend Ean had left on a spur-of-the-moment trip to Ireland with a family friend as a graduation present. After a couple of days, Jeff began calling again, leaving messages asking if Ean was still in Ireland and when he expected to return. He left longer and longer voice messages about needing to plan for the first semester of college and questions as to Ean's thoughts on housing arrangements.

"Jason, we should talk to him, tell him the truth." Emily said one evening after listening to another long message from Jeff.

"Don't worry dear, I've worked it out."

"Oh...?" she looked accusingly at him. Emily had been questioning her husband more about his decisions since Ean's absence.

Jason looked up from the news feed. "I contacted a real estate agent about purchasing a home near the University. I am going to visit with the Killwells and explain to them it is for Ean and Jeff to stay at while in college. Then I am going to send Jeff to Salt Lake City to set up the place."

"Jason McMurrin! How dare you think you can buy off Ean's friend? He deserves to know the truth: Ean is never returning and...and..." Emily collapsed into tears again.

Jason moved over to her and placed his arms around her. "Nothing is definite. He could be back sooner than we think. Have faith."

"Faith, you say?" Emily retorted, pushing back. "Faith in what? Jon Henric? No, there is no faith or trust in him. How could *you* trust him with our son?" The hurt expression on her face tore at Jason's heart.

"I was wrong about running from Jon--Ean had to discover what his destiny could be. I thought he didn't need to be worried about trying to be more than what he would be. "

"Well you may trust Jon, but I don't." Emily responded between clenched teeth.

"Oh come on Honey--"

"'Come on' what?" She pointed a finger at his chest. "No more secrets. No more lies. You will *not* lie to Jeff--you will tell him the truth and I promise you, Jason, if you don't, I will. We are going to Ireland to find the woman Elizabeth and explain to her what happened to her younger sister. NO MORE SECRETS."

Jason sighed in defeat, "Fine. I will stop by the Killwell home tomorrow and explain everything the best I can."

For a moment Emily was silent. Shaking her head, she pulled out her cell phone. "No, you can explain tonight." Within a few moments Jeff was on the phone. "Jeff," Emily started, "Could you come over? Jason and I need to tell you something." She paused for a moment to listen to his response. "Thanks."

She ended the call. "Done. He's on his way over."

They sat in stony silence until the doorbell rang. Jason answered the door, "Thanks for coming over."

"No problem, Mr. McMurrin." Tension was thick in the room, which was unusual for Ean's home.

Jason motioned for him to sit on the couch. "Please sit."

"Is everything alright?"

"Well...yes and no." Emily responded. She looked at Jason and nodded toward Jeff, "Explain."

Over the next few minutes they delivered a story so ridiculously fantastical they kept waiting for Jeff to call them crazy and leave. Besides a few interspersed questions, Jeff sat in silence--which was strange in itself for Jeff. Jason finished speaking and braced himself for the impending reaction.

Jeff shook his head and blew out a breath. "I *knew* it."

Emily glanced between him and Jason. "What did you know?"

"I *knew* there was something different about your family. I didn't know the specifics, of course, and wouldn't have guessed it in a *million* years, but...wow!" Jeff's eyes brightened with excitement. "Oh man! I wish I could go. That would be *so* cool!" Jeff stopped speaking when he saw the shock on their faces. "Oh come on Mr. and Mrs. McMurrin! How could I not believe you? So...when are you going to go? Can I go too?"

Emily's eyes met her husbands. They didn't even know if it was possible to follow Ean, but it was worth a try.

Jason stood. "Looks like we're going to Ireland."

Chapter 10

Blood Berry Bush

That evening Ean and Adair found another clearing, but this one was up a hill a distance from the path. Upon arriving, they discovered a small pond lined with trees and crimson berry bushes, interspersed with willows and tall grass.

Ean went to work clearing the area of rocks while grumbling, "I don't suppose there's a one-time overnight stay at a magical hotel, is there?" But he continued setting up two small tents, laying out sleeping bags inside when done. He also found a change of clothes for both him and Adair in the supply wagon, so he placed an outfit into each tent, along with new hiking boots for himself. While he was busy setting up the camp, Adair had wasted no time going through the food stocks and the cooking supplies. She found it interesting Ean remembered to add various spices to their supplies and realized he must have some basic concept of how food should taste.

Taking a business-like approach to the cooking and preparing of food, in no time at all Adair had three thick chicken breasts cooking on a grill over the fire and vegetables boiling in a pot on the side. Soon the three of them were eating their food. Smacking his lips, Ean made a show of complimenting the delicious food, hinting he was very interested in what she would prepare for breakfast in the morning.

Adair acknowledged his appreciation with a slight nod of the head. She stood up and spoke to Ean, "Those dishes won't wash themselves, you know, so you had better get to work or there will be no breakfast."

Ean stared at her retreating back, stunned by Adair's change to commander. Drake, still in his smaller size, chuckled as he curled up by the fire to sleep.

Leaving Ean to clean up, Adair moved to the pond where the thickest berry bushes grew and started collecting some wild berries for the morning meal. The setting sun glinted off the water and Adair's reflection caught her attention. She was amazed at how well-defined it was, the image of her standing by a berry bush, her hand raised in the act of picking fruit.

She could have sworn her reflection smiled and winked at her. Adair leaned forward and was studying her reflection more closely when all of a sudden something reached out of the bush and grabbed her about the waist. She looked down to spot a vine-like arm made of bark encircling her. She let out a high-pitched, terrified scream when her eyes followed the arm into the bush and realized the arm was part of the bush. The arm yanked, pulling her off her feet and into a gaping black hole which had formed in the center of the bush, where she vanished.

Ean and Drake, hearing the scream, ran to the pond. Ean was still holding the pot he had been about to clean. They started searching for her in every direction, yelling her name as they went. Drake was the first to notice Adair's footprint at the base of a berry bush. His wings flapping faster, Drake called out, "Ean! Come here!"

Running over, he shouted, "Did you find her?"

"She is gone. She has been swallowed by the bush."

Ean reached out to touch the bush, but Drake landed on his arm, "Do not touch it! This is a BLOOD BERRY BUSH...back away NOW!"

Ean did not like the sound of 'blood berry bush,' so he moved away. Fearing Adair's fate, he whispered "What happened to her?"

"It is my guess she was picking the berries from the bush. In revenge, the bush took her."

"Took her where?"

"Underground is all I know." Drake sounded sympathetic.

Moving over to the cart, Ean grabbed an ax and shovel, and then headed determinedly toward the bushes.

"Ean, STOP!" Drake growled, flying in front of his face.

"I have to save her!"

"Yes, I agree, but how are you going to do that?"

"I'll chop down the bush and dig down until I find her."

"Ean," Drake patiently explained, "She was taken by magic. There is no way to know for sure where she might be."

Frustrated, Ean demanded, "Then what am I supposed to do?"

"Wait until morning. These magical plants are more powerful during the night, so wait until it is light. Then we will figure out a way to free her."

Ean threw down the tools, "Fine, but we are getting her back first thing in the morning. Agreed?"

"Agreed," came the somber reply.

Adair remembered being pulled through a vortex in the middle of a berry bush. Where she landed was unexpected. Now she was lying on the sandy floor of a dark and spacious cavern, seemingly surrounded on three sides and overhead by rock. Black water lapped through the fourth side of the cavern, rippling up the sloped floor until almost touching where her feet were spread. She scurried to her feet, knocking sand off her clothes and began to walk around, observing the solitary light--only a glow really--was coming from a distance beyond where the mysterious water stretched.

Panicked, she began to run her hands along the walls looking for another way out. On the far left side, she found a large crack in the wall concealed by rock jutting past the entrance. A faint glow illuminated the two foot space between the sharply jagged walls of the crack. Adair realized she had two choices: attempt to swim out of the cavern or squeeze through the crack to explore where it went. Based on the fact she didn't know if anything lurked in the water, she chose to navigate through the crack instead, hoping it would lead her out of this nightmare.

Turning sideways, she entered the crack. After two quick side steps, the first jagged rock scraped across her rib cage. She held her breath as pain blazed across the wound. The next jagged rock was sharper than the first when it bit into the back of her thigh, causing her to jump forward and yelp in pain as she collided with another sharp point which jabbed her body, bruising her left side kidney. Wincing in pain, she paused and took a few needed shaky breaths.

Deciding to go much slower, she extended her right arm and felt around for some of the rougher wall angles as she slid further into the crevice. Many times her hands missed some of the worst points, but her body found them. Pointed rock made contact with her face, head, and all down her body. It was only uncomfortable until she slid her right foot into a sharp point, puncturing her boot and slicing the skin between two of her toes. She whimpered as tears coursed down her cheeks. A newfound claustrophobia made her imagine the walls were closing in on her and salt from her tears caused the scrapes on her face to sting even more.

She turned her head to the left--the way she had come and panic seized her due to the impenetrable darkness. She had no choice but to continue onward toward the faint golden light, which did not seem to be getting any closer. The slow process took so long Adair couldn't tell if it had been minutes or hours since she plunged into the crack in the wall, but fatigue began to have an effect on her.

Not long after something changed--the walls got smoother and a little wider. She continued another ten feet before feeling horizontal gaps lining the wall in front of her face. Each opening was about an inch high and two inches deep and they were consistent, as though scraped out of the rock surface.

Exploring one of the gaps, Adair lost her footing as her right foot gave way to open space below instead of ground. Without hesitation, she jammed her fingers into the open crevice, breaking two nails in the process, and held on until she could regain her balance. Her heart pounding, she placed most of her weight back on her left foot. Using her right foot to tap around, she found a ledge about six inches out from the wall in front of her and below the lines. The wall to her back appeared to be smooth as she pushed her back against the wall, otherwise, there was no footing at all--the ground dropped into nothing.

Panic and hysteria overwhelmed her. Adair scooted back four or five feet and sat down on the floor. Her back to the wall, she succumbed to emotional exhaustion and fear; wrapping her arms around her legs, she let herself cry until drifting into a troubled sleep.

∞ ∞ ∞

Ean tossed and turned all night. Sleep evaded him as his frustration and anger peaked to a new height. Just when everything was going right-- with food, supplies, and horses--everything went wrong. Ean took responsibility for Adair's misfortune. If only he had listened to Jon, if he had been rude to her back on the hill leading to Tara Stone, then Jon would be here instead.

Ean was still awake, staring at the inside tent walls, when there was a significant change in light, indicating the sun was going to be coming over the horizon soon. Before he had the chance to call the dragon, Drake's voice called to him, "Awake Ean. It is time."

Shoving past the tent flaps, Ean stepped out of the tent, determined that neither fear nor lack of sleep would hinder him from finding Adair. He ignored Drake and went straight to the weaponry tools. This time he also grabbed lighter fluid and flint. He was going to destroy the bushes in the most horrific way possible--cut them up and burn them, roots and all, until only ashes remained. In fact, he resolved to destroy *all* of the Blood Berry Bushes in Natura if necessary to find and rescue Adair.

He stomped up the hill to the pond and Drake landed on his shoulder, "What are you doing?"

Without breaking his stride, Ean responded through clinched teeth, "I am going to destroy every last bloody bush until I find and save Adair."

"I understand how you feel--" Drake began, but before he could continue Ean brushed him off his shoulder and continued onward, anger being his motivation and strength.

"Ean, STOP!" Drake commanded, growing to the size of a house to block Ean. "You do not know what you are doing! If you attack the bushes first, you will only be guaranteeing the death of Adair!"

Ean looked up at Drake, "What do you mean?"

"Attack one bush, *all* the bushes will defend themselves and the interconnected 'Mother Bush' will attack Adair. Let me explain.

"Blood Berry Bushes are so named because of their diet--they drink blood. The berry bushes around this pond are all seedlings grown from, and linked to, the original bush--the Mother Bush, which lives in a protected cavern somewhere in the Illusion Forest.

"Right now, the bush is likely waiting for Adair to die on her own before it feeds on her blood. If it squeezed her to death, her blood would saturate into body tissues and there would be less blood, or food, for the bushes. So the bushes wait for their prey to naturally die, or if prey wanders into water, the bushes will drown them. Now in order to help Adair, you need to find her first."

"You mean *we* need to find her."

"No. This is a challenge you must complete alone."

"What do you mean a challenge? Was this intentional? Look, I didn't sign up for any of this!" Ean yelled, throwing his hands out to indicate his surroundings and the berry bushes.

"You did not choose this, but it chose you. You were born to complete this task and more. Stop fighting destiny and focus on the task at hand."

Overwhelmed, Ean sat on a nearby rock. He looked up at Drake, his voice was pleading, "How do I do it?"

Drake took his time responding. Clearing his throat, he responded, "Do you sense the power within you? Better yet, have you used the power?

"What power?" Ean wondered as he looked at his hands.

Shaking his head with disappointment, Drake replied, "I know you felt it when you arrived--you glowed from within."

"I did?...I don't feel anything now."

"That much is obvious. Listen to me--this is what you are going to do..."

Chapter 11

The Cavern

*E*an stood in front of a Blood Berry Bush on the other side of the pond from the one Adair had touched. He carried a knapsack of supplies over his left shoulder and the machete in his right hand. *I have one shot at this,* he thought. Taking a deep breath, he raised his right arm and cut off a whole section of the plant with one single swipe of the blade. Faster than he had expected, a large and mangled vine-like hand reached out and grabbed the front of his shirt, yanking him into a black vortex that had suddenly appeared in the bush.

∞ ∞ ∞

Adair awoke shivering. Initially confused at the semi-darkness surrounding her and the throbbing pain throughout her body, despair overrode all other emotions as the weight of her current predicament came crushing down upon her. She was trapped in a rock crevasse, a painfully jagged corridor leading to a dead-end cavern on her left side, and on her right, a gaping hole in which she could--and almost did--fall to her death.

Now it was morning, or at least she thought it was morning. The golden glow she was following last night had become brighter and she could see some of the area around her. Looking down at the dark cavity a few feet away, Adair got terrified. She closed her eyes, took a deep breath, and leaned her head back against the wall behind her. Letting out the breath she had taken, she opened her eyes with her head still tilted upward. With the increase of light, Adair was able to perceive a ledge about 25 feet above her head. She stood to observe it better. The ledge continued along the wall toward the golden light. Her gaze dropped lower as she studied the wall in front of her; the horizontal line patterns repeated every couple of feet up the wall.

After considering her options, she decided to scale the wall to the ledge and continue toward the light, hoping she would find a way out. She placed her hands into the line above her head, but then pulled her hands out, wincing in pain. She had forgotten about the two broken nails she had gotten last night. To put less pressure on them, she pressed her back against the wall and placed her boots flat against the opposite wall. Shifting her body, then her legs, she made it six feet off the ground before her feet slipped and she came crashing down to the rock floor.

Frustrated, she yelled aloud, "Get me out of here!!!"

Waiting for her heart rate to slow, she turned to logic. Rethinking her approach to climbing, she realized she had been relying on the assumption she could exert enough pressure between the walls to hold herself up. She needed to attempt to climb the wall in front of her again, regardless of the pain it would cause. For a better grip with her feet, Adair took off her boots and socks. Stuffing her socks into the boots, she tied the laces together and threw the boots around her neck to keep from losing them.

She began her climb by inserting her toes into a crevasse two feet off the floor and her fingers in the gaps above her head. Hoisting herself up by supporting most of her weight with her toes, she then reached one hand, followed by the other, to the next space up. It took her more time to reach the ledge than she would have thought, as she frequently had to pause when tears of fear and pain blinded her vision and she had to blink numerous times prior to continuing.

She arrived at the top, pulling her body over the ledge, which was at least four feet wide. Adair laid there for a few minutes, the muscles in her body trembling from exertion and stress. When some strength returned, she sat up to put on her boots. She gasped at the sight of her bloody and sore feet; sliding up the wall and pressing her toes down inside the sharp grooves with her body weight had shredded the skin on both feet. As gingerly as possible, she put back on her socks and slid her feet into the boots, which only made the pain intensify. An agonized cry burst from her lips before she was able to bite her lip and regain control of herself. Battered and bruised, she hobbled forward in hopes an exit was near.

After an hour or two, she came to a point where the ledge curved to enter another two-foot crack in the wall. Peeking inside, Adair's eyes widened in wonder...

The crack gave way to an enormous cave lined with thick veins of gold and chunks of precious stones and gems. Throughout the oval-shaped room, the floor itself was heaped with mined piles of precious metals, diamonds or crystal and multi-colored gems. Realizing the light reflecting off the gems and gold had to be coming from somewhere, Adair looked up, disappointed to discover the hole in the ceiling of the cavern was at least a hundred feet above her head, too high to be reached.

Spellbound, Adair stepped into the room and was so distracted it took her a full five minutes to notice the trickling sound echoing in the room. Following the noise coming from the left side of the room, she found a section of wall seeping with water, which then flowed down into a small pool area in the center of the cavern. It was then she realized how thirsty she was and how parched her throat had become from lack of water.

Gingerly walking toward the pool, careful not to slip or fall on the loose rocks beneath her feet, she reached the water. Cupping her hands, she knelt and drank the cool water until her thirst had abated. Then she splashed water on her face and arms, washing away the grime and blood as the best she could. She carefully removed her shoes and the now bloody socks from her feet before slowly placing her feet into the water. Letting the cold water numb the pain coming from her feet, she gently washed her skin until the dry blood had been rinsed away.

She sat by the side of the pool, taking a closer look at the gold and diamonds surrounding her. Deciding they were the real deal, as far as she could tell, she slipped a few in her pockets; not that it would do any good if she never got out alive.

Shaking off the depressing thought, she got up and started hobbling around the perimeter of the room until she came to the narrow side of the oval room where two tunnels led out. She peered into one of the dark tunnels, considering whether she should explore it first, when she heard deep voice intone, "I wouldna' go through those tunnels if I were ye."

Jumping at the unexpected voice, Adair spun around and scanned the room. After a moment, her eyes caught sight of a seven-foot tall man standing on top of a pile of gold. He was holding a walking staff made of twisted roots and was wearing dark green trousers, a black shirt, and boots with pointed tips. The top of his head was bald, but framed by bushy red hair and a long red beard.

"What are...I mean who are you?"

"I am Brinston Denar, the Third, but everyone who knows what a devilishly handsome leprechaun I am calls me Brin." Now leaning on his staff, he quizzically looked at Adair, "And ye, young maiden, who might ye be?"

"I am Adair O'Conner, but you can call me Adair...and I'm lost. Could you please tell me how to get out of here?"

"Ye can't. Be truth, ye are the first one to visit this place in over a hundred years. All three routes from this cavern will lead to yer death. The route by which ye arrived was a deadly way to come."

Adair sighed, "Yeah, I almost fell down the opening in the floor."

"Well now, the fall isn't the worst of it. 'Tis the water at the other end where the Blood Mother drinks--she would have drowned ye within seconds of entering it."

"Blood Mother?" Adair looking concerned as a shiver ran down her spine, "Who is that?"

Brin eyed her with doubt in his eyes, "Ye do not know about Blood Mother, and yet ye are in the Illusion Forest?" Brin looked thoughtful, "How did ye go about gettin' down here anyways?"

"I was picking some red berries by a pond when I thought I saw something odd in my reflection. While trying to take a better look, an...'arm' came out of the bush and pulled me into it. I ended up in the cavern by the water."

"Well then, ye are lucky to be alive." Brin sat down. "So now, would ye be wantin' something to eat?"

The question caught Adair by surprise, "Um...yes, I am rather hungry."

"Good. 'Tis somethin' I can help ye with." He tugged on a leather and fur sporran pouch hanging around his waist. Opening it, he turned to Adair, "Would meat pies and gravy be sufficient?"

"Sure! I mean, that sounds lovely." Adair peered at the bag no bigger than a small purse and wondered how any food could fit in there. Then, right before her eyes, Brin disappeared then reappeared.

"Wha--how did you do that?" Adair looked quizzically at the bag as she took a cautious step back.

Brin grinned, "Ye do not know much about leprechauns, do ye? I can go invisible or camouflage to blend into me surroundings; being invisible is a convenience when one wants to hide. In fact, when ye entered this cavern I hid until I could size up the situation. But this is common information-- why does it surprise ye so?"

Adair took a deep breath and admitted, "I'm not from around here. I'm from a place called Earth. My friend Drake calls me an 'Earthling.'"

Brin was shocked. This young woman was not only an Earthling, but she mentioned Drake. There was only one individual he knew of named Drake, and he had been considered locked away in the city of Eden for a very long time now. "Well, me Dear, ye have a tale to tell. For now eat some meat pie--a full stomach helps any situation."

Brin pulled his hand out of his pouch, balancing two plates with large meat pies, one for Adair, one for himself. Adair took hers, sat down beside Brin, and began to eat the pie ravenously.

"Slow down, Dear, I have more if ye are still hungry." Brin laughed as food dripped down her chin.

"Oops, sorry. I didn't realize how hungry I was until I saw the pies." When finished, she glanced at the small water source, "Shall I clean the plate?"

"No, no. Me pouch will do it." He put the two plates back into the pouch. Adair leaned over and looked inside the pouch, but they were gone.

Seeing her surprise, Brin said, "They be ready when I need them again." He leaned in close to Adair, whispering, "This is a special magical pouch made by a powerful dragon."

"No way!" Adair was intrigued.

Brin straightened, "Well now, what do ye want to do? We could sing...I have a vast collection of books...or how about a card game?"

"Huh? Oh, no--I can't stay. I've got to go." Adair stood up. "I need to find my friends and go home."

"Ye can't. This cavern is sealed off. There is no way out."

"Brin, tell me about the other two tunnels. Where do they go? How did you arrive here?"

"Ah, 'tis quite the story, me dear." Brin leaned forward with wide eyes. He began in his bass voice, "It was over 100 years ago when I fell down that hole."

"Wait, you fell down the hole," Adair looked up, "and lived?"

"I was climbing down a rope when it broke. I fell only a short distance."

"Why were you climbing down?"

"Why, the gold o' course! Gold is the curse of a leprechaun. Though many of me people are generous with what we have, we always crave more. So when I peered down the hole and spotted the treasure in the walls, I couldna' resist; been harvesting it in me spare time." He gestured to all the piles of gold and gems.

Adair looked at the giant man calling himself a leprechaun and tried to reconcile her perception of him with what she would've thought a leprechaun would be. She wanted to ask him if all leprechauns were as large in stature as he, but was afraid she might inadvertently insult him by the question. Instead she said, "Well, I'd love to hear more about it, but I do need to leave..."

Brin cocked an eyebrow, "Well, ye be not gettin' very far." He looked down at her battered feet, which had started oozing blood again from a couple of gashes. "With the condition yer feet are in, 'tis a miracle ye are still standing. Here be some healin' oils that should fix ye up."

Brin reached into his pouch and pulled out a blue vial of liquid, which he opened and poured lavishly over Adair's feet and hands. Wherever the potion touched her, skin would steam as if touched by boiling liquid, yet there was no pain. Once the steam dispersed, her feet and hands were still red and tender, but the lacerations had healed. She put on her socks and boots again.

"Wow! Thanks...I feel so much better!"

"I'm happy to help. Now, what was I sayin'?...Oh yes, about the other two tunnels. That one there--" he gestured to the one on the left, "--leads down deep into the ground. At the end is a hole, even deeper than the one ye found in the tunnel ye came from. I do not know what is at the bottom, but judgin' by the noises coming from down below, whatever is there is likely worse than Blood Mother. The tunnel to the right leads to a painful death; it goes straight to Blood Mother's main chamber.

"Now ye asked me who Blood Mother is--'tis the only shrub practicin' hematophagy—meanin' it subsists by consumin' its victim's blood--hence the first part o' her name is "Blood." The term "Mother" comes from it reproducin' by off-shoots, so the multiple berry bushes surroundin' the area are interconnected to the parent shrub by roots. When ye picked the berries from one o' the shoots, the bush took ye to the water source for the parent, to be eaten at its leisure.

"So, put aside the idea o' leaving." Brin stood up and walked behind a pile of gems. He lifted up a wooden chest with checkered squares on top, "I say we play a friendly game of checkers instead. Loser shines the other's shoes." Brin clicked his boot heels together.

"What? No! I can't forget about leaving!" Adair began pacing the room. There *had* to be a way out, but how?

An earth-shaking screech filled the cavern. It sounded like someone-- or something--was in extreme pain. When it subsided, she asked in a muted voice "What was that?"

"It came from Blood Mother's cavern. It sounds like she's in a lot o' pain."

"She can talk?"

Brin set the game back down and joined Adair in apprehensively watching the tunnel entrance. "Not in a normal sense. She's alive and has an intelligence o' some sort, but she does not communicate with words. Legend has it Blood Mother screams when she faces a mighty foe. Only, leprechauns believe 'tis the way her leaves vibrate that make the sound."

Adair started walking toward the right tunnel, toward Blood Mother's cavern.

"What are ye doing? Do ye wish to die? If ye go in there, ye will not come back."

Adair paused. Then she heard an unexpected voice yelling, "Wait--no! You can't touch me, you foul disgusting plant! Ha, Ha! You'll never catch me...Adair? Where are you?" It was Ean's voice.

Adair turned to Brin, "Time to go!" She sprinted over and grabbed a fistful of his long red beard. If any of the mythological stories about leprechauns were true, then perhaps it was possible to control a leprechaun by holding their beard. She was about to find out.

"Unhand me, ye serpent in a fair maiden's disguise! How dare ye seize Brinston Denar the Third, from the clan o' MacCarlington? Let me go this instant! I will curse ye and me clan will hunt ye down if ye don't let me go!"

"Shh--be quiet! I'm not capturing you. I'm taking you out of here." She pulled Brin behind her, toward the direction of Ean's voice. The route lead upward and Adair's leg muscles began to burn as she ran uphill, her arm aching due to pulling Brin along, and her feet, though better because of Brin's help, throbbed with pain at each step. Exerting all her efforts to move forward, it only took a short amount of time for them to reach a ledge about sixty feet above a cavern floor. Adair and Brin skidded to a halt inches from the edge. The cavern, lit by inch-wide cracks in the ceiling permitting daylight, was circular and rather large--possibly seventy yards in diameter, and the ground was covered in berry bushes.

"Blood Mother," Brin whispered, raising a finger to point at the enormous shrub close to the farthest wall. More tree-like than shrub, Blood Mother was tall and wide enough to resemble a small hill. It had a weeping shape and whenever the thick black stems and branches swayed, despite the lack of a breeze, a wave-like effect rippled through the deep red leaves and berries, as if all plants connected to the Blood Mother made up a breathing animal.

Worried the bush might somehow sense them, Adair and Brin stepped back. Adair spied a tunnel to their left, carved into the wall. It spiraled downward around the cavern with archways overlooking the spacious cave every eight or ten feet. She let go of Brin's beard and waved at him to follow her.

As she was passing the second archway, Adair heard some labored grunts come from within the cavern. She peered down to see the cause of the sound and her pulse quickened: Ean was running, jumping and flipping off the walls and ground like an acrobat. Thorny green and brown vines snaked along the ground after him, trying to trip him and to knock him down. Afraid she would draw Blood Mother's attention if she made noise, Adair waved at Ean to get his attention.

∞ ∞ ∞

Even while outrunning the vines, Ean was still in shock over how responsive the bush had reacted to his attack. Drake's plan had been simple: get the bush mad enough to "swallow" him, neutralize any threat from Blood Mother, and find and rescue Adair. Getting the bushes mad was the easy part; they don't like it when someone hacks a bush in half. Before he had followed through on the swing of his machete, the neighboring plant had gobbled him up, bringing him to Blood Mother's cavern.

His first glimpse of it revealed piles of bones littering the floor amongst roots and vines. The bones, sometimes buried in dirt, were of various sizes, shapes and colors. A few twisted horns lay among the bones and Ean guessed they had belonged to unicorns. There was also a rather unique skull with spikes along the crown, causing him to suspect it was a dragon skull.

Then the roots and vines began to move toward him. One snagged his left wrist, which he lopped off with the machete before scrambling to avoid getting caught by the others. So far part two of the plan--neutralizing Blood Mother--wasn't turning out as well as he'd hoped. His energy had to be focused solely on defense, rather than offense.

He did not want to give the bush the upper hand (or vine, in this case). He had to be crafty with his strategy. He began to move in a pattern, causing the vines to tie themselves into knots. The bush did not catch on at first, but when it did its leaves began to shake hard as it tried to break itself free. Ean laughed at it and moved faster, trying to keep the bush distracted while strengthening the twisted knots of vines. The bush responded to his laughter, swaying and shaking its leaves furiously. *Hey! The bush doesn't like noise. I think I'll make some more...* Ean yelled at the bush and called for Adair as he flipped, spun and twisted above, below and around the vines.

Sweat appeared on Ean's brow and he slowed as his breathing became more strenuous. Worried about how long he could keep up his pace, he stumbled as the dirt beneath his feet started shaking. His heart skipped a beat as smaller blood berry bushes ripped their roots out of the ground. Stamping their thick brown roots, the waist-high bushes took up the chase, running after him like crazy little octopus plants.

"Agggh!" Launching himself off a large skull, Ean sailed ten feet up into the air. On the way down, a vine from Blood Mother snapped upward like a whip, slamming into his back. He came down hard, landing flat on his stomach. Losing his grip on the machete, the weapon went spinning out of sight. With a groan Ean rolled onto his back. More vines snaked their way toward him, followed by the small running bushes. Ean scrambled backward and his hand hit something smooth and hard. Grabbing it, he swung his arm to fend off the vines reaching for him.

He was pleased his impromptu weapon was a three foot long horn. As he fenced with the attacking vines, the horn began to give off heat. The tip Ean jabbed with glowed red, scorching any part of plant it touched.

"Whoa!" Ean began to counterattack in earnest, pushing first the vines, then the bushes back to the far side of the cavern. One enterprising bush managed to sneak along the wall until it was several feet behind Ean.

"Behind you!" The terrified voice penetrated Ean's concentration and he turned to see a small bush latch two of its branches on an overhead vine and swing itself toward him. Ean took two lunges straight toward it before he dropped, letting the momentum slide his body beneath the bush. He propped himself up, spotting two leather straps protruding from the leafy ground cover. Hoping for the best, Ean tugged on the straps, lifting free an oval shield with wickedly protruding sharp points.

Trying to figure out how to adjust the shield on his arm, he accidentally brushed the horn against the front. Soon the pointed barbs glowed as red as the horn tip. Since he couldn't figure the shield out, Ean gave up on it and instead flung it like a Frisbee toward Blood Mother. Soaring through the air, it became embedded into her trunk, causing her leaves to tremble to the accompaniment of her anguished wail. Ean jumped and whooped, "Point! You're going down!"

Blood Mother's response was a rustling sound. A long vine from the main trunk shot toward him and Ean reacted by pushing off into a back flip, dropping his makeshift horn weapon in the process. He arched back, catching a glimpse of Adair, waving her arms from an archway 20 feet above him. She was safe! With a sigh of relief that she was alive and well, Ean was ready to implement the rest of his plan. Leaning his head back, Ean began to laugh with all his might.

"What in the world is he doing?" Adair whispered to Brin. As she watched, the bushes vibrated and vines shot in all directions, intertwining with each other as they moved. The small mobile bushes began to bump into one another, knocking each other down or tripping over those which had fallen.

"He looks kind o' mad, if ye ask me," Brin commented. "Are ye sure this boy is right in the head?"

"Yes," she said distractedly, "Now hush, I want to see what he does next."

When the bush was entangled in knots, Blood Mother attacked. As a few untangled vines formed a circle around Ean, a branch with a sharply jagged, drill-like end slithered across the ground like a snake. When it drew near, the end reared up off the ground and the tip began to spin rapidly in a circular motion. "Oh crap," Ean muttered as he searched for his machete. Unable to find it, he reached toward a sword half-buried under human bones. Luck must have been on his side, he pulled it free in time to be ready for the oncoming vine.

The spinning vine hovered for a moment, then shot like an arrow straight toward his chest. Swinging the sword with all his strength, Ean severed the tip, causing the vine to thrash about in agony. The sword got knocked out of his hand by the flailing vine and Ean took off running again, laughing to taunt the bush. He needed to finish what he came to do--and fast, before he was overtaken by the vines. The thought had barely crossed his mind when he was tripped by a fast moving vine and went flying through the air. Out of control, he landed hard on the ground. He struggled to stand, but his legs wouldn't obey--they were bound by many small vines. All Ean could do was sit, struggle with vines, and yell.

The snapping sound of a branch breaking reverberated above his voice. Another vine was coming right at him. This one was more like an Anaconda snake--an immensely thick, open-ended tip filled with jagged twisted points, like deadly teeth. Ean, expecting he was most likely about to die, determined that no matter what, he would have to destroy the plant here and now to protect Adair.

The vine came closer and he brought his two hands together, pulling the cork top off a small bottle in his right hand. The vine lunged toward him, the gaping maw of splintered teeth aimed for his face and Ean plunged his arm into the mouth, emptying the contents of the vial into it. Ean screamed as it clamped down on his right bicep, piercing his flesh with jagged wooden spikes. Then, just as he thought all hope was lost, the vine released him and retreated back the way it had come. Another high-pitched screech filled the air--this time from Blood Mother. Its leaves began shaking violently, until they dropped off branches like rain falling to the ground.

An acrid odor filled the air, causing Ean to choke and cough. Ean looked around, noticing Adair had disappeared from view and the vines and roots surrounding him had shriveled to brittle husks. He broke off the vines surrounding him and stood up. All the plants had turned a sickly brown color as they shriveled; then they began turning a powdery white, burned from the inside out.

Ean got up and walked over to the Mother Bush, holding his injured right arm against his body. Except for the main trunk, the branches and vines had crumbled to the ground, leaving layers of white dust coating the floor. As he turned to look for Adair, something strange on the wall behind the massive remaining stalk caught his eye. He walked closer for a better look, placing his left hand on a patch of smooth, silvery wall. Solid rock melted away and a short tunnel appeared before him, leading upward toward daylight. The opening brought fresh air, providing relief from the decaying plant fumes. The increase in stark light gave Ean a better look at the cavern in which he had almost lost his life and the devastating effects his poison had caused.

Adair's muffled coughing echoed in the cavern. Ean called, "Adair?...Adair?... Where are you?" Due to the echoes, he couldn't tell where she was, so he scanned the upper walls of the room, hoping she would appear in one of the openings. Much to his surprise, a very large man stepped into view instead. He threw down a rope.

"Come Ean. Climb the rope."

Wondering how the man knew his name, he called back, "Who are you?"

"I am known by me friends as Brin, but there's no time to waste. We'll be needin' to get out o' this foul smellin' cavern."

"I need to find my friend first. Her name is Adair."

Stepping from the shadows behind the man, Adair waved to Ean with the hand not busy plugging her nose.

"Great, now ye can come up," Brin replied.

"I have a better idea," Ean raised his arm and gestured to the overlooked hole in the wall.

Noticing the daylight for the first time, the large man's face lit up with a large grin. "'Tis the best news in over a hundred years!" Motioning for Adair to climb down first, Brin then anchored the rope and descended after.

Crossing the room to Ean, Adair flung herself into his arms. "Oh Ean, I was so scared! I didn't know what to do to help. Are you okay?" She pulled away to look at him. "Your arm is bleeding! Maybe Brin can help you. How did you kill her?"

"Well I used a complicated potion I put together. What made it so effective was the core ingredient of dragon blood."

"Dragon blood?" Adair stepped back with a look of revulsion while Brin reached in the sporran at his side. "Ean, what did you do to Drake? If you hurt him so help me I'll--"

Startled that Brin was now holding an old double bladed battle axe and glaring at him, Ean backed away with both hands raised in the air. "Wait! Stop! Drake's fine. The whole blood thing was his idea. I swear!"

"What did ye do?" Brin roared.

Ean stammered, "I-I used some of the blood, I mean juice, from the blood berry bush, by crushing the berries you dropped last night. I mixed it with a few drops of Drake's blood--that he provided to me--along with some plant extracts and one very dangerous poison I got with the supplies. Then I heated the liquid to make an extraction and added a few more drops of dragon blood. This made the poison easy to absorb and more effective. Come outside—you can ask Drake and know I'm telling the truth!" Ean started toward the tunnel leading to fresh air and freedom then stopped and looked back to the other two.

"Ye go first." Brin commanded.

Ean led them to the tunnel. He slowed down to examine an intricate pattern lining the walls that looked purposeful. Unable to resist the desire to run his hands along the wall, Ean appreciated the wavelike ripples of the multi-colored rock surface, polished to a crystal-like clarity and smoothness. Ean couldn't help but think his mother would have loved this breathtakingly beautiful place. He glanced back at Adair's reaction. She was at the entrance to the tunnel, looking at something in her hand. Pocketing it, she started to follow.

"Move along," Brin boomed, now holding his battle axe over his shoulder with one hand.

"I was admiring the wall..." Ean stole another glance in Adair's direction.

"Sure you be...now stop lookin' at the lady and keep walkin'." The comment caught Adair's attention. Her head came up and for a moment their eyes met. Looking away, Ean was grateful she couldn't see his face flush red, though he did hear a snickering laugh come from Adair's direction, which only made him blush more.

Trapped underground for so long, Brin's excitement for freedom couldn't be contained and his stride overtook Ean's pace so he was first out of the tunnel. Ean and Adair caught up to Brin at the edge of a cliff jutting out from the mountainside. The leprechaun was leaning on his axe and looking up into the sky.

"Well, would ye look at that? 'Tis a rare sight." Brin said to no one in particular.

"What is?"

He shook his head. "See the greenish mass hoverin' up there in the sky? That, me Dear, is presumably yer dragon friend Drake." Brin said reverently. He continued, "A few hundred years ago there was a rebellion. Before it happened, all sorts o' dragons flew about--the 'living rainbows o' the world,' they be called. 'Tis because they be all shades o' colors--yellow, green, black, red, orange, purple, blue, gold, silver, any number o' those combined! Whatever color they be on the outside, they be on the inside, blood, bones, or fire.

"Ever since the rebellion, no dragons have been seen on Natura. To protect themselves and the knowledge they possess, they ripped their city right out o' the ground, they did. They stay within the protection o' a special shield around their city."

"Did you know any dragons personally?" Adair wondered.

"Oh, not personally. But me clan has always been close to dragons. Our colors are black and shades o' gray to match the first dragon we befriended." Brin looked at the horizon in the distance with a touch of sadness, "What a fine friend he was..."

After a moment, Brin spotted Adair studying an item in her hand. Sunlight reflected off the object. "Why Adair, what do ye have there?"

"Oh, um...something I found on the ground back in Blood Mother's den. It may be a key, but it...well, I'm not sure how to describe it," she held it up.

Brin whistled, "May I handle it please?" Taking it from Adair, Brin expertly examined the key. It looked like a metallic claw, made from intertwined patterns of silver, gold, and titanium, fluidly blended as if the three were one element. Carved runes ran along three sides with jagged marks and holes in odd places, and a pearl was perched atop the thickest part of the claw.

Brin marveled, "There is magic within..." He looked up in wonderment. "Adair, I think ye have found a Dragon Key!"

"A what?" Adair looked more confused.

"A Dragon Key," Drake's voice boomed as his huge mass blocked out the sun. With a start they all turned in time to watch Drake land on the mountain side.

The downdraft from Drake's wings blew loose dirt into Adair's eyes.

"Augh!" Turning away from the direction of the wind, Adair rubbed her eyes and unable to see her direction, stumbled to the edge of the cliff.

"No you don't!" Ean caught her arm as she lost her footing, pulling her into his arms to keep her from plunging to her death.

She gasped as she realized what had almost happened. "Ean...thank you!"

"No problem," Ean smiled, "I've saved your life twice today...But who's counting?"

Chapter 12

Flight to Ireland

*D*espite the late hour, Jeff bounced in his seat with excitement. Not only was he on cloud nine, he was above the clouds-- flying first class over the Atlantic Ocean on his way to Dublin, Ireland. By pure luck his parents agreed to let him come on this trip; it had taken fast talking from Jeff and reassurances from Ean's parents that he would never be out of their sight before they conceded to let him go. They were told Ean had gone on ahead with a family member to Ireland and was hoping his best friend could join them for some sightseeing fun. Of course, they neglected to mention Ean's real whereabouts and their hope to open a portal to another planet; definitely too much information for Jeff's parents to handle.

During the three days prior to the trip, Jeff spent hours researching the Tara Stone, black holes, native Irish folklore and legends. He even studied science fiction books for plausible ways to open the portal to Natura. A small part of him felt guilty for not telling his parents everything, but he figured it would be a trillion to one chance for their quest to succeed. Since he didn't want to worry his parents, or be grounded through college, he figured he was doing them (and himself) a favor by keeping them in the dark.

Jeff had talked nonstop during the first leg of the flight to Chicago, Illinois. Emily and Jason were now very familiar with Jeff's family camping vacations, including the time Jeff thought he heard a bear outside his tent and yelled loudly enough to wake up everyone in the campground. It turned out to be the generator from another camping site. Although he had been preoccupied reading or dozing during the final flight to Ireland, he was again wound up with excitement.

Jeff looked over to where Ean's parents sat together. The underlying tension between the two had softened somewhat. Since they were awake, he leaned across the aisle to whisper, "So...what's our plan after we find Elizabeth? Drop the bombshell and get it over with, or try to break it to her slowly?"

"It is always better to be direct and to the point," Jason opined. "Better to get all the cards on the table and deal with the reaction afterward."

Emily shook her head, "I thought we would do a more sensitive approach. She must be devastated her sister is still missing."

Realizing things were not as smooth as he first thought, Jeff decided to remain silent.

Emily continued, "When dealing with a woman you don't know, Jeff, it is best to not come off as a crazy lunatic for your first impression." She looked at Jason. "Believe me. I'm a woman."

"Alright," Jason said. "How do you propose we do that?"

"Well, after we find her, we introduce ourselves as the concerned parents. Once we bond over our common situation, we start from the beginning and try to sound realistic and plausible. Then we hope she doesn't call the authorities to charge us as accessories to kidnapping."

"Ah, I hadn't thought of that," Jeff admitted. After the brief image of being behind bars flashed through his mind, he changed the subject. "On a different note, I've been thinking about the Tara Stone. Mr. McMurrin, you mentioned when you turned sixteen Jon Henric took you to the Stone to see if you would be able to open the portal, which it didn't. Has more than one descendant ever touched the Stone at the same time?"

Jason's furrowed brows became more wrinkled as he considered the question. "No, I don't think so."

"Why not?"

"By tradition, Jon only took the potential Talent Master to the portal."

"I'm wondering if tradition was wrong."

"I agree with you," Emily interjected.

Interested, Jason turned directly toward him, "What do you mean?"

"Well...it's just a theory, but each male descendant from your family possesses talents of some sort. What if more than one of the royal bloodline, each with his own talents, touched the Stone at the same time? Could you trick the Stone to activate?"

"I don't know for sure, but I don't think so."

"Why not?" Emily and Jeff stated at the same time.

"According to family legend, a dragon cast a spell upon the portal so only a Talent Master could open it. A Talent Master is one person who possesses all the talents you could possibly imagine. So even if we had two or three generations of men from my family, I don't think it would be enough to work."

"Maybe," Jeff retorted, "But why try the Stone by yourself? That doesn't make sense."

"True." Emily spoke up. "The girl went with Ean and Jon; it would have made more sense for the entire family to have been there when Ean touched the stone."

Jason could tell Emily was still angry at the thought she could have been with Ean when he visited the Stone, and would therefore be with him now. With a sigh, he looked at Emily, "I'm sorry my love. It had always been done that way. I figured only the heir and Jon could go through, assuming the portal opened at all...I mean, when I tried it, the portal didn't open, so I didn't think it would for him, even with his talents."

The airplane began to descend and the conversation came to a quick close as they prepared for landing. Disembarking the plane, they headed toward the car rental counter. To Jeff's surprise, they walked past the counter to the parking area. Among a small list of names on an electronic board, the name 'McMurrin' was highlighted, followed by parking spot number. Jeff followed Jason and Emily to the spot, where a luxury SUV was parked. Stowing their luggage, they climbed in and Jason used the key-- ready in the ignition--to start the car and drive out of the lot.

"Um...aren't we supposed to check out?" Jeff questioned.

"There are perks when you travel a lot," Jason replied with a smile.

Once driving, Emily searched the GPS map for the address of Adair's father, based upon information from local media news and Elizabeth's interviews with the press. Within twenty minutes they parked outside a row of townhouses. No one moved. Jeff waited for the McMurrins to decide their first course of action. Jason looked at Emily with an expression that seemed to ask *'now what ?'*

Emily rolled her eyes, "Oh fine, I'll go."

Jason without missing a beat amended, "We'll go together." So the three made the short, but somehow also long, journey up the steps and Emily knocked on the door.

Chapter 13

Legions and Brigades

The saddle sores and bruises from his battle were driving Ean crazy. He kept shifting in his saddle, trying to find a better position, but the aching was unavoidable no matter what he did. After patching up Ean's wounds and getting the camping supplies, the group had continued traveling. Adair--with a small Drake resting on her saddle horn--rode at the front, while Ean on his horse and Brin, astride the Friesian pulling the supply wagon, trailed behind. Tired of handling the pain, Ean decided to call a break. "Hey, A--" his voice caught in his throat as he caught sight of her; a breeze had blown toward them, tossing her auburn hair in the sunlight and creating the illusion of fire radiating down her head and dancing off the tips of her hair. She stopped her horse and turned back, "Did you say something Ean?"

Ean shook himself out of his distracted thinking. "Uh, yeah. We should take a break. You know, so Brin can rest."

Brin's head turned sharply toward him, but before he could retort, Adair spoke up. "Good idea. We might as well grab a bite to eat...you know, while Brin rests," she said with a wink.

Brin grinned and rode up to be closer to Ean, "I suppose I am hungry enough to eat a horse."

Drake smiled, "I believe I could too."

"You two--especially you Drake--will stay away from my horse," Ean stated. "Unless you plan on flying us to Ferreglen yourself."

"Oh Ean, give it a rest," Adair commented, exasperated by his frequent complaints along the way about riding over flying.

Drake chuckled good-naturedly. "I believe I have explained why that wouldn't work already. As you recall, the Illusion Forest is magical and as a new visitor, it requires you to travel to Ferreglen by going *through* the forest, not over it. Furthermore, though I gave the three of you a short ride back to the horses from the cliff does not mean I am a pack animal meant for carrying creatures such as yourselves."

They pulled off the trail and Ean dismounted first. The ground was softer than expected and Ean's boots sunk into the ground about an inch. When he walked up to Adair's horse, a sloshing sound accompanied his steps.

"Here, let me help you down."

Surprised Adair teased, "What a gentleman! Why, I think I like this side of you best, Ean McMurrin."

"Did you want help or not?" He huffed.

"Ah, *there's* the side I'm used to." She lifted her leg over the saddle, so both of her legs dangled on the side of the horse by Ean, and leaned down so she could place each of her hands on his shoulders while Ean placed his hands on her waist. Acutely aware of how close she was as she slid off the Arabian mare toward him, Ean's face flushed yet again. He was doing that way more often than he ever had before.

Standing in front of him Adair cleared her throat, "Ean, you can let go of me now." His face flushed even more as he realized he still held her waist.

"Oh...sorry."

"No problem," she said with a sly smile, catching his hand as he pulled away and giving it a light squeeze before letting him go.

Walking over to Brin, Adair called back to Ean, "Could you unload the food and cooking supplies while Brin and I find a dry spot to build a fire?"

"Sure, not a problem." He went over to the cart and tugged back the canvas cover to remove a large carton of pots and cooking utensils, as well as two ham roasts (one would be for Drake's meal), then some cheese and bread. Then he hiked up the hill to where the other three stood.

Adair had her fists on her hips. "This would be the perfect spot. Look at how dry the ground is! Plus we have these trees for shade." Adair indicated the large trees providing them cover, then took in the inspiring view of flowers and trees carpeting the level ground below them. "Ean-- there you are. Why don't you and Brin go down to those trees and get some dry wood for a fire?"

"What? Oh...okay." Ean warily eyed Brin, still not trusting him with the battle ax.

"Back in a moment, me lady." Brin grinned at Adair and gave a short bow before walking down the hill with Ean.

"What was that all about?" Drake asked when the two were gone searching for wood. He was still small and curled up around her shoulder.

"I have no idea what you're referring to," Adair said loftily.

Drake admonished. "Giving orders to Ean and Brin. You know it will cause him to snap."

"Who?" Adair asked innocently.

"Play it how you will, but be warned--your game is not going to end well if you don't change your tactics." Drake took flight into the air. Gaining altitude, he grew to the size of two elephants (not counting the lengthy wings, of course) and flew away.

The brightness of the sun on his rippling green scales reminded Adair of her mother's jade earrings in the drawer of her home. For a moment Adair felt an aching sadness creep into her heart.

Drake's thoughts enter her mind: *Fear not. All will be well.* Startled, her melancholy feelings disappeared. Marveling at her newfound connection with Drake, she watched her dragon become a small receding speck in the sky until he disappeared. She set to work preparing the food.

∞ ∞ ∞

Stomachs now full, the four travelers rested around the diminishing fire. All evidence of the ham roast and roasted potatoes were gone. "Adair, ye be a superb cook." Brin commented. "'Twas a meal fit for a king...wait,

71

it was for a king!" Brin nodded toward Ean and began to laugh heartily at his own joke. Drake joined in, more due to the exasperated look on Ean's face than from the joke.

"Why thank you Brin. I'm glad at least *one* of you appreciated my cooking."

"What?" Ean said. "Oh, yeah, sorry--it was good...though not quite like my mom's cooking..." he said, as his thoughts had been turned toward his parents. As soon as he had made the comment, he regretted it, because Adair burst into tears. "Wait! No, that's not what I meant! I'm so sorry Adair--it was amazing..."

Adair wiped away her tears, sniffed loudly and stood up, her chin held high. "I'm going for a walk." Without looking at him, she added, "Ean, you'll clean up, won't you?" Not waiting for a response, she walked briskly away down the slope. Drake flew after her.

"Ye have done it now." Brin commented in a gruff voice. "In me clan, had I acted so thoughtless toward a lady, me father would have shackled me arms together and strung me up in the nearest tree for a couple o' days."

"First off Brin, I am sorry I was so tactless. My mom would have been appalled at what I said. And secondly--shackles?"

"Yes. It may seem a bit unorthodox, but I learned to control me tongue and ye have not."

After cleaning up, Ean moped around the clearing. After a good deal of time had passed and evening approached, Ean began to worry as Adair had not yet returned. He approached Brin where he was using his battle ax to chop larger blocks of wood into smaller firewood-sized pieces. Ean swallowed nervously as he watched the ax pass through the wood with ease.

"Brin, should we be worried they are not back yet?"

"No. She is with Drake. She will be fine."

"Well it is getting late. Why don't we camp here tonight? I'll go and get the tents and supplies."

"Yes, good idea. I will look after the horses."

Brin tended to the horses and checked their shoes while Ean set up tents and bedding for everyone. Then Ean prepared a stew in a Dutch oven over the fire and baked some biscuits in another. About the time the food was ready, Adair and Drake came back into the camp.

Ean stood, squared his shoulders, and walked up to her. He apologized again, "I am *so* sorry Adair. What I said was wrong on so many levels. It won't happen again. Please, *please* forgive me."

With a sigh she placed a hand on his shoulder, "It's fine; water under the bridge. We both miss our families."

Her response didn't make him feel better. It reminded him he was the reason she was on Natura, and it was his responsibility to get her home.

Adair looked around the camp. The stew's fragrance registered in her mind and her eyebrows arched up in surprise as she looked at Ean, "You cooked?"

"It was the least I could do after making a fool of myself."

"Huh. We'll have to see how you did."

"You might be surprised."

A short while later, Adair set her empty bowl down and gave her verdict. "You're right, I am surprised. The stew was passable and the biscuits buttery and moist. Overall, I'd give it a passing grade."

"What? Only passing?" Ean did his best to look offended, "What did you think Brin?"

He grunted, "Not bad. The stew had a nice, strong flavor and a tingle in the back o' the throat. 'Twas very much passable."

"And you Drake? What was your opinion?"

"It was okay."

"Wow, you are a tough crowd! Maybe you guys will be more grateful tomorrow night."

"You're going to cook again?" Adair asked. Somewhat territorial over the cooking duties, she was starting to think she had been replaced as chef and wasn't happy with it.

"It wouldn't be fair of us to expect you to do all the cooking. Besides, cooking is better than cleaning. And if I cook, then you clean, right?"

"Now wait a minute!" Adair's look was almost mutinous. "I believe you still owe me for what happened earlier. So *you* can clean the dishes."

"Water under the bridge, huh?" Ean muttered.

Adair sighed. "No, I love to cook and dishes never were my forte. So, while we're here, you can do all the cleaning and I'll do the cooking. Agreed? Great." She walked into her tent and closed the flap behind her.

"Now there is a strong-willed woman," Brin commented, looking at Drake. "I can guess why ye chose her as a Dragon Maiden."

"I've been meaning to ask you Drake, what is a Dragon Maiden?" Ean asked.

"During difficult or dangerous times, dragons would pick virtuous maidens to assist them during challenges. When you and Adair came to Natura, I chose her to help me help you, as well as for her own protection. Dragon Maidens are bestowed with gifts and she will learn what these are when the time is right or when there is real need. She has discovered we can communicate to each other without speaking out loud."

"Wait a minute--have you two been having conversations while we've been traveling?"

The lizard smiled in return. "One of her gifts. I won't give away all her secrets, however, since they are less likely to be taken for granted when one discovers it themselves."

"Drake..." Ean hated secrets.

"You will have to wait and see." Drake curled up on the ground under a tree and closed his eyes.

"Dragons," Brin chuckled. "Always wantin' to be mysterious."

"I heard that..." Drake commented.

"Good night, all." Brin walked to his own tent, leaving Ean to put out the fire.

Ean lay awake late while various thoughts bounced around his mind. Starting to drift off to sleep, he heard a faint sob. He realized Adair was still awake and crying in her tent. The weight of the world settled on his heart as he considered how she had been literally abducted to another planet against her wishes. Before falling into a troubled sleep, he made a personal commitment to make the journey more bearable for her and find a way to send her home.

The problem with sleeping is that oftentimes uncontrolled dreams can take over, and this night Ean's dreams were not pleasant. Once again he was someone else; this time a stout older man, with nubby fingers covered in blood. From his ragged clothes seeped his blood, dripping into a puddle at his feet. The slightest movement he made caused him agonizing pain, which was only overshadowed by fear of the oncoming monster.

Words, a distance echo, sprang from Ean's lips, *"You will go no further."* The monster roared in response, rumbling like a thousand boulders tumbling down a steep mountain, and Ean spotted what looked like a body made of boulders walking toward him. The head was flat, made of rock slabs sandwiched together to make a mouth, eyes, and ears. Every time it moved the ground shook and trees fell. Bodies littered the ground, as if an army had been stomped into the ground and the only one standing between the monster and the large vast city from his previous dreams was Ean.

Ean's hand lifted and he started waving a carved stick. A green hue began to glow from within the wood, getting brighter until there was a sudden flash of brilliant green light--too intense for him to look at-- replaced by a bush with long vines and roots. The plant scrambled upright, scuttling upon its roots like an octopus out of water until it launched itself at the monster, tackling it, winding vines between cracks and joints of the rock, encasing it like bandages covering a mummy. The monster fell with a tremendous tremor, only to writhe upon the ground.

Colorful figures appeared high in the sky, swarming together like a stream of colors before streaking to the battle below. Ean's breath caught in his throat as he watched the dragons pick up the entangled plant and monster and carry their heavy burden toward the vast mountain in the distance.

∞ ∞ ∞

Ean gasped and sat upright in bed, no longer the injured stout man of his dreams. He took a few deep breaths and lay back down, unable to shake the feeling there was something important about his dream he couldn't quite put his finger on. Letting the sounds of camp and smell of eggs and bacon calm him, Ean stretched before crawling out of his tent to spot Adair cooking over the fire. "Mm, I can't wait to eat!"

Adair's eyes widened as she spotted him. "Are you okay? You look like a zombie!"

"Great..." He grumbled, "That's how I feel..."

"How did you sleep?" She asked.

"I had a weird dream...nothing to worry about."

Shrugging, Adair went back to flipping the bacon, absentmindedly brushing her hair behind one ear.

Still tired, Ean sat on a rock and watched her cook. *Even in the morning she looks beautiful*, Ean thought. *Now stop that*, he chided himself, *you can't think those things; you have a duty to help her get home--nothing else.*

He glanced over to where Brin was stretching by his tent, and lowered his voice so only Adair could hear him. "I think I'll head over to the stream and clean up a bit. I should be back soon, but please save some food for me--I'm afraid Brin will be hungry enough to eat all the food if you don't."

She gave him a scrutinizing look. "Freshening up is a good idea. You're beginning to look more like the trail than an Earthling."

"Very funny." He replied with sarcasm.

"True none the less." She smiled as she turned her attention to the eggs.

Though he was unwilling to admit Adair was right, his arms were a darker brown than usual and the dark specks scattered on them proved the color was due more to dirt than a sun tan. He sighed and headed off to the stream he spotted before they pulled off the trail the day before. He figured since he was using cold mountain water to bathe, he would have to hurry fast and scrub a little harder than usual.

By the time Ean returned most of the food was gone, but he still had enough to fill his plate.

"Whoa, guys--" Adair breathed, "Look at those butterflies! They are *so* beautiful."

Ean turned around to look and saw something flicker in the sun rays filtering past the tree leaves. Several large butterflies flittered toward them.

Drake chuckled, "Those aren't butterflies. They are the fairies of the Forest. They don't bite...often..."

Awestruck, Adair and Ean stared at the twirling, dancing fairies, their sheer wings shining like diamonds in the morning light, their movements accompanied by a tinkling sound--like a crystal wind chime. The little figures were dainty, with sharp noses, chins, and ears, and their smooth skin glittered with a variety of colors. Ean knew his mother would have loved to have seen such a breathtaking sight and he found himself missing his parents again.

As they drew near, Ean was able to estimate their sizes to be between four to seven inches in height. The fairies began to encircle the group before closing around Adair. They sped up in excitement until they became a blur, and the tinkling increased to become a loud clanging racket. The travelers covered their ears as the blurred movements of the fairies became more concentrated into a rainbow tornado surrounding Adair's head. After a moment, the tornado broke apart, and the fairies slowed their movement down, moving away to encircle the group again before gracefully disappearing into the trees. Ean stared with amazement at the flower tiara resting on Adair's head. The flowers in the tiara shone like sheer crystals, mimicking the wings of the fairies.

"Those are female fairies, Ean." Brin explained. "They possess a lot o' magic and can do about anythin' in groups. The larger the group, the stronger the magic."

Ean scratched his head, more confused than ever.

Drake burst out laughing because of the look on Ean's face. In fact, he was laughing so hard a flame of green fire erupted from his nose.

"Now *that* is funny." Adair gasped while laughing. Together everyone laughed until tears threatened to form in their eyes.

When Ean managed to collect himself, he asked, "What are the fairies doing in the Illusion Forest?"

Drake replied, "If you recall Ean, I told you the Illusion Forest is home to magical creatures."

"Well I'd like to know more about them." Adair said, admiring the tiara now in her hands.

Brin spoke up, "Ye could say the female fairies are the gardeners o' the Illusion Forest. They fly around, creatin' and makin' plants grow and change. 'Tis their passion. In fact, there once was a fairy so in love with a flower she made, she stayed by it for weeks. Every time I passed by, 'twas a different color--whatever color fit her mood the best. Her obsession was so strong, the Brigade had to move her and the flower died."

"Why did it die?"

"Well, the fairy had nurtured the flower with so much magic, it came to depend upon it. When she and her magic left, it couldn't live."

"Oh how sad," Adair commented.

"Don't feel too bad. The flower sprouted seeds and its offspring still live in the forest."

Adair's eyebrows furrowed, "You said the 'Brigade' moved the fairy. Who are they?"

"Ah, the Brigade be the good male fairies--those that keep peace and order in the Forest. Not only is their magic different, but they look different too. They be taller..." Brin held his hands just over a foot apart, "and more camouflaged in color, to blend in with their natural surroundin's. They be leaner, stronger, and skilled in battle. As far as their magic...well, let's hope we never see one or there be trouble comin' our way."

"Wait," Ean chimed in. "You said they were the 'good males.' Are there 'bad' ones?"

Brin cringed, annoyed at himself for revealing something unpleasant. "I'm afraid there be rather devilish ones, too. They be the males who drink the nectar o' the flowers."

"What does the nectar do?"

"Nectar from flowers created by female fairies has special properties. To the male fairies, 'tis like a growth chemical or drug. The males who drink it get bulkier with disproportionate muscles and their huntin' and fightin' skills be magnified a hundred fold. One side effect o' this transformation is they lose their magical abilities. They call themselves the 'Giddian Legion'."

As if on cue, the forest was filled with a clamor as it became flooded with angry male fairies. Bulky fairies armed with weapons appeared on one side of the fire. Leaner fairies lined up on the opposite side. Ean guessed the first were Giddian Legion fairies and the others were from the Brigade.

Brin disappeared and Ean jumped across the fire pit, pinning Adair to the ground to shield her with his body as tiny projectiles flew through the air toward them. Growing in size to stand over Ean and Adair, Drake let out a roar and a blaze of green fire, his flames toasting some Giddian Legion warriors who had been aiming their blowgun darts at the Earthlings.

From the corner of his eye, Ean saw a large fairy sneak past Drake. Wielding a sharp spear, the fairy drew back his arm to aim. As he started his throw, he froze. His wings were pinned backward and his arm stuck, holding the spear over his head. Brin appeared behind him--it was his hands holding the fairy tight.

The battle continued with an intense skirmish. Drake swiped his claws and tail at Legion fairies within reach and burned others to ash--careful to avoid the Brigade fairies zooming through the fray. The air was filled with the buzzing sound of fairies attacking fairies in multiple clashes. Giddian Legion fairies who were dealt fatal blows turned into stone statues of themselves, whereas Brigade fairies killed turned into glittering puffs of dust. It was only a matter of minutes before the battle was over and the Brigade had won. The remaining Giddian Legion fairies retreated into the trees, followed by the rear Brigade guard, which continued their pursuit into the forest.

One large fairy separated from the Brigade and approached Drake off to one side. They conversed in quiet tones.

"Excuse me," came Adair's muffled voice. "Could you please move?"

Ean rolled off Adair in one swift movement. Getting up, he took Adair's hands and pulled her up to her feet.

Dazed, Adair demanded, "Alright, could someone tell me why we are in a war zone?"

"I don't know," Brin held up the Giddian Legion fairy he had captured during the fight, "But we be going to find out."

The Brigade fairies surrounded Brin's prisoner. The fairy talking to Drake flew over and placed the point of his golden spear against the prisoner's throat. Binding the fairy with cords, a few Brigade warriors pulled him away from the group while several others collected the stone statues of the Legion Fairies. The leader gave a brief nod to Drake, and within a flash all of the fairies had disappeared, leaving the travelers alone.

"Hey, where did they go?" Ean asked. Addressing Drake he added, "What happened?"

Drake's attention was elsewhere. A growling sound grew within his chest as he paced within the clearing, until he let out a tremendous roar, causing the other three to cover their ears. Seething, he grumbled, "Old decrepit body of Elders...*what* are they doing?" Whatever he was going to say next was lost to the roar of fire escaping his mouth, which singed the hair on Ean's head.

Afraid of the intense anger coming from Drake, the other three scrambled away from the sweeping range of his tail. After a few moments, Drake regained control of his temper and tail. He turned to address the three. "The band of Giddian Legion Fairies were mercenaries. They were hired by the Elder's Council of Ferreglen to terminate A... member of our party."

"Who?" Brin asked Drake.

Looking at Brin, he responded, "An Earthling."

Chapter 14

Assassins' Target

The large golden doors of the Council Chambers opened, allowing the departing Elders to pour into the hallway. Some walked deep in thought, while others whispered in small groups.

Among the last to leave was the ancient Elder Romearus, who shuffled while holding onto the arm of the sandy haired, hot-tempered Elder known as Augustus. "You don't fool me, young man," Romearus rasped to his younger companion once the others were out of earshot.

Augustus hid his alarm behind a calm expression. "What do you mean?"

"I mean it is obvious you do not agree with our esteemed Emperor."

"Do you always agree with him?"

Romearus's chuckle ended with a cough that made him stop to recover for a moment. "Once upon a time I thought I knew better than he in matters of Ferreglen. But time after time I found his rulings to be fair and just. I may provide an opinion or council to him, but because I know what type of man he is, I am content with his decisions." He turned to face the younger Arturian, shakily pointing his bony finger at him, "You would do well to be patient with him as well. You will find you trust him too."

I doubt that , Augustus thought, rolling his eyes. Movement in the shadows by the windowsill at the far end of the hallway caught his attention. He smiled and patted the old man's hand still gripping his arm for support. "Sage advice, Hakham Romearus," said Augustus, placing the honorary title for a wise and educated man before the Elder's name.

Spotting another council member conversing nearby, he interrupted, "Elder, would you be so kind as to escort our esteemed Brother? I have forgotten I had an appointment I must attend."

Handing off the old man, Augustus turned and walked down the hall toward the waiting messenger. Making sure he was unobserved, he changed his features and darkened his hair color, then slid into the shadows by the window and into a hidden alcove where a scrawny-looking Arturian was nervously hopping from foot to foot.

"What news have you?" He whispered.

The messenger cleared his throat. "The Legion Fairies attacked the group, but were thwarted when Brigade Fairies joined the foreigners."

"Any injuries? Deaths?"

"Several Legion Fairies were killed and a few were--"

"Not the fairies, you idiot!" Augustus barked at him. He dropped his voice again, "I *meant*, what about the *Earthlings* ?"

Trembling, he replied, "It appears they are unscathed, Elder."

Taking deep breaths to steady himself, Augustus considered the situation. "It appears they are more formidable than we previously thought. Very well, we can be formidable too. Here's what we'll do..."

Augustus issued new commands, and with a quick nod of his head, the scrawny man stealthily slipped out of the alcove and disappeared.

∞ ∞ ∞

Shocked at Drake's ominous announcement of the assassination attempt, Ean and Adair turned to look at each other. Ean's fear turned to concern when he saw how terrified Adair looked standing there, her face pale and her body shaking. Putting his arm around her, he reassured, "Don't worry--we'll be fine. After all," he gestured to Brin, "We have a leprechaun--who can become invisible, I might add--and a dragon to protect us." Trying to lighten the mood, he added, "And let's not forget I'm here, too--the one and only 'All Powerful Talent Master.'"

"Yeah, uh thanks Ean." Adair shrugged away from him and walked away.

Drake nudged Ean to go after her. Uncertain of what to do, he hesitatingly asked, "What do I say?" Drake gave an unbalanced wave of his wings, which turned out to be a shrug.

Sighing, he hurried to catch up to her. By the time he did, she was sitting on a large log overlooking the valley, brushing tears off her checks with the back of her hand. He sat next to her, "Hey."

She sniffled. "It's me, Ean. I'm the unwanted Earthling...the one who's not supposed to be here."

"Do you believe that? 'Cause from where I sit, it only makes sense I'm the target. My ancestors were slaughtered in this world. Now here I am...the heir to the human throne on this planet." Ean sighed and spread his hands helplessly, "If I ever learn to master my talents and magic, then I would be the biggest threat to the current rulers."

Looking out at the vista, she said unconvinced, "I guess it could be either of us. We'll have to find out at Ferreglen."

"Yeah, but should we even go there?" Ean asked. "I mean, if they issued some sort of death sentence for either one of us, we can't trust them."

"I don't know. I do know I trust Drake, and he wants us to go there."

"Yeah, but that was before we got attacked by fairies hired by someone at Ferreglen to kill us! I think we need to lay low for a little while, to lose anyone else who might be trying to go after us."

Adair thought for a moment before agreeing, "We should talk to Drake and Brin and see if there is somewhere we can hide out."

After explaining their idea, Brin was the first to speak. "Well, if ye are in need o' a safe haven, then there's no place safer than in me home town o' Glen-Delay! Ye'd be welcome to stay with me family clan--the MacCarlington Clan..." His expression grew wistful. "It'd sure be nice to visit me loved ones again. Over one hundred years can seem longer than ye'd think."

Adair couldn't stand seeing Brin look sad. "Sounds like a great option Brin. Are you sure your family wouldn't mind our company?"

Brin grinned, "They would love nothing more. It gives 'em an excuse to engage in festivities."

Adair smiled. "Sounds like fun."

"How far away is your city?" Ean asked.

"Not too far. 'Tis also in the Illusion Forest. I believe we can make it in about a week, give or take a day or two."

"Let's get going."

Despite Drake's reluctance to change their plans, Ean insisted they ready the horses and head back to the stone trail. This time Brin was in the lead and Drake flew overhead to scout for potential ambushes. Besides a brief stop for some food mid-day, their progress was steady. With dusk approaching, Drake descended. "There's a good place to rest for the night up ahead." Following him, the weary travelers went through the motions of setting up camp, taking care of the horses, and making a quick meal from their food stores.

After eating, they rested around the fire. Ean, exhausted after the eventful morning and day of travel, was resting with his back to a tree. His mind had been drifting, until he had a feeling something was not quite right. Listening, he didn't hear anything out of the ordinary. In reality, he didn't hear much of anything as it was quiet--almost too quiet. The usual evening sounds from native insects were absent, causing Ean's nerves to be on alert. Not wanting to appear overly paranoid about it, he casually asked, "Should we take turns on watch?"

"It wouldna' hurt," Brin agreed. "I'll take the first watch. Ean, ye be on second. Drake, third."

"What about me?" Adair asked.

"Consider me old-fashioned Adair--," Brin started.

Ean jumped in, "That's easy. You are over two hundred years old, aren't you?"

Brin glared at him, "Humph...as I was saying, I believe lady folk shouldna' be on the front line o' danger."

"Sweet as that is, Brin," Adair gestured to their encampment, "We all are on the front line of danger."

"I agree with Brin--at least for tonight," Drake added.

Feeling like a burden, Adair didn't agree with the verdict. Nevertheless she stopped arguing and turned in for the night.

It seemed like no time had passed before Brin was nudging Ean awake for his turn as lookout. Brin tugged his beard, "'Tis a quiet night...unsettlin' if ye ask me."

Ean stretched. A little more alert, he went to the cart and rummaged around until he found the sword he had ordered from Louie Lou's Shop. He stayed alert for any unusual sounds, and often got up to walk and stretch his legs. The third time he got up to pace, he was passing Adair's tent when he heard a soft rustle from behind. Heart pounding, he turned, sword held at the ready.

There at his feet sat several small rabbits--Ean did a quick count-- ten, in fact. Four squatted on their haunches, one tilting its head looking at him with big black eyes. The others sniffed the ground or twitched their noses. Wondering where they came from, Ean imagined Adair would have loved the cute, little bunnies. Knowing her, she'd probably fawn all over them.

He squatted so he wouldn't scare them. "Are you little fellas hungry?" He whispered.

All the bunnies now watched him with their wide eyes. Almost as one they opened their mouths and hissed, baring sharp tusk-like front teeth. Ean scrambled back. "Whoa! Not cute little bunnies! Not cute little bunnies!" He yelled.

One jumped forward onto his leg and Ean saw instead of paws, the rabbits--or whatever they were--had hand-like appendages, with opposable thumbs as well. Before the one on his leg could sink its tusks into his flesh, Ean brought his sword around and speared it like a kabob, causing it to screech. Flinging the body into the still burning campfire, Ean slashed the sword toward the others. Six were attempting to encircle him, while three jumped on Adair's tent wall, ripping the fabric with their teeth.

"Brin! Drake!" Ean screamed.

Heat flashed through him, starting from his heart and spreading throughout his body. His hand gripping the sword felt a vibration and when Ean looked, he saw the blade was giving off a silver flame. Then the six rabbit-demon hybrids attacked Ean. He swung at one, then hit another with the sword hilt. Another had grabbed his waist, and tried to bite Ean but missed, sinking its sharp teeth into his leather belt. He grabbed it by the scruff of its neck and yanked it off, throwing it into the fire as well. Rolling out of the fire, the now yowling burning rabbit took off into the forest.

Ean reached for one of the rabbits on Adair's tent, plucking it up by its tail as it entered through the hole it made. Spinning around he had time to register one rabbit was jumping toward his face. Swinging the rabbit he held in his left hand, he let go, letting the animals collide in mid-air. Without stopping he speared them and they disintegrated in the silver flame. Shocked, he froze for a brief moment. A movement to his right caught his attention. Slashing his sword to the right, he decapitated another demonic rabbit in mid-leap--reducing the body to ashes. Ean stabbed and dispatched the two racing toward the hole in Adair's tent, leaving three more. Heart pounding, Ean looked around wildly for them-- they were nowhere in sight. Not wanting to leave the hole to Adair's tent unprotected, Ean peered around the two sides, but they were not there.

"Ean?" Adair called.

"Stay where you are!" Ean yelled, looking around. Out of the corner of his eye, there was a slight movement. A patch of dirt was shifting, moving closer and closer toward Ean and the tent. Panic shot through him as Ean realized the rabbit must be underground, tunneling to the tent. He stepped forward, anticipating where the rabbit would be. Both hands on the hilt, he drove the blade downward into the ground and was satisfied when he heard the hiss of the blade as it seared the animal.

Searching the ground, Ean saw another fast moving patch of dirt to his right and one to his left. He pulled the sword out, jumped to the right and stabbed the ground. The patch of dirt skirted around the sword and kept moving forward. Ean stabbed at it again, sword at an angle, but again the dirt managed to dodge the blade. Forcing himself to be more steady, Ean raced the moving dirt to the tent. Taking a moment to gauge the animal's progress, he thrust the sword into the ground once more and heard the satisfying hiss of a fried bunny.

Turning to address the last rabbit, he watched the ground for movement. There was none. Frantic, he paced the side of the tent, looking for clues as to where the rabbit might be.

"Ean?" Adair called again.

"I said, stay there!"

"There's something coming up from under my tent--"

Ean ripped the hole in her tent wide enough to lunge through. Adair was huddled at the far end of the tent, a bulge was pushing up from the middle with tusks poking through, chewing and ripping the fabric of the floor.

"What is it?" She asked in a panic.

In answer, Ean stabbed the animal, charring it to death before it could fully emerge. Sensing movement behind him, he spun, sword ready.

"Whoa!" Brin held up his hands, surveying the pile of ashes. "I like me snacks a little less overcooked."

Adair emerged from her tent and Ean's knees gave way under him as his adrenaline subsided. The sword in his hand was no longer glowing with flames. In shock she surveyed her ripped tent and the scattered ashes littering the camp.

"What did you *do*?" She whispered.

Drake, curled up on the far side of camp, cleared his throat, "He single-handedly saved the camp from attacking syrabs."

"Did you say rabbits?" She questioned.

"Not quite," Ean replied. "They may look like rabbits, but there are a few differences." He thought about their tusk-like teeth and hands and shuddered. "Oh, and they have a *really* bad temper."

"Syrabs are hunters, trained to follow the scent of an animal and kill it." Drake said, "They pretty much go mad until they accomplish their goal."

Adair looked at them, "Were they after me?"

"Good question," Brin said, "Ean, where did ye find 'em?"

"I was passing Adair's tent when I heard them. I turned around and they were right there behind me. Couldn't their presence in our camp be a coincidence?"

Brin shook his head, "No, these animals be bred by gargoyles to kill enemies. The odd part is, gargoyles live in one remote area of the Forest far from here. I wonder why they be involved and how syrabs got here so fast."

"I don't care how or why. I want to get out of here!" Adair was wrapping her arms around her stomach.

Ean decided, "Let's clean up and move out. We can stop to eat later."

A few hours later, the tired travelers stopped in a grove of trees and made a quick breakfast.

"Brin," Ean started. "You mentioned gargoyles breed those animals. Are the gargoyles here made out of stone?"

"No. From what I remember, they be similar to what Earthlings call apes, except they walk more like solidly built, and very hairy, humans. They be short tempered, have no sense o' humor, and frequently fight to the death."

Imagining a group of Sasquatch-like creatures attacking each other, Ean asked, "Is that why they sent the syrabs after us? They think we're their enemies?"

Brin tugged on his beard again, "'Tis what is odd. They've no concern for what goes on beyond their home an' could care less about money or gold. This action goes against their nature."

It took Ean awhile to fall asleep as he wondered what was going to happen next. However, over the next four days, no more enemies appeared. They continued taking turns keeping watch, but this time Adair took turns as well, which made Brin unhappy. Watching Adair logically reason with Brin and Drake, Ean was reminded of his mom and smiled. She wouldn't sit by idly either; she would have wanted to do her part as well.

Unbeknownst to Adair, Ean stayed awake during her shift as well-- just in case she needed him.

On the fifth day Adair rode her horse alongside Ean. "Why do you think they have not attacked us again? Not that I'm complaining..." she added.

"It's possible anyone following came across the blood bath from the syrab attack and had second thoughts," Ean guessed.

"Oh, I hope you're right."

Overhearing them, Brin turned around in his saddle, "I doubt we've seen the last o' it yet. Keep a sharp lookout, because the Elder's Council is unlikely to give up. I'd be expectin' an attack around every corner." Then Brin noticed the fearful look on Adair's face. "Then again, maybe not and Ean is right." Brin turned back to face the trail, and mumbled "After all, miracles can happen."

Ean took first watch and Drake flew off again to scout the surrounding area, hoping to avoid another surprise attack. Adair and Brin turned in right after dinner, with Adair taking over Brin's tent and Brin sleeping in blankets on the ground. Ean was left alone with his thoughts, which were a replay of his fight with the Syrabs.

Besides the clacking sound of some native insects and the rhythm of Brin's snoring, the night was quiet. Then he heard what sounded like a chocking sob coming from Adair's tent. He realized she must be crying again, as she had been on and off since they had arrived in Natura. Her gasps between sobs sounded louder than usual, so after a few seconds Ean's guilty conscience made him get up to check on her.

"Adair, are you okay?" He waited for an answer, but only heard some thumping movement within. "Adair?"

Concerned she didn't answer, he lifted the tent flap to see it was crowded with Legion Fairies. Most held Adair down while two strapping fairies on either side of her head pulled on a cord wrapped around her neck. Adair's face was almost purple and her eyes started to roll back in her head.

Ean charged in with a war cry, kicking and punching fairies as he stormed the tent. Except for the two choking her, the rest let go of Adair to attack him. Surprised by the fairies' strength, Ean was even more shocked at his own. Even with the numerous warriors swarming him, they could not overpower him. In order to help Adair, Ean jumped toward the two fairies pulling the cord around her neck. Landing on her, he grabbed them, yanked them away from the cord, shook them and threw them out of the tent. A flickering green light, accompanied by a roar, told Ean the fairies he'd thrown out were now toast, thanks to Drake. Turning, Ean cleared the room, kicking, punching and back-handing the rest of the Legion out of the tent--where they met Drake's green flame.

Within seconds it was over and Ean was helping Adair out of the tent to where Drake and Brin battled the last few fairies. Adair, gasping for air and sobbing at the same time, was holding her bruised and sore neck.

Ean pried her hands down, "Let me see." He delicately brushed his fingers lightly over the maroon indents on her skin, his heart overwhelmed with sorrow. If only he had been faster, maybe she wouldn't have suffered as much. He wished he could take away her pain. Soon after the heartfelt thought entered his mind, his fingers began to tingle and a faint glow came from his hand. Adair gasped in surprise. She looked at him in amazement, "I feel better. It doesn't hurt anymore."

Ean moved his hands away to see her neck no longer showed any damage from the attack. He looked down at his fingers in amazement.

"Ean, what did you *do*?" Adair asked.

"I--I don't know," he answered truthfully.

With Brin's help, Drake finished dispatching the last of the Legion Fairies. He looked Adair over, "Ye alright?"

Trembling, she replied, "Yeah, I guess. But I'm pretty sure we now know who the target is...someone wants me dead."

Silence fell over the camp. Then Ean stepped forward, "Maybe so, but that is *not* going to happen." His eyes met hers, "Not in a million years."

"That's right," Brin added. "And next time Ean, stop hoggin' all the enemies." Brin swung his battle axe back over his shoulder.

Chapter 15

The Hermit

The next day they climbed to the peak of a mountain road. They came over the crest of the mountain to see the city of Glen-Delay in the distance.

Brin clapped Ean on the shoulder, almost knocking him over. "It looks the same since the last time I laid me eyes on it."

"How old are you Brin?" Ean asked.

"Within three cycles of our second moon, I will be 254 years old. Natura operates under a somewhat similar calendar to Earth, so I'd be roughly about the same age on yer planet too, give or take a few years."

"How long do leprechauns live?" Ean asked before remembering his manners, "That is, if you don't mind me asking."

"No, not at all. Most leprechauns live somewhere between 700 to 900 years o' age. A few reach an age o' close to 1200 years."

"Are all leprechauns as tall as you are?" Ean asked.

"No, I be the tallest. In me family, every other generation produces what they call a 'giant leprechaun.' Me great uncle is also a giant leprechaun." Brin pointed to the sporran at his side, "And he gave me this. This magical sporran has been in me family for as long as anyone remembers. "Tis family tradition to have the tallest member o' the clan carry this magical sporran." He grinned, "I'm taller than me uncle by a fingertip."

"So," Adair chimed in, "What is the normal height for a leprechaun?"

"It varies. They can range in size from below yer kneecap up to yer chest." He held his hand four feet off the ground. Then he chuckled, "However it means someone as tall as I be must watch where they step when around the smaller ones."

They all laughed, relieved to see their goal in sight. The laughter also relieved some of the tension they had endured the past several days.

They continued down the mountain. The tall trees became thick, casting dark shadows across the downhill trail. When they were almost out of the trees at the base of the mountain, the next attack occurred.

As Adair turned the bend, a dirty man dressed in rags dropped out of the trees above her. Brin, riding his horse behind Adair, spotted the man as he let go of the overhead branch. Brin spurred his horse into the back of Adair's, which in turn caused her horse to lunge forward and Adair and Drake scrambled to hang on. The man, face hidden by wildly long hair and beard, landed right where Adair's horse should have been and he was now in Brin's path. Pulling his battle ax out of his holster, Brin swung it in one quick movement, hitting the man over the head with the flat part of the ax blade.

To Ean's surprise, the ax maneuver just dazed the man. Even on horseback, Brin was hard pressed to control the stranger, who was now thrusting a rusted sword toward the leprechaun. Wielding his own ax, Brin yelled and jumped his horse toward the man. Agile and quick, the man rolled under the horse twice to avoid Brin's deadly swings, which would have cleaved him in two had they made contact. In the end, the attacker, with a few cuts and scrapes, pushed off a tree, vaulted off the rump of Brin's horse, and grabbed a limb 15 feet off the ground. Swinging higher, he was soon out of sight.

"Where did he go?" Brin demanded, turning his mount around in circles.

"He's gone," Drake commented from Adair's shoulder, where he liked to travel when not scouting ahead.

"Why, in all o' Natura," Brin exclaimed, "did a hermit attack us?"

"I do not know," Drake replied. "It is very strange."

"How come?" Ean asked.

The group continued to ride to the city while Brin explained, "Hermits began as humans who chose to live in nature, isolated from all others o' their species. Over time, hermits became a different species. When enough hermits existed, a male and female would come across each other, resulting in the occasional pregnancy." Ean blushed at what was starting to sound like a 'birds and bees' lecture.

Brin continued, "Once the child is old enough, they be sent away to live in large, hollow trees on their own. Once a hermit stakes claim to a tree, they stay. No amount o' monetary offer to kill someone would be enough to entice a hermit to leave their tree. Not that they won't kill—hermits be known to attack solitary travelers for clothing."

Ean rode in silence for awhile, considering all the unusual changes in the behaviors of the natives. Something, or someone, was behind all of these attacks, and it was up to him to discover the truth.

Chapter 16

Emperors Report

The day was hot in the city of Ferreglen and the warm breeze blowing through the open windows provided little relief. The doors to the Emperor's personal office burst open and a stout man hustled in, waving a strip of fabric and puffing, "The report is here! The report is here!" The Emperor looked up expectantly and Jon promptly rose from his own desk, where he had been working since his return to Ferreglen.

One of the reasons many citizens of Ferreglen were satisfied with their Emperor was his ability to make his people feel valued. So although he would have preferred to read it himself, the Emperor instead requested, "Would you please read it to us, Seritof?"

The man straightened with importance, "Yes Supreme Hakham...'To the Grand Emperor of Ferreglen. Report by General Alla-Galeson. Observations of the two Earthlings traveling from Omalla Mountain to Glen-Delay are as follows: The male and female Earthlings travel with two Natura natives, a giant leprechaun and a green dragon. Subjects spotted in possession of a dragon claw as they emerged from a cave on Omalla Mountain, which is reportedly the home of the plant known as Blood Mother. After they departed from the site, a quick survey inside revealed a large cavern with decaying vegetation. A footpath off of the cavern led further into the mountain and may be of interest for future exploration. Blood berry bushes outside of mountainside are shriveled and dead with no evidence of living bushes left.

"Tracked and located subjects again. Several attacks on the group have been witnessed: Possible magic used as the human male's sword glowed during one battle with Syrabs. Giddian Legion fairies have attacked the group two times, almost killing the female in their second attempt; all Legion warriors involved in the attack destroyed by male Earthling and Natura natives. Syrabs attacked one time; all killed outright by male human. Most recently, a hermit attacked the group and was driven away by the leprechaun.

"The subjects and natives appear to be heading for the city of Glen-Delay. I will watch the city gates and wait for them to continue their journey to the city of Ferreglen. This is the report I make. Your faithful servant, General Alla-Galeson.'"

Jon was shocked, "Father, did you send out an assassination decree on the girl?"

The Emperor rose from his chair, "I did not. I agreed, as did the Council, to determine her fate *after* the heir had been tested." He addressed his assistant, "Seritof, send a tracker and three guards to find the hermit. I want to know why he attacked them."

"It shall be done," Bowing, Seritof hurried out of the room to comply.

The Emperor murmured to himself. Then looking up, he said, "You know Henric, even if the boy isn't a true Talent Master, he could still be useful to the cause of freedom. He is still the living blood descendant of the human royal family. He could be used as a symbolic figurehead whom we could rally an army behind to defeat Abigor."

"Raising an army against Abigor without a Talent Master at the head would be suicide!"

The Emperor said gravely, "Victory comes at a heavy price."

Jon shook his head. "Give him time. He *is* the next Talent Master...I *know* it."

His father sat down leaning back in his chair. "Very well. We will wait and see."

Jon crossed to one of the open windows overlooking Ferreglen. Palms on the window sill, he leaned forward, looking into the distance. A green dragon...could it be Drake?

Chapter 17

Glen-Delay

"Welcome to the city o' me clan!" Astride his Friesian horse, Brin grinned and opened up his arms as if he wanted to give the city a giant hug.

Ean gulped as they approached the formidable stone walls encircling the vast spread of Glen-Delay. Towers dotted the sides of the walls and they could see many spears moving atop the walls, though no guards themselves were visible. The gate also appeared to be made of stone and Ean wondered how they could open it at all.

"Um, Brin?" Adair said. "Where are the guards?"

Brin smiled, "I assure ye the guards be there. They stay invisible most o' the time--unless they need to converse with one another."

"They can't talk when they're invisible?" Ean asked.

Brin replied, "O' course they can talk! But 'tis an insult if ye do not show yer face while havin' a conversation. Why, there have been clan feuds started over that very thing! Leprechauns be an honorable people, respectin' our own family clan rank and that o' the other clans. We be raised to protect our loved ones, develop our talents, and respect our cultural traditions. Leprechauns who lack proper manners could lose their privileges or a proper marriage, their inheritance, or even the right to live within the city walls. In one case, a leprechaun was banished from the Illusion Forest itself!"

Brin paused. Then, buoyed by the fact he would soon be reunited with his family, he proclaimed, "Enough o' these matters! Today ye enter the city o' me birth and will feast within me father's house and enjoy some real MacCarlington hospitality."

Upon arriving at the gates, Brin dismounted and walked up to the stone doors. Removing his leather gloves, he placed his right hand upon one of the doors and in a loud voice declared, "I am Brinston Denar the Third and I request entrance into the city o' Glen-Delay!"

After he spoke, a loud chime rang three times within the city walls. The doors began to glow a faint blue color before opening inward of their own accord.

As they rode into the city, people appeared out of homes and shops lining the streets. Once they recognized Brin, they started waving and calling out to him. Some followed along behind the newcomers to the hillside, where Brin led them to a gated estate. A short leprechaun inside the compound peered out to see the basis for the commotion. Seeing Brin, his eyes grew wide and he hastened to unlatch and open the gate. Entering the courtyard, the first thing the travelers saw was a large six-tiered water fountain placed in the center of a large circular courtyard. Cobblestones lined the ground around the fountain and tall trees, benches and patches of grass lined the large courtyard.

Dismounting, Brin was surrounded by the smaller leprechauns. Sure enough, some only came to Ean's knees, while others were a foot or two taller. Laughing joyously, they displayed an almost childlike enthusiasm and euphoria. Before Ean knew it, the travelers had all been pulled from their horses to shake hands. Brin was bent almost in half, giving hugs and conversing with others. He stood up and boomed to his traveling companions, "Welcome to me family home." The leprechauns cheered.

After a moment, they fell silent. An elderly leprechaun couple had appeared in the doorway of what appeared to be the living quarters. They locked eyes with Brin and the rest of the leprechauns began to fan out to give them space. Brin knelt in respect. With a choked sob, the woman rushed forward, embracing Brin with a hug around his neck.

"'Tis about time ye came home, son," she said huskily.

"I'm sorry I was away for so long, mama."

The old man nodded, "We have missed ye. But ye be home now, me boy. We shall celebrate yer return!" He addressed the other leprechauns,

"Me oldest son has come home. I declare a three day celebration!" The leprechauns eagerly cheered before rushing away to make preparations. A few leprechauns came forward to take the horse reins from Ean and Adair, reassuring them the horses would be fed, groomed and sheltered. The leprechauns then led the animals and cart to the stables on the far side of the building.

Once the other greeters had departed, Brin's father placed one thick hand upon his wife's shoulder and gestured to the others, "Brin, will ye introduce us to yer companions?"

Brin, still grinning, wiped away a tear from his eye. He leaned back from his mother and said, "These are me companions and friends, who rescued me from inside Omala Mountain...where I have been trapped for almost a hundred years." Brin's mother gasped and held her hand over her mouth in shock.

Brin continued, "May I present Adair O'Connor, an Earthling and Dragon Maiden who's bravery rivals that o' our most courageous warriors!" Adair blushed and curtsied. "I have the privilege o' introducing to ye the magnificent Drake, the only dragon on Natura for the past 400 years since Eden was removed!" Drake jumped off Adair's shoulder, enlarging to the size of a horse as he landed in front of the couple, surprising and pleasing them with his show. Then Brin clapped his hand on Ean's back, causing him to take a step forward, "And this young Earthling is known as Ean McMurrin. He is the descendant o' Azarion and is heir to Islandia's throne!" Brin's parents bowed to him with reverence, causing Ean to feel awkward.

Noticing Ean's discomfort, Brin whispered, "The sooner ye get used to it, the better." Then Brin walked to stand behind his parents. "May I introduce me esteemed parents: Brinston Denar the Second and Sarah Denar o' the clan MacCarlington." Ean, Adair, and Drake bowed to them.

Brin's father spoke, "When ye stay with us, ye be part o' our family. Me family calls me Dribbles, or Drib. So if ye use me fancy-shmancy name, I'll have ye shackled up by yer ankles in the highest tree." He looked Drake's large form up and down, "Or maybe I just won't answer ye."

Everyone laughed at his correction. "Now come inside and rest," he continued, "while the celebration is prepared."

For the remainder of the day the house was bustling with leprechauns. Even the guests lent a hand, chatting happily with the inquisitive clan members. Ean was pleased to see Adair laughing and enjoying their company as they prepared food (which cooked quickly, thanks to Drake) or decorated. It was the happiest he'd seen her since she'd seen her sister Elizabeth at the airport. Brin's parents kept Ean busy polishing utensils while he regaled them with details of his life on Earth, then of his adventures since his arrival in Natura.

After the travelers ate some refreshments, Ean and Adair were shown to rooms facing each other at the back of the manor, where they would be able to freshen up in a less noisy part of the home. Adair excused herself to her room, where a young lady leprechaun was waiting for her. Ean entered his own room to find a young leprechaun waiting next to a middle-aged leprechaun. Ean guessed the older one was likely twice the age of Brin. He was wearing a tailored suit while the younger one was dressed in working clothes with wet rolled-up sleeves.

The older one spoke first, "Welcome. I am Brog, the Tailor--"

"I'm Blog, the Fixer," the younger one interrupted, winning a sharp look from Brog. Blog continued anyway, "Yer bath has been prepared. The bathin' room is through those doors on the left."

"Thanks Blog," Ean said.

"'Tis me pleasure, Your Highness."

"Oh no... please don't call me that. I am a friend of Brin's, so call me 'Ean.'"

Blog ducked his head, "As ye wish, Mr. Ean." He gave a short bow and left the room. Ean turned to give his full undivided attention to Brog.

"Mr. Ean, Sir, I am Brog the tailor--the finest tailor in the city o' Glen-Delay," Brog puffed up his chest with pride. "I am also the personal designer o' the Denar family. I was asked by the Lady Sarah to make sure ye and the Lady Adair be fashionably clothed for the celebration. So if ye would be so kind as to let me take some measurements, then ye may enjoy the luxuries of the bathin' room."

Delighted and taken aback by all the treatment, Ean agreed, "Sure, what do I need to do?"

"Stand still while I measure ye." He brought Ean over to the mirror where he had set up a mini ladder. Climbing it, he pulled out a rectangular object from a tool belt around his waist. It reminded Ean of a television remote control. Holding it up to Ean, Brog scanned it along his body, pausing it from time to time. Then he climbed down the ladder, moved it in a semi-circle around him, and repeated the process.

"What is that?" Ean asked.

"'Tis a tailoring tool. Right now I am recording yer measurements." Brog continued working until he had completed a circle around Ean. "Now we can determine what will look best on ye." Brog showed Ean the tool, which now projected a 3-D version of himself above the screen. Colorful squares appeared next to him. "Here is where we choose the color for yer clothes." Brog touched a square and the image of Ean was draped in the corresponding color. After examining a few swatches, Brog decided on a rich blue hue.

Amazed, Ean said, "That is such a cool tool! How come most of the things in Natura aren't quite as...complicated?"

Grim faced, Brog replied, "We used to have many advanced items. Since the rebellion, the cities in the Forest regressed due to the lack o' cooperation with Islandia and the University o' Natura. Very few items such as this one remain in our cities." Brog straightened, "Well Mr. Ean, the bathin' room awaits. I will bring ye yer clothes shortly."

"Thanks Brog." Ean headed toward the bathing room doors.

Brog, heading out of the room, cleared his throat. "A recommendation Sir..."

Ean paused with his hand on the door handle, "Yes?"

"Me favorite is the Red Dragon," and with that Brog walked out, closing the door behind him.

Red Dragon? What did that mean? Unsure, Ean shrugged and entered the bathroom. "Whoa," Ean muttered, gazing around in wonder.

The room was large. A bean-shaped pool was situated against the middle of the back wall. He walked over to study the many ornamental faucets that surrounded the pools, intricately shaped as dragons, unicorns, lions, tigers, elephants, and other animals, configured to look as though each was about to step into the water. Shower-heads hanging from the ceiling came in shapes like fairies and birds, some of which he recognized and others he had never seen. Reaching up, Ean lightly touched a small bird faucet. It began to flutter its wings as if alive and a perfumed mist showered down. Deciding these were for females, he chose not to touch any more birds or other figures hanging from the ceiling.

He stooped over a faucet resembling a blue unicorn. He touched the horn and the faucet began to spout thick aqua blue foam into the water below. He touched the horn again and the faucet stopped flowing and the foam disappeared. Walking around the edge of the pool, Ean touched several of the figures. Some produced a syrup-like liquid, while others released foam or bubbles, but when touched again, whatever they were discharging would promptly disappear.

Remembering Brog's comment that his favorite was the red dragon, Ean entered the warm water of the pool and swam over to the far side, where all the dragon faucets were located. Finding the red dragon, Ean touched it and a red caramel-like substance oozed out of the faucet. Ean held his hand under the gooey stuff until it gathered around his hand, then spread up his arm to cover his body with a warm, tingling sensation. Once covered, Ean touched the red dragon faucet again and the goop disappeared from the water and his body, leaving him feeling fresh and clean.

The facial hair he had been growing for the past week and a half was gone and the remaining hair on his head was soft and silky. The smell lingering on his skin was the perfect balance between cologne and a fresh springtime breeze. Once he found the triggers for jet-powered water that massaged him from his neck to the bottom of his feet, he spent a significant amount of time enjoying the massage before swimming and resting in the water.

When he had dried off and returned to the main bedroom, he found the wardrobe chest open and stocked full of clothes his size. On the bed lay an informal evening shirt and slacks. He put them on to discover the clothes felt smooth and light and fit him well.

Not wanting to be late for the evening celebration, and wondering if he might have taken too long in the bath, he left his room. Heading down the hall, Ean admired for the first time the ornate doors, which consisted of various sized doors within each door frame, ranging from cat-sized to

Brin-sized. Each door had customized unique handles and materials; some were wood, others metal, and one even had a stone handle. He was so engrossed in the details that he hadn't paid attention to which direction he was heading and he realized he was hopelessly lost. He looked around, wondering where he should head.

After walking through three hallways and peeking down a couple of corridors, Ean found himself at a dead end. Prominently displayed on the wall was a large painting of a tall oak tree. Leprechauns of various ages stood or sat on and around the large trunk, and many more leprechaun faces peeked out from tree branches. Ean smiled at the whimsical portrait, then sighed and ran his hand through his hair.

"Great, my first day here and already I'm lost." He glanced at the painting, "I don't suppose any of you know where I am."

With a popping sound a tiny girl leprechaun materialized in front of Ean. Ean jumped at the sudden appearance of the girl, no larger than that of a garden gnome.

In a high voice she squeaked, "Sorry to disturb ye Sir, but ye be lost?"

"Uh...yes, I be...I mean, could you help me find my way back to Brin and my friends, please?"

"Certainly!"

"After you, my Lady," he said, gesturing down the hall. With a giggle, she took off running down the hall as fast as she could go. Ean easily kept up as she led him down hallways and a couple of staircases to a large great room. Comfortable chairs of various sizes were stationed in conversational settings around the room. At the far side where a large fireplace sported a hearty fire, Brin and Adair sat in chairs with their backs to him. Drake was also there, looking quite content from where he was draped on Adair's shoulders. When Ean and the girl arrived, Brin stood up to greet him.

"'Tis about time!" Brin commented with a smile on his face, "...I thought ye might have drowned in the tub."

"What you call a 'tub,' I call a pool," Ean responded.

"Yes, they be very spacious."

Adair stood up, "Ean, you look nice."

Ean replied, "And you look..." His voice trailed off as he got a good look at her. Radiant in a silver silk evening gown, her red hair piled in a bun and encircled with the flower tiara the fairies had made her, she positively glowed in the firelight. Drake, with his tail curled around her slender neck, looked like a shimmering emerald necklace.

Brin laughed at his speechlessness until he found his voice again, "Adair--you look stunning!"

Adair smiled sweetly, "Why thank you Ean, I'll send your compliments on to the ladies who assisted me, as well as to Mr. Brog for working his magic. And Brin, I need to thank your mother for all her hospitality."

"Me parents should be here any moment if ye wish to thank 'em." Soon after, Sarah and Drib entered the room and Adair and Ean expressed gratitude to Brin's parents for their kindness and generosity.

"Me dears, think nothing of it. 'Tis a small token of our gratitude for ye returnin' Brin to us." Sarah responded, "And besides, when ye be our guests, ye be family. Speaking o' family--Daisy, ye need to be getting' yer chores done now. Run along."

Dribs addressed the others, "Please have a seat. Refreshments will be brought and we can visit until the celebration begins." The group gathered to sit on the chairs near the fire. Brin assisted his mother with situating her chair and Sarah smiled at her son, patting his arm in gratitude for his kind gesture.

Late afternoon moved into evening while they enjoyed a friendly conversation. Drake contributed much to the conversation, but Ean felt that more passed between Drake and Drib than was communicated in words. As the sun was setting, they were escorted outside to the courtyard in front of the house, where many tables and chairs were set up on a grassy area. Brin escorted his parents to a table placed on a raised platform facing the rest of the tables. They sat at two small chairs elevated on tall legs with two Earthling-sized chairs for Adair and Ean on one side, and one large Brin-sized chair on the other.

Sarah explained that this dinner celebration included family clan members only, the next day's celebration would include friends as well, and on the third day the entire town would gather to celebrate with the Denar family. Adair and Ean learned that Brin was the oldest son, and although he had not yet married, many of his younger siblings had married and had large families of their own. Looking out over the leprechauns present, Ean guessed over 150 family members attended, not counting those serving the food or setting up music for entertainment.

The celebration began with a feast of dishes and sweets which were unfamiliar to Ean and Adair. Feeling adventurous, they both tried at least a bite of everything and Ean took seconds of many...sometimes even thirds. When Ean began to feel he couldn't eat another bite of food, the plates of food were removed, tables cleared and taken out of the courtyard, and all the chairs moved to the perimeter of the cobblestone. Leprechauns holding homemade instruments began to play.

To Adair's delight the music had a catchy tune and soon she was dancing with Denar family members, her silver dress swaying around her legs. After only a couple minutes of dancing, Drake jumped off of Adair and glided over to perch on the back of a chair. Much to his chagrin, several young children rushed over to him and began to pet him as if he were a puppy. Ean broke out laughing at the sight of Drake's expression, and was joined by Brin as he too caught sight of Drake. Drake did not find the situation humorous, but sat still while the little ones pampered him with attention. Even though he was a little irritated at being the center of attention, a slight throaty purr escaped his lips before he could stop it, causing Brin and Ean to laugh even harder.

After much revelry, the party slowly began to wind down. Adair was resting on a chair as she watched Brin dance with his mother to the last song. Her eyes flitted over to where Ean was dancing with a tiny girl no larger than a garden gnome and she smiled at the sweet scene. Ean enjoyed himself and interacted wonderfully with the pint-sized leprechauns. When the music ended with a flourish of beats, Adair stood up and walked over to where Ean had stopped dancing and was bowing to the young girl.

"May I steal him away?" Adair asked.

The girl giggled, "Of course, My Lady."

Smiling, Adair bent down toward her. "I should introduce myself; I'm Adair O'Connor. You can call me Adair. Who might you be?"

The girl shyly looked back up, "I am Daisy."

"Well, it is a pleasure to meet you Daisy."

"Likewise," came her soft reply. The tiny leprechaun turned and hurried off.

"I see ye have met me youngest sister, Daisy," Brin commented from behind them, causing them to jump and turn.

"Brin, you startled me!" Adair commented.

"That's me brother--full o' surprises," came another voice behind Brin. Brin turned around, "Zena!" He laughed and embraced the girl who only came up to his waist. Turning to the others with his arm around her, he proudly announced, "This is me oldest little sister Zena."

"Hmm, old *and* little in one sentence...should I feel insulted?" she asked Brin as she elbowed him in the leg.

"Ouch Sis! That always gives me a 'dead' leg."

"Yes, I know," she replied smugly.

She pointed to Brin and said, "Until his growth spurt he was no taller than Daisy. He would sneak around invisible for hours, and then pop up in front o' us when we least expected it." She laughed at the memory. "'Twas his favorite thing to do."

"Yes, I was a real wild child." Brin commented with a roll of his eyes, hoping to end the conversation.

"No, not 'wild' big brother, jus' a pain in the neck."

"Okay, stop pickin' on me. I missed ye too."

"About that, I am still mad at ye for bein' gone so long," Zena replied with one hand on her hip.

"I am sorry Zena."

Zena softened, "I know. Now you need yer rest, ye oversized brute o' a brother."

"Yes I do," he said as he picked her up and swung her around until they were both laughing.

"Now off with ye, Brin," Zena shooed him toward the house. Turning to the other two she said, "As for ye two, I will escort ye to yer rooms." She looked at Ean, "So ye won't get lost again."

"Again?" Adair asked, raising her eyebrow at Ean.

Sheepishly he admitted, "I took some wrong turns earlier this afternoon."

"Daisy found him in one o' our unused corridors, though I can only suppose she was there because she was followin' him." Zena winked at Adair over her shoulder.

Adair hid a grin, "Well Ean, it looks like you have made quite an impression on Daisy."

He shrugged, unsure how to respond without creating an opening for more jokes at his expense. He followed the girls through the house until they reached their adjoining rooms.

"Good night ladies," Ean said as he entered his room. Exhausted, he was grateful to see the sleeping clothes laid out on his bed. He changed and crawled into bed, asleep almost before his head hit the pillow.

The next two days were a blur to Ean. He remembered spending a large amount of time swimming in the tub every morning, often using a pearl dragon faucet he liked even more than the red one. He also discovered that out of all of Brin's sisters, Zena was the most informative and humorous. Daisy was the most energetic, enthusiastic, and accommodating, often appearing out of thin air whenever Ean needed anything. Though it was kind of unnerving to Ean to have that kind of attention, Adair thought it was cute that Daisy had an obvious crush on him.

What was more enjoyable than even the elaborate parties held in their honor, was the fact that for once in Natura, Ean felt safe; no one had attacked them since they had entered the city. When he inquired about it to Drib the previous night, he discovered that the magic around the city was so strong, no unauthorized intruders had been able to cross the city boundary in over two thousand years.

With the parties and their preparations over, Ean, Adair and Drake were invited to tour the rest of the city. Adair and Ean made plans to wander the city, though Brin and Drake chose to stay behind to visit some more with Drib and Sarah. Before the two left on their sightseeing excursion, Brin pulled Ean aside and handed him a large bag of gold and silver coins. "This is for ye to use while visitin' the city. Please feel free to spend as much as ye want--and make sure Adair gets everythin' she desires."

"I can't take your money," Ean whispered in a shocked voice.

"Yes, ye can. There be many great and wonderful stores in the town square. Oh, and if ye run out, tell them ye be staying at the Denar home and they will charge it to us later."

"This is too much. I--I...don't know what to say."

Brin grinned, "Say nothin' and enjoy yerselves." After patting Ean's shoulder, causing Ean to re-balance himself to avoid stumbling forward, Brin walked away.

Ean slid the strap of the bag over his head so the weight of the money rested against his side. Starting to think that it would be a good idea to exchange the heavy money for lighter goods, Ean met up with Adair at the front gate. They set off down the hill from the Denar home and entered the business district of Glen-Delay, all the while greeted like old friends by leprechauns they passed. Arriving in a street lined with shops, the two humans stopped, mesmerized by the merchandise displayed in wide open windows that stretched from the ground to the roof of each store. Since the roofs were often level with Ean's head, he often had to stoop to see inside the shops. He briefly wondered what Brin had to do to shop--he probably had to sit on the ground just to see inside the stores!

There were bakeries with delicious smelling foods, candy shops with more unrecognizable sweets, clothing for various sized leprechauns, hunting and military supply shops, blacksmiths, jewelers, leather stores, magic stores, pot makers, bag makers, fur stores, and many other splendid shops. What caught Adair's eye was a fabric store displaying kilt fabric for various clans. She bolted through the doorway, dragging Ean along by his arm. Once inside, she began looking at the different tartan fabric. She saw one like the O'Connor tartan, the one with a medium green amid a light blue and dark blue pattern, yet it was not quite the same. A wave of homesickness settled in her chest.

"That is a very nice pattern, me dear."

Adair turned to see a waist-high leprechaun woman with gray hair and spectacles on her nose standing next to her. "It is very beautiful," she replied. "May I ask what family clan is it from?"

"The Gunaltin family. They live on the south side o' town."

"What is the Denar family pattern?" Adair wondered.

"That is over here," she pointed to a wall with a large section of fabric. "Would ye like to see the daily pattern, the military pattern, or the formal dress pattern?"

Adair thought for a second, "The formal."

"Adair, what are you doing?" Ean interrupted.

"Shopping, of course," she retorted. "After all, it would be rude to return back to the manor without spending some of the money. I wouldn't want to insult them--they have been so great to us."

Ean had not considered they might be insulted if they didn't spend some of the money. "Just make sure that whatever you get doesn't weigh too much," he said hefting up the heavy coin bag a little for emphasis. He started looking around for somewhere to sit. "I'll be sitting over there. Let me know when you're done."

A short ring indicated the store door had reopened. A moment later he heard Adair exclaim, "Brog! What are you doing here?"

"Preparing yer wardrobes, me dear. What ye be up to?" Ean could only see the top of the tailor's head.

"The same...I was admiring the fabric and wanted to take a look at the formal pattern of the Denar family."

"Ah, that is an excellent design."

"Hey Brog? Can I speak to you in private?" Glancing over at Ean, Adair led Brog toward the back of the store where Ean couldn't hear them talking. They returned a few minutes later conversing with the older lady. Brog was smiling.

"Okay Ean. We're done. You can come and pay now." Adair called to Ean.

He stretched as he stood, then went to the woman to pay her before Adair decided to purchase any of the fabric she was currently admiring. Although he had nothing against it, he didn't want to spend any more time in a fabric store. The memories he had of being a bored young boy shopping with his mom in fabric stores were enough to last a lifetime.

The amount the woman stated owed was rather large, in Ean's mind, but Adair thought it was right, so he paid it. Turning to leave Ean asked, "Where is the fabric you purchased?"

"Oh, the shopkeeper will deliver it to the house later. You said you preferred to travel light, right?" Adair flashed him a smile.

"Uh, yeah." He decided it was thoughtful Adair would have it delivered so he didn't have to carry it through town.

For the rest of the morning and into the afternoon they wandered from shop to shop, often stopping for Adair to pick out and buy shoes and clothes for the two of them. Ean was very interested in the items displayed in a weapon shop, but Adair adamantly refused to let him buy a double edged sword and shield. Ean relented in order to avoid making a scene with Adair, but he left the shop a little annoyed with her. He was far more annoyed with her later when she spent his weapon money on a sturdy leather bag.

Ean's mood improved, however, after a trip to the sweet shop, where they both filled paper bags full of the most amazing sweets they had ever seen. By the time they headed back to the Denar manor, the gold coins were almost gone, though some silver still remained. Ean figured they had spent almost three-fourths of the money.

"Wow, what a day!" Adair commented as they walked up the hill to the Denar estate. She was absentmindedly rubbing her right hand over the soft leather of her new bag. "Huh...you know, to think of it, I didn't see any art galleries or bookstores in town today."

Good, less for me to carry, thought Ean as he tried to rearrange the packages he was carrying so they wouldn't continue to cut off the blood circulation to his arms. Instead he replied, "You're right. I didn't either. We should ask Brin. I am sure he knows where they are located in the city." They walked in silence the rest of the way to the gates, where they greeted one of Brin's many relatives. The leprechaun took the packages from Ean and as soon as he departed, another relative arrived to lead them to where the others conversed. This time they walked around the back of the manor, past a large pool, and up a steep mountainside stairway to a secluded pavilion, where Drib, Sarah, Brin, and Drake waited.

"It appears our adventurers have returned," Brin called. "Welcome back!"

"Yes, and thank you again for the means to shop and explore your business district." Ean commented to all the members of the Denar family, not sure if the gold they had spent had been Drib's or Brin's.

"Think nothing o' it," Drib commented to Ean. "'Tis a small thing among friends."

Ean smiled and nodded to Drib. Adair had walked over to Sarah and was showing her the bag she purchased as well as some of the items she had stored inside it. Ean wondered if they talked about him as the two whispered and glanced in his direction. Ignoring their behavior, he found an empty seat his size in the pavilion and sat back to rest after the long day of walking the city streets. Within a few minutes of their arrival, several leprechauns carrying trays of food appeared and soon the small tables between the chairs were covered with dishes brimming with food.

Noting Ean's confused look, Brin clarified, "Now that the formal feasting is over, we thought a more casual dinner was needed."

"Well I am delighted to have more time to visit with you both, Sarah and Drib," Adair commented. "I have many questions about the city that maybe you can answer for me."

"Anything me dear," Sarah responded, placing one of her small hands on Adair's arm. "How can I help ye?"

So as the hours passed, Adair asked question after question about the city history and culture of the leprechaun people. At times Ean jumped in, asking questions that came to him, but it was Adair carrying the line of conversation. Through the discussion, they learned Glen-Delay had been created and empowered with dragon magic thousands of years ago, with the help of a two-toned black and white dragon. This peaked Drake's interest, since he had never heard of a dragon helping to build a city.

Drake asked, "For what purpose did the dragon assist in the creation and protection of Glen-Delay?"

Dribs replied, "That, I do not know. It could be possible the curator o' the city history might know, but then again, he may not."

Silence settled over the group as they were each lost in his or her own thoughts. The torches lit around the pavilion did little to ward off the evening chill that had come upon them as darkness had fallen. Gazing at the two visible moons in the sky, Adair took deep breaths, drinking in the unfamiliar, yet comforting smells of the surrounding vegetation. As she was about to excuse herself to her room, Sarah spoke up.

"Shall we go down to the cultural center on far side o' the city tomorrow mornin'? We will introduce ye to one o' our eldest leprechauns, Limbora Himpton, the Art and Historical Curator o' the city. Lim was unable to attend the festival, so ye have not met him yet, but he has much knowledge and experience. He could tell ye more about the history and art o' Glen-Delay."

Adair paused as gratitude for Sarah's kindness and sincerity washed over her. Sarah's smile and sweet loving nature made her feel a part of Brin's family.

On the other hand, it also made her miss her own mother, who had passed away from cancer over ten years ago. Since then, Adair had built up a wall of defenses to protect her heart from future pain and grief. Only her father, Elizabeth, and her nephew and niece were allowed inside her protected heart. And now, on the verge of tears, Adair could feel the Denar family's tenderness and affection for her, and found herself returning her own love for them.

Her voice only wavered a little as she said, "That would be wonderful Sarah."

"Great, then that is settled. Let us all meet first thing tomorrow. Now, go get some rest dears. We will see ye in the mornin'."

After Adair left, Ean stayed up late visiting. When only Brin and Ean remained, Ean excused himself to turn in for the night, wondering what new experiences he would encounter the next day.

Chapter 18

A Kilt and Magical Paintings

*E*an enjoyed his morning swimming routine. After swimming several laps, he took pleasure in the crisp cleaning process provided by the dragon faucets before relaxing in warm bubbles from a faucet shaped like a strange fish. But upon entering his room and opening his wardrobe hutch for his clothes, he was surprised--and rather perturbed--to discover them missing. All of the clothes he had purchased the day before, as well as the outfits Brog had made for him, were gone.

Standing with a wet towel wrapped around his waist, Ean scanned the room for any sign of where they might be. His eyes landed on an outfit placed on the end of his bed; an outfit he had never worn before, nor even ever thought he would wear.

Realization donned on him that Adair had something to do with this. Since no other clothes were available, he walked over to the bed and pulled on the satin white shirt with a ruffled front and long ruffled sleeves. He picked up the kilt, strapped it around his waist and secured it with a thick black leather belt sporting a large silver buckle. A silver pin with a gem lay on the bed. When no undergarments were found, he attached the pin to the bottom of his kilt so that the weight would keep the front of his kilt from inadvertently flipping open while he walked. Needless to say, it was quite noticeable to him that this outfit would not prevent drafts.

He pulled on the matching plaid kilt hose, complete with ribbon garter, and slipped on the dress shoes. Unsure of how to correctly tie the long laces around his leg, he resorted to winding them around his ankle three times and tying a square knot in the front. Then he picked up the black leather and white fur sporran. Adjusting the chain around his waist, he hung the sporran in the front.

Fuming mad over Adair's audacity to force him to wear something so ridiculous, he threw his door open, stomped across the hall and pounded on Adair's door. After knocking several more times, without a response from within, he decided she had left earlier to meet up with the others. He marched down a couple of hallways, but realized he had been so caught up in his anger, he didn't know how to get where he needed to go. A thought came to him. "Daisy? If you are here, I need your help again."

A popping sound announced her appearance. She stood next to his left shoe, looking up at Ean. Surprised by her close proximity, Ean pulled his legs together.

"How may I be of service?" She asked in her high voice.

"I got turned around again. Could you help me find Adair?"

"Why, certainly. And ye do look very handsome," she commented as they began walking back the way he had come.

"Uh...thank you." Ean blushed before admitting, "But I'm not very comfortable. I've never worn a kilt before."

"Ye are wearing the formal tartan of me family. Ye look ready for a ceremony or a wed--I mean, another special occasion."

Ean couldn't be sure, but he thought he saw Daisy's cheeks blush. They traversed the rest of the way in silence until they arrived at the great room where Adair sat waiting for the others to arrive. "Thank you, Daisy, you have saved me again."

"My pleasure." And with a pop, she disappeared.

Ean wasted no time. Marching over to Adair he demanded, "Did you have anything to do with this?" His hands gestured to the clothing he wore.

"Why, Ean, you do look dashing," Adair's voice sounded sincere, but Ean could tell she was stifling her amusement.

"Why? What could I have done to deserve this? And where is my underwear?!"

"Well, first I recommend you be careful when you sit down. Or stand up. Or do anything, it is a sign of respect to the Denar family that the future king would honor them by wearing their tartan to a formal occasion--such as meeting one of the eldest members of the city. I too am wearing their tartan." Adair stood up so Ean would notice that she was indeed wearing a dress in which the shoulder sash and skirt section were made out of the same fabric as the kilt.

"Yeah, well, you can't spring this on me you know." He growled as he lowered himself into the chair next to Adair's, keeping his knees close together.

"Don't tell me you've never worn a kilt before!"

"Of course I haven't. If you recall, I am American. Kilts are only seen at Scottish or Irish festivals and parades. It's not like I've ever owned one."

"Too bad. I had hoped with the name 'McMurrin' you would have at least embraced some of your own history."

Feeling like she had slapped him, he retorted, "It's hard to embrace a heritage with which you aren't familiar. My dad didn't like to talk about his family history."

"Strange." Uncomfortable silence followed as they considered what the other had said until Brin and his parents walked into the room.

Dribs spoke first, "I see ye both be benefactors o' Brog's workmanship".

"Yes, he did a fine job," Adair commented as she rose and twirled for the benefit of Brin and his parents.

"My dear, ye are lovely," Sarah commented. Brin and Dribs murmured in agreement.

Brin looked Ean up and down. "Ye be missin' somethin'."

Embarrassed, he admitted, "Yeah, well, the underwear was missing."

Brin looked taken aback, then started laughing. Drib and Sarah both had to hide their smiles to save Ean more humiliation. After a bit, Brin wiped his eyes with the back of his hand, "'Tis not what I meant." He reached into his sporran and pulled out a small sheathed knife with a carved dark wood handle. "This is called a Sgian-Dubh. It goes into the stocking on the outside o' yer leg." He held it out to Ean.

Ean took it and examined it, "It's a--what?"

"'Tis pronounced 'skee-ən-DOO.' Although 'tis worn with formal wear, it could also come in handy at some other times."

Drib cleared his throat, "We should eat and leave soon. Lim indicated the best time for him to meet with us is one hour before noon at the art museum. I arranged for the family carriage to be brought out front and breakfast awaits us on the front porch, so we can eat before we take our leave."

"In that case, let us go," Brin said. He grinned as he saw Ean slip the Sgian-Dubh into his right stocking and try to stand up while keeping his knees together. "'Tis not yer style o' clothing?"

Following Brin's parents out of the great room, Ean said, "Well no. I would not pick it out myself, but I am honored to wear the Denar family tartan in respect for your family."

Adair nodded her approval for his choice of words, adding, "Since you are so amenable Ean, there are other ideas on how to change your looks. First off, you do need a haircut."

Though sure she was kidding, he could not resist glancing at his hair as they walked past a long mirror in the hallway. Brin caught his glance and had a hard time hiding a smile.

After a quick family meal, the group climbed into the open carriage, the smaller leprechauns using a step-stool with several steps to reach the carriage benches. Ean noticed one member of their party was missing.

"Adair, where is Drake?"

"He said he needed to stretch his wings and that he would be back tonight by dinner time."

And as they passed through the city, Dribs, Sarah, and Brin took turns pointing out landmarks. In spite of the interesting facts, Ean felt like the ride went on forever. By the time they arrived at the museum, Ean's legs tingled. The building they stopped in front of was more of an old cathedral, complete with buttresses and lots of small steps that led to a grand front door--outfitted with several various sized doors, of course. Ean, Adair and Brin could skip the small stairs by two, or even three, at a time. However they walked so Drib and Sarah could keep up. At the front doors they met Limbora Himpton, a leprechaun no more than three feet tall with white hair and a beard that wound down to his knees.

In a soft raspy voice Limbora introduced himself, "Welcome friends. I'm Lim the Curator. Come, let me show ye around." He ushered them inside the museum.

"'Tis good to see ye again, old friend," Drib commented, extending his hand to Lim's shoulder.

"Old?" Lim chuckled with a wheeze, "Who ye be calling 'old,' Drib? There are quite a few gray hairs on yer head, as well."

Drib chuckled, "The gray comes on faster than I thought possible."

Sarah shook her head. "Ye, two! There be visitors here who desire to learn the history o' our city; not to listen to ye old men go on about how old ye both be." Sarah's stern look of disapproval silenced the banter of the two older men.

"Yes, yes, ye be right. Please follow me." Lim led them through the hallways, pointing out various artifacts and spouting facts, oblivious as to whether they followed him or not. Ean saw many different styles of artwork: sculptures, pottery, metal work, paintings, and some things he couldn't even name. Some were inspiring, though others rather disturbed him. Lim took them to a preservation room, where precious art treasures were stored for safekeeping out of the public view.

They viewed even more intriguing pieces. One, in particular, was an oil painting of a meadow filled with flowers. Ean and Adair both leaned in for a better look. However, they found that the longer they stared at it, the more tired they got. Only when Lim pulled them away did they begin to get some of their energy back.

"What was *that*?" Adair asked, her mind still a bit foggy from the change in energy.

"That is one o' the museum's magical artworks. 'Twas painted using magical potion and paint compound mixtures."

"I could almost smell the flowers. They are not like any I have ever seen, yet familiar at the same time," Adair said.

"Ye could smell the flowers. It includes a potion designed to draw people to the paintin' by enhancin' odors. The fragrance places ye in a trance, so that ye never want to stop looking at it. This paintin' in particular was created over three thousand years ago. Throughout its history, many humans, leprechauns, Arturians and other species have ended their lives by lookin' at it--never movin' until they die from thirst, hunger or exhaustion. I, myself, spent a full day starin' at it until an assistant found me and snapped me out o' the trance...Ah, well, that was before the royal family o' Islandia removed it from public view, lockin' it up for the safety o' others."

"But if this is such a dangerous painting, why do you still have it?" Adair inquired.

Lim shrugged, "'Tis part o' our world history. 'Tis one o' only seven rescued from the Islandia palace by leprechauns during the revolution. We got them out during the invasion." Lim looked grim, "I shall never forget the moment General Mohann slayed King Azorian and Queen Isla."

"Wait, you were there?" Ean asked, astounded.

"Aye. As an ambassador from Glen-Delay at the time, I delivered some belated presents from our city to the royal family in behalf o' their baby, Prince Azarion. I was there when the assault on the palace began." Lim had a far-off look in his eyes, "The King himself gave me charge o' smugglin' the paintings out o' the palace and into the Illusion Forest. He was adamant that they be kept safe and protected. While leavin', I looked over the battlement wall and saw the King, Queen, General Mohann, and his guards in the courtyard below. I saw the moment the King and Queen were slain by the General's own hand..."

Ean's mind reeled. He had known about the revolution, but somehow it had been an abstract idea. Now, hearing the account from someone who had spoken with and had been in the presence of the last King when he was slain, the tragedy became more real and he felt a lump form in his throat. Trying to focus on something other than his murdered great-something grandparents, Ean blurted, "Did the other paintings have magical properties too?"

Lim tugged his beard, "Let me think. I cannot be sure, but I believe three more are magical. And one is so old, I could not tell for sure."

"May we see the other ones?" Ean asked hopefully.

"Yes, o' course. They be right over here." Lim guided the group to a back corner where six paintings hung close together. The group looked at the first hanging work of art, admiring the details evident in a lifelike tree within a coat of arms. A family pedigree moved outward along the branches, each name written in golden lettering.

As Ean examined the painting, it appeared as if the leaves stirred with an unseen breeze. Out of curiosity, Ean reached out to feel the texture of the tree in the painting. As soon as his finger touched it, the tree began to vibrate and a golden light shone around the outline of the tree in the painting. Ean removed his hand and stepped back in surprise. An audible gasp escaped from the rest of the group.

Adair saw Ean's confused look. She touched his arm and pointed at the top of the tree, "Look."

There at the top of the tree, his name, his parents' names, his grandparents' names--all his ancestor names had appeared, written in a golden script, connecting Ean all the way to Prince Azarion and the royal family of Islandia.

"What happened?" Ean asked.

Lim cleared his throat and responded, "When ye, a relative o' the royal family, touched the tree, ye updated the records, adding all the descendants o' the family since Prince Azarion.

"It means that ye have been officially declared heir to the throne of Islandia, Yer Highness." Lim added with a deep bow to Ean. Drib, Sarah, and Brin followed suit.

Speechless, Ean looked at Adair, hoping she would pinch him and he would wake up on Earth. Instead she gave him a small smile and curtsied, rather irritating him. "Please don't do that. I don't want people bowing or curtsying to me. I haven't done anything to deserve it".

Lim threw his arms out toward Ean, "But Yer Highness! The heir o' Islandia, has returned! The people o' this world need ye! Yesterday, I saw the king die. Today, I saw him return! What joy I feel, knowin' the hope o' Natura is restored!" Lim starting humming a tune and danced a jig in a small circle.

Blushing with embarrassment for all the attention, Ean decided to distract the leprechaun. "Limbora, should we move on?"

Lim, still bouncing up and down on his heels, agreed, "Oh yes, yes, indeed. Please, let us move on to the other paintings." The next two were of landscapes of Islandia and Eden, respectively. Adair was fascinated at the advanced cultures depicted on the fabric, unlike any they had seen so far.

Adair felt bad Drake wasn't there to see his home again, but realized it would be like her, seeing a picture of her hometown, reminding her of all she missed, but not being able to go there. Her heart went out to him as Adair realized that she and Drake had that in common, both isolated from their home and loved ones. Technically, Ean was too; but since Natura was to become his new home, he had no choice but to learn to leave his old home behind.

Adair studied the pictures. The landscapes and the cities architecture varied vastly from one city to another. "Wow," she breathed out, fascinated with the contrasting scenery.

Music diverted her attention to the fourth painting in front of Sarah. Obviously magical, the painted instruments moved and played music when observed. Tapping her foot, Sarah enjoyed the familiar melody. When it finished and started playing another tune, Sarah walked back to the group and the painting stopped playing, the instruments frozen on the fabric.

The fifth painting was the store front of a bakery. Delicious aromas wafted from the portrait, drawing the group to gather around it. Lim explained, "It smells o' breads or pastries, whatever food the observer desires most. The chef of Islandia's palace would often use it to know what to serve the family or guests for that evening's meal."

Hungry, Ean stepped closer to catch a whiff of mouth-watering donuts. A plate with a doughnut appeared on the ledge of the bakery's open window. "Hey, look at that!" Ean reached out to point to the doughnut, "I could smell--" as his finger touched the painted doughnut, it lifted off the painting and fell. Ean's quick reflexes helped him to catch the doughnut before it fell on the floor. Looking at the painting, Ean saw another painted doughnut, this one with a different topping, had taken the previous one's place.

"Well, that's new." Lim stated.

Everyone stared at Ean as he smelled, then took a bite of the fresh doughnut.

"Mmmm. This is good!" Ean said, his words garbled by the food in his mouth.

Lim shook his head, "I sat many times in front o' this paintin', smellin' the aroma from sweet bread. I even touched the paintin' a time or two, hopeful it did more than smell, but never once did anything come from it."

Drib straightened, "I propose an experiment."

"Oh? What did ye have in mind, Dear?" Sarah asked.

"Sarah, darling, move closer to the paintin' and tell us what ye be cravin'. Let's see if Ean can pull it out."

Sarah took a couple of steps toward the bakery image. Closing her eyes, she drew a deep breath of air. "Biscuits," she breathed out. "The ones like me mama used to make."

Looking at the ledge, the group saw a plate with two biscuits appear. Ean touched them and they lifted off the painting, landing in his outstretched palm. "My Lady," Ean said with a bow, bestowing the biscuits to Sarah.

"I'm next," Adair volunteered. Each person in the group got a chance to stand before the painting, reveal what food item they craved, and Ean would retrieve it for them. Once each person had received their bread or sweet, they drifted over to a nearby bench to eat it.

Dusting the powdered sugar from his cookie off his hands and beard, Lim said, "Now the final paintin' from the palace is the oldest o' them all, a rare and fragile piece of art. Legend states 'twas painted by Islandia's second Talent Master. No one knows if it has magical properties or not, but I have not seen evidence of any."

Even if only a legend, Ean tried to imagine a king sitting and painting this landscape of a lake front with various types of boats. An Asian-like palace rose up in the background on one side while a group of pyramids dotted the other. Far in the distance beyond the lake, a white snow-topped mountain glistened. Adair, equally captivated by the painting, stood close to Ean, looking at the details.

"You know, it sort of reminds me of home," Adair commented. "Hey, was that cabin there before?" She pointed to a small one-level log cabin, built on rocks jutting out from the lake shore. A watermill attached on one side turned slowly and the wrap-around deck led out to a dock floating on the surface of the lake. A row boat bobbing in the water was tied to the dock.

"I'm not sure," Ean replied. Entranced by the movement in the painting, Ean turned to ask Lim about it, but the rest of the group had moved to another part of the preservation room, looking at other artifacts.

When he looked back, the door to the small cabin was now wide open and a light from the inside flickered through it and the front windows. Only a moment ago the door had been closed and the windows dark. "Did you see the door open?" He asked Adair.

"What?" Adair asked.

"The door--I could have sworn it was closed a minute ago, but now it's open," he pointed to the cabin on the lake. Looking closer, Adair saw the change and gasped. Ean murmured, "I wonder if it will close if I touch it." His finger reached up, touching the door as Adair grabbed his elbow and said, "No! Don't!"

The next thing they knew, they stood in front of the cabin door. Rather than looking at the painting, they were *in* the painting.

Chapter 19

Oh, Hi Grandpa

"Aww, not *again*!" Adair turned and slugged Ean in the arm with her free hand.

"Hey, why did you do that?" He asked as he rubbed his arm with his other hand.

"Because you deserved it!"

Her response made no sense to him at all. "Do you care to explain what that means?"

"No! If you're too dense to realize you've done it *again*, I won't waste my time explaining it to you."

"Girls!" Ean muttered. They made no sense at all and always left him more confused than ever. He started to say as much to Adair when he was cut short by a different voice.

"Children, settle down and come inside--you are letting in the chilly air."

In surprise, Adair gripped Ean's arm more tightly, sending a pinprick of pain down to his fingertips. They peered inside the doorway to see a very old man with wispy gray hair and an old worn quilt laying across his lap, hunched in a rocking chair next to the fireplace.

He spoke and gestured with one hand, "Come...come have a seat by the fire."

With Adair still clutching Ean, they crossed the room and sat together on a small love seat just big enough for them to fit snugly side by side.

Adair found her voice, "Who are you?"

"I might ask you the same thing, young lady." Though when he spoke to her, he kept his bright blue eyes locked on Ean's face.

"I am Adair O'Conner and..." her voice trailed off as the old man turned his piercing gaze on her.

"Not your name dear. I want to know what an Earthling, and if I am not mistaken--a Dragon Maiden--is doing inside my painting?"

"Oh, that's his fault," she gestured with her thumb in Ean's direction.

"Hey, I didn't bring you here," Ean replied in his defense.

The old man spoke up, "As a matter of fact, you are responsible for her presence here. But I also see it was necessary."

"What's necessary?" Adair asked.

"Many things. But first let us deal with the Talent Master visiting me."

"How--how did you know?" Ean asked.

He smiled, "Because I am one too. What is your name, Son?"

"I'm Ean McMurrin, an Earthling as well. Wait--did you say *you* are a Talent Master?"

"Yes and no," he replied.

"What do you mean?"

"I mean that you are not an Earthling," he said, looking at Ean. He looked at Adair, "And, young lady, neither are you. Not anymore...and yes, I am--or for a better word-- *was* a Talent Master."

"What do you mean?" Ean and Adair asked at the same time.

Before the old man could answer they heard a loud whistle. Ean found the source: a teapot sitting inside the fireplace.

"Good," the old man said, "Refreshment is ready. Adair O'Connor, if you would please, I have some cups and saucers over on the wall. There are some thin wafers in the box on the table as well. Would you be so kind as to bring them here?"

"Aye." She got up, pausing only to extricate herself from the tight seating arrangement. Crossing the room, she found a silver tray upon which she placed three cups and saucers. From the box on the table, she pulled out a row of thin shortbread-like cookies and placed them next to the saucers on the tray. She brought the tray over to the fireplace and set it upon a low table next to some thick gloves. She slipped the gloves on her hands and picked up the hot teapot, pouring the caramel-colored liquid into the three cups.

"Ah, thank you, dear," the man said as he took a full cup and saucer from Adair. "These old bones get harder and harder to move these days. I appreciate your help."

"My pleasure, sir...?" Adair left the question in the air.

"Oh, yes, I am King Leonida...Leonida now, I guess. I gave up the throne of Islandia thousands of years ago. And now, my grandson, it is *your* responsibility." With a twinkle in his eyes, he glanced at Ean and raised his cup to him before drinking.

Shocked at the news that the old man was his ancestor, Ean sipped his drink--which vaguely reminded him of tea--absentmindedly. Questions tumbled inside his head and Ean wasn't sure where to begin, which one to ask first. When the cups were drained, Adair gathered the dishes and took them back to the table against the wall. She squeezed herself next to Ean on the loveseat. Looking at Leonida, she discovered he was asleep in his chair.

Ean called Leonida's name, softly at first, then louder and louder until Adair elbowed him in the ribs.

"Ow! Quit trying to beat me up! Why did you do that?" He asked angrily.

"Because you tried to wake him."

"Uh, yeah, that was the idea. Whatever gave me away?"

"Look, if you're going to be rude and sarcastic, I'm leaving." She got up and walked out of the cabin.

Ean sat there, not sure of whether to follow Adair out or wake up the old man, until he heard a voice he could have sworn was his mom's, telling him to go after her. So he got up and walked out to where Adair leaned on the railing of the dock, looking out over the water.

He sighed, "Look, I am sorry...for everything. And I..." he trailed off, not sure what else to say.

She replied, "I know you didn't plan on bringing me here." She gestured around, "Here in the painting and to Natura. But for one reason or another, here I am. Let's try to make the best of the situation."

"Thanks, Adair, that is mature of you."

Adair whirled on him, "Mature of *me*? Naturally you're surprised. After all, a boy like you would hardly make such a gesture!"

Ean held his hands up in surrender, "I didn't mean it that--hey, did you call me a boy?"

"Yes, I did. And for your information, it is well known throughout most of the civilized world that ladies are more mature and smarter than boys," she stated in a lofty, superior voice.

"Oh, they are, are they? Well in that case, it wouldn't surprise you if I did this..." And before Adair could react, Ean had picked her up and unceremoniously dumped her over the railing into the lake. Adair came up sputtering, shrieking and splashing. Ean laughed and called to her over her screams, "Well, it looks like "boys" are quicker and stronger."

"You immature brute!" Adair yelled at him.

"Yes...yes I am." Still laughing, he bent down to pull her up out of the water. Leaning over he started to lose balance as he slipped on the deck, wet with water from Adair's splashing. Adair took advantage of this, yanking him past her into the water. With a loud splash, both fell back into the water.

"Oh, it's on!" Ean sputtered, spitting out water. It was war; they splashed each other with the chilled mountain water like two bear cubs having the time of their life.

Soon they were worn out, and the cold water became very uncomfortable in the fading daylight. Hoisting themselves onto the deck, they hurried over to the cabin door and turned the handle. It was locked. Ean looked at the window, but the lights were out and all was dark inside.

"Great, now what?" Adair asked between her chattering teeth.

Ean rubbed his hands up and down his upper arms. "Well, we need to find some shelter and get warm."

"All right, lead the way."

They walked further up the shore until they reached the tree line. Finding a worn trail, they followed it, winding around trees and boulders. They continued along until the darkness had taken over, causing the two to stumble more often.

"Ow!" Adair's soggy boot had hit into a rock, stubbing her big toe. In frustration she said, "Can't we find somewhere to rest for awhile?"

"I'll start looking for a hotel," Ean said sarcastically before he thought better of it. "Sorry. I mean, I'm still trying to find some shelter."

Seeing a ravine to his right, he led her up it until they came across some boulders that created a shallow cave between them. A fire pit with ash inside and a large stack of firewood on one side of the cave was evidence the cave had been previously used. When he pulled a couple of pieces of wood off the pile, he noticed some items tucked behind the stack, indistinguishable in the darkness. He lifted them into the moonlight filtering into the front of the cave to view them better.

Pleased with his good luck, he set the logs in the fire pit and within a couple of minutes, had a good sized fire going.

"Wow! I can't believe you got that fire started so fast!" Adair said.

Ean held up what was in his hand. "To be honest, there was some flint and steel behind the wood stack. Since the wood is dry, it didn't take much to get it started...oh, and here," he tossed some fabric to Adair. "I found some rope and a few old wool blankets so we can dry off."

Locating some cracks in the boulders on one side of the cave, Ean placed an end of the rope inside, jamming some rocks around it to wedge it into place. He did the same with the other side of the cave, so the rope hung suspended above and to the side of the fire. They discretely undressed, wrapping themselves in blankets, hung the wet clothes over the rope to dry, and sat down by the fire to wait.

"How are we going to get out of this?" Adair asked Ean, not expecting an answer.

"I find solutions to problems come faster after a good night's rest and some food--which we'll have to find in the morning. We can return to Leonida's cabin and see if he can help us get out of the painting."

Adair was quiet. Ean reflected that even in the firelight, with wet hair and only an old blanket wrapped around her, Adair did look beautiful.

"You must keep focused on the task at hand." Ean started at the deep earthly-toned voice, looking around to see where it came from.

"Who is that? What task?" Ean wondered.

"You know what I mean. Stay focused on what you need to learn, not on the girl."

Ean looked at Adair to gauge her reaction, but it was obvious she hadn't heard the voice. That must mean the voice was inside his head. *"Great--it's official. I'm crazy!"* Ean thought.

"No, you are not going mad."

"Who are you?"

"I am you, and I am not you."

"Yeah, that makes a lot of sense...NOT."

He heard a deep chuckle. *"I am Velos, the dragon. I am he who picked your family to be rulers over the humans of Natura. I am also part of you, since my body is gone."*

"Have you always been with me?" Ean asked tentatively, not sure he wanted the answer.

"Yes."

"Great," he thought wryly. *"If you have always been here in my head, why haven't you talked to me before?"*

"You did not need me until now."

"I'm pretty sure I could have used some help when I faced Blood Mother."

"You had help."

Irritated by his offhand response, Ean wondered, *"He sounds just like Drake. Are all dragons this annoying?"*

The answering growl inside his head reminded him he wasn't alone with his thoughts. He winced, *"Sorry Velos. I didn't mean to offend you. I could really use your help right now. How in the world do I get out of this painting, and better yet, how do I get back home to my parents?"*

"First of all, Natura is your home. Accept it. Secondly, how would you get out of the painting?"

"I don't know! If I knew that, I'd already be out."

"What's your rush? Take time to explore. Have some fun and maybe you will learn a thing or two about yourself. Right now, rest...and remember the other paintings, like the bakery..."

"What do you mean?" But even as Ean asked the question, he could tell Velos was gone. Now more alert to his surroundings, he found the fire had dwindled down and Adair was asleep, curled up in her blanket. Exhausted, Ean added logs to the fire and lay down to sleep.

Daylight streamed into the cave entrance when Adair woke Ean up the next morning. "Wake up, Sleepyhead!" She tapped his foot with her boot.

Seeing the light, he said, "Oh sorry, I must have overslept."

"No kidding. But it gave me the chance to change while you slept."

Wide awake now, Ean was relieved his blanket still covered him from the waist down. "Great...uh, would you mind giving me a little privacy while I change?"

"No problem." She turned and faced the opposite wall.

Ean changed into his clothes, which were now dry with the exception of his damp shoes. "You can turn around now."

Adair faced him, "Alright, Sherlock, where to next?"

"We should go find some food."

"In theory that sounds good, but the last time I foraged for food didn't end so well. You don't think there are any blood berry bushes here, do you?"

"Remember the Painting!" Hearing Velos inside his mind again solidified the reality that the dragon did exist somewhere inside his mind and his conversation the previous night hadn't been a dream. On one hand, this truth was disturbing, now that he couldn't even think with privacy. On the other hand, he was relieved there was someone to whom he could ask questions, even if the answers were vague and confusing.

"Adair, do you remember the bakery painting from yesterday?"

"Yes, why?"

"Well, if it were here, what would you want?"

She stared at him for a moment, then huffed, "Fine, I like games. I would want a croissant, fresh fruit, yogurt and banana nut bread."

As she spoke, a transparent image of the painting materialized behind her. Ean walked past her and touched the air where the faded image of a buttered croissant and banana nut bread hovered. He turned around, holding the food in his hands.

"Where did you get those?" She demanded, looking at the food in Ean's hands.

"From the painting. Sorry, I can only do bakery items." He handed her the croissant and broke the banana nut bread in half, giving her one half and keeping the other for himself.

"Things keep getting stranger and stranger..." Adair commented to herself.

"You're telling me. This is only the icing on the cake. The cake was what happened last night."

Adair's eyes narrowed, "What do you mean? What happened last night?"

Ean took a deep breath and told her about Velos, except for the part where Velos chastised Ean for thinking about her, of course.

Let me get this straight--you have a *dragon* sharing your body?"

"Yeah."

"Great...we're doomed." Looking defeated, Adair sat down on the ground.

"What do you mean 'we're doomed?'" Ean asked, glaring at her.

"I'm at the mercy of a teenage American boy who's losing his mind! I mean, it's bad enough that you have the mental focus of a puppy--reading your mind would be like watching a ping pong ball bouncing all over the place!"

"She has you pegged. I like her."

"Oh shut up," Ean said out loud to Velos.

"What?" Adair demanded.

"Not you, Adair, I was telling Velos to be quiet."

"Yeah, sure...".

Great, thanks a lot Velos. When Ean's sarcasm didn't receive a response he was even more annoyed.

"We'd better move out." Ean said, returning the steel and flint to the spot he found them.

"Okay," Adair stood up and brushed herself off. "But let's leave the blankets. You never know who else might need them."

"Alright." Dropping his blanket behind the wood pile, Ean held out his hand to Adair. "Shall we go? We've got a painting to explore!"

Chapter 20

Pharaoh's City

*H*eading back out of the ravine, they realized the trail had changed. It no longer led back the direction they had come, it only led from the ravine toward where they had been heading the prior day. With no other option available, they followed it.

Around midday, they topped a mountain rise. Below them lay a triangular city in the middle of a valley. Three different and distinct pyramids were placed at each corner, connecting the tall city wall and accentuating the oddly shaped city.

As they descended toward the valley floor, a breeze began to pick up, bringing along with it the familiar scent of jasmine. Adair stopped, breathing it in. "How wonderful the smell of something familiar can be."

Ean agreed, but was unable to see any jasmine growing nearby, only the flowing red grasses that stretched across the valley. When they reached the bottom of the mountain, the dirt trail they had followed changed to a pathway of cut, polished stone. The granite-like stone, like that of the city walls, was as flawless as if new, without scratches or chips. Moving onward, the jasmine became more fragrant and the roadway noticeably widened as they neared an archway into the city. Soon they could hear the sounds of people cheering and yelling. As there was no sentry at the open archway, Ean and Adair passed through to find the streets empty and stores closed.

Wondering what was going on, they followed the noise until they came upon a large stadium, rectangular in shape, with tall stone walls that reached above the outer city wall. Each of the stadium's visible corners had stairs that ascended in a tight zigzag pattern.

"What should we do?" Adair asked.

"Let's check it out," Ean replied. They climbed the stairway and between pauses to catch their breath, listened to the swell of voices from a multitude of people. Reaching the top, they found a crowd of adults and children sitting on step-like benches that encircled the top half of the stadium. The bottom half of the stadium was submerged in water, upon which boats loaded with men engaged in battle. Men dressed in shabby armor on one boat tossed grappling hooks onto another boat that had drifted closer. Hauling in the line quickly, they started clubbing the men in the captured boat with primitive weapons. Though the men fought back, Ean and Adair watched in horror as bodies splashed into the water. The spectators roared their approval at the slaughter.

They found an open space a couple of rows down and sat next to a family. Turning to the woman next to her, Adair asked, "Who is winning?"

The lady gave her a strange look. "You must be new. No one wins until only one boat is left."

"Left where?" Adair asked.

"Floating on the water, of course. Once all the other boats have been sunk, the surviving crew of the remaining boat split the 10,000 gold coin reward."

"What happens to the crews of the boats that lost?" Adair questioned.

"They must remain in the water until the game is over. Many of them can't swim, so they don't last very long."

Nauseated by the brutal finality of fighting to the death, Adair replied, "Oh, I see. Thanks." She turned her attention back to the contest.

Every once and a while, two very large, rough looking men would grab a man from where he was watching the skirmish, drag him down to the water, and throw him in.

"What are they doing?" Ean asked Adair.

"I have no idea," she said.

The woman next to her overheard him and leaned closer to explain, "Those are the new players. The theater bouncers find replacements for the boat crews. As crew members in the boat get injured or killed, a man is chosen from the audience to be thrown into the water. He must swim to a boat and get inside. And as a new crew member, he must fight until they win or sink."

Stunned, Ean looked closer. The men in the boats fought with swords, axes, spears, and metal gauntlets with sharp spikes on the knuckles. It appeared that the only way to sink another boat was to have a crew member cross over to the enemy boat and hack away until a hole is created. And he must do this all while avoiding being skewered by the opposing crew. Once the job of sabotaging the boat was done, the enemies try to make it back to their own ship before they sink with their opposition.

Ean was appalled by the barbaric fight. Nevertheless, he couldn't seem to tear his attention away, watching until only two boats remained. The roar of the crowd increased tremendously. Some cheered while others shook their fists in anger. The blood lust of the people was unmistakable as they relished in the brutality of the deaths and losses. Dead bodies littered the boat decks and floated in the water. Some bodies were survivors in the water, bobbing at either end of the stadium, waiting for the contest to end.

Two bouncers down by the water looked in Ean's direction. One pointed toward him and the two began to climb up the rows, watching him as they ascended. Ean's back stiffened and his heart pounded in fear as they approached.

His mind raced with his options: should he grab Adair's hand and run? Should he try to fight the bouncers to avoid being thrown in? Should he go bravely and tell Adair that if he didn't make it she should go back to Leonida's? He sat frozen to his seat as they arrived at his row...and moved past him.

They grabbed a man sitting behind Adair and hoisted him to his feet. He protested loudly, but they gripped his arm painfully behind him until he had no choice but to stumble down the rows to the water. Ean's heart was still thumping as he watched the rough bouncers pick the man up and throw him in the water with a splash. The man sputtered and tried to climb out, but one of the bouncers kicked him in the head, so he fell backward. Flailing his arms, the man had no choice but to swim to the nearest boat, mount the side, and join in the fight.

One of the two remaining boats began to take on water as a large man chopped a hole in the side of it with an axe. He jumped back aboard the winning ship and saluted to the exuberant crowd. Once the sinking boat disappeared into the water, the remaining survivors were retrieved from the water. As the crowd got up and dispersed, Ean looked over at Adair, who was white-faced with revulsion.

She whispered, "Let's get out of here." Ean nodded his agreement and together they descended the stairs, heading in the opposite direction of the main crowd. They found themselves traveling toward the center of the city.

Ean guessed they had arrived in the city center when they entered an open large plaza. The light from the setting sun reflected off the gigantic obelisk jutting up from the middle of the space. It was centered in the spacious oval-shaped courtyard. At the far end three streets led away from the square. They had arrived along one of three streets that led to the square from this side of the oval, the other two streets were on their right and left sides. Walking around the perimeter of the courtyard, they could see down the six streets. Each one had a different feel about them, as they each had different architectural designs.

Adair took his hand, "Ean, where are we going next? It's getting late and I'm feeling tired."

"Which street do you want to try?"

"You're the Talent Master," she said wearily. "You pick."

Ean looked at each street in turn. As he did so, he began to notice themes: They had come from a street that consisted of dark, cold stone structures; the roadway to its right was filled with cabin-like wooden log buildings; and the one to the left had brilliant white marble buildings with gardens on their rooftops. On the opposite side of the courtyard, one street had Asian-like pagodas, the center street consisted of earth-toned homes and shops with potted plants hanging from windows with wooden shutters, and the last street had cottages with murals painted on their walls, grass roofs and detailed wood carvings over the doorways.

"That way," he pointed to the cottage-lined street. "It looks the most inviting." They headed in that direction. Not more than 100 yards down the cobblestone road, they were stopped by a woman with a thick accent.

"Who might you two be?" Looking around they noticed a middle aged woman with her hands on her hips, an apron tied around her waist, standing in the doorway of a cottage.

"Visitors, just passing through."

"Is that so? Well we don't get many visitors through here. What is your business?"

Ean opened his mouth to speak, but Adair cut him off, "We're not here on business. We were traveling through your city on our way home, and now it is getting late. Might you be able to help us?"

With wary eyes, the woman responded with a question of her own, "That depends, what kind of help do you need?"

"We could use a place to stay for the night, and some food to eat. Do you know where we could find those?" Adair asked with a hopeful smile.

She looked them up and down for a moment, nodded her head, "Humph...well come on in. I don't run a boarding house, but you can stay the night, and if you help with the meal and dishes...well, I am glad to share."

"Oh thank you! You are most kind!" Adair replied gratefully.

"You can call me May."

Adair smiled bigger, "Thanks, May."

They came in and set to work preparing a meal. As they worked, they asked May about the different streets of Pharaoh's City and learned they should avoid some areas at all costs. When they mentioned what they had seen at the stadium, May was stunned, "You have visited that horrid place? It is a miracle you made it out in one piece! The people inhabiting that part of the city are a cesspool of scum. It is why very few decent folk ever venture there."

After they had eaten and cleaned the dishes, the three settled down in the cozy room to relax. May got right to the point, "Now, tell me why you two children are walking around on your own."

Ean paused for a minute while he considered how to respond. He kept his explanation simple, "Though we did not plan to come, here we are, so we thought we would do some exploring."

Adair nodded in agreement.

May looked at him, "Your being here doesn't have something to do with the man in the cabin, would it?"

Ean was stunned, "You know Leonidas?"

May chuckled. "We all know Leonidas, child. None of us would be here without him. This is, after all, his painting."

Adair's jaw dropped, "Wait--you *know* you're inside a painting?"

"Of course. You can't paint a person into life. People from Natura chose to come here. Once inside, you continue to live life as normal. You can have families and die of course, as is the natural order of things, but one can live much longer inside the painting. That is why Leonidas created this painting in the first place--so he could live long enough to train future Talent Masters."

"Were you born here or did you come from Natura?" Adair asked.

May sighed. "My life in Natura was not an easy one. I experienced much heartache and difficulty. Though I knew life in the painting wouldn't be perfect, I felt a desire to come, like I was supposed to be here."

She leaned forward and confided, "I sometimes get little flashes of intuition. I learned it is best to follow these instincts. That is why I am here. And my instincts are telling me there is more about you than you are letting on." She raised her hand before they could respond. "I am not asking for information, but I have a gut feeling that you two need each other, not just here, but in Natura as well."

"Now, enough of my rambling." May stood to her feet. "Let's get some beds set up. I only have one spare bed in my room, so Adair will stay there and Ean, you will sleep in here." May crossed the room to a cedar chest and pulled out sheets, blankets and pillows. In no time at all she had helped Ean set up a make-shift bed on the hearth rug of the main room. Then she showed Adair to the back room where they would stay the night.

Even though he was tired, Ean was unable to sleep at first. He kept replaying May's words over and over in his mind, wondering if she was right. Well of course she was right--Adair did need him...to help her get back home to Earth.

Velos spoke up. *"Again, you have missed the point."*

"What did I miss?" Ean demanded.

"*That you need Adair as much as she needs you. At some point you are going to have to accept the fact that you need help from those around you, including her.*"

"Not an option," Ean dismissed the advice. "*I mean, she can help while she's here. But my first goal is to figure out how to get her home to her family again. I owe her that much.*"

"*You desire to go too,*" Velos commented dryly.

Ean ground his teeth, Velos's ability to read his thoughts was getting annoying fast. "*So what? Yes, I want to go home too. But I won't--I'll stay if that is the price I have to pay to get her home.*"

"*That is good. Remember Ean, personal foundations are not built upon one grand gesture of greatness, but on many little simple acts, each building upon one another to create the firm foundation of your character. You must build such a base that when the wind blows and storms pound upon you, you will be strong enough to prevail.*"

Then the dragon was gone. As much as Ean tried to continue the conversation, Velos would not respond and when he began to drift off to sleep, his last thought was that he wished everyone from Natura would stop talking in riddles and just tell him what he needed to do.

Ean couldn't believe their luck as he strolled down the streets of what was called by the people of Pharaoh's City 'Sector Six,' which is where May's home was. He was reflecting on how fortunate he and Adair were to have found such a wonderful and generous new friend in the city. Not only did May prepare an amazing breakfast before they said their final goodbyes to her, but she kindly found clothes for them to wear. Ean looked down at the baggy pants he was wearing. At least they weren't too small, and they were clean and comfortable. The two were also grateful to have the chance to wash off all the dirt and grime that had been sticking to them ever since they had fallen into the lake and slept on the cavern floor.

Ean could tell Adair was much happier today than she had been the prior day. It was amazing what wonders could be done by a good night's rest, good food, a hot bath, and clean clothes.

"Sleep well last night?" He asked to start a conversation.

She looked at him with a half smile, "I did. That is, after May and I had a nice long conversation...You know, our lives are never going to be the same again."

Ean had known that his happy ordinary life was over the moment he realized that he was heir to a throne and that people had expectations for him. He would have gladly relinquished his role in Islandia if he didn't know how bad things were for most of Natura. Even though he had never met any of the people of Islandia, his heart was touched by their plight and he knew that he was expected to do something about it. The only problem now was trying to figure out what to do and how to do it. However, Adair was a different story. Ean knew that he was responsible for getting her home, but besides memories, he didn't think it would change her destiny much. Wondering what she thought was different, he asked, "How so?"

"Well, for one thing, we are the only Earthlings here in Natura, which--by itself--makes us unique. And now, since we've been here, we've changed. I'm now a Dragon Maiden, and you're a future Talent Master and perhaps even king."

"What do you mean 'perhaps'?"

She gave him a little push and smiled, "Don't interrupt, I'm making a point."

Pretending to be contrite, he replied with an exaggerated bow, "My apologies, My Lady."

"That's better," Adair commented with a wicked grin. "Look at all that we have done: we've met a dragon, eaten in a restaurant inside of a tree, fought a ferocious magical plant, explored a cavern of gold--"

"You explored, I didn't get the chance."

"Okay, I explored a gold-filled cavern from which I took some souvenirs--"

"You what?! You never mentioned that before." Ean was shocked by her flippant confession.

"You never asked."

Ean made a couple of mental notes: One, don't underestimate Adair. Two, ask her more detailed questions.

She continued, "Now, let me finish...we've also befriended a leprechaun, been in the middle of a battle between good and bad fairies, fought off assassins who are determined to kill me, and oh yeah--now we are traveling through a magical painting where your grandfather lives."

Ean stopped. After another step Adair turned around, "What's wrong? Why did you stop?"

Ean paused. Not sure how to say all he wanted to say, he took a deep breath and blurted out, "I'm *so* sorry, Adair--"

Before he could continue, Adair stepped forward and placed her hand over his mouth. "Stop. There's no need to say it. I understand Ean. We were both brought here against our will. But I have to admit it's my fault, too. I didn't want to sit in the car while you two went to the Stone. And even though I miss my family, I'm beginning to feel like I belong here as well. Maybe it was a coincidence or accident that I came along, but it could have been fate. I like to believe that fate plays a much greater role in what happens in our lives."

"Fate?" Ean asked. "Well, tell fate I'm tired of all the surprises."

"I love surprises! Which reminds me, I would love a box of little powdered donuts about now..." She looked at him and coyly batted her eyelashes.

With a shake of his head, Ean smiled and focused his thoughts on the bakery painting, which materialized next to him. Seeing her box of donuts appear, he plucked them out and handed them to her.

She opened the box, breathed in the scent of fresh donuts and sighed, "I never get tired of that trick."

They walked for hours, winding through streets to enjoy different styles of buildings. Though May's home was more of an English cottage design, the majority of the sector had a different flare--with roofs framed with rounded wood-carved buttresses and gardens bursting with flowers lining the front of the homes and walkways, where fist-sized blossoms gave off intoxicating fragrances. Ean and Adair often paused on their sight-seeing tour to gaze at unfamiliar flowers. About mid-day, the sounds of children and laughter got their attention.

"Hey," Adair pointed further down the road to a fenced-in yard. "It looks like a carnival!" As they approached the commotion, they could see people playing various games, each separated by low walls covered in vine-like plants. A young girl greeted them at the gate.

"Welcome to the annual education fundraiser for Sector Six. Half of the proceeds from today will be given to the school," she stated in a programmed speech. "Thank you for your support and have fun." She stood to the side so they could enter.

Ean and Adair were surprised to recognize some of the games found traditionally on Earth. There was a dunk tank, discus throw competition, popping balloons with darts, foot races, and knocking over bottles. Entertainers sang and danced on a stage in the center of the yard. Unfamiliar games also vied for attention: Shrink-your-parents, eat-your-friend's-schoolwork (which was a baked pastry that looked like a writing tablet for homework), a game of jumping over a two-story high wall (Ean had no idea how they did it), and a variety of other competitions. Adair was surprised to see a giant falconry cage, where children could hold predatory birds on thick gloves while inside a large domed enclosure.

They wandered past the activities and entered the food area of the event. The booths of food and beverages seemed endless! The pastries were so light, they could imagine them able to float above the plates. Sweets with frosting disappeared as soon as they touched the tongue—leaving only a sweet taste behind.

Ean practically drooled when they came across the meat section. Cooks offered steaks, three meat shish-kabobs, pork, lamb, duck, goose, mammoth, saber-tooth tiger jerky, and a three-horned fish he had never heard of before. A woman holding a tray of samples handed him a piece of the savory fish and Ean found that the tender morsel dipped in a Hollandaise like garlic-butter sauce was delicious.

Following the meat booths, they came to a booth where a young girl, perhaps seven years of age, and boy, about ten years old, sat behind a table which was empty, except for a scattering of crumbs. The girl was crying into her hands and the boy was wiping a tear away from his face with the sleeve of his shirt.

Adair walked around the table and knelt down next to them. "What's wrong?"

"We...we ran out of bread," the boy said, his voice cracking from the emotional confession. "We had more bread to sell, but on the way here the wagon overturned and the rest of it got ruined." He looked miserably into Adair's eyes, "If we don't raise enough money for the fundraiser, we can't have the same booth next year. We use our portion of the money we earn from today to provide for our family until next year."

"Oh, you poor dears," Adair groaned, giving the kids each a one-armed hug. "What are your names?"

"Eva," came the girl's reply.

"Fierusk," said the boy.

Ean pulled Adair aside, "I've got an idea..." As he whispered his plan into her ear, she began to grin.

"Let's do it!" She exclaimed when he was through.

They prepared the booth, telling the kids what they needed help with. Though baffled by the instructions Adair and Ean gave, the kids obeyed, bringing them a long length of dark fabric and rope. Ean and Adair hung the fabric a couple of feet behind the table so that it stretched from the top of the booth walls to the ground. Adair coached the kids on what they should do, assuring them that everything would work out.

Standing on a chair in front of the table, the boy called out, "Draw near, one and all! We offer you edible enchantments to purchase! For the next little while, we will deliver your bread wishes! Tell us what bread you desire and we shall provide it!" People who had been passing by paused to listen as the boy repeated his speech.

A crowd began to form by the time he finished and his little sister stepped up on the table. Pointing to a burly man with a thick black beard she asked, "What bread would you like, sir?"

After a moment of thought, he called out, "Two loaves of rosemary olive oil bread!" Behind the curtain, Ean concentrated on the request. When the bakery painting appeared, he pulled the two loaves out and handed them to Adair, who walked around the curtain to evoke gasps from the crowd. She handed the loaves to the stunned customer, who pulled out a silver coin to put in Eva's little outstretched hand.

A woman at the side of the crowd called out her wish for 10 rolls and Adair disappeared behind the curtain, only to reemerge a moment later with a bag of the rolls. Suddenly, the orders started coming in from all directions and Ean was hard-pressed to keep up with them. For the next hour of time, he pulled breads, pastries, and sweets out of the painting as ordered. Adair was exhausted from being in constant motion and the two kids preoccupied with collecting the customer's money. The crowd remained thick as most of the people lingered to behold what they called "the bread miracle."

The orders began to slow as most of the crowd had received what they wanted and Adair announced there would only be time for one more order. Turning to Eva and Fierusk, she said, "And what do you two want?"

A big smile lit up Eva's face as she pointed to a boy in the crowd holding a box of pastries, "Could I have a Berry Sweet Cream, too, please?"

Smiling, Adair turned to Fierusk. "Would you like that too?"

Looking down, he scuffed his boot into the dirt. "I was hoping for a couple of loaves of bread--enough to feed my family for dinner."

Adair's smile faded as tears came to her eyes. She cleared her throat and managed to say, "Coming right up."

She made it behind the curtain before a tear escaped from her eye. As she wiped it away with one hand, Ean gave a squeeze to her other hand. "I've got this." He pulled a large box of the creamy pastries and a bag with three loaves of bread out of the painting. Adair followed him out front as he presented it to the excited kids. Ean walked over to the wall and tugged on the rope overhead, letting the curtain fall to the ground. Murmurs and exclamations erupted from the crowd as they saw that there was nothing there--no bread, machines or anything at all.

Still amazed, the onlookers began to disperse. Eva and Fierusk hugged Adair and Ean before launching into dozens of questions.

"How did you *do* that?"

"Where does the bread come from?"

"Are you magic?"

"Can you only do that with bread?"

"Can you do it again?"

"Can you show me how to do that?"

The questions were so fast and numerous that Ean and Adair could only chuckle in response to their seemingly endless queries. Ean patted Fierusk on the back, "We're glad we could help out. Now, would you like some help counting your money?"

The kids emptied the bags holding the coins and proceeded to separate the denominations. After it had been counted, the kids jumped up and down in excitement. Fierusk explained the good intake also meant that not only could they keep their booth, they now qualified for an even better location the next year.

As the two children scurried off to pay their fundraiser dues, Ean and Adair moved on to other fair booths. Soon they came across a large group of people gathering at the end of the street. A short beep got their attention and a magnified voice called out, "Don't miss your chance to win $1,000 gold coins! This is the last and final call for those wishing to compete in the 5K race. Remember, all contestants must register at the race booth prior to the race. We'll see you at the finish line!"

Adair grabbed Ean's arm. "You should enter the race!" Adair grinned at him. "You know how to run, right?"

"Of course I know how to run. It goes like this..." Ean pretended to run in slow motion, causing Adair to giggle.

"Yep, that's it all right. Though you probably don't want to show off those skills in front of everyone else."

Ean chuckled. "True. I guess I could show them how I ran while on track team in high school. Not as cool to watch though."

Taking this as his consent to run, Adair said, "Great! This should be fun to watch!" She practically dragged him with her to the racing booth situated under a large banner that simple said "5K Race."

A thick, muscular middle-aged man stood behind a table with a clipboard in one hand. He glanced up. "Race is in five minutes."

"Here," Adair said breathlessly from her efforts to pull Ean behind her. "He's going to run."

"Great, sign here." He stabbed his paper and handed Ean a feathered pen. "All runners meet over by the town clock."

Having signed the paper. Ean took a deep breath. "Wish me luck." He started jogging toward the starting point.

"Good luck, Hotshot!" He heard Adair call after him. When he arrived at the beginning of the course, Ean approached a rather distracted man, figuring he must be a race official.

"I checked in over there," he said, pointing to where he had signed in.

"Of course, of course!" he replied. "Name?"

"Ean McMurrin"

"Fine. Your starting circle is that one over there." He pointed out where he wanted Ean to stand. Thanking him, Ean walked over and began his regular stretching routine, like he always used to do before high school track practices and competitions. The last race he had run felt like a lifetime ago.

"Racers, take your mark!" Boomed a magnified voice. Ean and 29 other hopeful runners lined up on their circles. The voice spoke one more word, "BEGIN!"

There was a loud 'BOOM' as a cannon shot blue smoke into the air. A little startled by the abrupt signal, Ean started a fraction of a second after the other racers. But he soon transitioned to his racing pace, behind the front five contestants. The track for the race went the length of the school ground before veering through the cobblestone streets of Sector Six.

After an easy one and a half miles down the street, the pathway led up and down several steep hills. Pushing himself to keep up his rigorous pace, Ean passed three more racers, so he was in the third position. As he pushed himself over the final hill and was starting to descend the slope, Ean's back was hit with a hard object, throwing him forward. Feeling the loss of control, Ean tucked himself into a ball, allowed himself to roll once, and as his feet started downward again, he straightened his back, bending only his knees. Planting his feet on the ground, Ean pushed upward, letting the momentum of the jump take him a few feet down the slope. Skidding to a stop, he looked back to see what had happened.

There, on the hill above him, lay a black brick that hadn't been there before. Realizing that the pain shooting from where he had been hit was caused intentionally by someone made Ean flush with anger. It was obvious that someone did not want him to win and they were willing to cheat to stop him. His rage ran through him until his blood boiled; Ean let out a yell and took off running with the single-minded focus of winning.

His emotions running high, his body reacted instinctively to the changes in terrain, increasing his speed until Ean was surprised at his swift pace and stamina. He had more energy than he had ever had in a race before, with more building up inside of him until he thought he would explode. His arms and legs tingled and became hotter by the second. When he felt that he couldn't hold in the energy any more, he released it, taking off like a missile. Within seconds he caught up to, then passed, the racers in front, leaving them far behind.

He laughed out loud with exhilaration when he saw the finish line no more than a hundred yards in front of him. Out of habit, he pushed himself to reach beyond the ending line, flying along almost effortlessly even though he could feel the muscles working and stretching with every sprint. Within seconds he had crossed the end of the race course to the sound of the cheering crowd. Out of the corner of his eye he saw Adair jumping up and down, excited over Ean's win.

There was a brief award ceremony in which Ean was congratulated and handed a sack of gold. Walking away from the podium and dispersing crowd, Ean murmured to Adair, "I don't see why we need all this gold."

"Just take enough to cover any expenses, like somewhere to stay, shopping and food. We can give the rest away."

"Good point. I think I saw an inn in the main square yesterday. Let's see if they have room for us tonight."

On their way to the inn, they spotted a statue of what looked like a monk next to a church. People were dropping a coin or two into a slot on the side of the statue. As they neared it, they saw a plaque at the feet of the statue: "Orphanage and Widow's fund. May you always be blessed for giving to those in need."

Ean and Adair turned to each other. Simultaneously they said, "Let's give them the money." Their eyes lingered for just an extra moment, blue on hazel, hazel on blue. Then with big grins, they both emptied the bag of coins into the slot for those in need.

∞ ∞ ∞

The exterior of the Dancing Crane Inn was a simple white, wood-trimmed building. Inside, however, was a different story. Maroon velvet curtains framed each window, resting atop the richly polished cherry wood floors and contrasting the smooth light stone countertops. An elegantly dressed man, the host of the inn, welcomed them at the door. After a brief inquiry about prices and availability, Ean reserved a two-room suite and ordered a full buffet to be brought to the room.

Upon entering the suite, they were amazed by the continued elegance of the surroundings. Golden framed pictures and mirrors adorned the walls, a comfortable looking couch with round end tables faced two dark brown leather chairs flanking an elaborately embellished side table, upon which sat two gold cups and a golden pitcher that held what looked like grape juice. They peeked into the two bedrooms off the seating area to discover that each consisted of identical king-sized canopy beds with four posts draped with white lace. Each bedroom had a fair-sized bathroom attached.

After cleaning up (Ean was grateful for the chance to take a shower following the race), they rang a bell to inform the kitchen staff they were ready for the food. Within minutes the door was opened and several servers dressed in white marched in, carrying silver trays. Ean tried to give them each a metal coin as a tip, but the servers refused, insisting it was part of their job.

Ean and Adair dug into delectable meat, fruits, and vegetables. Each of the items was paired with several types of dipping sauces to enhance the flavor, and among recognizable dishes rested unfamiliar items with unusual tastes. Some of their favorites were the trays of sweets consisting of hand-dipped chocolates, pastries, cakes, and miniature hard candies.

Once full, they felt very drowsy. Ean rang the bell again and the servers appeared to remove the trays. Closing the door behind them, he collapsed onto the couch next to Adair, who had curled up on the end.

She sighed with a smile on her face, "That sure was some meal...I can't remember having a meal quite like that one."

"Tell me about it," Ean agreed. "But don't tell my mom I said that-- she prides herself on her cooking."

"I'll keep that in mind if I ever meet her."

"Oh, you will." Not sure why he had said that, he blushed and changed the subject. "Do you think it's time to return to Grandfather Leonidas?"

"Hm, good question," she mumbled.

When she didn't say anything more, he looked over to see that she was asleep. Figuring she would get a sore neck from sleeping on the couch, Ean got up and walked into her room. He turned down the bed sheets and returned to the seating room. Lifting her into his arms, he carried her to her bed, laid her down, and covered her up with the blankets.

"Good night, Adair," he whispered. On his way out, he closed the door behind him.

"That was kind of you."

Ean was relieved to hear from Velos again. *"I knew she was tired and she would be more comfortable in her own bed."*

"Still, chivalry is the mark of a man."

"And it surprises you that I'm chivalrous? Since you can read my thoughts, you should know that this is the kind of person I am."

"Ah, but thinking about being kind and acting upon those thoughts are separate. It was pleasing how you chose to help others this day. Such actions prove you possess great values and character...and by the way, you ran like a dragon today."

Pleased with Velos's praise, Ean climbed into his bed and fell asleep as soon as his head hit the pillow.

∞ ∞ ∞

The next morning Ean and Adair walked toward the outside perimeter of Sector Six, having decided it was time to look for a way back to Leonidas.

"You know what I wondered?" Adair asked. Her voice dropped as she whispered. "Why do you think the people in the painting are here? If they were born in Natura, then why come? If they were born here, why stay? It is strange that people would live their whole lives inside a painting."

"No stranger than us living outside of it. To those born here, this is all they have ever known. Who can say what is normal or not?"

"What an insightful perspective. I am *impressed*." With the last word she added a quick slug punch to his arm and darted away.

"That's it! You're in for it now," Ean yelled as he chased her down the street. Adair was much faster than Ean expected and she kept out of his reach until they reached the end of the street. "Gotcha!" He grabbed her arms from behind.

"Look!" Adair nodded her head to the city wall. A small archway, partly hidden behind a pile of crates, allowed access out of the city. Eagerly moving forward, they saw a dirt pathway heading into a forested area. "I don't remember seeing a forest around the city before."

"Do you want to try this exit or should we try the archway we came in?" Ean asked.

Adair shuddered, "I'm not going back through that sector!"

"Let's try this way."

They followed the path for much of the day, only stopping to rest and eat bread Ean conjured up from the painting. It was late in the day when the trees opened up to reveal the path ended at a lake shore. In the distance a speck of light floated as if on the water. Close by, a white row boat with two oars bobbed on the shore.

"Shall we?" Ean gestured to the boat. Looking apprehensive, Adair climbed in, followed by Ean.

As soon as they sat inside, the boat moved away from the shore of its own accord. Ean took up the oars and began to row, but it made no difference, the boat was traveling at its own speed, cutting through the water toward the distant light.

As they got closer, they realized that the floating light was not actually floating, but it was a lantern hung on the dock that extended from the lake to Leonida's cabin. Their boat came alongside the dock, stopping without so much as a bump. It stayed where it was while Ean and Adair disembarked. After scrambling out, they turned to look at the boat one last time. To their surprise, it was gone.

Chapter 21

Becoming a True Talent Master

They walked around the deck and came to the front door. Ean tried the handle and the door opened.

"Did you kids have a good swim?" an old, soft voice asked as they walked across the threshold. Instantly their clothes became soaked through. Looking down, they both wore the outfits Brog had made them the morning they had left the Denar family home to visit the museum.

"How--what?" Ean stuttered, looking from Leonidas to Adair, who wore the same shocked expression on her face.

Leonidas chuckled, "You fell into the water and by the sound of it, you two had some fun."

Ean wondered if the whole journey in the painting had been a dream. Trying to wrap his head around everything made Ean feel like the room was spinning, so without waiting for an invitation, he sat down on the hearth rug to avoid getting the furniture wet.

"This is too much, I think I am losing my mind..."

"You and me both," Adair commented as she walked closer to the fire, sitting down on the stone mantle.

Leonidas smiled, "You two are not going crazy. Time is different in a painting. For example, in some areas time stands still, while in other areas time either moves forward or in reverse. It is all rather inspired, if I do say so myself." He chuckled, "Of course, I am the artist, so that is how I designed it. My cabin here is the anchor for the magic that brings this painting to life, so here time remains frozen, unchanging. It is why I lived here from almost the moment I entered the painting, and it is the reason I am still alive."

"If you don't mind my asking, why are you here?" Adair asked, curious as to why he chose to come into the painting.

"I am here to make the transition easier for the next Talent Master. I am here as a teacher, guide, friend, whatever the next Talent Master needs."

"Let me get this straight, you are living forever in this cabin, in your own painting, in order to help the next Talent Master?" Ean asked.

"Yes."

"Okay," Ean got excited; maybe going home would come sooner than later. "Would you teach me how to be a full Talent Master and how to open portals to Earth?"

"Yes and no, I cannot."

"What? Why not?" His excitement turned to dismay.

"I will give you the knowledge to be a full Talent Master, but the creation of gateways is the secret of the dragons. Very few Talent Masters earned the trust of dragons to be given that knowledge, but I will tell you this: it's is not about impressing them, it is more a matter of need and trust that you could attain that knowledge. I never had the need in my lifetime as the ruling Talent Master, so I did not seek out that skill."

"Oh..." Though disappointed, he was not going to give up--the responsibility remained his to get Adair back to Earth. An idea came to him; if the dragons knew how to create portals, then Velos should know how. He tried to mentally contact Velos, but of course Velos was never around when Ean wanted to talk with him. Putting his questions aside for later, he decided to address his next question.

"Leonidas, how do I become a full Talent Master? What do I do now?"

"It depends, what talents do you know you possess? Can you use magic yet?"

As Ean collected his thoughts, the cabin became quiet, only the sound the fire crackled in the background. Hesitantly he began, "Well, I fought the Blood Mother bush with acrobatic-like stunts, took bread out of the bakery painting, changed the family tree painting by touching it, and ran super-fast during a race--I mean faster than I have ever run before, it was amazing! I felt like I could run forever!"

"Ah, the talents you are naturally drawn to and excel in are creative and artistic ones. However, you have yet to exhibit many logical and analytical talents. That doesn't mean you won't-it means you will need to work harder to develop them. Remember, the potential to do anything you desire is there, though the strength and magnitude for each talent is limited to your weaknesses. You will need to focus on improving that which you are not good at--but if you work hard to develop them and use them with magic, you will be able to do miraculous things."

Leonidas looked wistful, "I remember my first experience with magic and talents. It was amazing...and she was so beautiful."

Adair perked up, "Oh, please do tell."

"It was a day long ago...the sky was clear and..." he paused for a moment, then shook his head. "This is not the time to relate such tales. Maybe another time."

When Leonidas stopped short of telling his story, his cheeks were blushing, but maybe it was only the light of the fire.

Leonidas continued, "Where was I? Ah, yes, you need to learn how to harness the power of the dragon inside you. After you find many of your talents, the magic will begin to flow from you--like music in the air--just by the way you think, feel and act. So here is my one warning," Leonidas looked into Ean's eyes, "If you rely upon magic to do ordinary tasks, you will begin to take for granted those around you and what they do for you. You will become cold, unfeeling, and displaced. Only use magic when necessary, when something can be done no other way.

"That is enough for tonight, children. Rest here and tomorrow we will continue." Leonidas closed his eyes and started to breathe deeply.

Ean turned to Adair and whispered, "What do we do now?"

She smiled and mouthed, "Sleep." She stretched out on the couch and went to sleep, leaving Ean to sleep on the hearth rug.

Ean kept busy the next morning doing various exercises. One was a mind exercise where Ean would first picture in his mind what he wanted to accomplish and then he had to will himself to create it. Not as easy as it sounded, he had to create items he didn't want, such as twigs, paper, smoke, onions, and clothing. The jeans and polo shirt he conjured from nothing seemed rather easy to do, since he wanted to wear something more his style than the kilt he had been dressed in. Despite the success he had creating objects, Ean was still unhappy he didn't know how to create a portal to Earth. Each day he tried to reach Velos, but of course the dragon didn't answer--that would be *way* too convenient.

Leonidas assigned him physical exercises as well. Leonidas explained that along with the importance of working the mind and imagination, the body also needed strength in order to create stronger magic. Ean was being pushed harder and harder each day to become more focused and to stretch, flex and bend his body in ways he never thought it would, or should, ever bend.

Adair joined in with the daily exercises. She loved coming up with new things for Ean to create with magic. The small cabin filled fast with weird odds and ends, and one day he even created a floating tree right off the cabin dock. As the weeks flew by--which of course, they didn't, since time stood still--Ean became very adept at creating things within an instant of his thought. Sometimes he would flourish his hands as he made it, while other times he held still as the new object appeared.

Leonidas explained, "The same thought process that creates these objects is also the same for becoming anything you want to be. For example, if you want to be a painter, swimmer, runner, doctor, or scientist, take this desire and combine it with the visualization techniques you learned, and you will become it." At Ean's skeptical look, the old man said, "Try it. Do not doubt it. What you used to believe was impossible has become second nature for you to accomplish."

Ean asked a question that had been weighing heavily on his mind, "What if all this becomes too easy for me? Will my magic stop growing?"

Leonidas smiled, "Your magic will always be there. It being too easy is not the problem--that would be complacency and taking your talents for granted. Such attitudes will corrupt or lessen who you are. That is why it is so important to know yourself--because only you can decide if your actions are out of careful thought or a reaction to inner rage. In the end, it is why you do what you do-that makes all the difference in the world."

The daily workouts and lessons continued until one morning Leonidas told Ean he had one more lesson to teach him. He took Ean aside and discussed how he had created the magical paintings, including this one. "This knowledge is not given to you for you to practice, but I give it to you for knowledge and for remembrance." Then Leonidas offered Adair a wooden box carved with flowers and vines. When she opened it, she saw two dragon keys inside. "These are for you."

"I will keep them safe," she replied. "Thank you very much." She leaned forward and gave him a kiss on his cheek.

Leonidas beamed, "It is my pleasure, my dear." He looked at Ean, "Keep this one around. Now, keep practicing and remember--being a Talent Master is who you are. You are the next king, my grandson. The people need you, and most importantly, you need them." He gestured to the door. "To leave this painting walk out the door and you will return to where you entered."

Ean nodded, a lump in his throat. "I will miss you Grandfather. Thank you for teaching me about becoming a Talent Master."

Leonidas shook his head, "You already were a Talent Master, Ean; I showed you how to unlock your potential. You did everything else yourself. Now, travel safely and remember--no one but you can tell you what and who you are."

With final words of goodbye, Ean took Adair's hand in his own and they stepped out the cabin door to find themselves back in the museum, the painting with the cabin behind them. Turning, they looked back at the painting. This time the cabin door was open and Leonidas, stooped with age, stood at the door, waving goodbye.

Chapter 22

Walking Shopping Mall

"here have ye been?" Brin's voice boomed, startling Ean and Adair. They spun around to see him striding toward them, followed by his parents and the museum curator.

"What?" Ean asked.

"Ye heard me," Brin replied. "We looked for ye two for hours. Where were ye?"

"Uh..." Ean wasn't sure how to explain.

"Oh Brin, give 'em a break. I remember a time or two when ye disappeared with a young lady." His mom, Sarah, commented.

"Mama! I never--" Brin's face turned red.

Drib chimed in "...so ye never spent time with Tizzy Hegney, or Luticia Dobhailen, or--"

"Papa! I was only friends with 'em."

Sarah crossed her arms, questioning his truthfulness with one look. Brin was reduced to mumbling, "Well, I suppose we did kiss..."

"Mmmm hummm," she replied.

Ean liked the idea of sneaking off with Adair and wished they had been doing what everyone thought they had been doing.

Thoroughly embarrassed by the innuendos about them going off to kiss, Adair pulled her hand out of Ean's and blurted, "Ean and I have never...I mean we *would* never...That would be ridiculous!" Ean's ideas on the matter were snuffed out. Ean sighed and reminded himself that the only thing she needed him for was a way home.

Sarah patted Adair's arm, "Love is normal, dear. No need to deny it."

Adair flushed with embarrassment. "Sarah, nothing happened--well that's not true--lots of things happened, but not what you think--I mean..." Adair looked at Ean for help.

Catching her silent plea, he walked over to Sarah, moved his hands with a flourish and produced a large bouquet of two dozen roses, holding them out to her. It was the perfect distraction Adair needed from the conversation.

Sarah gasped and took the flowers from Ean's outstretched hands, "How be it possible?"

Ean grinned, "I picked up a couple of new tricks."

"Where from?" Brin interjected. "I havena' seen ye do magic like that."

Ean turned to the historian Limbora Himpton. Pointing to Leonida's painting he declared, "Out of all the paintings, this one is the most important. Use all your resources to protect and guard this painting. Countless lives could be lost if harm were to ever come to it."

The leprechauns looked somberly at the painting, wondering what Ean had meant.

Lim bowed, "I will do as ye say, Your Majesty. I will dedicate the remainder of me days to makin' sure the paintin' be guarded." Satisfied Lim would keep his word and the inhabitants of the painting, including his distant grandfather, were protected, Ean relaxed.

Curious, Drib stepped forward and placed his hand on Ean's forearm. "I suspect there be something ye aren't telling us."

Drib's sincerity pierced through his protective wall and Ean let out a deep breath. "In short, Adair and I have spent the past month inside that painting, where I was taught how to use the dragon's magic inside me."

"A month?!?" His statement caused the rest of the group to simultaneously ask several questions. Ean realized explanations could take a while. He held up a hand to get their attention. "Let's find a more comfortable place to discuss this. And I'm sure Drake will want to hear about it, too."

"O' course," Brin agreed. Without delay, Brin and his parents thanked Limbora for his time and ushered Ean and Adair back to the coach.

As Ean climbed awkwardly into the carriage to maintain his modesty, he huffed, "I, for one, am looking forward to a change in wardrobe again."

Adair sighed. "I did like some of the outfits you made for me at Leonida's cabin. I do wish I had been able to keep them when we left."

Ean shrugged, "Don't worry, whenever you want I can make more for you."

Adair's eyes lit up and she smiled her sweetest dimpled smile at Ean, "That's right! You're my own personal shopping mall! Every girl's dream come true!"

Ean groaned, *What did I do?* He couldn't tell from the look in her eyes whether she was serious or kidding.

Back at the house, the carriage entered the gate and came to a stop by the water fountain. As Adair exited, she greeted Drake, who landed on her shoulder and wrapped his tail around her neck. Adair relaxed now that Drake was nearby. Although Ean didn't know what kind of connection the two had, Adair was happier with Drake around.

After everyone had entered the home and found soft chairs in the great room, Drib sent for some food to be brought to the group. While waiting, Ean felt everyone watching him. Before he could start explaining what happened, Drake spoke.

"I see you've found your magic; It's about time--you kept us waiting long enough."

Drake's comment struck a chord with Ean, "Wait, you were waiting for this?"

Drake smiled. "What happened at the museum that made such a change?"

Deciding it would be best to give the cliff note version of what happened, Ean began, "It all began when I--I mean we," Ean indicated Adair with a nod, "touched the last painting. We met someone unique who taught me what I needed to know."

Drake shook his head, "That is the shortest, least informative story I have ever heard."

Everyone started to laugh, lightening the mood in the room.

"That's okay," Adair chimed in. "I can explain..." Over the next couple of hours Adair explained what had happened, though she did keep Leonida's identity secret. Ean contentedly sat back and listened.

When she finished answering some questions after describing their experiences, the room became silent.

"Well, now what do we do?" Brin asked.

Ean looked at Drake. "I am going to leave tomorrow and find the City of Ferreglen. I am going alone."

Noise erupted in the room as everyone except Drake started in with their objections. "How dare you consider leaving me behind!" Adair accused him.

"We be companions," Brin added. "I will see this quest to the end!" His booming voice carried over the objections his parents made to Ean's statement. The arguing started attracting the attention of other clan members and more leprechauns entered to see what had caused the commotion.

Ean looked at everyone, understanding their concerns, but he felt firm in the belief that Adair would be safer if she stayed within the walls of the city. He figured he would come back for her as soon as he could figure out how to get her home. Because of their connection, Drake should stay with her to protect her. He was trying to formulate his arguments in his head when Adair stood, walked briskly over to him, and with one quick motion, slapped him across the face. The room fell silent.

With her hands balled into tight fists at her side, Adair reprimanded him between clenched teeth, "How *dare* you Ean McMurrin? Don't you think for one moment you are going to dump me here or anywhere else in Natura. You and I are seeing this through. Any plans to abandon me are selfish and inconsiderate! Just because you are a Talent Master now doesn't give you the right to toss your friends aside. This goes to show you still have a lot to learn." She paused, then narrowed her eyes and said, "Now, you listen to me: If you leave, I leave. Am I clear?"

Her intense glare left Ean speechless; he could only nod wide-eyed in response.

"Good!" She turned on her heel and walked back to sit in her chair. "Now that's settled, when do we leave tomorrow and how are we going to avoid those nasty assassins waiting for us?"

"Father," Daisy popped into view right in front of Drib. "They could use the secret passageway through the mountain."

"Daisy, yer not supposed to be listenin'," Drib replied.

"But Father...the entire house can hear, so I thought..."

"That be a brilliant idea!" Brin chimed in to stick up for his littlest sister.

"What secret passage?" Ean asked.

"Oh, I forgot all about it--but thanks to Daisy here," Brin winked at his sister, "we have an escape from the city. The assassins will not even know we left."

Drib took over the conversation, "The passageway be a protected family secret. Our home be built right up to the mountain for a specific reason: our home marks this passage. When the city was built with the magical border, the dragon helpin' our ancestors also created a passage for escape--in the event the city ever became breached by an enemy. The magic protectin' the city passes right through the mountain, so we be still protected. No one knows about the passage except us."

"Which dragon created this magical border?" Drake asked.

"I am sorry, but that information has not been passed down. However, I imagine a record o' it was kept in the city o' Eden."

"I'll have to look into that when I get home," Drake said thoughtfully.

"Drib, where does this passage lead?" Ean asked

"The passageway exits the mountain about five days' ride from the front gates o' Ferraglen, assumin' the Forest lets ye reach the gates."

"It will, I am sure of that," Drake commented. "Now that a Talent Master is among us..."

Ean looked at his friends in turn. "Okay, Adair, you are coming," he said as he rubbed his cheek. "But Brin, you are finally home after being gone for so long; I can't ask you to leave your family again."

"Ye don't have to ask--I am coming," Brin commented. He looked to his parents for their approval, which was met with a nod from his mother.

"I'll come too," Daisy added.

"Ye certainly will not!" Drib chimed in. "This journey be no place for ye, Daisy."

Daisy pointed at Ean, "But...what if he gets lost again?"

Adair got up and walked over to Daisy. Kneeling down, she looked into Daisy's eyes, "Would you trust me to look after him?"

"Well, I suppose so. But..." Daisy leaned in real close and whispered loud enough for everyone else to hear, "Ye won't slap him too much, will ye?"

Adair held back a smile, "Only if he deserves it. And if you would like, I could send you letters from time to time to let you know how he is doing."

"Oh, would you? That would be great!" Daisy said, bouncing up and down.

The indignation on Ean's face caused Brin and Drake to chuckle. Though annoyed the ladies conspired to monitor his behavior, he realized he needed to be the better man in the situation. An idea began to formulate in his mind.

Getting up and striding over to the girls, he asked, "So, you two think I need looking after, do you?"

"Yes, we do," Adair said defiantly. Daisy agreed in her squeaky voice.

"Just how are you going to send messages?" Ean asked. "It's not like we have the postal service here. And a runner may not be feasible, nor reliable."

"I didn't think of that," Adair said, sadly.

Daisy added, "What be a postal service?"

"A way to send letters to homes around the world--on Earth, that is."

"Ohhh..."

Ean smiled. Unable to contain his excitement any longer, he held out both his hands with his palms up. A bright ball of light shone on each of his palms, fading to reveal two small dark cherry wood boxes. He handed one box to Adair and the other to Daisy. "These two boxes are magically linked. Whenever you put a letter or object in this box, it will appear in the other one."

Adair was speechless, "Ean, this is amazing!" Her wide eyes admired the beautiful box. She opened the lid and fingered the soft red velvet lining. She looked up to see Ean grinning at her.

"What's so funny?" She demanded.

"I could put the postal service out of business with boxes like these." Ean said. "There's no way they could ever deliver mail this fast."

Not the best joke, but Adair smiled.

"I guess 'tis been decided," Sarah commented. "Except for when ye plan to go."

"Tomorrow," Ean said.

"No," Adair disagreed, "The day after tomorrow. We need to plan and make sure the wagon is fully stocked."

"Why? We've got me!" Ean said confidently.

"It's always better to be prepared. What if we had to split up? Besides, as I recall, you were told not to take your magic for granted or use it for everyday tasks."

Annoyed at the reminder, Ean conceded, "Fine...we'll prepare tomorrow and leave the next morning."

After a few more minutes of sporadic conversation, the group began to disperse to their own rooms for the night. As Ean started down the hallway, Daisy caught up to him. Looking up at him with moist eyes, she said, "Thank ye for the gift, Yer Majesty."

Kneeling down on one knee, Ean said, "Daisy, you are my friend. Always, and I mean always, call me Ean."

"As ye wish...Ean," she replied with a grin, shifting the little box she had cradled in her arms. Ean patted her on her arm and wished her a good night.

Once he arrived in his room, Ean sat down on a chair next to a small side table across from another identical chair. Still in shock about the recent events in his life, Ean tried to mentally process all that had happened when someone knocked on his door.

Too tired to get up and answer the door, Ean called, "Come in."

Sarah peeked in, then entered and crossed over to him. "I wanted to thank ye for the gift ye gave Daisy."

He gave a half-hearted smile, "My pleasure. If it helps make it easier for everyone when we leave, then I'm glad." He fell silent, lost in his own thoughts.

Noticing the change in his demeanor, Sarah asked, "How are *ye* doin'?"

"Honestly? I'm confused."

"About what?" She asked, as she sat on the chair opposite from him.

Sarah's concern for him was obvious and he couldn't help but feel like she had adopted him into her family. He sighed, "I understand my duty now as a Talent Master and well, I sort of accept it. But Adair...I can't figure her out. I mean, I know it's all my fault that she's even here, but I didn't expect...I don't know...ugh!" Unable to explain what he was feeling, he put his head in his hands.

"'Tis not yer fault," Sarah said gently.

Ean shook his head and looked back up, "Sorry to disagree, but if I had let Jon Henric push her away like he was trying to at the Tara Stone, then she wouldn't even be here right now. I thought Jon was being so rude that I invited her to come with us and now here she is--far from home with assassins trying to kill her." Ean hung his head in shame, "All her pain and suffering is my fault. I'm the alien that abducted her."

"Alien, huh?" She reached across the table, took Ean's hand in hers and gave it a squeeze. "Look at me." She waited until his eyes met hers. "I've lived long enough to learn a few things about life, one of which be that 'tis the same story when love be involved."

"What do you mean 'love be—I mean, is--involved'?" Ean asked, afraid of her answer.

"Love, plain and simple." She paused, "Keep in mind that Adair be here, and ye be the only link she has to Earth. Ye be someone she can relate to, and even though ye might not notice it, she does have feelings for ye."

"Yeah, I noticed it all right--she's pretty mad at me. And I think she might have some anger management issues."

"'Tis not anger. 'Tis love."

"Well then, love hurts," Ean said as he touched the cheek Adair had slapped.

Sarah laughed, "Yes, it can sometimes, though the reasons why may be different."

Ean then asked what he had been wishing he could ask his own mother, "Could you please explain the mind of a girl to me? I keep messing up with Adair."

"I'm sorry, I can't. The mind o' each girl be as different as snowflakes. Ye need to figure out what she be sayin' without her sayin' it...and never, *ever* underestimate her."

"Okay." Ean's eyebrows furrowed.

Sarah reached over and placed a hand on Ean's knee, "I will tell ye this, first stop blamin' yerself--not everythin' is yer fault. Like ye, Adair has been through a lot o' changes since comin' to Natura. She was chosen to be a Dragon Maiden and she be going to need ye as much as ye need her. Keep her close and Ean--she *does* love ye, even if neither one o' ye be ready to admit it yet."

Sarah stood and left Ean alone, watching the door close behind her. Though he still didn't understand Adair any better, he felt more relaxed and some of his tension melted. He knew he liked Adair. Whenever the light lit her hair visually on fire, he couldn't look away. Despite the fluttering in his stomach whenever she was around, he enjoyed her company. When he lay down to sleep, he wondered if his own feelings could be described as more than 'like' and if Adair felt the same about him.

Chapter 23

Passage

S aying goodbye to the Denar family clan was hard, since they didn't know when they would see them again. Brin gave bear hugs to all his family, then turned and led Ean, Drake and Adair to where the mountain's secret passage began. Finding the opening behind the sliding rock panel would have been almost impossible if Brin had not already known where the brass lever was hidden in a crack of the wall. As they entered, excitement and anticipation for the upcoming journey pervaded the group. They coaxed their horses and supply wagon into the large, well-lit tunnel, which was tall enough for them to ride while on their saddles. Drake, in his lizard-sized form, sat possessively on Adair's shoulders.

Before closing the entrance, Brin reached into his sporran and pull out two bags of powdery chemicals. As he mixed them together, he explained to the others that since torches would use up the precious oxygen of the passageway, the group would use this concoction in lanterns instead. Sure enough, the mixture started to glow faintly at first, then more brightly as he divided it into three lanterns, which efficiently gave them constant light.

The wide passage walls curved like a cylinder up to a high ceiling and the left-hand wall had a hollow ledge about three feet high, running the length of the tunnel passage. Acting as a natural retention basin, it was filled with water formed by drops of moisture that collected from condensation on the mountain tunnel walls. Due to the noise of the horse hooves clomping on the stone floor, it was only when they paused to drink from the refreshing, mineral-rich water that they could hear the constant dripping sound of water echoing around them.

Based on how painful his leg and back muscles were after extended time in the saddle, Ean estimated that their journey had covered most of the daylight hours. They stopped to eat food from their saddlebags once, and every hour or so, they would come across a lever in the wall, which when pulled, would move a pivoting rock enough to let in fresh air. Brin explained that the fresh air likely flowed through some of the cracks in the mountainside, which acted like a conduit or air duct.

After some time, Brin bellowed, "We're about there!"

Adair looked around, "Where?"

"The end of the passageway," Brin announced.

Relief and excitement rippled through the travelers as they spotted the small speck of dim light in the distance that signified the end. It still took a fair amount of time to reach it, but as they got closer, the light got a little brighter. Then the tunnel opened into a cavern glowing from the moonlight filtering through large overhead cracks. Covered barrels held feed for the horses and non-perishable food for the travelers. Extending out from the wall at the far end was another brass lever, similar to the one that opened the door at the tunnel's beginning.

After some debate they decided to rest for the evening within the cavern and leave the safety of the tunnel early the next morning. Having prepared bed rolls to sleep upon and a quick cold dinner, Ean and Adair sat together, gazing up to admire what stars could be seen through the larger cracks.

"Ye two might as well rest," Brin commented. "We have no idea when we will again have a peaceful sleep."

Drake looked down from where he was perched high in the cavern. "Brin is right, it is time to rest. Once we emerge from the tunnel tomorrow, I think I will go hunting for a real meal."

Brin nodded and said with a smile, "Bring back some wild meat for us...if you catch anything, that is."

Drake looked at him scornfully, "I don't think there will be anything left. You will have to do your own hunting."

Curious, Ean asked, "What can you hunt in a magical forest?"

Brin responded, "We don't hunt magical creatures, if that be what ye wonder. Normally we hunt deer, elk, mammoth, tigers, rabbits--that kind o' game."

"I didn't see any signs of wildlife, well, except for the syrabs that is."

"There was no need to see 'em," Brin commented. "We be in a magical Forest after all."

"Hold on a minute--there's no need for us to kill animals," Adair said, glaring at them in turn. "We have plenty of food in the wagon. And even if we didn't, Ean can create plenty more." Drake huffed and turned his back, Ean found a speck of dust floating in the air suddenly fascinating, and Brin had the sheepish look of a little boy caught with his hand in the cookie jar.

After a well-rested night, the group awoke to sunlight streaming down on them. As one they began to stir, falling into their routines and doing what needed to be done like a well-oiled machine. They bustled about; Ean rolling up the bedding, Brin looking after the horses, and Adair cooking up a hot meal with Drake's fiery assistance. The meal was delicious and everyone made sure Adair knew it. Even without being told by Adair, Ean cleaned the dishes.

As they finished their morning chores, Drake turned to Adair. "How many Dragon keys do you have, Adair?"

"Three," she replied. Pulling out the box Leonidas gave her in the painting, she opened it to reveal three ornate claw-shaped dragon keys, each covered in a different metal.

"Drake, what do these go to?" Ean asked.

"They are magical keys that can unlock anything. They can be used individually or together. The more that are used at once, the stronger the magic that is applied. However, each key can only be used once."

"Wow!" Adair said. "So I can unlock any lock, but I can do that only once, twice or three times, depending on if the keys are used together or separately."

"Yes, precisely."

Brin asked, "Why didn't ye mention this earlier?"

"She only had one key," Drake replied as if that explained everything.

When the group was ready to travel, Brin pulled the lever, opening the rocky door a crack so Drake could slip out. He was gone for about twenty minutes before he returned to signal all was clear. As a group, they exited the cavern and let the door swing shut, so it blended again with the natural rock formation in the mountainside.

"Whoa!" Ean commented, looking back at their exit door, "If we didn't know it was there, we wouldn't be able to find it."

Brin smiled, "That's the idea--so no one else can find it." He frowned as he looked down. "However, we'll need to cover our tracks or it may not stay hidden. Let's grab some branches and use 'em to rake the ground."

"Good idea." Snapping off a couple of tree branches, they began to rake the ground. In no time most of the evidence of their passing was gone and they continued their journey. Riding their horses down a slope, they emerged from the thick trees of the mountain range to the spectacular view of the valley stretched out before them. A pathway, different than the one they had been on before Glen-Delay, led through the Illusion Forest-- which no longer looked like a forest, but a grassland, dotted with scattered groups of trees. Cutting through the middle of the valley, the pathway became dark, smooth granite tiles framed with interwoven trees. As soon as they started along the path, their horses made a clip-clopping sound.

Looking at the vegetation surrounding them, Ean said,"I've seen something like this before."

"Ye have?" Brin asked.

"Yeah, in France. Not the trail, but the trees. My dad said the process of interweaving trees is called 'pleaching.'"

"Pa--what?" Adair asked.

"'Pleaching.' An ancient art of weaving the branches of multiple trees or plants together so they become one living unit."

"So each side of the trail is like one long row of the same tree?"

"Yes." Ean replied.

For the rest of the day they traveled, seeing no one else besides a multitude of birds perched along the trees lining the trail and valley. Some trees were so laden with them, the trees themselves were in constant motion. Periodically, a flock of the birds would shoot out of the trees, fly together in formation, then dive back into another set of trees.

Ean thought the noise of their chattering and calls was enjoyable at first, but as the day wore on, the consistency of the noise began to give him a huge headache. Adair looked pained as well, but Brin paid them no mind.

That night they camped off of the trail, in a small grassy area. Brin was happily whistling while the group worked to set up camp. As he was stoking the small fire he had built, Ean grumpily turned to Brin and asked in-between songs, "Doesn't the sound of the birds bother you?"

"Not really. They would, the sound o' that many birds shrillin' be enough to drive a man crazy, which is why I stuff small strips o' fabric in me ears to block out the noise."

Taken aback, Ean and Adair stared at him--surprised and dismayed that they didn't think of doing that themselves. "Why you didn't mention that earlier?"

Now it was Brin's turn to be surprised. "Sorry, I didna' know they bothered ye."

"They do!" They exclaimed in unison.

"Well, then here." Brin reached into his sporran and pulled out a sheet of fabric. Cutting off four strips, he handed two each to Ean and Adair so they could plug their ears. He stuffed the rest of the fabric into the pouch.

Ean studied the pouch around Brin's waist. Curious, he asked, "Brin, the fabric you took out of the pouch...where did it go? I mean, I know you put it inside, but there is no way it could have fit."

Brin frowned in thought, "I am not sure. 'Tis a magical sporran that has been in me family for generations. When I need somethin', I think about what I want as I reach into the sporran, and 'tis there. The storage space inside is endless as well."

Remembering the first time she had seen Brin use the sporran to offer her meat pies, Adair asked, "Who made it? What else is in it?"

He shook his head, "I am not sure. I do know that the dragon that helped make our city's magical wall also helped with this sporran. Since then it has become a family heirloom, passed down amongst the tallest livin' leprechaun o' the Denar family." He smiled, "Which at the moment, is me, o' course. I must say that it sure came in handy when I became stuck in that cavern."

Listening to their conversation intently, Drake jumped off of Adair's shoulders and stretched before enlarging to the size of a big dog. He moved over to Brin and examined the sporran.

"I remember those meat pies you gave me." Adair said. "It's too bad you couldn't pull a ladder from it."

"True. There does seem to be some limitations with size."

"Still," she said, shaking her head, "it is amazing!"

"Yes, it is," Drake murmured, still examining the pouch.

Uncomfortable with all the attention, Brin huffed, "If ye are all done starin', I think 'tis time to turn in for the night."

"Good idea," Ean said.

"And don't forget to put out the fire," Brin ordered Ean. "Ye don't want to burn up the entire valley."

Ean wondered when everyone got the idea that his being a Talent Master translated into treating him as if he served them. Ean sighed and doused the fire.

$$\infty \quad \infty \quad \infty$$

Asleep, Ean was dreaming that he was being chased by something or someone. The faster he ran, the closer he came to being caught by his pursuer. He heard heavy breathing behind him and knew they were close on his heels. Just as he felt something jerk him back, Ean jolted awake, heart pumping with fear, chest heaving as if he had just stopped running.

Then his ears picked up a sound—a real one this time--and Ean tuned in to what sounded like loud footsteps; someone was running toward them and they were coming quickly. Ean slipped on the sneakers by his bedroll and slipped out of his tent. Seeing Drake and Brin whispering close by, Ean joined them in time to see a figure appear about one hundred feet down the trail. Heading toward them, the nine-foot tall slender man was running with determination, focused totally on the trail ahead. His white shoes glowed, almost like headlights, and with each step he leapt forward--covering immense distances fast. He swept past them, sprinting on.

"That can't be good." Drake commented. To answer Ean's unvoiced question, he explained, "That is an Arturian messenger. There is likely trouble going on somewhere nearby that we should be aware of. I'll go and grab him."

"No, let me," Ean said, though unsure of why he would want to go, he felt an urge to run.

Drake looked at him dumbfounded. "You think you can catch an Arturian in a full run?"

"Yes, I do...as long as I don't give him too much of a head start." With that, Ean took off, leaving the Drake and Brin behind. Once his feet hit the stone pathway, he let himself go, feeling the renewing energy of his talent flow through his body.

Sprinting as fast as he could push himself, he caught up to the runner within a couple of minutes. Veering to the right side of the runner, Ean asked as casually as he could while running full out, "Where are you going?"

Startled, the wide-eyed man looked down at him, "Wha--...who...how?" Distracted, the stranger stumbled over his own feet and went flying face down onto the granite path.

Ean stopped and dashed over to him. "Sorry to startle you. Are you okay?"

The runner stood and brushed himself off. "Yeah, I'm fine," he grunted. "But how in all of Natura did you catch up to me?"

Ean shrugged, "I like to run."

"I've never even seen another Arturian run that fast, let alone a humanoid. What are you?"

Hiding his smile, Ean replied, "Human."

The man looked stunned. "Not possible. No human can run as fast as me..."

Ean realized he needed to take charge of the conversation before the man started asking more questions about him. "Who are you?"

"I am the First Commander of the Emperor's Private Guards, Ax Starling."

"Pleased to meet you Ax, I am Ean," he extended his hand for a handshake.

Ax gazed at Ean, but did not extend his own hand. Ean dropped his hand and tried again, "So...where were you running so fast at such a late hour?"

"That is for the Emperor's ears only-- Imperial business."

Ean shook his head and tried to seem in command, "Well, I am afraid my friends and I insist you tell us."

The man gave a snort of derision and straightened to remind Ean how much taller and stronger the Arturian was, "You might be a fast runner, Ean, but you have no power to restrain me."

"We will see," Ean said with a half-smile before glancing at Ax's feet.

Ean turned, calling over his shoulder, "Don't move, I'll be right back." He started back toward camp.

Ax shook his head at the young human's boldness. Ignoring Ean's command to stay, Ax started to move forward, only to find that his feet were stuck fast to the granite stone beneath him. "Wait! What have you done to me? I can't move!"

"I know," Ean called back. "Stay put." Ean took off running.

Arriving back to camp, he found Brin pacing and Drake landing from where he had watched Ean from high above the camp. "Well, who is it?" Brin asked as Ean approached.

Catching his breath, he said, "I believe he said he was a commander of the Emperor's private guard."

"*What*?!" Brin exclaimed.

Drake added, "What is he doing so far from the city of Ferreglen?"

"I don't know," Ean shrugged. "Shall we go and ask him? He's waiting for us up the path a little."

"Should we wake Adair?" Brin asked.

"No, let her sleep," Drake responded. "We can handle this without disturbing her."

Together they walked, or flew, in Drake's case, back to the commander.

Brin sized him up as they neared, "'Tis one big fellow."

"Coming from you, that is saying something," Ean commented. Drake flew higher within the dark shadows above the tree line to have a better vantage point.

"It is about time you came back," Ax barked. "Now let me go."

"I would be happy to assist you as soon as we get the answers we need," Ean said.

"My allegiance is to the Emperor himself! You have no authority to demand anything from me!"

"True," Ean drew out the word. "Still, you are stuck where you are. Since I won't help you until I know what you know, then the Emperor won't get a chance to hear it either. I guess it depends on how *important* the news is for him." Ean was starting to feel a little guilty about trying to extort the information from him. In a way, he kind of felt like a bully and didn't like that at all. Still, Drake said they needed to know what was going on, so for now, this was the only way Ean could think of to get the information. "All you have to do to be on your way is to answer our questions."

"Never!" Ax sneered.

"Do it the other way," Velos commented from the back of Ean's mind.

Surprised Velos was getting involved, Ean asked in his head, *"What other way?"*

"Remember what Leonidas has taught you. The mind is tricky, but not hard to break. You must look for the right opening."

Ean reflected on what he had been told by his ancient grandfather. If he concentrated, truth could be discerned from lies and he could pluck thoughts from the minds of others if needed. Ean let his mind relax until it felt like it was drifting away. It was an out-of-body experience--his mind felt free as a part of his awareness left his body. Though he had the ability to use his mental acuity, he could also perceive what was going on through his own eyes, though that view had a filmy texture to it, as if he were looking through a dirty window. He thought about wiggling his fingers and toes, and he was pleased when his body responded.

He wondered at how he could be two places at once and how far he could travel from his body with his mind. Worried he might cause a fatal mistake, he decided to make the journey a quick one.

His concentration centered on Ax. Looking at him through this focused awareness, Ean did not see a body in front of him, but rather a steel, human-shaped exterior. His grandfather had told him that every mind protected itself differently. A mind might be protected by wind, fire, rock stone, steel, gems, or a multitude of other shields. The trick, Leonidas taught him, was that *every* shield had a weakness. Find that weakness and you can penetrate the protective exterior. Ean began searching. He didn't know quite what he was seeking. A crack? A hole? He had never tried this before, so he hoped he would recognize it if he saw it.

"There...right there. Do you see the small curve by his left hip that is transparent? Through there you can gain access to his mind," Velos said helpfully.

Utilizing his newfound mental abilities, Ean probed the small curve above Ax's hip bone. As he applied pressure, it was like pushing against a strong wind. After a moment of resistance, he found himself inside of Ax's mind and was able to instinctively sense his strengths and weaknesses. He also realized that there was nothing Ax could do to stop him. Ean could take total control over his body.

After relishing the power trip, Ean moved on to where the brain synapses sparked. The initial flood of information was overwhelming, but he sifted through it, finding some thoughts he expected and some that surprised him. Realizing that the guy had way too much information about Ean and his group of friends, Ean decided to remove select parts of Ax's memory. With the right adjustment, all memories of them were gone. After a moment of analysis, Ean interjected a command into his brain; an urgent thought that he must run home as fast as possible.

Searching around, Ean discovered where the synapses were for controlling the vocal cords. After a couple of minutes of trying to figure out how to direct Ax's brain, Ean was able to work his vocal chords and breathing so that he could speak to Brin and Drake through Ax.

"H--h---hide."

Drake took off high into the air and Brin led Ean's body into the dark shadows of the grassland. Once he was satisfied everything was in order, Ean exited Ax's body through the weakness in his side. Floating above Ax, Ean released the magic holding Ax in place and headed back to his own body. Looking bewildered, Ax took a quick glance around before continuing his sprint down the path toward Ferreglen City.

"Wow! What a rush!" Ean gushed as he entered his body again.

Brin looked at him, "What in the blimey was that? 'Twas like ye were in a trance!"

Ean grinned, "No, I visited Ax's body for a little while."

Shaking his head, Brin growled, "If ye ever do that again without some warnin', I swear, Talent Master or not, I *will* strangle ye...Ye scared me half to death!"

Having the good sense to look abashed, Ean said, "Sorry, once it was obvious that his loyalties were firm and I realized he wouldn't be persuaded to talk, I decided to try this alternative method."

"How did you get the idea in the first place?" Drake probed.

"Oh, um, it came to me. Kinda like a hunch."

Ean could tell Drake wasn't convinced, but he didn't elaborate further.

"So what did you learn?" Drake asked.

"A lot, but I think we should wake Adair, or at least wait until she is awake so she can find out what happened too."

Deciding that she would be in a better mood by waking on her own, the others waited for her, staying awake until sunrise. Stepping out of her tent, Adair was surprised to see everyone already up.

"Good morning. Did I sleep in?"

"No," Ean responded, "We had a late night visitor of sorts, whose mind I probed for information."

"Literally," grinned Brin.

"Okay," She said. "Does anyone else want to explain what happened?"

Drake flew over and landed on Adair's shoulder. She relaxed, which Ean assumed was due to the special connection they had. Then Adair's eyebrows raised and she looked at Ean expectantly.

"I see," she said after a moment. "Someone ran by and Ean ran him down."

Ean grinned, remembering his race at the school fair. "Yep, I ran him down, but I also learned a lot from him."

"Yes, ye keep sayin' that." Brin said. "And now that the lovely Adair has joined us, perhaps ye are willin' to share yer newfound knowledge with us?"

Ean leaned back against the trees behind him. "Let's see...well, you all know that a death sentence was placed on...one of us." He deliberately avoided saying Adair's name. "The order for the assassination came from the Emperor and is based on some ancient law--which I know how to supersede, so no problem there. I just found out there are more assassination orders, ones that even the Emperor doesn't know about. These orders call for the death of *any* Earthling."

Brin grunted, "Not surprisin'."

"Another intriguing fact is that they know about you, Brin, and you, Drake. One of the Emperor's generals has been following us until we entered Glen-Delay. You may be interested to know that he is still outside the gates, watching and waiting for us to continue our journey to Ferreglen." With a grin, he added, "I suppose he will be waiting for us to come out of the front gates for a very long time."

Brin jumped to his feet and began pacing now. "I can't believe it! 'Tis a violation o' our boundary treaty with Ferreglen! I must get word to me family as fast as possible!" Brin was looking around wide-eyed, not quite sure what to do next; should he stay with the group or ride as fast as possible back to Glen-Delay?

"Oh, for goodness sake, sit down!" Adair commanded. "We can send them a letter."

"What?" Brin looked at her with a blank stare, as if he did not comprehend what she had said.

"I'll show you." She got up and walked into her tent, returning with a small wooden box in one hand, a pencil and sheet of paper in the other. "Here," she handed him the paper and pencil. "Write a letter. We'll place it in the box and Daisy will get it...I call it my 'Mail Box.'" Adair grinned and flourished her box.

Ean laughed. "Good idea Adair! I forgot you had that since I last saw it in the tunnel. Do you still use it?"

"Yep. Every evening I send a letter, sometimes two--one for Daisy and another for Sarah."

"Oh." Ean wondered what she could be writing about. Then he wondered if she was writing about him and what she was saying about him if she was. Adair smiled and began stroking Drake's head, since he had returned to sitting on her shoulder.

Brin wrote furiously on the paper. Folding it, he wrote Drib's name on it and handed it to Adair, saying, "'Tis done."

Adair placed it in the box and closed the lid. Then she opened the lid again to show Brin that the letter was gone.

"Wonderful!" Brin's mood completely changed. He almost looked gleeful when he crowed, "The Emperor will pay for this treaty violation."

"Well," Adair got up. "If there isn't any other news Ean would like to share with us, then I'll make breakfast so we can get on our way to Ferreglen. How about you boys break camp while I cook?"

Ean and Brin agreed and set about clearing the campsite. Ean noticed that Adair was withdrawn during breakfast. So while packing away the cooking supplies, Ean stepped up behind Adair as she was at the wagon and asked in a tone low enough so only Adair would hear, "How are you doing?"

Keeping her back to him, she replied, "I'm fine. Just another day in the Illusion Forest, so why wouldn't I be?"

As soon as her hands were free, Ean turned her around by her shoulders. "No, I mean it. How are you doing?" he asked her earnestly.

Tears welled up in her eyes. Her voice quivered as the wall she put up to mask her emotions came tumbling down. "I miss my family. And I miss feeling safe."

Before he could think about what he was doing, he drew her into a hug. "Me too...But I'm working on how to fix that. I promise I'll find a way to keep you safe and send you home."

Despite the fact that she had been enjoying the comfort his hug gave her, Adair withdrew from it. With a small smile, she said, "I know you will try, but please don't make promises that you might not be able to keep."

"Okay," He held her gaze, "Then I *promise* I will get you home."

Adair stared at him, unsure of what to say or believe. Finally she murmured, "I don't want to get my hopes up."

She turned and walked away.

Chapter 24

Time to Outrun the Outlaws

Throughout the day they rode down the granite trail, following the same direction as Commander Ax. Besides the birds, which were thinning in numbers, everyone rode in silence, lost in their own thoughts, which was fine for Ean since he was having a long argument with Velos.

"Leonidas told me that dragons know the secret to inter-world travel. And I need to know how to send Adair home. Could you show me how?"

"You don't need that information."

"Look, Velos, you can see into my mind. You know I will not use the knowledge for my own desires. I am staying here, for better or worse, but she has to go home. It's wrong for us to keep her here if we have the ability to send her back."

"Ean, this information gives power that you have not yet felt. It could change you, it could change what choices you make. We dragons do not share it lightly."

"I understand that knowledge is power and comes with responsibility--I get that. Isn't that why dragons created Talent Masters in the first place? To have both and manage them at the same time?"

"Yes, but your predecessors who received this knowledge had a hard time not using it. You must be careful--you could change the balance of worlds, wipe out civilizations and even change history as other worlds know it. Such tampering is dangerous, which is why the Great Creator only gave this power and knowledge to the dragons of Natura. There are no others who possess it."

"I see." After a long silence, Ean questioned, *"Then am I to be judged by my predecessor's choices? I am not the same as them. I come from two different worlds and it is obvious the balance of life is leaning in the wrong direction here. I need this power and knowledge to reverse the wrong of bringing Adair here. I might be able to someday fix what is wrong here and perhaps even become the leader of humans. But if I do not correct my own mistakes, then how can I fix all the others in this world that are not my fault?"*

After a long silence Ean realized that Velos would not respond. His first instinct was to get angry with him, but he decided that Velos would hear his frustrated thoughts, so he put his emotions on the back burner to give the dragon time to think about what he had said.

When the travelers stopped for lunch, they found a small stream from which they restocked their water supply and gave the horses a chance to drink. Ean was sitting on a large boulder, enjoying a better view of the valley. A breeze played around them, bending the supple grass blades and causing the trees to sway back and forth. Seeking some privacy, Adair had moved into the waist high grass, running her fingers along the tops of the bent grasses. Ean watched as she settled herself on a large rock and pulled out a paper and pencil. The sun above reflected the red highlights of her auburn hair, causing it to shimmer as the wind tossed it backward. She was beautiful and for a moment Ean just stared.

Sensing someone watching her, Adair looked up and made eye contact with Ean. Embarrassed he was caught watching her, he gave her a small smile before climbing off the boulder. He headed to the cart to pull out food for a quick lunch.

As he passed Brin, who was brushing down the horses, Brin piped up, "Ye know, if ye be staring at her all the time, ye might as well admit ye like her."

"I do not stare at her!"

Brin chuckled, "That ye do. Ye should tell her."

Ean sighed. "Not like I could with an annoying little lizard on her shoulder all the time..." Realizing what he said could be taken the wrong way, he tried to explain, "That didn't come out right--what I meant was that although I like Drake and all, it's just that he's always there...like he's a bodyguard or something. And...well...it is so *annoying* sometimes..."

With a grin, Brin replied, "I can help ye there. I'll distract Drake while ye make yer move."

"What? No!" Ean was embarrassed by Brin's suggestion. Why did he and Sarah think Ean and Adair should be more than friends? In fact, it would be better for both of them to keep their distance. Ean fully planned to find a way to send Adair home and becoming more than friends would complicate things, making their separation that much more difficult.

"When yer ready, say the word. I am happy to distract Drake anytime."

"Thanks, but no thanks, Brin." Ean commented over his shoulder as he continued on toward the cart for supplies.

After a fast cold meal, they started out again. Drake took off flying to scout the trail behind them. When he was far enough away from the horses so he wouldn't spook them, he grew in size until he was large. Less than ten minutes later they saw a jet of green fire shoot down toward the ground in the distance, with Drake following it in a downward dive. Despite how far away they were, they heard and felt the ground shake when he landed.

"What's he doing?" Adair asked.

"Probably huntin'," Brin replied offhandedly.

"What?" Adair looked annoyed. "I thought we talked about this. We have plenty of food, so there is no need to senselessly kill innocent animals." Suddenly she gasped, "He's coming back and he is *angry*!" Through her connection with him, she could tell Drake was flying back toward them; He was moving very fast and growling with anger.

Unable to see him, Ean's head swiveled as he tried to find him. "How can you tell? I don't even see him."

"He's coming, I can tell. Look! There he is!" She pointed up when she spotted him.

Drake was dropping like an angry missile. His wings folded in and at the last second he extended them, using the force of the wind against the scales on his wings to slow his descent. The dragon, still larger than a small hill, landed in the grasslands off the pathway. "Move," he barked. "Move fast!"

They kicked their heels into the sides of the horses until they moved at a fast gallop. The horses pulling the cart lagged behind.

Brin yelled, "Blast this cart! Quick, stop and pack the essentials in yer saddle bags. We must cut the cart loose if we wish to travel faster."

"What is it?" Ean asked, as Drake touched down nearby.

"Mercenaries. Hundreds of them are following us. A mercenary only has one goal--to kill their target."

"How come we didn't know they were there before?"

"They must be only moving at night. But since I set fire to their camp, I don't think they're worried anymore about being spotted. We need to race to the city where the walls and guards will protect us."

Stuffing food into his saddle bags, Ean asked, "Can't you take care of them, Drake? I mean, they wouldn't be much of a match for a dragon..."

His voice trailed off when Drake reproached him with his eyes. "A dragon does not commit acts of unnecessary violence. If we have an opportunity to escape, we will."

Having been humbled by Drake, Ean blushed. Then another thought popped into his mind. "Not to bring up an obvious solution, but wouldn't flying be faster?"

"Yes, have you grown wings yet?"

"No. I thought you could--you know, take us?"

Drake shook his head impatiently. "As I've mentioned before, it is the way of the Illusion Forest for your first trip through to be on land, not air. I'm going to distract your 'friends' back there. You must go. Now!"

Ean looked at Adair and saw her face was pale with fear. He stepped over to her, "Hey, it's going to be fine. We have a head start and thanks to Drake's warning, we'll go fast."

"Yeah, I guess..." she replied in a small voice.

"Come on, saddle up."

To block the path of the mercenaries, they left the cart sideways on the path and scattered the remaining cooking supplies and food to further impede them. Taking off on a full run, Ean led the way, with Adair in the middle, and Brin bringing up the rear. Conversation was almost impossible, but the men had an unspoken agreement that Adair's protection was priority. For even though Ean was the heir to the throne, and therefore his life of paramount importance, he knew his abilities as Talent Master would protect him in an all-out fight, whereas Adair had no such advantage.

Having created a slight lead, they had to slow down and walk their horses to avoid overexerting them. Despite their anxiousness to arrive at the city, they also realized they couldn't do that if they ran the poor animals to death.

Drake, who had shrunk to the size of a large dog again to avoid giving away their position, was flying level with them. "How close are they?" Adair asked him.

"I will check." Shrinking even smaller, he flew up into the clouds. It was about thirty minutes later when he returned, "They are still coming, but their mounts are tiring and they move slower as a large group. If we keep up our pace, they should not be able to catch up to us."

"So what's the plan?" Brin asked, walking his horse. "Eventually the horses will be unable to go any further. Do we hide and let them pass or turn and fight?"

"We keep going." Drake replied. "I am guessing we are two days away from Ferreglen City. If any of the mercenaries break away from the group and try to chase us down, then we will have to deal with them. For now, to save the horses, we will have to walk them at night and rest them occasionally. Otherwise, we will have to keep going as fast as possible."

"Should we move off the trail?" Ean asked.

Brin answered him, "No. The granite is noisy, but the grass will slow us down and leave a trail that is easily followed."

"Oh."

"We should pick up the pace," Adair said anxiously. "Is it my turn to take the lead?"

"NO!" Three voices responded. Adair raised her eyebrows at the forcefulness of their response.

Brin cleared his throat, "Adair, right now all o' us be in danger; we want to keep ye safe." Adair hung her head, feeling like a burden rather than a contributing member of the group. She felt guilty she didn't have the ability to keep the others safe.

As they quickened their pace, Ean moved to be in the lead again. Daylight sped onward and soon it was time to walk their mounts as darkness fell. Giving their horses a short drink of water and a few oats, they ate a small ration of food before pressing onward. Shortly after, they walked alongside their horses. Adair was dragging her feet in exhaustion and her mind felt dulled. She had to focus to push herself to move forward, so at first she didn't register the faint sound as being out of place. But something within her realized it was important. Stopping, she held up a hand, "Shhh! Do you hear that?"

Brin and Ean stopped to listen as well. The clip-clopping sound of horse hooves was increasing in volume, indicating it was coming closer.

"Go!" Brin cried. Adair and Ean scrambled on their horses and egged them on to a full run. Brin led his horse into the dark of the grasslands and laid in wait for the pursuer. Drake took to the trees on the side of the path to help Brin if the newcomer was an enemy.

Ean and Adair continued to race forward until Drake swooped forward and overtook them. Flying low, he told them to stop and wait for Brin. Dismounting, they stroked their trembling horses until their heavy breathing abated. "Who was it?" Ean asked.

"An assassin. But you don't have to worry about him anymore, Brin took care of him."

Ean and Adair waited uneasily for Brin to return. It took a little time for him to catch up, but when he did, he was leading three smaller horses behind his own. He was in a rather good mood as he sauntered up. "Poor little animals seem to have lost their rider. Figured I couldna' let 'em get lost as well, so I brought 'em along."

"There were *three* assassins?" Ean exclaimed.

Brin chuckled, "Nope, just one. Now we can use them to our advantage. As we travel we'll switch off between horses so they can rest from the extra burden of a rider." Still grinning, he gestured to himself, "Especially this one."

They remounted and continued on, changing horses often. Halfway through the night Brin called for a stop.

Drake flew over, "We can't stop now."

"We have to," Brin replied. "The horses must eat before they collapse."

"The horses are hungry, or you?" Drake teased.

"Both."

Brin rummaged in his sporran. "If ye do not mind meat pies, I have some." He pulled out four eight-inch meat pies. With the allure of food, even Drake couldn't resist taking a brief break. After making short work of the pies, they fed their horses.

"Let us keep going," Drake said.

The night dragged on as they moved, keeping an ear out for unwanted visitors. By morning, it was harder for the horses and riders to travel in a straight direction due to exhaustion. When the first rays of sun peeked over the distant hills, Drake scouted both directions of the pathway from above. Satisfied they had a sufficient lead on the mercenaries, the travelers and horses took a brief nap and rested before continuing the journey. All three meals they ate that day were either Brin's meat pies or Ean's bakery bread. Ean wondered if any other kinds of food could come out of Brin's pouch, but he didn't ask so as to avoid sounding ungrateful for the food.

The next night, Adair began to fall asleep in her saddle. Since her balance was not the best, she would start to slip to the side whenever she began to doze off. When she almost fell off, Brin looked at Ean. "Ye know Ean, I think it might be wise if Adair rode on the same horse as ye. That way ye can hold yer arms around her nice and tight to keep her from slippin' off." Brin wiggled his eyebrows up and down suggestively.

Catching the hint that Brin was trying to help him put some "moves" on Adair, Ean blushed and choked when he swallowed at the same time he tried to breathe. He hoped the moonlight didn't show the redness of his cheeks. He overcame his coughing fit, but before he could respond, Drake spoke up.

"I'm not so sure that is a good idea." Ean looked up to see Drake looking at him. "After all, we wouldn't want to weigh down one horse too much."

That sounded like a lame excuse to Ean, but he didn't challenge it. "How about if I ride next to Adair to help her if she starts to slip off?"

Adair sleepily smiled at Ean. "Thanks."

Ean felt warmth spread through his fingers and toes and he felt a little lighter in the saddle.

After a couple of hours, Ean asked, "So, Drake, how are we doing on time?"

Drake stretched his wings before taking flight to assess the progress of the enemy. He flew back, a little breathless. "Not the best. They are getting too close for comfort. We must hurry faster." Ean nudged the horses faster, causing Adair to startle fully awake. They galloped through much of the night and into the early dawn. As the sky lightened, the group paused to give the horses water.

"Uh, guys, do you see what I see?" Adair asked, tilting her head back the way they had come. Ean turned to see a multitude of ruffians in the distance, closing the gap between the groups. Ean wondered what types of weapons the mercenaries had and whether they were still out of harms reach.

"Let's go!" They took off, riding their horses hard enough to keep their lead.

By mid-day, they crested a small hill and could see in the distance a small mountain. Standing hundreds of feet tall, large stone walls surrounded the base, broken only by formidable steel doors large enough for Drake to walk through in his full size--well, at least as large as Ean had ever seen him. With the army of Assassins hot on their tails, Drake flew back toward the enemy, trying to scare their horses into a panic. He only managed to slow them a little bit. Meanwhile, Ean, Adair and Brin rode straight to the doors and began banging as hard as possible on the closed doors.

One little peep hole opened on the side between two large stones of wall blocks. "Who goes there?" demanded a squeaky voice.

"I, Brinston Denar the Third, from the city of Glen-Delay, and me companions here seek safety within the walls o' the great city Ferreglen."

"No." The voice responded and the stone was replaced in the peep hole.

"No?...Did he actually say no?" Adair asked incredulously.

Brin's face was grim. "He did."

"But how will we get in?" Adair could feel panic start to well up within her.

Ean answered, "If here, Drake could break the door down; but as he is busy buying us time, I think it's up to me."

"Don't count me out," Brin added.

"Believe me, I'm not. I need you to guard our backs." Then Ean turned and faced the large gates, *"Any ideas, Velos?"*

"If you knocked the door down, that would let your enemies follow you in and cause the Emperor to be outraged about the damage. Regardless, the decision is up to you."

As he studied the gates, considering the easiest way to get in, he imagined what a dragon would do instead of breaking them down. *"A dragon can fly, so he'd fly over the wall,"* Ean thought to himself. Since leprechauns and Earthlings don't fly, maybe he could--

"Ean," Brin called over his shoulder, deflecting an arrow shot toward him with his broad ax, "They be almost upon us. Whatever ye be goin' to do, please do it now!"

--after his experience with transporting his consciousness into Ax, Ean began to wonder what other capabilities he had. Leonidas said the limit was his own imagination and willpower. Thinking about teleporting--a superpower he had always wished he could have--a plan began to take shape.

Having no idea if he could carry it out, he shouted, "Grab the horses and take my hand!" Only able to grasp their own three horses, Adair and Brin released the smaller horses and held tightly to Ean's arms.

Ean used all his concentration toward imagining the group inside the gate. As he felt the tingling sensation in his legs travel up his body, he yelled, "Hang on!"

He felt the whizz of an arrow whip past his head and a sharp sting on his ear as the arrow feathers brushed it. He ignored the sudden pain as he realized his body had begun to glow. A shiny bubble of pure magic, originating from Ean's body, pushed outward, enveloping the travelers and their three horses. Another arrow hit the bubble with a dull thunking sound before rebounding off and falling to the ground.

The scenery around Ean began to growing increasingly brighter until he was no longer able to see. Panic swept through him as he realized his attempt at teleportation was dangerous and could very likely result in tragic consequences.

His eyes closed against the dazzling light, so he felt the flash of light rather than saw it. When the light filtering through his eyelids decreased again, Ean peeked. No longer on the outside of the city walls, they were on the inside of a walled area.

Due to his unfamiliarity with what was on the other side of the wall, Ean was unable to properly visualize their destination, so they appeared haphazardly in a corridor on the other side of the massive doors. The now agitated horses had landed upright in the middle of the open passage and Adair was sitting on top of a cart full of hay. Ean, on the other hand, was standing inside a barrel, waist deep in a liquid combination of fish and vinegar. Brin was sitting on top of a small fellow.

The muffled voice spoke from underneath Brin, "Pardon me, could you get your large rump off of me? Oh, never mind, I'll do it myself." The small man increased in size, growing in size and girth until Brin was no longer the bigger of the two. With one shove, Brin was thrown off; and the now giant man jumped up to land nimbly on his feet.

The man looked down in disapproval at the unexpected travelers. His deep voice boomed, "I said you could not enter! How *dare* you force your way in?!"

Though shocked by the man's complete change in appearance, Ean climbed out of the barrel, steeled his nerves and steadily gazed back into the man's glaring eyes. "Technically we did not force our way in. We teleported."

"We must see the emperor!" Brin cut into the conversation.

"Impossible!" The giant man responded. "You are unwelcome intruders. It'll be the dungeon for you until I decide otherwise."

Sloshing and dripping, Ean walked over to the hay wagon and helped Adair descend.

Brin's face was turning red as his anger at the gatekeeper rose. "I don't like yer attitude. What is yer name?"

Bristling at his demand, the man raised his chin even higher. Trying to convey his superiority, he replied, "I am Gregory Vongilbert, Gatekeeper of the great city of Ferreglen! I don't answer to any leprechaun or human."

"Well, Gregory--"

"--Sir Vongilbert to you."

"-- *Greg*, we must speak with the Emperor at once."

Gregory Vongilbert was about to reply when a clash of arms hit the gate with full force. Alarms sounded and soldiers began running along the top of the city walls.

Ean looked up, a green glimmer catching his eye as it descended rapidly toward them. "Oh good, here comes Drake."

As Drake got closer Gregory Vongilbert's eyes grew wider. Even though the inhabitants of Ferreglen hadn't seen a dragon for over 400 years, since Eden had been lifted from the surface of the planet, they could still recognize one. Gregory was speechless, with his mouth gaping wide open.

Drake diminished to the size of a horse. Landing on the pavement, he greeted them, "I am glad you were able to get into the city safely. I was unable to convince that force to slow down."

"Actually, we had a bit o' difficulty gettin' into the city," Brin commented.

"Oh?"

"Yes. Unfortunately *our friend* here--" Brin indicated the giant Arturian and smirked at the gatekeeper's reaction to his reference. "-- refused to let us in."

"What?!" Drake roared, blowing a puff of smoke from his nostrils. Swiveling his head to focus his large cat-like eyes on the gatekeeper, he began to grow in size, crowding the giant man against the wall behind him.

The gatekeeper's voice quivered as he asked, "Who-Who are you?"

Seeing the wind knocked out of the arrogant Arturian, Brin relished the turn of events. With a wicked grin, he responded, "People who don't like to be kept waiting. Now take us to the Emperor at once!"

Chapter 25

Elizabeth

*E*lizabeth paced the living room floor of her father's town home, trying to figure out if the McMurrin family was crazy or not. She held the sleeping Rosemary in her arms in an attempt to calm her own nerves while she replayed what they told her. The bizarre tale they concocted was so unbelievable that it couldn't be true. Yet Emily's sincerity showed she believed its truth and she was clearly upset the two teens were still missing.

Emily's husband had sat on the sofa, holding his wife's hand as she tried to explain what they thought happened to them. The man had Ean's handsome looks--or was it the other way around?--but it didn't matter, Elizabeth trusted one McMurrin male and now her sister was gone. She wasn't willing to trust another one.

She stopped pacing to listen to the conversation now going on in the kitchen. Her father, Kevin O'Connor, being his charming self, used his Irish brogue to befriend the McMurrins and the young man who accompanied them. Quite the storyteller, Kevin spent most nights socializing with his buddies down at the local pub over a pint or two of ale. At least it gave him somewhere to go since he retired the previous year.

Clinging to the hope that he would find his younger daughter, he was intrigued by the tale. Adair's disappearance had been hard on her father. When she didn't return home the day Elizabeth arrived, Kevin locked himself in his office, going over rare family documents. Elizabeth supposed everyone had their own way to cope with emergency situations, but seeing her level-headed father withdraw caused her heart to ache even more.

One evening, as he passed through the hallway, she'd asked him what he was doing. He responded, "Call it faith, Lizzy. I am going to find my Adair. If the authorities can't do it, then our roots will." Without further explanation he walked into his study, shutting and locking the door behind him.

Now here he was, visiting with strangers like long lost friends. It didn't make any sense.

She had enough. Walking into the kitchen, she glanced at Jason before speaking to Emily. "I understand why you are here looking for your son. And I wish we could help, but we can't."

"Why not?" Surprisingly the question came from her father of all people!

"What do you mean, why not? Of course we can't help! These people claim that in order to help Adair, we must help them figure out how to travel between worlds. What can we do to help?!"

Kevin winked at his exasperated daughter and said, "More than you might think."

"Would you care to elaborate on that father?"

"You wanted to know what I have been doing in the office. I am reading old Celtic writings passed down from generation to generation for thousands of years...information our grandfathers wrote down for safe keeping."

She shook her head at the mention of the family records he referred to. All she knew about them was they were the reason she had been lectured on more than one occasion as a child. She remembered the admonition 'Watch yourself Lizzy! You know you're not allowed to play in here. It's where we keep the records of our people.'

Putting a hand to her head to ward off the threatening headache, she said, "Why are you reading them?"

"Our family is different too--not like the McMurrins here, but still...special. We are descended from *druids*!"

She groaned, "Oh please not those stories again." Her father had recently been telling Jacob bedtime stories about the ancient druids.

"Not stories--our history. We are one of the last few families that can prove they are of druid descent."

Knowing she couldn't dissuade him from that belief, she tried another tactic. "Fine, let's say I believe you. How is this going to help with getting Adair and Ean back?"

"I am not sure yet, but I am working on it."

"And how are you working on it?" She asked in a weary tone.

"I am reading the Celtic record of the Druids."

"Wait, I thought the Druids didn't keep written records."

Looking somewhat abashed, Kevin cleared his throat and said, "Yes, well, my great-great grandfather did not quite keep that particular vow. He committed everything to memory, like he was taught, but when he reached an old age he secretly wrote it down. He figured that someday memory alone would not be enough, a record needed to be kept. His record has been passed down every generation to a male heir. I possess it now and someday it will be Jacob's."

"Amazing!" Jeff, quiet until this point, joined the conversation. "What a cool history! Could I see the papers?"

Mr. O'Conner looked at him thoughtfully. "I suppose it would be fine. It's all in Celtic language, so you won't be able to read it."

"That's okay, I have an idea."

Together, Jeff and Kevin left the kitchen and entered the study, shutting the door behind them.

Elizabeth plopped down onto an empty chair, hopelessness and fear showing upon her face. "I can't take any more surprises, I just can't. I might have a nervous breakdown."

Emily got up, walked over and put her arm around Elizabeth. "I'm sorry. I know it's a lot to hear and try to comprehend. But somehow, we are going to find a way to get them back."

Chapter 26

Two Faces

*E*an and his group were escorted up the main street by the recently humbled gatekeeper. Still in defensive mode, Drake decided to remain large while taking up the rear.

Nobody else tried to stop their progression in the city. In fact, the Arturians moved out of their way, surprise evident on their faces at the sight of a dragon. Ean looked back at Drake and remarked, "The streets are larger than I expected. I never thought we'd find a city you could walk through while that size."

Drake chuckled at Ean's observation. "In years long past, we dragons visited the Arturian capital many times. Ferreglen was designed to make us feel welcome--as much as it was built for the peculiar nature of Arturians."

"What do you mean?" Adair asked.

"Arturians can change to any size or shape within their same gender. Therefore, the buildings are designed to accommodate almost any size of customer."

"I see." Adair looking around at the citizens watching them and noticed they were indeed a mixture of body heights and shapes.

As they arrived at the city capital building situated on the peak of the mountain, Drake shrank and returned to his favorite spot on Adair's shoulders. The group dismounted, leaving their horses tied to a bronze-like statue depicting an Arturian changing from a small boy to a tall and prestigious looking man. Once at the front doors, they met more hostility.

"State your business." An official-looking man demanded to Greg, though he was eyeing the small Drake with care.

Greg stepped forward, "I bring these, ah, visitors to see the Emperor."

The man checked his clipboard, "Do they have an appointment?"

Greg looked at Ean and Brin, then back at the man, "No, they don't, but they do insist it is of the upmost importance and--"

"No appointment, no entry. You must leave." He dismissed them with a wave of his hand.

"What?!" Ean was about to express his opinion when Brin placed a hand on his shoulder.

"Not yet," he whispered.

The capitol official looked at Ean, not missing the restraint from Brin. "Does the young one think he has the right to speak to an Arturian?"

Ean looked at Brin. "Please." He whispered.

Brin, sensing his determination, nodded once and took one step back. Ean walked up to the official doorman. "I'll give you one chance to move." Ean said evenly, but with authority in his voice.

The guy frowned down at him. "I'm not going to move, young one, not for the likes of a human like you."

Ean glanced at Drake for the briefest of moments. *A human like me, huh?* He thought, then he curled his hand into a fist and spoke one word while lifting it, "UP!"

The man shot up like a rocket until he collided with the underside of the roof extension, where Ean left him floating, clinging to the wall three stories above the ground. The doorman uttered a string of foul language, some of which Ean didn't recognize, and shifted to grip the side of a window. The doorman peered in to where he could see the Emperor and his son going over papers. Ean watched as the floating man knocked on the window and gestured to Ean and his companions below him.

Jon Henric stuck his head out the window and looked down, "It's time you arrived! What took you so long?"

Ean's mouth dropped open in shock, "Jon...you're here?!"

Looking confused, Jon responded, "Yes, why wouldn't I be?"

Seeing Adair's icy stare directed at him, Jon said, "Hold on. I will be right down..." He glanced over his shoulder, then amended, "*We* will be right down."

The exhausted travelers decided to go into the capitol building through the now unobstructed doors, as the doorman was still floating outside the building. They helped themselves to the comfortable seats in the foyer while they waited.

Adair leaned over in her chair toward the couch where Ean was sprawled lazily. "You should let him down."

Ean shrugged. "I don't know about that. He *was* very rude."

"Yes, but do you want to be known as a Talent Master who throws his weight around?"

Ean realized she had a point. He sighed, "Okay. Come on."

"Be nice." She warned as they stepped outside again, though he saw the smile she was trying to hide.

Arturians had assembled at the capitol to learn if the dragon rumors were true, but discovered instead the floating official and excitedly pointed up at him.

Ean's thought had been to spin and flip the annoying man while lowering him, but when he saw the embarrassment the proud man was going through, he decided the doorman had been punished enough. Ean relaxed his concentration and lowered him very slowly to the ground.

His eyes bulged as he gasped, "Who are you?"

"Ean!" A voice behind Ean stated. Turning, Ean saw Jon Henric standing alongside an older man.

After introductions, the group made their way up to the Emperor's council room. Ean tried not to look impressed at the size of the room with a domed, vaulted ceiling. They were led past two large desks and chairs belonging to the Emperor and his son to the other end of the room, where a kidney-shaped table was surrounded by scoop-like chairs. Sitting in one of the odd chairs, Ean found he could either sit up straight or recline, and the push of a button would lock the chair in place. It was the most comfortable chair he had ever sat upon. After rocking back and forth a few times, he chose to recline slightly.

The Emperor and Jon sat in two chairs facing them. On one side of Ean sat Brin, on the other Adair, with Drake still perched imperiously on her shoulders. Looking up, Ean caught Jon watching him. Though Jon smiled, Ean just nodded to him. He was still trying to decide if the man across the table was Jon or a shape shifter impersonating him.

"Let us settle some matters," the Emperor said. "Jon--as you know him--tells us that you will be the next Talent Master."

Ean sat as tall as he could. Gathering his courage, he declared, "I *am* the Talent Master. I know your plans. You are planning to have me tested to prove it. That will not be necessary; nor would I ever consent to such a test."

He held up his hand to keep the Emperor from interrupting. "As I understand it, I am--as rightful heir to the kingdom of Islandia--the only person on Natura who controls inter-world travel. Therefore I grant permission for Adair to be here in Natura. Moreover, should *any* Earthling come to Natura, their presence would also be under my jurisdiction. Only *I* have the authority to choose to accept or reject them."

Though he had spoken politely, he had also been bold and confident. He hadn't known it was his right to give permission for inter-world travel until he had read it in the mind of the Emperor's messenger back on the trail to Ferreglen.

The Emperor's face was impassive, but he was steaming--this impudent boy had cut him off and already assumed he had the authority of a king! Further, he was bothered the boy knew about the test. Was there a spy in his midst that had given away confidential information? Glancing at his son, he saw Jon holding back a grin. It was obvious Jon was proud of the boy.

Still focused upon the Emperor, Ean continued. "I have been given one detailed version of events in Natura." He gestured to his companions, "Now we need a full report of Natura's condition from your perspective."

That did it. The insolent boy had confirmed his suspicions of a spy in the capitol. The Emperor fired back, "Now wait a minute! You are in *my* city and you will not dictate to me what you are 'entitled' to have! I say you *will* be tested before you can claim Talent Master status."

Ean shook his head. "I am afraid that is not in your authority, Emperor. I am here in Natura and that alone proves I *am* a Talent Master. You saw me toss your doorman around. Would you like a more personal demonstration?" He held out his hand toward the Emperor to prove he was willing to give him a taste of what the doorman had experienced.

Furious, the Emperor's eyes narrowed. Clearly his idea to use Ean as a figurehead for a revolution was misguided, given Ean's unwillingness to be subject to his directions. He obviously was not meek enough to be merely a figurehead. "That won't be necessary..."

Standing, Ean slammed his hands on the table and leaned forward. He growled, "Did you, or did you not, agree to have Adair killed? Did you order an attempt upon her life?"

The Emperor was taken aback by the sudden accusation. He spoke carefully to avoid an out-of-control situation. "I agreed that she was to be safe until after your testing. If unable to prove yourself as Talent Master, I had no choice but to concur with the law that her life would be forfeited."

At hearing how callously her life was considered disposable, Adair drew in a sharp breath and reached up to touch Drake for reassurance. Drake responded with a growl directed at the Emperor, who rushed on defensively, "There were no orders given to execute her. Having heard of your difficulties during your travels, I had launched a full investigation on the matter. Indeed, I even sent guards to apprehend the hermit that attacked you in an effort to discover who was behind the forged orders..." He paused before speaking, "I want to assure you, Ean--we are on the same side."

Ean straightened. "That is yet to be seen. From where I stand, you have been involved in planning my friend's death. That alone does not help in starting a partnership, wouldn't you agree?"

The Emperor leaned back in his chair. Frowning, he said, "Someone undermined my mandates. I am sorry that there may have been hardships for you because of it."

"To make sure it is clear," Drake added, "Adair is under *my* personal protection."

At those threatening words, the Emperor nodded his acknowledgement.

Jon spoke up, "I am glad that is settled." Standing up, he walked around the table to pat Ean on the back. Grinning, he said, "I *knew* you had it in you! You just had to find your powers on your own."

Facing Jon, Ean clenched his fists. "Where have you been this whole time? Here?!...You know what's funny? I trusted you...I left my parents with the impression that you would be there for me...that you would guide me. What a joke! I see now that I was your free pass to get home. Well, you're here. Congratulations."

Jon shook his head. "I needed to pave the way for you here at Ferreglen."

"Pave the way? Interesting choice of words, since the gatekeeper wouldn't even open the gates for us!"

"Ah, yes. I am sorry about that." Jon said, chagrined. "Nevertheless Ean, you *can* trust me. That is why the queen of Islandia entrusted me to take her only surviving son to safety. It is why I have watched over your family for generations..."

Adair couldn't take any more of his self-praise. She bolted out of her chair, storming up to Jon. "You...you..." Adair proceeded to give Jon the sharpest tongue lashing he had ever had in his life. By the time she was done, she had backed the very wide-eyed Jon halfway across the room.

"Remind me to avoid getting on her bad side," Brin murmured out of the side of his mouth.

Then the door to the room burst open as soldiers stormed in, dragging a few chained men to the middle of the room. The Emperor was on his feet instantaneously. "What is the meaning of this, Captain?"

"Our walls were attacked. These are the prisoners that we captured for interrogation."

"Very well...take them down to the dungeon. Send General Alla--never mind, we'll deal with them later. Send in Seritof with a report of what is going on at the city walls."

"As you command." The soldiers marched the prisoners out. The Emperor sank wearily back into his chair.

"Maybe now we can get to the bottom of the assassination attempts," Brin said.

Looking at each of his guests in turn, Jon noted how exhausted they appeared. Making up his mind, he cleared his throat, and said, "We have much to discuss. However, it may be best to adjourn to give everyone a chance to rest. I have taken the liberty of having rooms prepared for you. Please, follow me." He started toward the door.

Adair and Brin paused, waiting for Ean's reaction to the invitation. Though Ean felt that not enough headway had been made as of yet, he recognized the importance a good rest would be in negotiations and dialogue with the Emperor.

"Thank you. That would be appreciated." He was glad the manners instilled deep within him by his parents overrode his unpleasant opinions of the situation.

They followed Jon to the wing of the building where the family and honored guest living quarters were located. "That did not go as smoothly as I'd hoped," Jon said wryly. "Though I must say Drake, your intimidating skills are quite remarkable. Perhaps you would like a position in Ferreglen as a negotiator?"

"Not likely," Drake grunted.

Jon chuckled. "That's what I thought." Then he turned to Ean, "You should know, Ean, our kingdoms have been allies since the founding of the human kingdom. My people desire for your return to the throne of Islandia and for peace and prosperity to return to Natura."

"Oh? And when I do return to the throne, what other benefits await your people?" Ean asked, interested in what the Arturians' ulterior motives would be.

"Freedom to leave the Forest again." Jon sighed, "Apparently the University took over most of the planet during my absence. Any Arturian discovered outside the Forest is killed. Though we live rather long lives, our race does not have children often, so the loss of any Arturian is a travesty..."

Ean was silent as he absorbed what Jon had said. He realized it would be almost impossible for each Arturian to fully share memories and knowledge gained over a lifetime of a thousand or more years.

He did notice something different about Jon, or perhaps he was viewing him with a different perspective, but Jon's demeanor was more sad and contemplative. He wondered if it was due to all the changes on his home planet. Stepping into the room assigned to him, Ean turned to Jon. "I disagree with you...the loss of any life by unnatural means--no matter how long or short it was--is a travesty." Ean shut the door between them, ending the conversation.

A little while later, after he was sure Jon had gone, Ean walked across the hall to Adair's room and knocked.

Adair answered, "Ean! Come on in, we were about to come and get you." Brin was there, and of course, Drake was still on her shoulders.

Ean looked at Drake, "Okay, we are in Ferreglen now. What do you want us to do?"

"Why ask me?" Drake responded.

Irritated, Ean tried to remain calm. "If you remember, it was *your* idea to come to Ferreglen in the first place."

"True. I only suggested the journey to get you into the Illusion Forest before the troops arrived from the capital city."

"Troops? You never mentioned troops to us!"

"It was not necessary. You entered the forest and thereby evaded them, since they cannot enter. Or, I should say, they can enter but would likely be unable to find their way out again." Drake explained.

"How did they know we were here?" Adair asked.

"They didn't, except the light show caused by your arrival was rather noticeable. Abigor would have sent troops to investigate."

"True," Brin nodded in agreement.

"For now," Drake continued, "You should learn more about Ferreglen and its citizens. Find out if you might be interested in partnering with them...that is, if you can control your temper and not throw everyone in the air..." Drake added with a chuckle.

"Did I go too far?" Ean wondered.

Brin answered, "No, he deserved it, just don't make a habit o' it. It wouldn't look good for ye to start a reputation as a heavy-handed ruler."

"See, I told you," Adair said.

"Fine!" Ean had never thought in a million years that he would have to worry about making the right impression for an entire city...no, make that an entire world. "Do I also need to apologize to Jon?"

Adair's emphatic, 'No!' contrasted to Drake's, 'Yes!'

Drake looked at Adair, "You both should apologize."

"What?" Adair responded indignantly. "He deserved everything I said!"

"Maybe so, but remember--he spent over 400 years away from his home and loved ones. Not only did he fulfilled his duties, and beyond, but he did so at a cost far more than he should have had to make."

"What do you mean?" Ean asked.

Drake jumped off of Adair's shoulder and landed on a soft chair. Once settled, he gazed at them steadily in turn as he explained. "As you may be aware, Jon--as you know him--is the heir of Ferreglen. On the day of the attack on Islandia, he had been busy fulfilling some duties on behalf of his father. We unexpectedly met up that morning and chose to travel together while accomplishing our responsibilities. I was with him when a messenger arrived from his father, asking him to check on the king and queen of Islandia.

"You see, the Emperor had heard some rumors of civil unrest and he wanted to verify whether they were true or not. As we rushed toward the capital, we came across an Islandian messenger heading toward the Forest. Stopping him, we discovered his message was one of vital importance: Queen Isla was beseeching the Emperor to send a trusted Arturian to Islandia for assistance in smuggling her children away from the city. We amended the message to inform the Emperor we intended to assist the Queen, sent the messenger on toward Ferreglen, and hurried as fast as possible to the capital city Islandia." He paused. "We were too late to save all the royal children; only one remained..." Drake looked at Ean. "Your ancestor."

"We took the child to the city of Eden, home of the dragons. Under the protection of the dragons, the prince would be in the safest place on the planet. Yet Zatarion, ruler over all dragons, was wise and sent Jon and the prince to Earth, where Jon was to watch over the royal line until a Talent Master was born. I was instructed to seal the portal so no one could follow or return unless they were a Talent Master. Jon was imprisoned upon another planet until some future time. He gave up *everything* for you and your family. So holding a grudge against him is pretty selfish, I would say."

He paused to let them consider his words. "And, I believe you both can guess how he felt about wanting to go home during his years on Earth."

His guilty conscience burned him from within and Ean felt bad for how he had treated Jon earlier. Maybe he could trust Jon. He realized he needed to apologize to Jon when he saw him again.

Their conversation turned to lighter matters as Brin started teasing Ean about the way his magic had put two difficult Arturians in their places. The banter was still going on when a knock came at the door. A young woman standing outside the room greeted him with a curtsy, "As honored guests, you have been invited to dine with the Emperor and his family. I have come to assist the Lady in her preparations for dinner."

"Alright gentlemen--out!" Adair commanded. "Time to get cleaned up for dinner...you most of all Ean..."

"Ha, ha, very funny."

It didn't take Ean long to bathe and dress in the formal clothing supplied to him in his wardrobe room. It was an unfamiliar style of clothing, with a long loose tunic that reached halfway down his thigh and loose fitting pants, but the outfit was nicer and cleaner than anything he had with him. To top off his formal wear, and also to impress Adair, Ean even dabbed on some cologne-like oils available for his use.

"Excellent, you look much better," Drake remarked. The lizard had joined Ean in his room to give Adair privacy. It appeared he had also scrubbed up a bit, as evidenced by his gleaming scales.

"Look who's talking. Should we wait in the hall for the others?"

Drake answered by jumping on his shoulder. Walking out of his room, Ean almost bumped into Brin, who was pacing the hall looking cross. "What's wrong Brin?"

Brin huffed and waved his hand over the Arturian formal clothing, "This--this is what's wrong! I take off me britches for a moment while I wash up and THIS is what I return to! 'Tis not right for a man to wear! Now a kilt, on the other hand, a kilt is what ye wear to a formal dinner..."

The sound of Adair's door opening caught their attention. Ean sucked in his breath when he saw her standing in the doorway, draped in a flowing gown of creamy white, curving around her figure, her flame-colored hair intricately winding from the top of her head down over one shoulder.

Seeing the jaws drop on the two men, Adair flashed them a sweet smile, complete with dimples, which only intensified her beauty.

Realizing his mouth was gaping open, Ean shut it and struggled to say something nonchalant, yet gallant. "Y--you look nice...I mean good...beautiful, even...that is to say..."

Brin chuckled and took over, "What he means to say me dear, is that not even the beauty o' Natura's shores, nor the visions o' the Illusion Forest could compare to the splendor before us. Ye are looking as lovely as ever." Blushing, Adair took hold of his outstretched arm as a young Arturian arrived to escort the party to an exquisite dining hall packed with seated people. As they entered, everyone stood and watched while they walked the length of the room to the head table.

Adair smiled charmingly at the Emperor as she and Drake sat to his left. Brin and Ean sat on the other side of Jon, who sat on his father's right. Once seated, the remaining guests sat down as well and servers streamed from doors lining the walls, each carrying plates laden with exotic foods. Ean waited in silence along with the rest of the diners until the Emperor took the first bite of food: a signal that everyone else could eat. All at once, the room became full of clamor and noise as the guests enjoyed the feast before them.

Ean leaned closer toward Jon, who sat on his left, and started, "Uh, Jon? I'm sorry about earlier, I--"

"Don't mention it Ean." Jon waved his apology off with a hand. "Consider it 'water under the bridge.'" He leaned a little more toward him and murmured, "I hope you don't mind, but I told my father that you had sent him an apology for your earlier words to him."

Ean was shocked, but rather than get upset, he let the annoyance at Jon's audacity slip past him. Trying to be the better man, he whispered, "Don't you think I should apologize personally?"

He shook his head. "All is forgotten."

After a moment of quiet chewing, Ean swallowed and asked the question lingering in his mind, "How did you know I would apologize?"

"After 400 years with one family, one learns to read personalities. That, and your family is rather predictable."

Adair had started a conversation with the Emperor. Both smiled at something the other said, which was a good sign.

Catching his eye, Jon said, "Take a moment to enjoy yourself."

Ean nodded and scooped his utensil into grain dish. "Do you always eat so much food every night?"

"No, this is a special banquet in your honor."

Ean began to study guest with more attention. He noisily dropped his utensil when he saw some of their facial features change.

He heard a chuckle coming from Brin, who was sitting on his right.

"I wondered when ye would notice," Brin commented in an undertone.

"What's going on?"

"They are having a conversation, of course." Brin replied. "They play a political game at the same time. Ye see," he lowered his voice even more, "as Arturians are shape-shifters, they can change their facial features when communicating in order to show or hide feelings while discussing sensitive matters. By doing so, they can hide what they are thinking. It makes their politics very complicated."

"What a strange thing to do. Won't other Arturians think that a person who changes their appearance is dishonest? How can anyone tell who to trust?"

"Part of the game," Jon cut in. "A little intrigue can spice up the most tedious conversation. However, there is a way to tell if someone has been unlawful in their past dealings. Any Arturian found to be guilty of breaking the law in Ferreglen is taken to a medical center and injected with serum that will alter their genetic coding, such that their face will be divided by two different and random facial structures. From then on, they can no longer alter their facial features, but are stuck with the two forevermore. For obvious reasons, we call them 'Two-Faces'."

"Ouch! Rather harsh punishment, don't you think?" Adair said, leaning back in her chair to overhear their conversation.

The Emperor joined in, "It might seem that way to you, but for our race it is the only way to mark who is honest and who is not. Watch this..." Making sure she was watching, he morphed from his middle-aged prominent features and grey-speckled dark hair to a tow-headed, blue-eyed boy, no older than six, sitting on the Emperor's chair, swinging his little legs. His childish voice belied the fact that he ruled the city, "See? We can hide many things."

Fascinated at how different he could look, Ean watched as the Emperor morphed into a dozen other appearances--all male of course. Various human ethnicities flitted across his features as he demonstrated how versatile an Arturian could be. He settled on the appearance his guests were accustomed to seeing and said, "If it can be proven that an Arturian broke the law, we must be able to know they are not trustworthy. They lose the right to hide their true character from the rest of the world."

Ean piped up, "It must be hard for the Arturians who get caught breaking the law to lose the ability to change."

"True," the Emperor agreed. "Yet it deters many others from being dishonest. Now, enough of this gloom!" Standing, he raised his crystal goblet and his voice to gain the attention of the room. "A toast! To the new Talent Master and the hope of a better tomorrow!"

Picking up their own goblets, the guests repeated the words, leaving the last word reverberating throughout the hall as they drank from their cups. Ean raised his goblet in acknowledgement to the toast and was pleasantly surprised by the familiar taste of sparkling grape juice.

As they finished their meal, servants cleared the plates. The guests and royal family remained seated as other dinner guests left the room in small groups.

The Emperor cleared his throat. "I am sorry for your first impressions of Ferreglen. Please allow us the chance to redeem ourselves. We insist that you tour the wonders of our city tomorrow as our guests. Tomorrow evening, I would like to discuss future possibilities with Ean."

Still determined to be charming, Adair said, "Thank you, Your Highness. We appreciate your hospitality." Ean and Brin nodded their agreement, pleasing the Emperor.

Standing to leave, he smiled, "While you are here, please call me Marcus."

After he left, Jon stood as well. "If you would be willing, it would please me to be your personal guide to Ferreglen. I must admit, it would be somewhat self-serving. It has been a long time since I have seen much of Ferreglen," he said with a wry smile.

Ean and Brin agreed first, Adair hesitated a moment before nodding her head. Jon escorted them to their rooms before bidding them goodnight. Standing across the hallway from him, Adair's eyes lingered on Ean, as if she wanted to talk to him. With Brin and Jon waiting for them to retire for the night, however, she murmured goodnight to them all and slipped into her room. Realizing how tired he was, Ean yawned, gave his own farewell, and entered his room. Not even bothering to get ready for bed, Ean kicked off his shoes, flopped on the giant firm pillow in the corner of the room that served for a bed in Ferreglen, and fell asleep.

Chapter 27

Sweet Memories

The next morning, Ean, Brin and Adair arrived at the foyer of the capital building to wait for Jon. With the doors to the building open, they could see that the doorman from the previous day was standing rigidly at his post, trying very hard not to make eye contact with anyone in the group.

Amused, Ean pointed him out to Adair. She, however, was not amused.

"Oh Ean! You scared him half to death yesterday! Come on, let's go make sure he's okay."

Ean reluctantly followed her over to him. She spoke first, "Excuse me. I don't think we got a chance to introduce ourselves yesterday, I'm--"

"Yes, my lady," he interrupted. "I know who you are now. I want you to know I am very sorry for my behavior yesterday. I beg your forgiveness for the disrespect I showed you."

Adair looked at Ean as if to say 'Go on.' Ean rolled his eyes, then replied. "I am the one who should apologize. I should have found another way to work out our differences. It was wrong of me to react the way I did."

The doorman knelt on one knee before Ean and bowed his head, "No, Your Highness, I don't think any other way would have worked quite as well. You were within your right to punish my offensive behavior."

"Well, it was still wrong," Ean commented. "For that, I am sorry."

Jon's voice from behind startled Ean, "Wonderful! I am glad everyone is moving forward."

Half joking, Ean said, "Have you ever considered wearing bells on your shoes?" Seeing Jon's confusion, he added, "That would warn us you're coming."

Though Jon chuckled, Adair chided, "Now, Ean, play nice." He sighed in mock defeat to her words.

Velo's voice echoed in his thoughts, *"Well done. There is hope for you yet."*

"Ah, Velos! Now that you're around, how about we start an old conversation again? I need to know how to make a portal to Earth."

He could almost hear the dragon's groan. *"Not that again! As I have told you, there is no need. Besides, you should try paying attention to others right now. You missed a question from Jon..."*

"Ean, did you hear me?" Jon asked, looking at him with concern.

Adair had seen that Ean's attention had shifted and remembered when he told her about Velos. She realized he had probably been conversing with him and decided to cover for him. "Don't mind him. He loses his attention once and a while. I blame it on a short attention span."

Having heard her, Ean was offended. "Hey!"

She smiled, "Oh good, you're back."

"Are we heading out or what?" He asked, trying to change the course of the conversation.

Looking at him with concern, Jon said, "Yes. The carriage will take us to the city and then I thought we could walk."

"Fine by me," Brin piped up.

Everyone else agreed and they settled into the carriage that was awaiting them at the bottom of the stairs, with Adair, a small Drake and Ean on one side, Brin and Jon on the other. As they rode down the road to the city, they oohed and aahed over the amazing view of the expansive valley below. Though the group had traveled to the capitol only the day before, due to the perilous events they had encountered, Ean had missed seeing the jetted, spiky peaks peering from behind and through the capital building. He couldn't tell if the building was coming out of the mountainside or if it was located inside a small crater.

He marveled as the sights around him grabbed his attention: the intricate patterns on the roads made from light and dark stone blocks, white-washed buildings encircled by layers of dirt troughs from which green vegetation hung, and the multitude of trees interspersed around the houses, each tree covered with unique flowers--various sizes, shapes, and colors of blossoms, all blooming on the same tree.

A spacious pathway for pedestrians ran parallel to the road and was rather busy with the daily activities and meanderings of the residents. Ean watched as a forty-something balding Arturian with a smattering of brown hair on the sides of his head in a brown tunic recognized an older woman cutting flowers from a tree. The man transformed into a teenager with shaggy blond hair in a bright orange tunic before raising a hand to greet her by name. She turned, smiled, and started chatting with him. Ean shook his head; he thought it would get rather hard to keep track of everyone if they kept changing their appearance. A new thought popped into his head.

"Jon, isn't it possible for an Arturian to pass one of his or her own family members in the city and not recognize them?"

Adair and Brin listened closely as Jon nodded and replied, "Yes, it is possible. Normally, however, an Arturian chooses a select few forms as their favorites and their family members are familiar with them. However, if an Arturian chose a form unfamiliar to them, then yes, not even a family member would recognize them."

"Sometimes when an Arturian changes form, their clothes will change too. How do they do that?" Ean asked.

"It is part of our abilities. Our pliable genetics rearrange our appearances, but our ability to change our clothes comes from the magic within our race."

Brin spoke up, "It is much like our race as well. Leprechauns have the ability to be invisible, including whatever clothing we are wearing and any objects we are holding if we choose it to be."

"I wish humans could change their clothes by thinking about it," Adair sighed.

Ean couldn't help but add, "Me, too. It would sure cut down on the time it takes a girl to get ready every day." Adair gave him a sour look and stuck out her tongue. Brin snorted, trying to hold back his laugh, but only Drake and Jon managed to hold their composure.

Ean turned back to Jon, "And how do you know how old an Arturian is?"

He chuckled, "If they are of an adult age, then asking is your best bet since you won't be able to tell by their appearance. However, if the Arturian is a youth or even a baby, they cannot hold an appearance beyond their own true form for very long. It is something that takes practice, patience, and focus, which is in short supply for youngsters."

"Oh." After a short pause, he blurted, "Is this your true form?" Recognizing he could have potentially offended him, he blushed, embarrassed he had asked the question.

Jon's expression became serious and he looked out the window of the carriage. "Very few besides my father know what my true appearance is. My father the only family I have left..."

Unsure what to say, Ean turned back to study his surroundings. The road had become level as they entered the valley portion of the city and they passed buildings similar in architecture to the homes surrounding the capitol building. Gardens sprawled anywhere there wasn't a building, which was pretty much everywhere, since the buildings were spaced far apart. Pathways led from one amazing garden to another. Ean's jaw dropped as he spotted a garden filled with stone statues of dragons. Small spurts of fire flared from within the statues' mouths, synchronized to match the accompanying battle music in the background. The next garden they passed had fountains that sprayed water, followed by one that had multicolored gems hanging from the trees to catch the light of the sun, refracting it around garden to create rainbow mosaics of color.

While admiring the passing scenery, Ean felt Adair lean across him to look out his side of the carriage, then move away as she looked out hers, then back again. After several times of her moving from side to side to see everything she could, Jon chuckled, "Don't worry Adair, there is plenty of time to explore the city. Trust me."

She sighed, "It's so amazing, I don't want to miss any of it."

Arriving at the main city square, they exited the carriage to discover the square was designed to make an impression. An area the size of almost three football fields was divided into smaller sections by the interconnecting walkways and barriers of rocks, bushes, and walls. The sections held pavilions for sitting, play areas for the few children Ean saw, large grassy fields with shade trees, and an ice skating rink. Ean did a double take when he saw the ice--the weather was warm enough that ice would melt, but there were Arturians skating around the rink on what looked like flat soled shoes.

"Whoa, this is amazing!" Ean commented.

Next to him, Jon smiled, "Welcome to my home."

Ean studied him. The edginess that Jon had shown while on Earth was gone and he was more relaxed and friendly. "I am glad you are home with your family, Jon," he said before looking away. "I wish I could say the same."

Putting his hand loosely on his shoulder, Jon said, "Look Ean, I am sorry for your loss, but life here in Natura will be wondrous. Give it time. In the meantime, we can focus on what is most important: taking back your kingdom."

"I was wondering when that would come up," Ean murmured.

Feeling the sudden increase in tension, Adair cut in, "Hey, we will have a fun day if it kills us, so come on!" She tugged on Ean's arm, "Let's go find a sweet shop, then we can explore!"

With Adair attempting to keep the peace, Ean's guilt came back. Like him, she had been separated from her family, yet she was making an effort to avoid pouting, complaining or making a scene. She was trying to put a positive spin on the day. "*See Velos*," he thought, "*she deserves to go home.*" Naturally, the dragon didn't reply.

Eager to avoid hostility as well, Brin agreed, "Something sweet sounds great."

Jon nodded, "I suppose I could show you one of my favorite shops."

They followed Jon down a path that passed some shops and a few smaller gardens until they turned the corner to a garden that smelled amazing. Before Ean's eyes, Jon had transformed into a younger version of himself, likely about the age of a ten year old Earthling. Ean did a double-take as he took in the sight of the carefree boy with thick, dark curly hair bounding ahead of them.

On one side of the path was a bakery, on the other was a candy shop. Along the edge of the walkway, a row of unusual plants grew--bubble gum flowers held up by licorice stems with leaves too thin to be real. Though not like the kind of flowers to which Ean was accustomed, the aroma of the plants was intoxicating and rather delicious. The smell alone caused Ean to salivate and feel the effects of a sugar rush, as if he had eaten the whole plant. Jon grinned, and said in his young voice, "Watch this." He bounced over to a dark green plant, plucked one of its leaves, broke it in half like he was tearing paper, and stuck one half on his tongue. "Ooh, minty..." He grinned again.

"You stop right there young man!" Everyone turned to see an elderly man about Ean's height thumping down the walkway toward them, leaning some of his weight on the wooden cane he held in his right hand. "By the Maker! I thought I was rid of you!" He thumped right up to Jon and shook his left pointer finger in his face. "I see you have not changed one bit! You and your sticky fingers are hurting my plants, you scoundrel. At your age you should be ashamed of yourself, setting such a bad example for these young visitors!"

The man appeared to remember Jon, and Jon had not left behind pleasant memories for him.

"Ah, Mr. Sweetness..."

"You know very well my name is not Sweetness." Exasperated, he looked at the rest of the group, settling his gaze on Adair. He said, "I am Krane Dulsa, at your service."

"Pleased to meet you, Mr. Dulsa," Adair replied with her dimpled smile.

"Now, young lady, be sure you don't follow his example. My shop is through the garden, come along, I will show you." Before turning, he shook his cane at Jon, "Go on then, you know the drill, you go first. If you even think of touching one of my plants, boy, I will smack you over the head with this cane, I will."

"Sir," Adair asked as she fell into step behind Jon and next to the old man, "how can picking a leaf hurt your plant?"

He elaborated in a whisper, "My plants are special. They contain special flavor properties that are the secret ingredient to all my custom candies. They must be harvested in a particular way, or else the whole batch of candy will be ruined. Don't get me started on the preparation methods..."

"Oh yes, please don't--" Jon started. Whatever else he had been going to say ended when he received one solid smack on his head with the wooden cane. Ean winced, but Jon shook it off and smiled mischievously back at them over his shoulder.

"I spent years trying to teach this boy how to care for, and harvest, my plants correctly, but he is as stubborn as molasses is thick. He has no talent for being a Sweet Master."

"Wow!" Adair said, looking at the building--of sorts--that was before them as they exited the garden. It was three stories tall, pulled, twisted and bent in a taffy sort of way. As they followed Mr. Dulsa inside, they gasped in amazement at the tall glass shelves lining the walls of all four levels, holding glass jars, wooden boxes and buckets, all full of the most colorful sweets he had ever seen.

"Come in. Take a bag and fill it up with anything you want. The sweetest candies are on the lowest level, the next--" He jabbed his cane toward the misshapen staircase in the center of the room. "--has the savory, then come the sour candies and the hot and spicy ones are on the top level. Why don't you youngsters go on and explore. But, not you," he said, pointing his cane at Jon. "I want a word with you. Come with me."

They watched as Jon strolled behind the old man as he thumped through a door marked 'Office--Keep Out.' Once they left, Ean blew out the breath he hadn't known he'd been holding. Trying to sound nonchalant, he said, "Well, shall we explore?"

"I guess..." Adair looked worried as she added, "I hope Jon will be okay."

"Don't worry yerself about him." Brin said. "Ye can be sure he can take care o' himself."

"I'll pick him up some candy too, just in case." She said, grabbing an extra bag.

"Hot and spicy for me." Drake said, jumping off Adair's shoulders and flying up the stairway to the top level.

"Figures that the fire-breathing lizard likes it hot and spicy," Ean commented under his breath.

"Don't knock it until you try it," Drake called out from above.

Wandering around, Ean wasn't sure what to pick, all the candies smelled so good. Hesitating over what to choose, he saw Adair filling her bags with one or two of almost everything she saw. Ean decided that sour or savory might be more to his liking, so he took the stairs up a level and started collecting candy from the containers on the shelves. He realized that if he'd had a fear of heights, he wouldn't have left the main level, because all that kept him from falling off the ledge to the bottom floor were glass railings running along the walls at each level. Ean looked up to see Brin was up at the sour level. Because his bag was full, Brin was adding some to his sporran for good measure, causing Ean to stifle a laugh.

Meanwhile, down in the office Jon had returned to his original appearance. He spoke softly, "I am sorry for not visiting."

"I should say so! Back for weeks and never once coming to my shop! I was beginning to wonder if you had forgotten about me," Krane huffed as he sat down in his office chair.

"I could never forget about you! It's just that, well, with what happened, I..."

"Don't even speak of it," Krane snapped. "I don't believe it...she is still alive...she has to be!"

Jon shook his head sadly. Krane's denial of what happened was clear and Jon didn't think he could convince him that the reports were true. He himself didn't want them to be true, but the evidence spoke for itself. "What was she thinking?"

"That someone had to do something. She never was one who could sit still and watch all the injustice take place. Then, after *you* disappeared...well, she became more determined than ever." He huffed and cleared his throat. "In any case, I am glad you're back, my boy. Now maybe you will visit from time to time, eh?"

"Of course," said Jon, speaking from his heart. "Besides, I don't think the guests--" he gestured to the door, "will feel that one visit is enough to sample your candy."

Krane chuckled, "Well we'd better make sure they get a little of some of the more unique items." He gave Jon his own mischievous smile.

Jon smiled back, "Yes, please! I'll take a bag of those as well!"

"Well, what are we waiting for? Let's go help them."

∞ ∞ ∞

Overwhelmed with all the walking they did to explore Ferreglen's gardens, shops and city streets, Ean returned to his room sweaty, exhausted and sticky.

Ready to freshen up himself and his clothing, Ean was still thinking about what a wonderful city Ferreglen was when he walked into the bathroom. The room itself had the similar functionality he was used to back at home, though from all his experiences on Natura, it was the bathing room at Glen-Delay he would miss the most. After he had washed and dressed in a clean tunic and pants, he returned to his room to relax. As he settled down on the pillow bed, a knock came at his door.

Opening it, he saw Brin, Adair and Drake. They looked concerned. "What's going on?"

Adair held up a letter, "This arrived."

"Is it a letter from Daisy?"

"Oh, no. Though I did send her some candy from the shop earlier and she was quick to respond that she absolutely loved them and--"

"Then, who is it from?" Ean cut in.

"Actually there are two letters," she glanced down the hall. "We should talk inside your room."

"Oh, sorry, come in!"

Once everyone had found a seat, Ean closed the door and said, "Okay, what's going on?"

"Do ye remember the letter I sent to Drib?" Brin asked.

"The one about the general from Ferreglen that was spying on Glen-Delay?"

"That's the one. This is his update."

Suddenly no longer sleepy, Ean asked, "What happened?"

Brin settled further into his chair, "The general was well hidden, but they found 'im. He is in a cell at Glen-Delay. A messenger is here to deliver the demands o' me city."

"What demands?" Adair asked.

"First, I want to impress upon ye the seriousness of this situation. A military representative from another city violated terms o' the Illusion Forest Treaty. The consequences be quite serious--Glen-Delay can collect a tribute for this breach o' contract. Or, on the other hand, Glen-Delay can choose to let the atrocity pass, if the clans were cowards and rolled over like poisoned syrabs."

"It sounds like Glen-Delay isn't interested in forgiveness. What tribute do they want?" Ean asked.

"One-half o' Ferreglen's wealth in gold, gems and grain."

Ean's eyes bulged at the cost. "Whoa!" He couldn't imagine a similar thing happening on Earth. There's no way a country there could handle such a demand without a complete collapse of economy. "That's a lot!...
Why ask for grain? I mean, I get asking for gold and gems, but grain seems like an odd choice."

"Gold and gems affect the financial standing o' the city, whereas grain affects the food supply, so the citizens will not forget the actions o' their leaders. A leader with any sense and a city full o' hungry and angry citizens will not soon make the same mistake."

"Oh...I can see how that makes sense."

"The other letter is from the city council o' Glen-Delay; for ye, Ean."

Ean turned to Adair as she handed him the letter she was still holding.

Ean opened and read the letter, then looked at Brin. "I can't do what they are asking of me. It's your place more than mine."

"What are they asking of you?" Drake asked from Adair's shoulders.

"They want me to be their chosen representative for the city of Glen-Delay in the negotiations for the tribute. They authorized me with the authority to forgive the debt or to demand some or all payment owed them." He looked at Brin. "They say they will accept whatever I decide."

"That is a great honor," Brin responded somberly.

"I agree." Drake concurred.

"I don't," Adair said. She looked at Brin. "It's not right to force so much on Ean's shoulders. After all, he is only sixteen years old. Neither he, nor I, for that matter, understands the underlying politics or the economic impact his choice would make on the cities. Why did they ask him rather than you? Why not send a proper representative with the messenger?"

"I do not know the reasoning behind their request," Brin began, addressing Ean, "but I believe ye can do it. Whether ye decide to accept or reject the city's request, I will support ye as a friend."

"Uh...thanks." Unsure what to do, he said, "I think I'd like to wait and see what happens after the messenger arrives."

A knock sounded at the door. This time it was Jon. Everyone excused themselves out of courtesy to give them privacy, so Ean found himself alone with the Arturian.

Jon tapped his fingers on an end table as he sat in awkward silence in Ean's room. After a few moments he spoke, "So, what did you think of our city?"

Curious as to why Jon came to him, Ean tried to play it casual by shrugging and saying, "It was different."

"Different?" Jon asked with a half smile.

"Well, the gardens and buildings are amazing, but we had to walk *a lot*."

"I don't suppose walking ever hurt anyone. We keep them far apart because we don't see why we should live so close together. We do, after all, live long lives and have few offspring to fill the empty spaces."

"I hope you don't mind me asking, but how do you keep your identity straight? The people of Ferreglen change their appearance based upon whom they are speaking to, or sometimes as a reflection of thoughts during a conversation. How do you know who you are supposed to be and when?"

Jon chuckled, "It's an Arturian thing. We practice the art of changing as soon as we realize we can control it. I'm afraid I am a bit out of practice due to my long absence from Ferreglen."

"I suppose you didn't change too often on Earth. I still think it's weird to drastically change your appearance. Why not stick with your true form?"

"It makes sense that you find shape-shifting strange since you don't have the ability to change your own features; but there is something liberating about being able to express yourself on another level or to show the different personalities within yourself. Think of it this way: Have you ever felt so restricted by your parents that you wanted to rebel and be independent? What would you look like on the outside if you could show that side of you? Or have you done something that you enjoy, that makes you feel like a carefree kid again and you don't care who sees you feeling that way? If you could--you would show your youthful side. It's another way we express ourselves, because we can."

"I suppose you've been repressed, being on Earth and all. Doesn't that make you glad to be home?"

Jon looked away. "Not particularly."

Ean couldn't have been more surprised. At the Tara Stone, Jon couldn't wait to get back, and here he was saying he wasn't happy being home. Despite his polite upbringing to not intrude on other people's business, Ean's curiosity got the better of him. "Why not?"

Jon continued to avoid eye contact. "It's not the same. So many people have sacrificed their lives attempting to help others. Not even my father is the same after living through 400 years of oppression."

"What are you going to do now that you're back?" Ean asked.

Jon looked back at Ean and said with fervor, "I will continue my mission to ensure you fulfill your destiny, Ean McMurrin. I *swear* I will do everything in my power to help you take back your throne."

Ean scoffed, "What throne? What claim can I make on a throne after 400 years? I mean, be serious! Not that I don't appreciate the fact that everyone gives me respect here, but let's face it: I am not a king and will probably never be one."

"It was *your* family that was chosen by dragons, the most ancient of races. Regardless of how much time has passed, the fact that you were chosen hasn't changed. It is your right to claim and take back the throne that is rightfully yours to rule. I'm not saying you should do this for yourself. I'm saying you *have* to do this for the good of the people who believe in you, the same people that are suffering today under the chains of tyranny."

"How would you recommend I take back the throne?" Ean retorted. "Should I march in, declare who I am, and tell Abigor to leave? That wouldn't work." Ean shook his head and started pacing, "Hey, I know! Maybe Drake could gather the dragons together and we could destroy Islandia! Then I would be the king of a dead land with dead people. No, better yet, I could unleash monsters from other worlds to roam Natura and destroy everything in their path--"

Standing, Jon's voice thundered as he cut Ean's ranting off, "Don't even joke about such a thing! You might be surprised to learn that very thing happened. A portal to another world was created, unleashing a monster that rampaged across Natura; many species were likely to be destroyed by it until your Talent Master great-something grandfather was able to trap it."

"What are you talking about?" Ean asked, confused.

Jon took a deep breath and let it out. "That is a story for another time, perhaps. As to the matter of regaining the throne, I am not yet sure how to do so, but as Talent Master you have the power and authority to do it." He hesitated before adding, "There are even some who expect you to raise an army and fight for what is yours."

Ean shook his head and started pacing again. "No. Never! I refuse to treat people like pawns, to let them die fighting my battles so I get what I want...if it is even what I want...I would rather abdicate the throne than have the blood of Natura's inhabitants on my hands."

"I was not saying I recommend it, I meant that is what some are expecting you to do. But you need to remember that every single day the citizens of Islandia are kept under the chains of bondage by their leaders. Countless lives were lost because Abigor decided they were the wrong species or because they didn't do something his way. As long as he remains in power, all in Natura are prisoners.

"So Ean, as of today the blood of every person who dies due to his tyranny is on *your* hands, because only *you* can do something about it. You are the one with the power and abilities needed to overcome the enemy. Now, Your Highness," Jon said with a mock bow, "what are your priorities? Are you going to turn your back on your people or are you going to stand and fight for their freedom?"

Ean sat down on the corner of his pillow top bed. "I need to take things one at a time. There is more going on here than we are aware. For instance, who disobeyed your father by ordering Adair's death, and why? Because we don't know the answers to those questions, I think my first priority is to learn how to send her back to Earth, so she will be safe."

"Would Adair be returning by herself?"

"Yes. I will not abandon the people here. You were right in that I have talents and magic--abilities that may be helpful. But I don't know what to do and how to do it."

Jon was silent for a moment before speaking. "Natura needs you," he sat down next to Ean. "You have changed a lot since you came here. You are already showing signs of growing up and taking on adult responsibilities."

"I didn't have much of a choice..." Ean commented dryly. "Before I can figure out a way to help the people of Natura, I need to find a way to get Adair home. Once she is home, she'll be safe."

"And if Adair refuses to go?"

"Why would she?"

Jon smiled patiently, "Let's say she doesn't want to go back. What then?"

"I'll cross that road when I come to it."

"So how are you going to make a portal?"

"I'm working on it. I'm not sure yet."

"Until you figure that out, let us take things one step at a time. Why don't we get some dinner first? Then we can meet with my father and see if we can figure out the answers to your other questions."

"That sounds like a plan."

Despite consuming so many sweets, Ean was hungry again.

Chapter 28

Computers and Druids

*J*eff was antsy with excitement as he waited for Elizabeth and Mrs. McMurrin to arrive back from their shopping errands. The McMurrins and Jeff had been staying as guests at the house with Elizabeth, her kids and her father for the past three weeks. The housing arrangement had been a debate at first, as the McMurrins were determined to not be a burden upon the family, but Mr. O'Connor stubbornly persuaded them he needed Jeff's help as much as possible.

Of course, that argument would have been stronger if they had been told what the two were doing, but in the end it was agreed that the Americans would stay. Now that their research was done, Jeff couldn't wait to share it with everyone else.

"Sit down, boy," Kevin O'Connor said. "If you keep pacing, you'll wear down the floorboards! It won't speed up two women who are shopping. I don't know anything that can do that."

"Sorry. I can't wait to tell them what we might be able to do!"

"It's still a long shot...don't go getting them too riled up. Remember, we're piecing information together. It might mean nothing at all."

Jeff froze for a second as he considered whether Kevin was right. Deep down, however, he had a feeling they were onto something big. "No, I believe we've figured it out."

"I'm sure you do. But your impatience is enough to drive a man to drink! I swear, this generation has no patience whatsoever..." He swept his arms behind his head. "You've got to learn to enjoy the moment when waiting for a lady," he said with a wink. "You might as well get some practice for that now. You can save yourself a lot of frustration if you learn a bit of patience. A good first step would be to relax."

Jeff decided Kevin might be right, so he took some deep breaths, sat down in the armchair by the fireplace, and took a few more deep breaths. After about 30 seconds, Jeff realized relaxing wasn't going to work. He was too antsy and fidgety, so he was up pacing the room again.

Then he heard the front door close. He practically raced into the foyer, but when he turned the corner, he stopped short. "Oh, it's just you," he said, disappointed.

"Yep, just me," Jason McMurrin said with a lighthearted smile. "Sorry to be a disappointment."

"No, it's just that--I mean, we're waiting for Elizabeth and Emily to come home so we can share the big news."

"More like a theory..." Kevin called out from the other room.

"What news do you have?" Jason walked into the den and took a seat across from Kevin.

Kevin snorted, "We found a puzzle and Mr. Computer Wiz-Kid here thinks he solved it."

"You have my interest. What is it?"

"All we have are bits and pieces of information that Jeff thinks he has been able to make into something we might be able to use." Kevin shifted in his seat. "I'm not so sure about it. I don't want to get everyone's hopes up."

Jason nodded sagely. "That makes sense."

They sat in silence, aware of Jeff's constant pacing about the room and the passing of time kept by the prominent ticking of the clock on the wall.

Finally! Jeff thought when he saw Elizabeth, Emily and the kids drive up. Not patient enough to wait for them, Jeff threw open the door and announced, "We found something!"

"*Might* have found something," Jason corrected as they gathered in the den. Emily had confiscated the sleeping Rosemary and little Jacob ran to sit in his grandpa's lap. Kevin gave him a puzzle made of metal intertwined rings, which the boy happily examined.

"Father, what did you find?" Elizabeth asked apprehensively.

"Not what I found. This is Jeff's discovery. You'd better ask him."

All eyes turned to Jeff, "As you all know, we have been spending some time in the office."

"Yes, we noticed." Emily commented with a smile.

"Any-hoo," Jeff continued, not wanting to lose his concentration, "we scanned all of Kevin's dad's documents into my computer and used a software program to convert the scans into digitized text, and used another program to translate the text to English."

He subconsciously began speaking at a faster rate. "We then started reading and categorizing terms used, cross-referenced similarities, and checked duplication to see if they were used in the same context. Although it was fascinating, we began to feel we weren't getting anyplace, so I went back to the original documents. Though I can't read Celtic, I did notice a difference between our translated documents to the originals. The translations had straight sentences and no tears on the pages, whereas the originals were somewhat askew and had folds and tears that looked purposeful.

"So I treated the old pages like a puzzle. I began laying the documents down and matching the tears together. But that didn't seem to do anything. Then I noticed that some pages had different folds than others. So I began folding the pages and as I aligned them, a pattern began to form. Since I didn't want to fold all the old documents and take a chance of ruining them--"

"--meaning I wouldn't let him," Kevin interjected.

"--I took the digitally translated documents and overlaid them on the computer, so the English version was beneath the Celtic. Then I warped the text to match the skewed text of the original, digitally folded the English version to match the creases in the originals, and placed them all together making this..." Jeff pushed a button on his computer, sending an image through the projector to the wall.

"Wow!...What is it?" Emily asked.

"A Triskele, which is a tripartite symbol composed of three interlocked spirals," Jeff responded. "Some suspect that it represents the time a baby is in the mother's womb, nine months of time."

Elizabeth walked up to the wall, "What does it mean?" She twisted her head left and right, trying to figure it out.

"Wait...it has words with it. Here they are," Jeff moved his computer mouse and clicked a couple of times. All the words disappeared except for the ones in the image. Elizabeth, standing closest to the projected image, read the words out loud:

> *Gateway to wend,*
> *Hope to bring;*
> *Relief found in friends*
> *With ax and wing;*
> *Portals, cycles of life,*
> *Are limited to the first of three,*
> *Journey repeated by Bandruidh during strife,*
> *To find her love and set broken heart free.*

Silence followed her reading of the words.

Elizabeth spoke. "Okay, I give." She looked from Jeff to Kevin. "What does it mean?"

After a couple moments pause, Jeff said, "I think that the first lines refer to Ean. According to the McMurrin legend, the Talent Master, or Ean in this case, is supposed to be the hope for the throne of Islandia. I don't know what the 'friends with ax and wing' means, but I still think it refers to Ean in some way. Maybe he makes friends with some...unusual people or something.

"As for the second part about the cycles of life, the best I can tell is that the Triskele symbol found in the documents represents the growth of a fetus in the womb, hence the cycles of life. When my mom was pregnant with my younger brothers and sisters, she counted their growth in trimesters--first, second, and third--just like the Triskele, which has three distinct spirals as part of the whole. So I was thinking that the next part of the poem, the 'limited to the first of three,' means that the ability to travel through the portal is limited to within the space of a trimester--or three months--from the time Ean left."

Silence permeated the room once again. Then Emily broke the silence. "Do you mean to say that we can still use the portal? But only within the three months since he left? How?"

"Let us remember," Jason cut in, "That we have no idea if this even relates to our situation. It could be random gibberish--no offense Kevin."

Kevin grinned, "None taken."

"I do think there is something we can do..." Jeff said timidly, now looking at Kevin for support.

"Go on, son, it's your idea."

"What idea?" Elizabeth asked.

Jeff started fidgeting and pacing. "Uh, during the research there was lots of information on rituals and prophecies, as well as incantations. They gave amazingly detailed descriptions of how herbs, soil, water and animals are used to heal people, stop wars and cast spells--and even create miracles! What's more, though I'm not sure I understand everything the druids did, I think that with a little luck and a blend of modern technology and ancient methods, we might be able to open the portal."

No one spoke, the only sound the occasional clinking of rings as Jacob played. Elizabeth, Jason and Emily digested the ray of hope Jeff had thrown out to them. Was there any hope of seeing Ean and Adair again? Or were they grasping at straws? No one spoke, not knowing what to say. Emily ended the silence, "What do we need to do?"

Jeff did a mental fist pump. *Excellent!* Jeff was sure that if Emily were on board, then he had at least a small chance of trying out his idea since he thought she would be able to convince the others to try it.

"Alright, here's what we do." Over the next hour Jeff explained his idea. "Do any of you have questions about your assignment?"

"Yes," Elizabeth said. "What if my part doesn't work?"

"My dear," her father addressed her, "it is in your blood. Since Jeff and I have studied the manuscripts, I realize now that my grandfathers and I have been misled as to whom we may share our traditions. We learned in our research that women have been an integral part of this religion and way of life since it was brought to our world. I should have taught you our Druid knowledge a long time ago..." He leaned toward her, "I have the utmost confidence that you will do well."

Rosemary woke up and started fussing. Elizabeth took her from Emily and started rocking her. "I sure hope you're right."

Emily sighed. "How about some dinner everyone? As Jeff explained, we have nine days to prepare until the moon is in the best position for the ritual to work. So, let's eat and get to work. We'll do the best we can and see what happens."

As she stood up and headed to the kitchen, all Emily could think about was that in nine days, she could be in the same world as her son. To her, that was all that mattered.

Chapter 29

Interrogations and Negotiations

*A*s the days went by, Ean began spending a significant amount of time with Jon and Emperor Marcus. The interrogation with the hermit had been quick, but not very effective. A hooded figure had forced him out of his tree and threatened that if he didn't kill the girl, something horrible would happen. What that horrible thing was, Ean didn't know. The hermit was too terrified by the thought of it to speak of it. Later in the council chamber, Marcus told Ean that the threat had likely been that his home tree would be burned down. Ean didn't think that was a valid reason for committing murder, but in the culture of hermits, it was apparently acceptable.

"What about the council members who issued the death sentence without your knowledge?" Ean asked.

Marcus's eyebrows drew together in concern. "That is still a mystery. I have met with each member of the council and they all have given oaths that they were not a part of it."

"What about a polygraph test, you know, to detect lies?" Ean asked.

"We don't have those," Jon said. "Remember, this is not Earth."

"A polygraph?" Marcus asked in confusion.

Jon turned to his father and explained, "It is a machine on Earth that reads blood pressure, pulse, respiration, and skin conductivity to tell if someone is lying."

"Oh," Marcus responded. "That would help, but we don't have anything like that here." He sat back in his chair, "I wish we could pluck the truth from their mind. That would make everything much less complicated."

The idea of plucking the truth from someone's mind reminded Ean of his newfound abilities.

"Would you mind if I asked the council members some questions?" Ean asked before adding, "In private?" He didn't want to divulge his ability to Jon or Marcus.

"Why? What did you have in mind?"

"It might be they would act differently or let something slip if they are talking with me rather than their Emperor."

Marcus raised his eyebrows. "You wouldn't threaten them, would you? I don't need my entire council floating at the top of the ceiling..."

Ean chuckled, "No, nothing like that. A friendly one-on-one conversation."

"Very well," Marcus responded. "I'll set the interviews up for tomorrow morning."

"Thank you. It's getting late and I would like to turn in." Ean commented, standing up and stretching.

"I'll walk you to your room," Jon added. They bid the Emperor goodnight and left the room.

"Okay, fess up," Jon said as they walked back to the Ean's room. "What is the real reason you want to visit with the council?"

"What do you mean? I told you why."

"Oh, come on Ean! I know the McMurrin family too well. What is the real reason?"

"Look, you might know my ancestors, but you don't know me. I gave you my reason and that's it."

They walked in silence the rest of the way to Ean's room. Reaching his door, Jon said, "I see I still need to earn your trust. I hope in time you will come to know you can trust me."

In time, I hope so as well, Ean thought. "Goodnight," he said out loud. He closed his door, not moving until he heard Jon's footsteps fade away. Counting to sixty as an additional precaution, Ean slowly opened his door, tiptoed down to Brin's door, and knocked. He waited an agonizing 30 seconds, but Brin did not answer. So he moved to Adair's door and knocked.

The door flew open by the end of his last rap on the door and Adair was standing there looking flushed, yet beautiful. She was wearing a perfume with a soft floral fragrance that Ean wanted to drink in. Feeling woozy, and a little weak at the knees, he started to speak, but his voice squeaked. He cleared his throat and tried again, "Do you know where Brin is?"

"Yes."

"And..."

"And what?" Adair asked.

Ugh!, he thought. *She's messing with me again.* She wasn't even trying to hide it, as evidenced by the dimpled grin crossing her face.

"And *where* might Brin be?" Ean asked.

"He's in my room, of course."

How was I supposed to know that?, he thought impatiently. Instead, he said, "Can I come in? We need to talk."

"Sure." Adair turned and let Ean shut the door before following her to a sitting room that adjoined her main bedroom. Her tunic was made of a more silky fabric that flowed around her as she walked. The effect was flattering and decidedly feminine.

"I should think you would keep your mind on the task at hand," Velos chided him.

Ean gritted his teeth. *"And I think you should stop spying on my thoughts!"*

"If you don't want me listening, then don't shout them all over the place."

"I was not shouting," Ean insisted, though the dragon was silent again.

"What brings ye around?" Brin asked as Ean approached. "For awhile, I thought ye had forgotten about us."

"I've been rather busy today. If you want a full report, Brin, I would be more than happy to give it to you. Detail, by excruciating detail." He sank down in a seat facing them.

"How about the condensed version?" Drake cut in.

Over the next 30 minutes or so, Ean gave them a run down on what he had discovered and his plans for visiting with each council member the next day.

"In private? Do you think that's safe?" Adair asked in a worried voice.

"No, in fact I'm not at all sure it's safe. That is why I wanted to talk with Brin." He focused on Brin, "I was wondering if you would join me, but with a catch: I don't want anyone besides our group to know that you are there."

Brin smiled, "I get to spy on council members?"

"And, be my bodyguard," Ean emphasized.

"It'd be me honor!" Brin replied. "I think I'm going to enjoy this..."

∞ ∞ ∞

The next morning everything was going as planned. Brin left the common dining table first and once he was alone in the hall he went invisible. Then he followed Ean into the room in which Emperor Marcus escorted him. Brin waited in a corner for the Emperor to leave.

Once he did, Ean looked around the room and asked in a whisper, "Are you here?"

"Right here," the voice came right at Ean's left shoulder, causing him to jump. Even though he had expected Brin's voice, he didn't expect him so close.

Catching his breath he muttered, "I sure hope this works."

"Me too."

Soon a council member wearing a dark robe over his tunic was ushered into the room. "Please, sit." Ean said, pointing to the chair opposite him. He could tell that the Elder was irritated he hadn't stood up to greet him. Adding to his injured ego was the way Ean commanded him to sit, even if he did do it politely.

"What can I do for you, Your Majesty," he slurred the title in contempt.

Ean smiled nonchalantly. "I wanted to ask you a few questions."

"Ask away."

"First off, I would like you to take a few minutes to tell me about yourself and about your current position on the council."

The man had started to phase into another appearance by habit, but reconsidered and phased back. He wanted to ask Ean some questions of his own, but restrained himself. The Emperor had made it clear that no council member was to interrogate or irritate the young Talent Master. So he began a synopsis of his life history.

As he was talking, Ean was busy working on his own magical ability to separate his conscious mind from his body. His consciousness hovered above the man and what he saw surprised him. This man's mental shield was not solid, but a shield of encircling flames of fire, as if he radiated a power of his own.

Remembering that every shield had a weakness, Ean searched him thoroughly. It was as he was searching near the base of the Elder's neck when he saw a flame of fire a bit dimmer than the rest. Steeling his resolve, he drove right at it. At first, he thought his own consciousness would burn up in the intense heat, but then the area gave way and he slipped right into the Elder's mind.

It took a few minutes of searching his mind before Ean was satisfied he knew enough about the man; he was arrogant, no real surprise there, and he held people he viewed as in stations below him in obvious contempt. However, there was no treason there, so Ean wiped out his memory of their meeting, leaving only the recollection of a pleasant conversation, and he returned to his own body again.

"Well, I think that will do it," Ean said, cutting the man off in mid-sentence. I can see you are loyal to your Emperor, but let me give you a piece of advice: be kinder to the people around you, or they might rebel against you."

Taken back by Ean's comment, he stuttered, "I–if that is all, I have more...pressing things on my agenda."

"Of course, thank you for coming," Ean responded. The man stood, turned with a flourish of his robe, and left the room out another door to Ean's right.

"How can the Emperor stand him?" Brin commented from where he was in the room. "He was an arrogant boor."

"True, but he is an innocent arrogant boor...at least based on our concerns."

The morning passed in a blur as Ean met with one Elder after another. Each one had his own unique shield; such as stone, brick, steel, wind, fire, water and even some that Ean could not describe. Each shield did have a weakness where he could enter with only minimal resistance. Whenever he had a hard time finding one, Velos would step in and direct him on where to find it. During one of his 'interrogations,' Ean realized that of all the minds he had searched, every single one had been that of an Arturian. He began to wonder if humans and dragons had similar mental shields.

"*Yes, and no,*" Velos answered his unspoken question. "*The shields are similar, but the race does affect the shield. Human, dragons, even leprechauns are very different.*"

During lunch, Ean did not leave the room, instead choosing to have the food brought to him, which he shared with Brin after the server left.

"I don't know if this is worth our time," Brin commented.

"It is." Ean said adamantly. "Someone ordered Adair's death and I will not rest until I know who and why they did it. I am sure it was not due to the laws of inter-world travel."

"Maybe so, but I am gettin' tired o' listenin' to these so-called 'Elders.'" Brin said with a look of annoyance on his face. Ean laughed.

"What's so funny?"

"You," Ean replied. "Relax my friend, we only have three left, then we are done."

"That's a relief."

After lunch, a very old man shuffled in and introduced himself in a raspy voice, "I am Romearus, the oldest member of the council."

For some reason he couldn't pinpoint, Ean, for the first time all day, stood up and shook the man's hand. "Pleased to meet you. Would you like a seat?"

"That would be a relief." As he took a seat, he smiled. "I am not as strong as I used to be. I believe that means I am feeling my age."

Ean returned the friendly smile, "We won't take too much of your time. Tell me about yourself and how long you have been on the council."

As Romearus was speaking, Ean prepared to enter the man's mind. However, the Elder did not appear to have a shield at all. With such easy access, he was, in essence, an open book. Ean could not find any secrets. In fact, he was the most loyal of all the council members, with no ulterior motives at all. While he was searching the man's mind, he was surprised to see that Romearus knew about Ean's mind reading abilities. Ean didn't bother to erase the interview from his mind.

As Ean returned to his own body, he saw the man watching him placidly. "So, young Talent Master, did I pass your test?"

"I--yes. And I am surprised that you are aware of what I can do."

"Why is that?" he asked.

"Well, I have not told anyone except my closest friends."

He chuckled, "I have been close friends to another Talent Master myself. I know many things about your potential abilities."

For the first time all day Ean felt like he was the transparent one. "Really?"

Romearus responded, "You are young, but you are trying to do some good. I hope you catch the ones you are looking for."

"So do I," Ean responded. Then without thinking he blurted out the question burning in his mind. "How come you have no wall?"

"I have a shield, one you would not be able to penetrate," Romearus responded with a smile. "I am one of very few in the world who can control their own shield."

"How can you do that?"

"Years and years of practice. I also had assistance from one of the last great Talent Masters."

"Who?" Ean asked with interest.

Romearus struggled to his feet and Ean stood to assist him. "Come to me when you are not busy and we will talk. I believe you have someone else waiting to see you."

After the Elder left, Brin spoke up, "What was that all about?"

"I'm not sure, but that is one man I can trust. I know it."

The next Arturian walked into the room like he owned the place. Ean took in the sight of the tall man with dark wavy hair and decided he did not like him. "Have a seat," Ean said bluntly, pointing to a chair.

"What am I doing here?" The elder demanded, still standing.

"Did the Emperor not explain it to you?" Ean asked in a business-like tone.

"He was brief and vague. I will not sit until I know what is going on."

"It's simple. I have asked to meet and get to know the council members. So," Ean said with a forced smile, "please sit down."

The man took a seat in the chair with a flourish and sat in icy silence.

"And who might you be?" Ean asked.

"I am Augustus, son of Dillverta, leader of the Arturian army."

"Now then, Augustus, please tell me how you became a member of the council."

Ean wanted to find entrance into the man's mind as quickly as possible. Due to the dangerous vibe Augustus gave, Ean was worried about leaving his body for very long in the Elder's presence and was relieved Brin was in the room for protection.

Disgusting! The irony of finding Augustus's weakness in his armpit, of all places, was not lost on him. A repulsive weakness for a repulsive man. But if he thought the armpit was disgusting, his mind was ten times worse. Augustus had many things to hide, some Ean wished he hadn't discovered. Yet he dug deeper down and discovered that he had found the man who ordered the attack on Adair.

With the new information, Ean was desperate to speak to the Emperor. The pieces of the puzzle started to come together for Ean: from the messenger they met in the forest, to Augustus and his father Dillverta. There was a conspiracy in Ferreglen and he had found a key player. Ean cleared Augustus's mind and made some alterations to his long-term memories. Then he exited the cesspool of Augustus's mind and entered his own body again.

"Thank you for coming. You may leave now."

Augustus sneered and was out the door before a moment had passed, slamming the door as he went.

"Not very subtle, is he?" Brin commented.

"No, but he is the one I was looking for. I had been hoping it wasn't a member of the council, but I suppose I'm not surprised it was. Emperor Marcus has a major problem of which he was not aware." Ean replied.

"One more council member is comin' in. Better get ready." Brin whispered, standing invisible at Ean's shoulder.

As the man entered, the Emperor stormed in right behind him. Stepping past the council member, Marcus marched up to Ean. "What is the meaning of this?" He demanded, waving a letter from Glen-Delay demanding tribute.

Acting innocent, Ean looked up at him and asked, "The meaning of what?"

"This ransom note! Don't tell me you don't know about it. You know very well what it is asking for!" Marcus boomed.

"Let's assume I don't. Would you kindly tell me what it says."

"It says that my general is being held as a prisoner in Glen-Delay."

"Why would the people of Glen-Delay take *your* general prisoner?" He could tell his pretense of innocence about the matter was getting under Marcus's skin.

Marcus responded through clenched teeth, "Because the general was watching the city gates."

"Are you at war with the city?"

"No," the Emperor replied.

"Was he sent on a diplomatic mission to visit the leaders of Glen-Delay and seen at the wrong place?"

"No."

"Was he on a recreational trip? Is that why your general was outside the city gates?"

Exasperated, he thundered, "No!"

"Then enlighten me, Marcus. If not there for recreation, diplomacy or war, why *was* your general outside the gate of Glen-Delay?"

The Emperor turned to avoid Ean's gaze. "He was sent to watch you. I needed someone I could trust to report on your abilities."

"I see," Ean said, his voice low and dangerous. Although what Marcus had revealed wasn't new to Ean, he decided he didn't want to reveal all his cards yet. "How long had he been watching me?"

"Ever since you left Blood Mother's cavern...I meant to ask you, what happened with Blood Mother? Did you move her?"

"No, I destroyed her. But don't change the subject. You mean to tell me that during all the attacks on us, your military leader was within range to offer assistance?"

"He was instructed not to interfere; only to observe your actions."

Now Ean was getting mad, "So you say you did not order the assassination, but if it had been successful, you would be fine with that? You would let your general stand by and *watch* it happen?"

"I was of a neutral option about you. I needed someone I trust to let me know if you were a Talent Master, or not."

"Is your son not trustworthy enough for you?"

"As he has been involved for over 400 years with your family, some felt that there could be some bias in your favor. I cannot risk my people, or this world, by relying on the wrong person."

"I see." Ean got to his feet and looked Marcus in the eye. "Are you willing to risk your people and this world on me now?"

Marcus met his gaze and said without hesitation, "Yes."

"Now, back to the note. What are the demands of Glen-Delay?"

"Half of all my gold, gems and grain."

"Or what?"

"Or the general dies, and we are officially at war."

"What are you going to do?" Ean asked.

Marcus frowned. "The letter says to negotiate the terms with you."

"Then do you accept their demand or do you have a counteroffer?"

Marcus's appearance blurred as he fought the temptation to change appearance. "Half of the gems. That's it."

"What? No gold or grain?" Ean asked calmly.

"No. Gems, and only gems."

"Unacceptable," Ean replied coolly. "Gold is most precious. They will want half of your gold, you may keep your gems, but add one fourth of your grain."

"What?!" Marcus spit out angrily. "I will not give gold to any greedy leprechauns, nor will I part with the grain, which will cause suffering to my people." Ean thought the insult to leprechauns was slightly amusing given the Emperor was unaware Brin was only a step away, holding his battle axe. If he wanted to, he could cleave the Emperor in half.

"Will any of them die with this price?"

Marcus frowned, "No. But it will cause discomfort and we would have to ration the grain supplies."

"Ah, what a shame." Ean stated flatly. "I guess the life of a human doesn't matter, but discomfort to an Arturian does." His voice hardened with finality. "I set my terms. Accept, or the general dies and you find yourself at war."

The verdict came out a bit harsher than he had intended, but now that he had said it, he was committed. His eyes were locked on the Emperor's as he stared him down.

Silence fell, emphasizing the thick tension building in the room. Then, the Emperor surrendered, "Fine! I'll pay. I'll draw the terms up and the penalty will be ready by this evening."

The tension dissipated, though the wall that had always been between Ean and Marcus remained.

Ean nodded, glad the negotiations were over. He hoped the leprechauns would be happy with his choices. "I'm afraid we have some other important matters to discuss...in private." He inclined his head and glanced over the Emperor's shoulder to where the council member had stood frozen like a statue throughout the men's exchange.

Ean spoke to him, "We can meet later. Thank you for coming."

"I can leave now?" the council member asked, looking at the Emperor for approval.

"You are dismissed, Neal. Do not mention anything about what you heard to the other council members, or any other person, for that matter."

"Yes, Your Excellence," he said, bowing low multiple times as he walked backward to leave the room. Before he exited, Ean spoke.

"Neal? Could you please find Jon and ask him to meet us here?"

"Y--yes. Yes." His face pale, he turned and practically fled the room.

"I think we have shaken up your council member a bit."

Marcus half smiled, "It is good for them to get their blood going from time to time."

Within minutes, Jon entered the room. He would have arrived a couple minutes earlier, but it had taken time to pry basic information regarding what had happened from the poor, gasping council member who had run to find him.

"Is everything alright?" Jon asked as he walked in.

"No," Ean turned to Marcus. "You have a serious problem on your hands."

"Yes, I know," he said, looking back at him.

"Oh, not me, I'm the least of your worries. There is treason within your own organization. Your council member Augustus wants to replace you with his father Dillverta, who cares only about power and nothing about Ferreglen."

"What?!" Marcus and Jon chorused. Then Marcus continued, "Those are serious accusations! What proof do you have to go around accusing some of the highest leaders in Ferreglen of treason?"

"Oh, I have proof." In order to share his knowledge, Ean had to reveal his abilities to the Arturians. He provided them with all the details he'd garnered from reading the minds of the messenger and Augustus, explaining that Dillverta is the true ring leader behind the treason.

Though they believed Ean, there was a catch. "Ean," said Jon, "you do realize that you wiped out the minds of the messenger and Augustus, destroying any supporting information to your claims. Only Dillverta still has his memories of the treasonous acts, and, as such, it will be his word against yours."

Marcus was pacing about the room, so Jon tried to reassure his father, "All will be well, Father. Now that we know about this we can watch him closely and catch him, and anyone helping him, in the act. Then we can prove his treason."

The floor beneath them began to shake. Stumbling toward the table, Ean yelled over the rumbling noise, "Do you have earthquakes here?"

"No!" Jon called back. "Natura itself does, but never in the Illusion Forest!"

Then an explosion happened with such force that the sound wave crossed the entire forest, bending trees in its path and breaking many of the windows in the capital building. The men crouched and threw their arms up to protect themselves from falling glass shards. Ean stood and looked through the now gaping windowsill to the horizon beyond. It looked like the mountain had exploded. Black smoke and gray ash billowed up and outward into the sky. Smoke clouds spread toward Ferreglen, coating everything with a thick layer of ash.

"Volcanoes..." Ean said, eyes wide in shock at the aftermath of the explosion.

Marcus shook his head. "Omalla Mountain is not a volcano...wait!" He turned to Ean, "Earlier you mentioned that you killed Blood Mother. What did you do with her prisoner?"

"Adair?" Ean asked confused. Then Drake came shooting out from the approaching clouds. Due to his large size, he landed heavily on the ground in front of the capital building.

Between heavy breaths, he gasped, "The Lucrus...the Lucrus has emerged from Omalla."

"What is the Lucrus?" Ean asked the wide-eyed dragon.

"An alien creature that came to our world thousands of years ago by mistake, when a Talent Master created a portal to another world. It is impossible to defeat, even armies could not stop it. Only your ancestor was able to subdue the creature. I had hoped it would be damaged enough to be unable to recover and would remain under the mountain...but I was wrong."

"How did my ancestor subdue the creature where others failed?"

Marcus replied, "He created Blood Mother. She fed from the life force of the Lucrus, keeping it weak so it could do no harm." He looked angrily at Ean, "And you, his descendant, killed its guard; the only thing keeping it from destroying everything and everyone on the planet. You have brought doom to us all." He turned his back on Ean and stormed out of the room.

Ean was speechless with guilt. He was supposed to help the people of Natura, not unleashing an invincible monster on them! Seeing the look on Ean's face, Jon grabbed him by the shoulders and said adamantly, "Ean, it was not your fault. Don't listen to him. We can figure this out."

"Brin?" Ean asked.

"Yes?" Brin appeared next to Ean.

"Please send a message to Glen-Delay. They need to release the general and get him here as fast as possible. Then bring Adair here when you return."

"On it," Brin replied.

"What is your plan?" Jon asked after Brin ran back to their quarters.

"I'm working on it." He was, but how do you explain that you are having a conversation with a dragon stuck in your head?

Chapter 30

Tara Stone vs. Druids

*E*lizabeth woke from her nightmare, gasping and shaking, the prophesy echoing in her head: *'Journey repeated by Bandruidh during strife, To find her love and set broken heart free.'*

She had been tormented since she realized what the prophesy was saying: she was going to die when she opened the portal. After Kevin explained that a Bandruidh was a female Druid, it became obvious that Elizabeth, being of Druidish descent, was the only option as Bandruidh. The strife was obviously Adair being separated from her family. Even the last line pointed to her, no--mocked her. *'To find her love and set broken heart free.'* Jeff triumphantly proclaimed that it meant she was to open the portal and find her precious sister, Adair, whom she loved so much, thereby setting her broken heart free.

Only Elizabeth understood what it meant. Her heart had been broken before Adair disappeared. It had been broken ever since the military lieutenants showed up on her doorstep, bearing the news that her husband's army helicopter had been shot down in enemy territory, exploding upon impact with the ground. There had been no survivors. That was when her heart shattered into millions of pieces. The only way to release her from her grief would be for her to be with him again, and the only way that would happen is if she died too. No one else recognized the clue and understood its implications, but she did.

When she realized opening the portal was a death sentence for her, she almost refused to take part in the plan. There is no way a mother would willingly die, leaving her young children orphaned. Unless...unless there were something of greater worth, something that would make such a sacrifice worth it. When she saw the tears coursing down Emily's cheeks, when she thought of how terrified Adair must be in a strange and foreign world, that's when she thought she saw something more important than her life. That's when she thought her sacrifice would be worth something.

∞ ∞ ∞

It was two days until the moon would be in place for the ceremony. Jeff was positive this was the answer to their prayers. He had researched it, prepared well, and made the necessary modifications. They collected mistletoe, sacred oak, white outfits, and even collected bull blood at a local butcher shop. They obtained a wreath tiara from Kevin's old aunt, who used to make them when she was younger. She had one stored high in her coat closet she was willing to lend them. They had made an excuse to her about needing it for a photo shoot, choosing to not admit that Elizabeth needed it so she could be the Druidess of an ancient prophesy that would reopen a portal to another world.

Wanting to make sure they prepared for anything that might be encountered after passing through the portal, Jeff had the others gather and pack outdoor gear and clothing for winter or summer. Though no one complained, he suspected that the others were as leery of being stuck eating freeze-dried food for the long term. Ultimately, however, dried food was better than no food. Elizabeth prepared a bundle of cloth diapers for Rosemary, since it wasn't practical to assume disposable diapers were available on the other side.

That night, as they sat around the table finishing their dinner, Jeff scanned the forlorn faces of the McMurrin and O'Connor families and tried to lift their spirits. "Cheer up everyone! In two days time, we will be in Natura with Adair and Ean."

"'Dair! 'Dair!" Jacob tugged on his mom's sleeve. She gave her son a small sad smile.

Jason could see that Jeff was trying to lighten their moods. He raised his glass, "A toast! To new friends and the journey to a new world!" The adults raised their glasses in a toast and each took a sip of their drinks. "Well," Jason said, "Get a good night's sleep. Tomorrow will be our last day here before we leave."

Elizabeth looked ready to cry. Kevin assumed she was nervous about her role as Druidess. "Lizzy, my dear, you will do great. Being a druid runs in your blood."

She sighed, knowing they misunderstood her sorrow, "I guess." Emily, sitting next to her, put an arm around her and Elizabeth laid her head on Emily's shoulder.

Since their time with the O'Connor's, Jeff had noticed that the two women had developed a close bond. Kevin explained to him that Elizabeth had taken over as the matriarch of the family since her mother had died of cancer. Having Emily there eased the weight of such responsibility off of her shoulders. Jeff then asked a simple, but inappropriate, question. "Why didn't you get remarried?"

Kevin became quiet for a few moments before replying, "I can never replace her...never." The conversation over, Kevin walked up the stairs to his bedroom and did not come down until the next day. Jeff realized how insensitive his question had been and vowed he would never make that mistake twice.

Bringing his mind back to the dinner table, Jeff said, "Well, I hope everyone packed their bags, because tomorrow we load up the SUV." Even as he spoke, he thought how strange it was to be speaking so lightheartedly about an attempt on inter-world travel as he would about one of the road trips his parents would make with him and his siblings every couple of years.

"Why the rush?" Jason asked with a smile. "We don't have to be at the stone until after the moon rises in two nights. We have all day tomorrow, and the next, to pack the car."

Jeff shrugged, "Call it my scout training. You know, 'Be Prepared' is my motto. I want to make sure we don't miss anything we might need."

"Don't worry, we'll be ready." The other adults nodded in agreement.

Jeff slept like a log that night, and after breakfast the next morning, he packed, and repacked, the supplies to make sure everything fit.

"Are we ready?" Kevin asked from behind Jeff as he closed the trunk.

"I think so."

"You *think* so, Mr. 'Be Prepared?'" Kevin joked. "I expect a 'yes sir!' attitude from you, soldier!"

Catching his humor, Jeff turned and saluted stiffly, "Yes sir! We are ready, Sir!"

Kevin nodded. "Good. I hope the old magic works."

"It will," Jeff assured him. He may not be of Druid descent, but he was confident and optimistic that their plan would work.

"Good. Now turn in."

Jeff dropped his salute in consternation. "What about dinner?"

"Well, now that you've asked, I suppose I should tell you the ladies sent me to get you, even if I had to hog tie you and drag you behind me, because dinner is ready."

"Great! I'm starving!"

"I should think so! You've spent all day packing the SUV," Kevin replied with a smile. "Now, are you coming or do I get to hog tie you?"

Walking into the kitchen, Jeff sniffed the delicious aromas in the air. "What's for dinner?"

"Steak and potatoes," Emily replied from her spot by the stove. "Jeff, after you wash up, would you please set the table?"

"Sure thing." Jeff went to the sink to wash with soap and water. Emily watched him and bit her lip for a moment, not quite sure how to broach the subject on her mind. But now seemed like the best time to speak to him.

She leaned toward him, "I know you want to go with us; but if it works, I think you should stay here. I know how hard it is to be away from your family and I don't want your mother to go through what I have been going through ever since Ean left."

Jeff froze with his hands still under the running water. He tried to objectively consider her recommendation, which meant he had to push aside his own excitement at the prospect of going to a new world. He had been feeling guilty whenever he thought long enough about the implications of leaving his family and leaving the familiarity of Earth for whatever Natura was like, but there was a small voice inside him that assured him that going was the right thing to do. He couldn't understand it enough to explain it to the McMurrins, but Jeff knew his parents would understand when they read the FedEx letter he would drop in the mail tomorrow--maybe not like it, but they would understand.

He turned off the water and began drying his hands on the nearby hand towel. Turning to Emily, he said, "I understand your concerns about leaving family, which is why I am calling my parents first thing in the morning and I'm sending them a detailed letter, explaining everything. I assure you, Mrs. McMurrin, my decision to go was made carefully and I believe it is the right thing for me to do."

Emily looked at him solemnly, "All I'm asking is for you to reconsider your choice. Keep in mind, I will be reuniting my family while you would be leaving yours."

"I'll think about it."

She nodded. "Good. Now, you'd better get that table set or we will be eating cold steaks and potatoes."

"Yes, Ma'am."

∞ ∞ ∞

The next day, they implemented their plan. They left by four in the afternoon to arrive early at the Hill of Tara, making one short stop at a FedEx drop box for Jeff's letter.

They waited by their vehicle until dusk. Once certain the area was deserted, they started unloading the baggage. Elizabeth insisted on carrying Rosemary and holding Jacob's hand while the others lugged bags to the top of the hill. Kevin pulled white robes out of one of the bags and handed one to each adult.

Taking the children with them, the ladies moved several feet away from the stone to pull on their robes and get ready. Watching Jacob entertain Rosemary by bringing her wild flowers to destroy, Elizabeth was oddly quiet as Emily helped her pin the wreath to her hair.

"Still nervous dear?" Emily asked her.

"Terrified." Elizabeth's shaking fingers dropped another pin.

While some people would try to say something reassuring, like 'It'll be okay' or 'You'll do great,' Emily did not. She somehow knew those words would not lessen Elizabeth's concerns. Instead, Emily wrapped her arms around the younger mother and held her while she trembled. Silent tears coursed down her cheeks, which she wiped away with the back of her hand. Emily pulled a tissue out of her pocket. "I guess it's good to 'Be Prepared' after all."

Needing a release from the built up tension inside of her, Elizabeth laughed longer than necessary at Emily's quip. "Thank you," she managed.

The two finished getting ready, gathered the little ones, and walked back to where the three men were waiting by the stone.

"The moon is out, but it's not dark enough yet," Kevin cautioned. "However, I think the first part can begin."

They formed a circle around the stone with Emily cradling a sleepy Rosemary and Jacob sitting tall on Jason's shoulders. Kevin began an incantation in Celtic as the others stood as silent sentinels. He held a jar of bull blood in his right hand and read from pages Jeff illuminated with a flashlight. Jacob got bored and laid down on the blanket and pillow his mother had prepared within the circle before the ritual started. The incantation continued for almost an hour. When he finished, Kevin nodded to Elizabeth. She stepped forward and placed one finger in the jar, then she walked over to the stone and drew a spiral of blood on the stone. Jeff could see that this was difficult for her--she was repulsed by the blood.

She picked up a piece of oak wood and mistletoe from where they had been placed by the stone. She sang the Celtic song she had memorized, hitting the stone with the wood and then the mistletoe. When the song was done, she waited with her eyes closed, her head tilted skyward.

Only the buzzing sound of insects responded in the night.

She opened her eyes and looked at her father questioningly. He shrugged and motioned for her to do it again. She repeated the song and tried the wood and mistletoe again. She squinted intently at the stone, trying to discern whether there was anything different about it. The only difference was that the blood had dried on the stone as a brown marking, but besides that, nothing magical or remarkable had happened.

When it was obvious nothing was going to happen, Emily's hopes were dashed and she began to cry tears of grief and anger. She turned on Jason. "Your family is from Natura! Open the portal!" She demanded, her mascara smearing beneath her livid eyes.

He held up his hands to fend off her fury, "Dear, I told you I tried it when I turned of age. It did not work for me."

"Try again...and this time *mean* it!" She yelled.

Jason complied. He walked over, placed his hand on the stone and bowed his head with a silent plea for it to work.

Still nothing happened.

Around the lump forming in his throat, Kevin uttered, "By my Irish roots, I thought this would work..."

"Maybe we missed something?" Jeff offered.

"No, Jeff," Jason said. "You did all the research you could have done. But it is sealed by dragon magic from the other side. We cannot enter. None of us are a Talent Master."

They stood silently in the dark around the stone.

Chapter 31

Full of Surprises

*I*t had been two days since the Lucrus announced its presence by exploding from the ground, blasting a good portion of what had been Omalla Mountain into rubble. For two days, the city of Ferreglen had been swarming with action, busier than a provoked beehive. The army was gathering and preparing in full force and the council remained in constant meetings with the Emperor and Jon. Looking over the battlements of the city walls, Ean could see an endless line of people and creatures seeking refuge by making a procession into the city from the smaller cities closer to Omalla Mountain. Needless to say, the influx of refugees meant that the city as a whole was rather chaotic. Letters from Drib reported that Glen-Delay was in no better condition, their gate now kept wide open, allowing anyone in who chose to pass through the magical border into the city.

Yesterday, the fairies, both female and Brigade, arrived. Ean was surprised when they refused to speak with anyone other than Adair and Drake. Though he knew it was childish, Ean was secretly satisfied by Marcus's bewilderment when he was sent away by the Brigade. These new refugees kept Adair rather busy, and the fairies made sure Adair was constantly adorned with fresh flower tiaras and leis.

As for the Lucrus itself, reports indicated that it had not attacked the smaller cities yet. It continued to wander the mountain range, tearing up trees and letting out roars heard in the farthest corner of the Illusion Forest.

Ean looked up to see Drake descending toward him from the sky. This time the dragon was so huge that when he landed on the ground outside the wall, his head still towered above where Ean stood on the battlement. Adair, surrounded by some fairies and wearing tall boots, trousers and a blouse, was straddled on the beast's shoulders, which were now level with the wall. She stood and jumped onto the battlement, where Ean caught her hand to keep her from stumbling. Steadying herself, she announced, "Except for the trees and areas affected by the initial explosion, there is no real damage yet."

Ean looked at her in chagrin, his eyes apologizing again for the whole mess.

"Stop beating yourself up; it isn't your fault. If anything, it was mine! I picked the berries from the Blood Mother Bush and was snatched, causing you to come rescue me."

During the last couple of days Adair had been trying to reassure him that he shouldn't feel guilty about the Lucrus. But Ean knew that everything bad that had happened to Adair-from her being captured by Blood Mother, to the assassination attempts on her life, to the presence of the Lucrus--all had been because of him. He couldn't help the recurring thought that kept floating through his mind, '*If I had not brought you to this world, you would be safe.*' Now she stood close, the sunlight causing her face to shine more radiantly, showing off hazel specks in her blue eyes. She was beautiful. He admitted to himself that even though he was determined to send her back, he didn't want to.

Taking a deep breath, he blurted out the decision he had made on his own. "When the time comes, I have to be the one to confront the monster."

Adair's eyes opened wider in surprise and objection. "No! Ean, the army will do that--not you!"

Ean shook his head and turned to look toward where Omalla Mountain had stood. "No. This is my fault and mine alone. It is my responsibility to face the Lucrus and to stop it...or die trying."

Adair stared at him, speechless. The stark reality of his potential death slapped her in the face. She found her voice, which wavered as she commanded, "Absolutely not! That is not an option, you hear me? You can't die on me, do you understand?" Grabbing him by the arm and turning him to face her directly. "You and me, *we* are going home. This is not your fault, *nor* your fight! Let this world take care of itself!" She stated her convictions with such fierceness and command that Ean began to question his decision.

Then his resolve returned. Promises had been made. He could not back away from this challenge, no matter how his heart felt.

Wanting to reassure her, Ean pulled her into a hug. Her idea of getting out of Natura together, leaving the monster behind for someone else to eradicate, was tempting, but Ean knew he wouldn't do that. He was instilled with a sense of responsibility and commitment and he knew that he would stay and face the consequences of his actions. "Would you do something for me?"

"If you're asking me to fight by your side, then yes, I will. We're in this together."

For a moment Ean paused. 'Together' did have a nice ring to it, but there was no way he was going to let her put her life in further danger. She was going home to Earth. He would make sure of it, even if it was the last thing he did.

He pulled back from the embrace, "Would you hold these letters I have written to my family and friends?...You know, in case I don't make it?"

She wanted to protest. She wanted to scream at him that he was wrong, that he would leave with her, or he would fight with her alongside him, but she knew it wouldn't make any difference. Natura did need him, as she felt she needed him. He was her security blanket in a strange world. He was her protector from danger. He was the one with whom she wanted to explore the unknown. However, Natura laid claim on him. He was a Talent Master and he could be the difference between life and death for many of Natura's citizens.

Her voice heavy with emotion, she replied, "I would be honored." She took the leather bag he slipped off his shoulder. "Ean, I--"

"One more thing, Adair." He interrupted. "When we visited the city with Jon, do you remember the jewelry shop we visited?"

"Yes."

"Well, I have a gift for you."

Despite her dismay that she didn't have anything to give him in return, she was surprised and curious about his announcement. She wasn't disappointed by his surprise. Her heart skipped a beat when Ean opened a silk cloth to reveal a stunning diamond necklace, the center of which held a ruby pendant the size of a robin's egg. "It's beautiful! How did you buy it?"

He shrugged, avoiding her questioning eyes. "It was a trade, of sorts. Will you wear it?"

"Yes," she breathed. She pulled her hair back and turned around so Ean could place the necklace around her neck, locking the clasps together in the back.

Ean was relieved. He had been afraid she would refuse the gift. Now that it was on her, he could rest easier. Turning, she gave him a quick kiss on his cheek. "Thanks."

At that moment, a loud roar reverberated throughout the valley and city. They turned to face the mountain.

"I think it's beginning to move," Adair said, needlessly.

"We had better get back to the capital."

"Get on!" called Drake. They leaped onto his back and settled on his shoulders. He flew them back to the capital building where Jon met them on the front staircase as they landed. He looked worried, "It is coming."

Ean climbed down, turning to help Adair. "What is the plan?" Ean asked Jon.

"My father has assigned the general to bring the archery troops to the battlements. Augustus and his Father were assigned the ground troops, with strict instructions to lead the attack."

"Why in the world would he trust them?" Ean asked, exasperated.

"He doesn't, but they are still astute leaders of military strategy and highly skilled in battle. Besides," he added with a grim smile, "it could be that this arrangement might rid my father of two of his current problems."

At the sound of horns blowing in the distance, Brin stepped out of the doorway. "The ground troops be on the move." The dragon, Arturian, leprechaun and humans stood together, waiting to see what would happen.

They watched the troops head into the forest until they could no longer be seen. In the distance, they could make out the indistinct form of the Lucrus, taller than most of the trees, moving erratically toward Ferreglen.

Brin spoke up. "The troops from Glen–Delay started arrivin' last night." He shook his head. "How they moved so fast, I am not sure, but they plan to meet up with the Ferreglen ground troops to encircle and surprise the monster."

With his superior eyesight, Drake studied their target. "The monster has changed since being imprisoned."

"How so?" Ean asked.

"When it first arrived on Natura, it was a creature made of stone. Since captivity, it has morphed into a creature with thick, twisted vines for a body, a mound of soil and rocks for a head, and it moves upon eight snake-like vine appendages."

"How is that possible?" Jon asked.

"I am not sure. It came from an unexplored world...not even the dragons had a record of it. It appears, however, that it can change down to its molecular structure, or perhaps magic is involved. Either way, it has taken on some of the characteristics of the Blood Mother Bush..." Drake craned his neck to get a better look.

"How did Blood Mother keep it trapped?" Ean asked.

"She used the creature as the foundation for her roots. She held it in one place by feeding from its nutrients, keeping it weak."

With a furrowed brow, Ean queried, "If it looks more like a twisted version of Blood Mother Bush, does that mean it has the same appetite as the Blood Mother?"

"Let's hope not," Brin added. "That would be terrible."

"It is damaged, I think." Drake commented, still focusing upon the monster. "One half is twisted and black, as if the wood of the trunk had become diseased, and three legs are dragging. The remainder of the trunk and limbs are dark green and fully functional."

"Maybe that was an effect of Blood Mother feeding on it," Jon conjectured.

"Could be," Brin agreed.

The troops from both armies converged, forming a ring to block the Lucrus from moving forward or backward. The silence was intense and the seconds felt like hours as they watched for the next move.

Suddenly, several smaller vines shot out from the Lucrus, grabbing the first row of the closest troops, pulling them all into a cavity of the trunk. The monster froze in place momentarily, shuddered, then grew larger in size.

"Ah, that proves we are dealing with another Blood Mother variety, though this portable one is much worse." Brin commented.

"Your Highness, here are the things you requested," a new voice spoke behind Ean. Everyone turned to see that it was the Emperor's assistant who had spoken.

"Thank you, Seritof. I appreciate how quickly you brought them."

"Is there anything else you require?" The assistant asked, bowing to Ean.

"No. Go to your family and comfort them, this should be over soon."

Looking confused, he replied, "Yes, Your Majesty." He turned and left.

"Ean, what is all this?" Jon asked.

"Some supplies I may need," he responded, as he emptied out the leather bag Seritof had given him. He was soon surrounded by gauntlet gloves, wicked looking double-edged knives with long handles, a pair of boots with steel spikes on the bottom--as if he were going to climb a glacier, and a long shirt made out of what looked like liquid metal, rather than fabric.

"What are these for?" Adair asked.

He started sorting the items. "I told you, I must confront the monster. Magic, alone, might not be enough. I don't think what I did to defeat Blood Mother will work on this creature." He pulled the shirt over his head and let the length of it fall to his knees.

Adair was shaking, "You're not serious about confronting the Lucrus on your own, are you?" As she saw him preparing for battle, she realized she wasn't ready to let him go.

He pulled on the boots and strapped the knife and sword on his belt. As he tugged on the gloves, he calmly responded, "Yes, I am."

"OH, NO YOU'RE NOT!" Adair yelled back. She stepped toward him, grabbed his belt and started tugging at it, trying to remove it. "You can't go after it alone...I won't let you!"

"I don't want to fight with you, Adair, but I must do what I can." He held her wrists to restrain her attempt to remove his weapons.

She looked at him in horror. "Do what you can? It killed a bunch of trained troops in seconds! You think you can stop it by yourself?"

"I think so... I hope so. I had a dream--no, maybe a vision. It is hard to describe it, but I know I saw the Lucrus when it first came to this world. I saw what it did and I saw it stopped by one man--a Talent Master, like me. No matter what, I have to try to confine or destroy it."

"Ye won't be going alone," Brin's gruff voice interrupted. "I am going with ye."

"I am too!" Jon and Adair added, simultaneously.

Ean looked at his friends, his loyal companions. Seeing the concern and love on their faces made him realize that what he was about to do was going to be harder than he thought. He knew that they would all come with him if he asked, but it had to be him. This was the only way his plan was going to work. He had spent past day working out the details with Velos, but none of them knew about that. "I'm sorry, my friends. I am the only one in the world who can do what must be done. It is my responsibility."

"You mean *our* responsibility," Adair stated firmly. "We are both from Earth. We are a team." Her voice cracked with emotion. "I can make a difference. I have magic, too, as a dragon maiden. We have to work this out together."

Ean looked at her sadly, knowing it was time to do what must be done. Why is it sometimes difficult to do the right thing? "Adair..." Ean guided her away from where the others stood. "You came to this world, against your will. Even though it was a mistake, I'm grateful for it. I know it would have taken me years to get to Ferreglen without your help."

"True," she agreed, determined to keep eye contact with Ean. She was determined to not relent. No matter what, he was not going without her.

Ean smiled briefly, then continued, "The time has come to part ways. Your life is yours to live again. Live and be happy. Please remember your promise," he glanced down at the bag of letters by her side. He looked back into her eyes, "I will always remember you."

He let go of her hand and stepped away. Turning, he leapt, elevating himself with magic, and landed on Drake's large shoulder, making sure the spikes from his boots didn't scratch the dragon (though with Drake's scales, it probably wouldn't have hurt him).

Adair was stunned. Did he just say goodbye? She felt like Ean had neglected to tell her something important; yet she couldn't quite figure out what. She knew there was no way she was going to let him leave her here alone.

"Ean! You're not going to die!" She called to him. "You hear me? You *must* come back!"

Ean looked at her one last time. The sunlight warmed her auburn hair like a gentle flame of fire. She was the most beautiful person he had ever known, and what he did next, he did with a heavy heart, knowing it would change their lives forever. Raising his voice and focusing on his command, Ean yelled, "IT IS TIME FOR YOU, ADAIR O'CONNOR, TO *RETURN HOME!*"

In that instant, she froze, wondering if he could mean what she thought he meant. Then she realized the world around her had a red glow to it. "No, no, no, no--" She realized he must have figured out a way to send her home...without him. When Ean had said goodbye, he meant that *she* was the one leaving. *Forever.*

She yelled out to him, "Stop it! I don't want to--" Her last words were lost as, in a flash, she was gone.

"What have ye done?" Brin asked.

From his perch on Drake's shoulders, he swallowed the lump in his throat. "I sent her home to Earth, where she will be safe."

Drake raised his head, roared and let out a long blast of fire into the sky. His emotions spent, Drake stood where he was, shaking, whether from grief, frustration, or anger, Ean didn't know. Regardless how many of his friends were against his decision, Ean had done what he knew to be right. Even if it meant breaking hearts...including his own.

Chapter 32

The Letters

*E*mily had collapsed to a sitting position on the ground, unwilling to move. Every time Jason approached her, she shooed him away. Once she even went so far as to throw one of her shoes at him. Elizabeth was still trying to console Rosemary, as she started to cry when Emily had wailed her frustration. Dejected, Jeff walked around the stone, looking for any missed clues. Jacob had awakened and was busy climbing the pile of gear next to the stone. Kevin was mumbling to himself in Celtic. At least, that was what Jeff thought he heard.

Despair was so thick, no one bothered to clean up the gear in preparation for leaving the stone. To leave would be to admit defeat, removing all hope of ever seeing Adair and Ean again.

The moon had risen to its highest point in the cloudless sky, illuminating the hilltop with white light.

Jason cleared his throat, "Maybe we should move the gear back to the car."

No one even commented on his suggestion.

"I guess it can wait." Jason conceded.

Then, it happened: the Tara Stone began to glow a bright red color. A silhouette was standing next to the stone. When the red light vanished, Adair was left standing in its place.

Adair stared wide eyed at the motley crew, then cried, "Nooooo!" She turned and grabbed the Stone, hysterically crying and screaming at it, screaming at Ean. Elizabeth, cuddling Rosemary in one arm, was now trying to calm her sister, as well as the baby. Trying to pry Adair's fingers from the stone, she said, "Adair, you're home now! It's going to be okay!"

"No! Leave me alone!" She pushed Elizabeth away. "Ean, how could you!" she yelled. "If you die, I'll kill you! You hear me?" She began hitting the stone, crying, "Take me back, take me back!"

Emily's scared voice broke in, "Die? What do you mean, 'die'?"

Adair shook her head, "Go away!" She waved everyone away. "I shouldn't be here! How could he be such a clueless American boy?!"

"Yep, she must be talking about Ean." Jeff commented.

"Adair," Kevin turned her around until she was facing him.

"Let me go! Let me go! I need to go back!" She tried pushing him back. "How dare he send me back right when he was going to go take on the monster...and I won't even be there to help him! What if he dies because I'm not there? Ean!!!" She yelled, even though it did no good. They were worlds apart.

Kevin pulled her into a bear hug. "My Adair, I thought you were lost." Tears of joy ran down his face. Holding her in his arms, he murmured, "My little girl...my angel...my Adair."

She pulled back enough to plead with her Father. "I have to go back!"

Jason stepped next to her, searching her tear-streaked face for the answer he needed, "What did you mean Ean might die? "

"The Lucrus--a-a creature--was advancing on the city. It took out parts of the army and Ean is going to...or is...or did...try to take out the monster himself to save Natura." Her knees crumbled beneath her and she collapsed on the ground, crying again.

Jason and Emily exchanged looks. They were scared but knew they needed to be with their son. Jason turned to the stone and banged on it until he cut his hand on the rough edges, causing his blood to stain the rock. Nothing happened.

Jacob walked over to Adair. "Aunt 'Dair?" he asked, touching the tears on her cheek. "You crying...where you go?"

She looked at her innocent nephew and took a steadying breath. "I went away..."

For a moment, she calmed down, as Jacob gave her the biggest little bear hug he could muster. "I love you, Aunt 'Dair."

"I love you too," she replied.

"You happy now?" Jacob asked.

"Yes, Jacob, your hugs make me happy."

"Yay!" Jacob clapped, "Mommy, I made Aunt 'Dair all better."

Elizabeth had tears running down her face, "Yes, my big boy, you did."

For a moment, the air was thick with silence.

Emily walked over to Adair. As she sat down next to Adair, she whispered hoarsely, "Please Adair, I need to know what is--or was--going on."

Adair focused on her and realized she was looking at Ean's mother. A mother had a right to know what her son was facing, whether or not it was pleasant. Then Adair remembered her promise and realized Ean's letters could help his parents know what he was facing. Pulling the leather bag off her shoulder, she handed it to Emily. "This is for you...from Ean." Then she leaned back on the Tara Stone, folded her legs to her chest and closed her eyes.

Kevin had taken Rosemary from Elizabeth so she could sit with Adair. She wrapped an arm over her sister's shoulders and spoke softly to her.

Emily took the bag over to Jason and together they pulled out the letters. One was labeled 'Mom,' another 'Dad.' There was also one each for Jeff, Elizabeth, and Adair. Emily wasted no time--she ripped open the multi-page letter and read, then reread Ean's words. She had a hard time getting through it, as the tears running down her cheeks made it harder to see the words clearly in the moonlight.

Jason also read his letter, with eyes moist. He choked out, "My son. So brave. I am so proud of him."

Kevin walked over. "Does he say anything about how we can reach him?" Jason was touched by the simple, sincere gesture. Even though Kevin had his daughter back, he was still willing to help Jason for Ean's sake. He glanced over to where Adair was sitting with her back to the Stone, her head down on her knees. Maybe it would be for her sake, too.

"No, there were no instructions on how we can get to him. Just an explanation and a loving farewell." Jason voice sounded raspy in his own ears. He cleared his throat. "There are some more letters here." He handed

Jeff, Elizabeth, and Adair their letters. Silence prevailed as they opened and read them.

Emily walked over to Adair and knelt down. "He cares for you," she said.

Adair sighed, "Yeah? Well, he has a funny way of showing it."

"Sorry, but that's his fault." Emily pointed to Jason.

"Dear, I said I was sorry..." Jason responded.

Ignoring him, she turned her back to him and asked Adair, "What does he say?"

"Everything he didn't have the courage to say in person."

"May I see it? Please?" Emily asked.

"Sure," Adair handed her the pages of her letter.

Emily read them, surprised to see the depth of his letter. Obviously, Ean had formed feelings beyond friendship for Adair. She said as much to the Irish teen.

"Not enough to keep me there." Adair commented, still bitter.

"Maybe he was thinking of protecting you," Emily countered.

"Agh! Men!" Adair commented, "What do they know?"

Emily smirked. "Tell me about it." She agreed, glancing toward Jason.

Exasperated, he said, "Again, I'm sorry!"

"What does this mean?" Emily asked, looking at what he had written on the last page under his signature. "'Like a dragon key, if your heart is ready and willing, the ruby egg will open the way.'"

"What?" Adair asked, taking the page back from Emily. Her eyes grew wide as she reread what Emily had said.

"What's a dragon key?" Jeff asked.

"Shh!" Adair said to him.

"Just asking," Jeff looked a little affronted at being shushed.

Getting to her feet, Adair began pacing while she considered what he meant. He mentioned a dragon key. Dragon keys could open locked doors. Could the stone be like a locked door? No, she shook her head. Drake sealed the door--no one but Ean could open that door, no matter what kind of magic they had. Ruby egg...what ruby egg? She couldn't figure that out.

Jacob walked over to Adair and held up his arms, indicating he wanted to be picked up. Adair automatically responded by lifting him up on to her hip. He started to play with her necklace. "Mommy look! Pretty rock."

Adair reached up and touched her necklace, the one thing Ean had given her...her eyebrows shot up. "I'll bet he didn't think we would figure it out so fast!"

"Figure out what?" Jason asked.

"The necklace Ean gave me; it's the key to Natura!"

"A Dragon Key?" Jeff asked confused.

Adair glanced at him, "Don't be silly, it doesn't even look like a Dragon Key...it's a ruby egg key."

Jeff looked at her like she had lost it. "But..."

Adair cut in. "Grab the bags, everyone! We're leaving."

"Where are we going?" Emily asked, not moving.

"Back to Ean. If he isn't already dead, I'm going to kill him." She stated firmly.

Emily reached out and squeezed her hand. Adair returned Emily's squeeze. A common bond was being formed.

"Well, gentlemen, what are you waiting for?" Emily said. "Grab the bags."

Jason, Kevin, and Jeff were quick to throw the packs on their backs and grab the extra bags. Adair turned to Elizabeth. "Are you sure you want to come and bring the kids? There may be danger there right now..."

Elizabeth shook her head. "I've lost enough family members. I can't stay behind and watch you go. We'll be all right."

"All right, everyone, grab hands and hold on tight." Elizabeth held Jacob and Rosemary tightly while Kevin and Adair held her arms. Everyone else held hands.

"Ean McMurrin," Adair called, "this better work!" She grabbed the necklace, closed her eyes and concentrated with every last molecule of her heart, her very soul. Speaking out loud, pouring into her words her conviction and heartfelt desire, she declared, "We want to be where Ean McMurrin is right now!"

She knew it would work before she opened her eyes because her fingers holding the stone began to tingle and become warm. Her words must have been enough, because she once again saw red around her. In a flash, they had left the Tara Stone.

Chapter 33

Dooms Day

The wind blew in Ean's face as he and Drake flew above the clouds of the Illusion Forest. To say the battle below was going terribly wrong would be an understatement...it was a disaster! The uniformed Arturian and Leprechaun forces, along with most of the other creatures that call the Illusion Forest their home, had originally joined together to fight the Lucrus, but order had turned into complete disarray. The beast was attacking their encircling army from all sides, vines shooting out, pulling soldiers into the body, trampling others underneath its gigantic mass.

Drake flew toward their target, but at an angle, so they would be hidden above the clouds. Seeing the sheer size of the creature as they neared, Ean's fear kicked up a notch. "*Velos*," Ean thought, looking for reassurance, "*will this plan work* ?" The silence was long and Ean was almost sure Velos was not going to respond, when he heard his voice again.

"*There is no guarantee Ean, but it is the best option we have. In fact, it is probably what your ancestor should have done in the first place, had he not been too stubborn to listen to my advice..*".

"Well, I'm listening now--and I really *don't want to die.*"

"*I know...nor do I want you to...there is still so much we must do.*"

It was a gentle reminder to Ean about the other pressing concerns on Natura. He was having a hard time focusing beyond the immediate danger of the Lucrus and the sense of loss he felt since he sent Adair back to Earth. Although he knew that the overall action of sending her home had been the right thing to do, he wondered if the timing had been wrong, given his friends' reactions to her departure. Then again, every time he thought of her staying here, where she could be hurt in battle, he knew that even if he could, he wouldn't have changed his choice to send her when he did. He tried to tell himself it didn't matter when he had sent her, but deep down he knew it would always matter. Drake, who had not spoken to Ean since Adair disappeared, had taken it the hardest. He also wondered if Drake was hoping he wouldn't make it through the fight after all, that he had changed his mind about helping him remove this monster from Natura for good.

"Are we going to get to work, or not?" Drake snapped, ending his silent treatment and pulling Ean out of his reverie.

"You remember what the plan is?" Ean asked.

"Of course, a dragon never forgets...but I still think you're foolish about the approach."

"Crazy might be a better term!" Ean yelled back over the wind. Ean felt Drake tense up. It was time to live or die. Either way, he was committed. The air was pulled from his lungs as Drake tucked his wings against his body and dropped into a stooping dive, down through the clouds. With the wind tearing at his skin, as if it wanted to rip it off of his body, Ean clung tightly to Drake's back, feeling like he was trying to hug a shooting missile. He felt his hands starting to lose their grip just as Drake opened his wings, catching the wind current as he leveled out. The sensation of stability only lasted a moment, long enough for Ean to wonder if his stomach was going to return to its rightful spot, when Drake flipped, dropping Ean in a free fall.

Ean tucked his arms against his chest, holding them steady and still as he shot downward toward the head of the Lucrus. Ean wanted to check to make sure Drake was heading to where he was supposed to be, but the risk of losing his focus was too great, so he forced himself to concentrate on his target. Angled to come down from behind the Lucrus, Ean waited until the last moment to spread his arms. The metallic shirt he wore had a thin layer of webbing between his arms and upper legs to his body that caught the wind current, so he was no longer falling, but gliding. The metal of the fabric reflected the sunlight, causing him to shine brighter than a falling star. Ean was sure he was blinding everyone who looked up at him, but it couldn't be helped. The only one he didn't want to see him was the Lucrus, and thankfully it was distracted by Drake, who was flying in front of him to keep him preoccupied. The scene was somewhat comical, a gigantic tree trying to swat an annoying fly.

As he neared the creature, he knew his positioning and timing had to be perfect. During his approach, he focused on the looming back of the Lucrus, imagining how he would tilt upward as he landed, how he would place his hands and feet so to cushion his impact and grip on the back. Then he did it for real. He tilted, spread his hands and feet, and landed. The initial hit was painful, but the boots and gauntlet gloves helped him grip the vine-covered trunk, preventing him from falling the long distance to the ground. The vine-like appendages of the Lucrus retreated from attacking the surrounding army.

For a moment, Ean thought: *Great! This is going to work!* Then the unexpected happened: As he was analyzing where the weakest spot of the creature would be, a glowing red light appeared on the field behind the Lucrus. To Ean's shock, several people appeared within it before the light disappeared and the newcomers remained. What scared him most of all was the sight of Adair, standing next to his parents and Jeff, behind the monster.

Distracted, he didn't see the large vine headed toward him. It smashed into his forehead, throwing him backward. Instinctively he tried to twist toward the trunk to grab on, but then he ended up hitting into it with his left hip, rebounding far enough away that he couldn't get a good grip. Disoriented, he flailed his limbs, trying to stop his fall when he felt something grab his arm, halting his plummet. Somewhat relieved, he looked to see what had saved him. There was a vine from the Lucrus wrapped around his right arm. As he dangled there in the air, he got a better view of how perilous his situation was.

All the numerous vines that had retreated from fighting the army were now snaking their way over to him. Some wrapped around one leg; others started wrapping around the other. Before they could wrap around his left arm, Ean grabbed his sword from his belt. As he hacked at two vines headed for his left arm, Ean worried that the vines were like the heads of a Hydra from Greek Mythology, and each of the damaged vines would grow into two more. But they did not, the damaged vines retreated and other vines approached. He cut the ones around his chest and the one around his neck next, as they were cutting off his air supply. He felt a tremble and realized the vines were bringing him around the body of the trunk to where the gaping cavity awaited him. He started wildly slashing with his sword, hoping to stop his advance toward certain death. Once he had cut enough vines, his liquid metal shirt was slippery enough for Ean to pull out of the Lucrus's grip.

After cutting the vines wrapped around his right arm, and freeing his body, Ean switched the sword to his right hand while falling toward the mass of vines waiting below. Reaching with his left arm, Ean snagged a vine and swung against the trunk, to the side of the hole. Using the blade points of his shoes, Ean secured himself to the trunk and prepared to fight. Vines surrounded him, ready to strike. Ean had to bob and weave, sometimes using his grip on the trunk for leverage, sometimes sliding down the trunk to avoid a trap. He slashed and hacked at the appendages as they whipped toward him. It was a deadly game of sword fighting, but Ean moved with such grace and precision that the vines were unable to capture him again.

It was only when the burning smell hit his nostrils, causing his eyes to water, when Ean noticed the sword blade once again glowed with a silver aura; not only cutting off the vines and deflecting their attacks, but burning the Lucrus at the same time. Even though the creature was trying to kill him, at that moment Ean felt sorry for it. The Lucrus wasn't even supposed to be on Natura in the first place, as it had been accidentally transported there by Ean's ancestor.

Ean was jarred back into the fray as he slipped on the trunk, sliding a couple of feet before he could regain his footing. He turned and started climbing up the twisted trunk that served as the Lucrus's body, heading for the top.

A baby's cry echoed in the background. It was mixed with screams coming from where his parents and the other visitors had appeared. The name 'Rosemary' crossed his mind, but Ean brushed it aside as a vine wrapped itself across his face. He was trying to pull on it and cut it with his sword without removing his own nose or head in the process. *No more distractions please!* Ean begged in his head.

Once he sliced through the vine and came free, he spotted Drake shooting out of the sky toward where his parents stood behind the Lucrus. The enormous creature paused, following the dragon with its head to where he landed. Then the Lucrus lost control of its footing, falling forward toward the ground. Ean dropped his sword and grabbed the knobby trunk with both hands before the creature impacted the ground. Ean would have been thrown free from the monster if he didn't have his boots and gloves, but as it was, it was a miracle he was able to hold on as the shock waves jarred every bone in his body. Ean looked up from where he was clinging to the trunk under the head.

To his surprise, the army had surrounded the head, swords and spears drawn, ready to attack the monster. Ean raised his hand to stop them, signaling instead for them all to retreat. For the space of a moment, they froze, processing what he was asking them to do. Then they all turned and fled into the coverage of the forest as Ean began to glow brighter and brighter. This time the light wasn't from a reflection of the sun or the flame of his sword, but the full power of a true Talent Master.

Drawing the long dagger from his belt, he focused his magic into a jewel on the hilt until the stone itself began to crack. Focusing on his desire, Ean raised the dagger and plunged it into the Lucrus's thick body. Having prepared himself beforehand, once the dagger pierced the Lucrus, Ean transported himself to the safety of the forest cover. The Lucrus began to stand up when the jewel exploded. An intense flash of bright light was followed by darkness.

Ean felt time itself had stopped. He saw that the area where the dagger had been plunged into the creature had been replaced by a black void, which swallowed the Lucrus, along with some loose debris nearby, with a loud suctioning noise. Then the vortex shrunk, closing and disappearing with a pop. The Lucrus was gone.

Chapter 34

Finding Home

ollowing the explosion, the army's surprise magnified the silence. Once the shock passed, the deafening roar of cheers was overwhelming. Ean and the army amassed in the clearing where their foe had vanished. Laughter came from all directions, and others even cried with relief. Fairies zoomed around, throwing colorful dust that caused plants to grow and change color as they passed. During the celebration, numerous leprechauns reappeared from where they had hidden with their invisibility; some waved at him, others nodded and smiled. None of them approached him or congratulated him. Ean didn't mind. He was glad the danger was over and he survived.

His relief was short lived. He remembered Adair's abrupt appearance during the battle. He thought he remembered seeing other familiar people with her, but he couldn't remember who--everything had happened so quickly. Before he could put his finger on identity of the newcomers, the hair on his neck stood up, an instinct warning him he was being watched or that danger was approaching.

A shadow crossed overhead; Drake was descending. Due to his large size, his bulk blotted out the sunlight on the field below as he neared. Seeing the dragon coming, the armies dispersed to give him plenty of room, leaving Ean standing in the field by himself. Coming in for a soft landing, Drake tilted his right wing for a moment to adjust to the wind current and Ean caught a glimpse of red hair behind Drake's shoulder.

That specific color of red was branded on his mind. It was Adair; the girl he had splashed with lake water inside a painting...the girl with whom he had trekked through a magical forest...the girl he had saved from peril and death a number of times...the girl he couldn't stop thinking about...the girl he had fallen for...the girl who was now very angry with him...the girl who had arrived on the back of a dragon to confront him...and he realized danger remained. By making one choice, he had placed himself in hot water and now must face the firing squad of her wrath.

Ean looked around, hoping for an escape. Not finding a suitable place to escape, he stood where he was, waiting for the assault that was sure to come. He felt as if the armor he was wearing wasn't enough protection.

Adair climbed off Drake and stood in his shadow, watching Ean. Although he couldn't see her facial expression, he could see from her body language she was upset. She folded her arms, then let them fall to her sides, then folded them again. He wondered if she was waiting for him to speak first, or if he should wait until she did. Hesitating, he opened his mouth to say her name, but instead he closed it, at a loss of what to say. He wanted to reach out to her, to calm her, but when he thought of walking over to her, he remembered the slap she had given him what seemed like a lifetime ago in Glen-Delay. He waited for the attack.

Then it came. Adair dropped her arms to her sides, her hands clenched into fists. She set her shoulders back and charged him. It happened so fast, her actions were blurred into one. Ean flinched and stiffened before turning and ducking his head, anticipating the blow. He felt her body slam into his, followed by the tight, crushing grip that pinned his arms to his sides. His eyes opened wide as he felt her sobs rack through her body while she squeezed him tight. He hadn't expected her reaction to be this. Looking over her shoulder, he caught Drake's eye. The dragon was grinning at him, amused at his shock. He put his arms around her waist (he couldn't raise them further) and murmured in her ear. "It's okay...the monster won't be able to hurt you."

She pulled back from him, so that she was gripping onto his arms with her hands. Surprised, she said, "Hurt *me* ?"

"Isn't that why you're upset?"

"No--you..." her voice caught and she bent her face downward so as to avoid seeing his face and vice versa.

"Me, what?"

"Ean..." She took a breath and spoke quickly, her fears spilling out, "It was terrifying, seeing you on that...that huge monster! It seemed hopeless from where I was watching, that such a monster could be taken down by something so small!" Ean wondered if he should be offended by her reference to him being small. She continued, "Then it kept hitting you and wrapping itself around you, trying to eat you...and you fell...you could have died!...I was afraid you were going to die..." She gasped, taking in jagged breaths of air.

"You were worried about me?"

"Of course!" She gripped him tighter, as if she never wanted to let go.

He liked hearing about her concern for him. Though of course she cared--she cared about everyone. It takes a special kind of wonderful person, after all, to love an annoying, oversized lizard. With that thought, Ean glanced at Drake to see him talking with some leprechauns and fairies in the grassy field.

He ruined the moment by speaking without thinking, "How did you get back so fast? I thought it would take you a lot longer to figure out the note."

She let go of him and stepped back, folding her arms across her chest. "I shouldn't have had to figure it out if you had listened to reason in the first place! I told you we needed to do this together...But I guess you didn't need my help after all." She looked at him searchingly and hinted, "But I wonder if perhaps you had someone's help after all?" Her voice dropped low, like the growl of a lioness. "One of these days that dragon of yours and I will have a talk about proper advice."

Ean felt Velos shift uncomfortably inside his mind and Ean smiled, pleased he wasn't the only one afraid of Adair. Then, because he wanted to know enough that he was willing to risk her wrath, he asked, "Why did you think we needed to battle the Lucrus together?"

Adair's eyebrow raised, "You have magic, talents and a dragon living inside your head, but you can't do everything by yourself all of the time. You need to rely on others and work as a team with them. After all, I do have talents and abilities that could have helped in defeating the Lucrus if only you had let me help instead of sending me away. You know, sometimes--"

Something he had forgotten during the heat of the battle jumped into his mind and Ean cut in. "Wait a minute. You didn't appear in the field by yourself. Who came with you?"

Her train of thought derailed, Adair frowned. "Are you trying to change the subject on me, Ean McMurrin? Well it's not going to work. You're still in big trouble. But since you asked..." She tilted her head and half smiled, "Why don't you come and see for yourself?" Turning on her heel, she walked over to Drake. "I think we should head back."

Drake nodded in acknowledgment and ended his conversation with the leprechaun to whom he was talking. He stood and stretched, raising his neck and head high.

Grinning, Ean decided to take advantage of the situation. He ran to catch up to Adair, grabbed her around the waist from behind, causing her to gasp in surprise. Drake turned to watch them, as continuing forward, Ean push off the ground, using his momentum and a fair amount of magic. They shot in an arch upward, reaching about forty feet above ground level, then descended downward, smoothly landing on Drake's back.

Her heart pounding, Adair exclaimed, "Whoa!" She turned her head toward her shoulder, "That was awesome! But next time, warn me first."

Ean felt giddy. She said 'next time.' She wasn't mad at him! "You bet."

It was Drake's turn to leap into the air with the massive flapping of his wings. The wind and momentum almost sent Ean tumbling off the dragon's back, but he was saved when he slid into one of the large hard scales sticking out of Drake's back.

"Ouch!"

Drake chuckled, "I suppose I should have warned you to hold on! Don't get used to this. I'm not a pack mule to carry humans everywhere they want to go."

The flight back to Ferreglen seemed shorter than the flight to the battle. Free from the worry of a life and death situation, and with Adair in front of him, Ean enjoyed the view of the forest. As he relaxed, he figured that a dragon this size could travel the globe in a matter of days, more or less.

Adair was quiet. Ean imagined she was enjoying the flight as much as he was. He supposed that enjoying the moment was sometimes necessary.

As they passed the city walls to Ferreglen, the cheers of the Arturians could be heard. Even though he looked like a speck on Drake's back, he waved to the people below.

Drake began to descend to the courtyard of the capital building. Ean tried to look down at the people gathered there, but Drake's wings blocked his view. He could only hear the sound of voices echoing up to him. Drake landed with a small thump and stretched his leg out for his disembarking passengers. Adair thanked Drake through her connection to him, then turned and smiled her dimpled smile. "Come on. There are some people I want you to meet."

Ean returned her smile before sliding down Drake's leg. He caught Adair's hands to steady her as she joined him and together they jumped off of Drake. Ean squeezed Adair's hand, she returned his squeeze, and they walked around Drake to face the crowd.

The first people Ean saw were Emperor Marcus and his council of Elders. Unlike his earlier experience when he attended meetings on how to deal with the Lucrus and he received angry glares from the council members for his mistake in freeing the monster, they smiled at him and called out their greetings and congratulations for his victory. Marcus shook his hand and said, "Thank you, Ean."

Feeling awkward, Ean said, "It was the least I could do. Now if you'll excuse me, I have some people I must greet."

A thoughtful glint entered into the Emperor's eyes and a slow triumphant smile spread across his face. "Yes, of course." With a calculating gaze, the Emperor stepped aside to let Ean pass and Ean felt cold chills run down his back.

"Velos, let's watch that one. I don't trust him." Though he didn't get a response from him, Ean could sense the dragon watching the Emperor more closely.

Adair turned to face him and tugged on his hand to get Ean to follow her. Ean looked at her and smiled again. He couldn't believe that she had chosen to come back to him! He felt as thrilled as a kid on Christmas Day. Even though he had not intended to come to Natura and he would never see his family again, here was someone who represented Earth to him. She was a link to all he had ever known up until he touched the Tara Stone. All he could think was; *'She came back!'*

Then it hit him. *Why did she come back? What if she came back for Drake?* For a second, the world around him darkened. Then he shook the thought off. *No, she said she cared about me.* Now she was holding his hand, leading him toward the capital building.

Other Arturians in the crowd pressed closer to him; for some reason they felt the need to touch Ean on the arm or pat him on the back as he passed. But when they saw his attention was not on them--it was searching the crowd for other faces, they parted, creating a pathway to a spot where a group of people stood away from everyone else.

Ean spotted Jon standing in front of the group with a huge smile on his face. He moved to the side and Ean locked eyes with his dad. He stopped in shock. He never thought he would see his father again, especially not here on Natura. "Dad?!" His focus shifted, "Mom?! Mom! And Jeff!" His eyes grazed over the middle-aged man and Elizabeth with her children. "You're here! I can't believe you're all here!"

"*You* can't believe it?" The man Ean assumed might be Adair's father scoffed. "*I* can't believe that the first flight I've ever taken with my grandsons was on the back of a dragon!"

Too caught up in his emotions to respond, Ean focused on his parents again. Seeing the tears streaming down his mom's face, Ean started running toward her, tugging Adair along until she caught up. Reaching the group, they fell into embraces with their loved ones. Ean's mom sobbed as she clutched him to her. His dad put his arms around them both, trying to hug them at the same time. "My son...my son, I am so proud of you..."

Ean felt like time itself had stopped; only he and his family existed in their own little moment of time. He was brought back to the moment when he heard little Jacob exclaim, "Auntie 'Dair, we rode a dragon!" Rosemary squirmed in her mom's arms and started to fuss.

Ean smiled. They were here--all of them. No matter what happened, Adair and Ean had their families with them. At that moment, Ean remembered one of his mother's favorite sayings, which she repeated every time they moved: "Home is where your family is." Ean had brushed it off as his mom's way of trying not to feel guilty for the frequent moves, but he now understood it as it was meant to be understood.

It didn't matter where he was or what he needed to do. At this moment, in his mother's arms, he was home at last.